rock the dream

B.B. MILLER & LESLIE CARSON

Cover Design by:
Jada D'Lee Designs

Cover Image by:
iStock Photo

Editing by:
Lauren Schmelz, Write Divas

Interior Design & Formatting by:
Christine Borgford, Type A Formatting

For Mandy

chapter one

kennedy

"DON'T YOU WANT MORE?" MY voice sounds disembodied, dry, and raspy, like I'm a seventy-five-year-old chain smoker who doesn't give a shit about what a lifetime of nicotine has done to his lungs.

A booming bass fills the penthouse suite at the San Francisco Fairmont, where my band, Redfall, and a host of strangers party into the night. "Mmm . . . You're so fucking hot." It's a slurred and intoxicated whisper against my neck from some nameless groupie sitting on my lap. Gin and desperation roll off her in waves. She licks the curved chaos of ink snaking down my shoulder and grinds her skinny, naked body against mine. I shudder at the feel of skin and bones against me. She pushes her tits forward, and breathes in my ear. "Touch me, Kenny."

"I always want more. So do you." The voice of my tour manager, Brodie Dixon, drifts to me from somewhere far away. I lean back against the couch, trying to open my eyes in an attempt to find him. I feel like I'm floating in a dream or a nightmare; it's hard to tell which. I'm stuck somewhere between reality and a fucked up fantasy.

"Name's Kennedy," I mumble.

"Kenny, Kenny, Kenny," she chants as she rolls her hips against mine.

I turn my neck in the direction I think Brodie's voice came from, making a feeble attempt to brush away the hand flattening against my stomach, and drifting south. I can feel her jagged nails scratching over my hip, fumbling, as she attempts to unhook my leather belt.

Her hot, liquor-laced breath fans over my exposed chest, and her fingers lazily drift along the tatt that covers my neck. She doesn't give a shit about me. She's just here because I'm Kennedy-Fucking-Lane and she wants to say she fucked me.

Somehow, I manage to open my eyes. Through an intoxicated haze, I can make out Brodie—at least I think it's him—bent over a table, slowly moving his face along a mirrored surface. I lift the dead weight of the bottle of Jack to my lips, welcoming the burn as the whiskey hits my throat.

Muted light filters in from the gaps in the curtains, catching the glare from the mirror and splaying prisms of color over Brodie's body. He leans back in the chair and lifts his hand to his nose, snorting back any excess coke he may have missed. He cracks his neck like he always does when he's finished, and pats his thigh.

It feels like I'm watching in slow motion as a groupie appears like an apparition out of nowhere and floats to his lap, immediately wrapping her arms around his neck and crashing her lips to his.

I shut my eyes, guiding the heavy bottle back to my lips, hoping the magic liquid will block everything out. It hurts to swallow. My throat feels like it's on fire. I wonder how much is enough to numb the pain.

"No. I mean more than this," I say, setting the bottle back on the couch.

"I've got more right here, man." The unrelenting music pounds in my head, and I hear the sound of the chair scraping across the hardwood floor as the room spins.

Shuffled feet make their way across the room. I hear a crash, broken glass hitting the floor, and then a fit of giggling.

"I fell. Kiss it better, Brodie." That high-pitched voice is like nails on a goddamn chalkboard.

I open one eye to find Brodie leaning against me. "Mmm . . . You've got more, too, I see. What's your name, sugar?" Brodie gives a lazy grin to the blond perched in my lap.

"Whatever you want it to be," she says slowly, leaning forward to press her lips to my neck.

I try to roll my eyes, but it's too much work in my current fucked-up state. From the floor, the giggles continue and Brodie laughs, big and boisterous, reminding me I'm, in fact, still alive.

The girl on my lap rolls her head back, her bleached hair spilling against my jean-covered thighs. Pouring a stream of whiskey over her tits, my tongue lazily follows the trail. "Mmm . . . More, but not real. I miss real tits."

"They're tits, man—real, fake, what's the difference?"

"More . . . The difference is more."

Brodie leans over me and cups her breast in his hand. "Well, I like them, sweetheart. Come here."

It doesn't take much coaxing to pull her from my lap. She squeals while I try to make my escape, pushing off the cushions a few times to get somewhat vertical. The room sways, and I stumble back against the arm of the couch.

My vision blurs to the point I can only make out shapes—changing, shifting, and morphing shapes that seem to deliberately block my path.

I take in the bodies currently grinding together in an erotic, tempting dance. They're everywhere and nowhere at the same time. Against walls, windows, furniture, molded to the floor. It's like a fucking funhouse in here.

"I'm just gonna . . ." The world tilts, and my eyes slide shut.

"You're high as a motherfucking kite, Lane," Brodie yells from the couch.

My grip tightens around the neck of the bottle as I step over a pair of endless long legs pushed into high-heeled fuck-me boots. I register something slicing into my foot, and I welcome the pain.

I stumble to the black grand piano where there's a couple of plastic bags open, their powdery contents spilling out. I can almost hear them calling my name.

Somewhere in all the haze and drug-induced madness of my currently fucked-up, fried brain I know if I take another drink or do another line, it may be my last. The scary part is that some-where in there I kind of want it to be.

Through my blurry vision, I see a solid mass of muscle standing ready in the hall. I think it's Tucker Pearson, my secu-rity guard, and one of the only real friends I have left. He shakes his head in my direction, and makes the decision for me.

Leaving Brodie and the rest of my band to the squealing groupies, I shuffle my way to the first door I find, push it open, and welcome the softness of the bed as I collapse face first into it.

Welcome to the life of a motherfucking rock star.

"GET UP, ASSHOLE."

I groan from a tangle of covers and pillows. Maybe Tucker will go away if I just lay here. It hurts too much to move any-way. The warm covers fly off me, exposing my bare back to the assault of the cool air conditioning.

"Fuck, man. Give me a second."

He opens the blinds to the terrace, and I blink at the harsh sun streaming in. My head pounds and I burrow my face into the pillow, waiting for the welcome darkness to descend. I made it to another day. Halle-fucking-lujah.

"You look like shit."

He grips my hair, forcing my head back as I fight to open my eyes. Even in my fucked-up state, I can see the disappointment in his face. He shakes his head and tightens his hand in my hair.

"Is this what you want, huh? This is what you worked so hard for?"

"Fuck off, Tucker."

"You've got the meeting with the charity today. Did you forget about that? The dream for the sick little boy?"

"Mmm . . ." It hurts when I try to shake my head. "T'morrow." I try to push him away. It's almost impossible at the best of times, given Tucker's sheer size and strength let alone trying it after a night like the one I just survived.

"It *is* tomorrow, idiot."

He pushes my head forcefully into the pillow. The bed dips with his weight. "This has got to stop, man. You want to be *that* cliché? Musical genius who drank and snorted himself into oblivion?"

"What I don't want is a lecture from you right now." My voice is muffled against the pillow.

"You're better than this, Kennedy." His voice is quieter, and I manage to turn my head in his direction, opening my eyes.

"Not anymore."

"You are. Why don't you let me check out that rehab place? The one in Malibu?" It's not the first time he's suggested it.

"Right, 'cause that's not a cliché at all, is it?"

"They deal with celebrities all the time. They have confidentiality rules and—"

"And what? You want me to sit and talk about my goddamn feelings like the last time I tried rehab? That's bullshit, man." I wince as the jackhammer rattles in my head. "Fuck, where's the goddamn Oxy?"

He moves from my vision, and I close my eyes, welcoming the quiet. I stretch my arm out beside me, my hand making impact with warm skin. The room spins as I turn my head, glancing over at the body beside me. I think she might be the giggler from the floor last night, but I'm not sure.

"Shit." I manage to push myself up and lean back against the plush headboard. I don't want to see her half-naked body draped over the rumpled bed. At least I still have my jeans on. Little victories amuse me, and I try to laugh, but it hurts too much.

My stomach rolls as she lets out a moan, lifting her head just off the pillow, her eyes glassy and unfocused as she stares blankly at me. "Ready again so soon, handsome?"

In the cruel, harsh light of the morning after, everything is different. Here I am, in a lush penthouse suite with a strung-out junkie, whose name I don't even want to know beside me.

The raccoon eyes are in full force as she clumsily wipes them, leaving more mascara smudged beneath her lashes. "I just need a little something first. Got any smack?" She tries to push herself up, but doesn't seem to have the strength. She dissolves back to the bed with a giggle.

I close my eyes and swallow down the razor blades lining my throat.

"Tucker?" I strain to hear him moving around in the bathroom. I think I doze off right there, leaning up against the headboard with my head feeling like a tire iron has been rammed through it, until ice-cold water splashes down over me.

"Jesus, fuck!" My body convulses when I try to push off the bed. I glare at Tucker as he holds an empty ice bucket. The giggler squeals louder in hysterics.

"You—in the shower. Now." He scowls at me, daring me to defy him.

The frigid water drips from my damp hair as I push off the soaked bed. He shakes his head, his lips curling up into a knowing smile. I think Tucker's patience is running out, but for now, I know I'm forgiven for another night of debauchery.

"Do something with that, will you?" I tilt my head in the direction of the giggler. He knows the routine. Wipe her phone, pay her well, and remind her of the confidentiality agreement she no doubt has forgotten she signed when she was sober.

"I'm on it," he replies, while I drag my sorry ass to the bathroom. I curse as pain shoots through my foot, and I struggle to remember what happened last night.

It's not unusual for me to have blackouts where I have absolutely no idea what I did or how I got to be in the place I wake up in. I know I'm existing on a very thin and unstable line. I've been looking to the bottle to fill up a gaping hole in me. If left unchecked . . . the siren call to make the pain go away is too strong for me to resist.

It's one of the reasons I'm grateful for Tucker. He's the one who pulls me back to reality after a night of excess. Why he hasn't left me is a miracle. But he's here, dealing with what I can't. I can hear shouting from the giggler behind the closed door while he cleans up my mess one more time.

Leaning against the cool marble vanity, I squint in the harsh lighting. I hardly recognize the gaunt face staring back at me. Fumbling with the tap, which is harder to figure out than it should be, I finally get the cold water to turn on. I lean over the basin and splash water on my face.

I hate myself for admitting that Tucker is right. I'm getting too old for this shit. You could easily mistake me for an addict on the street instead of a successful musician who should be on top of the world.

Under the glare and buzz of the fluorescent lights in the luxury of the bathroom bigger than my first apartment, it dawns on me: I've just used the word I have always refused to associate with myself. *Addict.*

The bathroom door opens, and Tucker steps into view in the mirror beside me. He's the picture of health and life. A sharp contrast to what I'm becoming.

"What are you doing? If she was here, if she could see you—"

I meet his eyes in the mirror. "Don't go there, man. Just don't."

"I have to."

I glare back at him. "If I piss you off this much, why the fuck do you stick around?"

"You know damn well why. I promised Rob—"

"Don't. Don't you dare say her name." I clench my teeth, feeling my jaw set.

He glares at me in disgust. "Do you think this is what she would've wanted for you?"

We stare at each other in the mirror in a silent standoff, neither one of us wavering.

"Oxy is beside the sink. Drink this." He tosses me an energy drink—some pink colored shit that tastes like hell, no doubt. "All of it. Shave the forest you've got growing on your face, and take whatever you need to appear somewhat alive and coherent. The charity team will be here at one."

My hands shake as I go for the pain meds. It's a fight to get the lid off. Finally, I pour a couple of pills into my wet palm and lift my gaze to meet his in the mirror.

"You're really living the dream, Lane. Living the dream."

abigail

"GOT A MINUTE, BOSS?"

My eyes pop up from the spreadsheet I've been struggling with. Tessa Baker, my assistant, is poised at my doorway. Grateful for the interruption, I smile.

"Sure. What's up?"

She strides into my office and hands me a sheaf of papers. "We have the final report on the Peterson Dream."

"Oh, good. We really lucked out on that one." I still can't believe we'd been able to fulfill ten-year-old Ryan Peterson's dream of being with his beloved Seattle Seahawks when they won the Super Bowl. The lucky part hadn't been sending Ryan to the game—the Seahawks and NFL had been only too cooperative. It was whether Ryan's bone cancer, which had accelerated, would allow him to attend. It had been a race against time.

I scan the report with my usual mixture of pride and sorrow; pride because we were able to provide this for a spunky young boy who sorely deserved it, and sorrow because he had lost his fight with his illness only three weeks after the event. As the executive director for *What's Your Dream*, I'm more than familiar with the emotions.

Although we'd only been in existence ten years, we'd already fulfilled more than three thousand dreams of children with terminal or life-threatening illnesses. Since I'd become director three years ago, we'd doubled the number of chapters. Soon, we'll have one in every state.

"His parents were so grateful," Tessa comments, her eyes

full of understanding.

I nod again, my brow furrowing as I recall his mother's voice when she'd called to let us know about Ryan's passing. I couldn't help but cry with her over the phone as she'd described his last days. How happy and thankful he'd been to not only attend the game with his family, but to also have the chance to hold the Lombardi trophy—with the help of a few of his favorite players. It had been all he'd talked about, right up until the end.

Moving the report aside, I take a settling breath and stand, smoothing my black pencil skirt. "Okay, then. Everyone waiting for me, I suppose?" I look at my assistant.

Tess ticks something off on her clipboard. "Just April, of course. But the others are on their way."

We leave my office and Tess follows me down to one of our smaller meeting rooms. April is seated at the table, texting someone. I swear, the girl was born with a phone in her hand.

"You're late." She doesn't look up.

Smirking, I take the seat opposite her. "Happens to the best of us once in a while, April," I quip as the rest of our group files in and take their places.

"Yeah, yeah," she retorts with a sigh, and places her phone on the table. She flips her glossy, straight black hair over her shoulder. April Morrison is our public relations director and damn good at her job. I'd managed to coax her away from Make-A-Wish last year, and I constantly thank my lucky stars. She's sharp, tireless, and loyal, and her penchant for punctuality has become legendary.

"So, what do we have this week?" I open the folder in front of me and glance up to our giving director, Nadia Baskov, sitting next to April.

"Sixteen dreams were already approved by the Eligibility team this week"—she takes a sip of her tea—"but they bumped these seven cases up to us."

I hum in understanding. Although our Eligibility team is responsible for evaluating each request, they only implement the relatively straightforward dreams, such as those for new pets, birthday parties, or trips. The more complex requests are sent upstairs where the four of us—April, Nadia, Duane Allen, our finance director, and I—deliberate on the possibilities and appropriateness of the requests.

I skim through the seven cases before sitting back to let Nadia take us through each one. Her fingers toy absently with a lock of her silky blond hair. With her sharp green eyes and stylish navy suit, she looks the epitome of a cold, calculating businesswoman, but underneath her austere demeanor beats a sensitive and compassionate heart.

A twelve-year-old girl with a brain tumor wants an audition with the Moscow Ballet. Hmm, that's a little tricky in the current political climate. However, Nadia's cousin is a trainer with the San Francisco ballet . . . maybe that could work instead. A six-year-old boy from Colorado with a degenerative lung condition wants to score a goal against his favorite hockey star. A ten-year-old boy with MS loves airplanes and dreams of being a pilot; my contact at Alaska Airlines can provide a complete tour, everything from the tarmac to the cockpit. Maybe we can throw in a trip to one of the flight schools, too.

We work through the cases, discussing the merits of each and formulating initial plans. The children's faces that peer up at me from the folder look happy and hopeful, but when I read their stories . . . I glance out the large window at the bright blue sky, blinking back tears. I hate that so many virulent diseases threaten so many young lives. So many futures at risk. So many poems and symphonies to write, or planets and species to discover. One of the children we see here could hold the key to solving the world's greatest problems, but may never get the chance.

Ever since I was fifteen, when I saw what cancer could do, I've wanted to do something about it. Science has never been my forte, so I knew I wouldn't be the one who would find the cures. But I could do something to ease the patients' suffering and bring a little joy to their lives, as well as the lives of their families.

"You okay there, Abby?" I glance up to see April's concerned face. We all have our moments when the stories and the kids behind them break through the professional veneer we try to maintain during these meetings. Last week it was Tess who'd had to excuse herself during the discussion of a six-year-old boy with Non-Hodgkin's Lymphoma, who simply wanted to take his grandfather to Disney World. The grandfather had been an illustrator for some of the Disney movies back in the sixties.

I suddenly become aware that I've brought the discussion to a halt. "Yes, I'm fine," I assure her and nod at Nadia. "You were saying?" I smile encouragingly, and she continues, holding the last profile aloft.

"Now, I think I sent to you the details on the meeting we're having today a few days ago, Abby, but I haven't heard your thoughts on it yet." Nadia fans the pages out on the table. She takes a breath and slowly lets it out, her eyes lingering the last page.

"This is Parker Jensen," she begins, indicating the grinning blond boy on the top sheet. "Eleven years old with leukemia. He lives right here in San Francisco, and his dream is to enjoy a day as a rock star with . . ." She taps the second photo in the set, and there is a collective intake of breath around the table.

"Oh, my," April says appreciatively. "He's aged well, hasn't he?"

"Kennedy Lane?" Duane questions. "Isn't he a little old for the preteen crowd?"

Nadia's eyeing the photo like it's a triple-decker hot fudge sundae. "He's not *that* old," she scoffs. "He's only thirty-six. Apparently, Parker idolizes him. He's learning to play the guitar and wants to be just like Lane when he grows up." Her expression becomes wistful. "And I hope he has the chance."

We're silent for a moment. The thought Parker may not get a chance to grow up sobers us. Then April sighs, a smirk curving her lips. "Well, Parker has excellent taste in music. I don't remember how many awards this guy has won, but he's incredible. And when you throw in that *face* . . ." She points to the publicity photo. "I think spending a day with Kennedy Lane would be my dream, too." Tess giggles in agreement; Duane rolls his eyes at her. "Oh, please. Get over yourselves. You don't see Abby getting all swoony. Besides, when was Redfall's last hit? They're never on the radio anymore," he complains.

"Abby never gets swoony. And, Redfall has a new album coming out soon," April shoots back, peering at Duane over her chic cat-eye glasses.

"Oh, what? I suppose the money's running low, so he's going to squeeze out something to make the teenage girls and their mothers scream? Then he'll take his money and run back to wherever aging rock stars go when they retire?"

"What's got into you?" A frown mars Nadia's lovely features. "We deal with celebrities all the time."

He shrugs. "I just don't think he'd be a good influence, that's all. The kid should idolize someone more worthwhile."

"They can't *all* want to go to Disneyland." April waves her hand at him. "And Lane is more than a rock star; he's an artist. At least, he was."

Their sniping fades into the background as I peruse the two pages. Parker is adorable with bright blue eyes and an infectious grin. Lane is . . . Actually, I'm not sure what Lane is. Handsome seems inadequate when you consider his chiseled jawline and sensual pout. But, April is right; he's so much more than his looks. The complex rhythms and cerebral lyrics that have always characterized his sound set him apart from his contemporaries. His band was a staple during my college years and beyond; in fact, I have dozens of Redfall's songs on my playlists now.

But how wise would it be to fulfill this particular dream? Parker's treatments have left him in a fragile state. Is Kennedy Lane the type of man who would understand—and respect—that?

I'd started researching him as soon as Nadia had sent me the report, but had come up with mixed results so far. His older interviews revealed an intelligent, whimsical mind that appealed to me. He sounded like someone I'd love to sit with for a beer and conversation. His more recent comments in the press, however, had sounded so angry. Arrogance and negligence had replaced the whimsy and playfulness. Maybe he succumbed to the pampered celebrity lifestyle, or maybe it was just a bad day. Who knew?

I flip the promo photograph over, focusing on the more recent paparazzi photos Nadia included in the packet. The photos captured him leaving a club with his entourage. He was obviously annoyed and probably drunk. But more than that, there was something in his eyes . . . something familiar in that glazed stare . . .

I manage to suppress a shudder when a particularly unpleasant memory leaps to mind; a memory of screamed threats, desperate begging, and a final, terrifying good-bye. My ex, Lucas, had hid his addiction before finally slipping up. After months of pleading and empty promises of rehab, his inability to change led me finally to wipe my hands clean of the mess his addiction had made of our lives.

It's funny how having a gun pressed to your temple can

make everything so clear.

"Abby? What do you think?" My attention snaps back to the here and now, and I see all eyes trained on me. I take a deep breath to compose myself, and lock the past where it belongs—in the past.

"Actually, Duane has a good point." I ignore how he puffs up his chest at my comment. "I'm not sure if exposing a young boy to this *scene* is a good idea. You know, the whole sex, drugs, and rock 'n roll' thing." I hold up a hand when I see Nadia getting defensive. "I know—it's a stereotype. But, I'm honestly concerned why Lane dropped out of sight for so long. Was he in rehab? Or was he off on some spiritual journey meditating with the Dalai Lama or something?" I pause and thoughtfully tap the photos with my fingertips. "All that aside, granting wishes is our mission. If we can make this happen, we should. We'll have a better idea once we meet with his team today."

"*We?*" There's no mistaking the annoyance in Nadia's voice. "Well *I* have an appointment with his manager and a representative from his record label at the Fairmont at one. The record label was very enthusiastic."

"Will Lane be there, too?"

She adjusts her glasses, looking like the cat that got the cream. "There is that distinct possibility."

I share a quick glance with April; she cocks an eyebrow, and I know she's also noticed Nadia's odd demeanor.

"I'm going with you."

"Oh, uh . . ." She falters, drawing my gaze up to hers. Nadia rarely hesitates. "Are you sure? You don't usually attend these sorts of meetings, Abby."

"I know, but I want to ensure this goes smoothly." At her sharp look, I add, "I've heard Lane's manager can be difficult, and you might need the extra firepower." I don't want her to think

I doubt her abilities. Nadia is extremely skilled at her job. I'm probably misreading her—she's too professional to fuck around with a case, literally *or* figuratively. "And, given what we've just discussed about the potential negative influences in his life-style, I'd like to hear for myself if his team understands Parker's situation."

She hums, sounding mollified, and peers at me speculatively. "This is one of those cases for you, isn't it?"

I sigh, knowing that she's right. Sometimes, a dream fulfill-ment will hit you just the right way, and it becomes "yours." And apparently Parker Jensen, with all his struggles and his soulful eyes that touch my heart, has become one of mine.

"I guess you're right."

"Okay," she replies, with a touch of resignation. "I'll send the appointment over to Tess so she can arrange your calendar."

Duane deflates with Nadia's statement, and we quickly ad-journ. I exit the room, pretending not to hear Duane calling my name. I'm not in the mood for whatever he wants to say, espe-cially if he's going to complain about my decision. I swear, the man can pout worse than a thirteen-year-old girl.

Back in my office, I tuck a stray hair back into my perfect chignon and adjust the collar of my crisp cotton blouse. Not bad for thirty-four, but still, April is right. 'Swoony' is definitely not a word I subscribe to, not even for fuckhot rock stars.

Sitting at my desk, I pull Lane's promo photo out of the file and stare at it. Peering out from beneath a mop of thick black hair, those deep blue eyes seem to leap off the page to see right through me. It's disquieting. Suddenly, the only word I can think of to describe Kennedy Lane is . . . *dangerous* . . . in more ways than one.

But how can I say no when he's a little boy's heart's desire?

chapter two

kennedy

I'M IN HELL WHERE THEY play "Flight of the Bumblebee" over, and over, and over again. It's muffled and sounds like it's coming from somewhere far away, but still; it's torture to the fucked-up state of my head right now.

"Shit, shit! Double shit!"

A panicked, and highly amusing, female voice reaches in and pulls me from the darkness. I stretch my legs out on the sofa and crack an eye open, peering out to the awe-inspiring San Fran skyline from the suite at the Fairmont. Thank fuck I kept my sunglasses on. The sun blazes through the terrace doors, doing nothing for my headache.

Tucker's form is evident on the terrace, and in a rare display, he looks relaxed as he sits in a lounge chair, peering out over the city.

The annoying ringtone slices through the solitude of the vast living room, and I can't help but grin. Why the hell would anyone use that tune on their phone?

I hear rustling from across the room and something being

dropped on the piano. There's a series of jumbled and erratic notes that stirs something deep inside me. Finally, thank fuck, the ringtone silences.

"Mom!" It's a whisper-yell from the same woman's voice, and I slowly lift from the cushions to peer over the top of the couch. "You're on speaker, but I can't talk right now."

"I just don't know where all this uptightness comes from," another female voice complains through the phone. "Even your father lets his hair down once in a while now. Tell me, how are things in the love department?"

"I'm not uptight!" I take a scan across the room, and the woman slowly comes into view. She's leaning against the piano, her fingers hovering over the keys, her dark hair swept up to expose the curve of her neck. I drop my eyes over the back of her tailored black suit: a fitted blazer hiding her ass, and a conservative knee length skirt with black stockings. The shoes give me pause. They're high and black and really the only thing I see that would put into question the uptight description I heard being bellowed from the phone. "I'm the director of a respected charity. I can't just go around yapping about my sex life all the time."

Charity . . . It's all coming back to me now. The meeting that Brodie and Tucker reminded me about this morning. This morning, when I was barely lucid and woke up with a nameless groupie in my bed. I should have been alone. Alone is good. Alone is fewer problems and potential fuck-ups.

"Ah-ha!" the echoed female voice crows. "You *do* have a sex life! Does he treat you well? You know, satisfies you—"

I watch as she takes the phone off speaker, disappointed I'm not going to get to hear the rest of the conversation.

"I can't talk to you right now. I'm about to go into a meeting." Her fingers trail across the keys, and from deep inside, I hear another few chords beckoning me over. "Because I'm nervous and . . ." Her voice trails off as she listens to whatever is being said on the other end of the phone, and I get a minute to appreciate the tempting curves of her body—real curves—not plastically enhanced.

"I know I'm never nervous. You know what? Never mind. Is something on fire or is someone dead?" I squeeze my eyes shut, trying to hold onto the notes that are tempting me, but her conversation is too damn distracting to focus.

"You called me to set me up? Mom! How many times do we have to—"

I open my eyes to watch her once more. Clearly, her mother is a source of frustration. She's wired tight, this one. I could do something about that.

From the terrace, I see Tucker move to the door, his eyes trained on the woman, ready to take her down if need be. I hold up a hand, silently stopping him.

"What kind of a name is Beau? Was his mom a Dukes of Hazzard fan or something?"

She stares up at the ceiling, shaking her head. "We can talk about this later. I have to go." Another pause as her eyes move back to the piano. "I love you, too." I watch her shoulders sag as she presses a button on the phone to end the call and tosses it back into her bag, before sinking to the piano bench.

I'm up and off the couch, crossing the room to the piano before I can stop myself. Sliding in beside her on the bench, my fingers still over the keys. "Oh! I'm so sorry. I had no—"

"Shhh . . ." I pause, trying to focus, and I wonder if it's ever not going to hurt when I think about Robin. She loved when I played. She always said it was where I wrote my best songs. She used to sit and watch me, offering her honest and unique commentary on whatever I dreamed up.

"I'm just going to leave—"

"Stay right here." I feel the tension release from my shoulders and brush my fingers across the keys, igniting my adrenaline.

"Do you have a recorder on your phone?" I see the notes come into view behind my closed eyes. I play as the melody finds me like it always has. It's the one thing that never fails. The one thing I can always trust.

"A what?" she whispers.

"Just record this."

I play the same few chords, feeling her stiffen beside me, and hearing a little huff of aggravation. "Okay. I'll video it. Will that work?"

"Do you have something to write on when I'm done?"

"How's this?" I finally open my eyes as she thrusts a file folder in front of me. I see my name on the tab at the side, along with another underneath it. Parker Jensen.

"Perfect. Start recording." I play the simple melody that will end up being the foundation for the song. I don't know how many times I repeat it, altering and weaving when it wants to take me somewhere else.

The words come spilling out of me as I hit what will be the chorus.

"If you let me take your hand, I'll wrap you in my arms
And I'll make sure you're safe tonight underneath a sky of stars—"

"Fuck!" I lift my fingers from the keys in frustration as the lyrics fade off. "I fucking had it." I rake my hand through my hair. "I hate that." I turn to look at the woman beside me. "You know what I mean?"

Behind my sunglasses, my eyes lock to her big, hazel ones. Even with the hangover from hell, those eyes hold me. Vibrant amber gold flecks play in caramel brown, deep green around the edges. She looks like she's in shock, her pretty mouth dropped open slightly as she stares at me in an awkward silence that yawns between us.

Now that I get a chance to really look at her, I can appreciate how gorgeous she is. Soft features, perfectly full lips, a natural color blushing her cheeks. She's real in a way I don't get to see much these days. Real, and looking at me like I just dropped down from another planet.

"Sort of? I mean not with this, obviously, because that was just . . ." She pauses, searching my face. "I don't have words for what that was. But, I know it's frustrating when you want something, and it just doesn't work out like you hoped."

"Yeah. That was kind of shit, wasn't it?"

Her eyes widen. "No! That's not what I meant. That was amazing."

"Really?"

She passes me the folder. "You should write it down, or whatever it is you do now."

"It doesn't sound cheesy? Robin would always . . ." I stop that thought before it goes any further, my heart stabbing me in the chest just to make sure I don't say her name again. I take the folder, and set it on top of the piano. I can't go there right now, back to memories of my sister. Not with the headache from hell, and certainly not with a perfect stranger who probably thinks I'm certifiable at this point. "Do you have a pen?"

"Yes, here." She fiddles around in her purse, holding one out for me. I give her a grin of thanks, and lean over the keys to start writing.

"Thanks for this. How are you in here, just out of curiosity?" A long few minutes pass before she answers, and I feel her watching me, probably trying to decide if I'm a nutjob or not.

"Brodie told me to wait in here. He's giving one of my colleagues the tour."

"You didn't want the tour?"

"No. He said you were sleeping and to wait in here."

"Well, I was *trying* to sleep." I glance over at her.

Her brows knit together. "You heard all of that conversation with my mother, didn't you?"

"Mmm . . . Want to talk about it?"

"No. I'm going to probably need therapy with the knowledge that you heard any of that," she says with a groan.

Finishing the lyrics on the folder, I hand the pen back to her. "So, I'm Kennedy Lane." I wish there was more to write, but this happens all the time. You have something, and then it's just gone. It might never come back, or it might hit me at four thirty in the morning.

She takes the pen from me, but says nothing. I lean into her slightly, holding her gaze, not wanting her to look away. "This would be the part where you tell me your name."

"I'm sorry. It's Abby. I mean, Abigail Walker. I'm the director of—"

"*What's Your Dream*. Yes. I know. Brodie said you were, let me get his words right, 'Like a dog with a bone,' I think he said."

She lets out a nervous laugh. "I know how to get what I want."

"Is that right? And what is it exactly that you want, Miss Abigail Walker?" Fuck, she's fun to tease.

"Well, right now . . . You."

An unexpected shiver runs through me at her words that I'm quick to tamp down. "Abby, I know you've probably heard a lot about the rock 'n roll lifestyle, but we just met."

She rolls her eyes at my smirk. "Please. Like you're rock's biggest angel."

"I have my moments, so I've been told." I open the folder and my eyes fall to a picture of a blond boy. He doesn't look very old. "Tell me about him."

"His name is Parker Jensen," she says, all sarcasm and play-fulness gone from her voice. "He's eleven, and he has leukemia." He's so young. Life is fucking not fair sometimes. "He idolizes you. He's even learning to play the guitar."

I meet her eyes once more, and I can feel her assessing, judg-ing. It doesn't sit well with me. "Really?"

"Yes. He has all your records, posters . . . the whole nine yards."

"What would something like this entail, exactly?"

"If we go ahead with this, we'd decide that together. He'd like a day as a rock star. I was thinking maybe a studio tour, a lit-tle concert at the hospital."

"*If* we go ahead?"

Her smile fades, and she shifts away from me on the bench. Out of reach. Unattainable. "Yes. If."

"Why wouldn't we?"

"Well, to be honest, I'm not sure if your type of lifestyle is . . ." She pauses, her scrutinizing gaze running over me. " . . . healthy for him. He's in a very vulnerable place right now, physically and emotionally."

"What exactly about my *lifestyle* exactly are you worried about?" I ask, my jaw set as the anger rises.

"Do I really need to spell it out for you?"

"Well, to be honest, *Abby*. I think you do."

"Your partying for starters." She gives me a pointed look. "That sort of thing wouldn't be tolerated when you're with him."

I can't help my scowl. "Of course not. Jesus Christ. Do you really think I would let a kid into a party?"

"I don't know. But pictures don't lie, and I don't have to tell you that the press has painted you in a rather unfavorable light of late—"

"You honestly believe photos in a fucking gossip rag?" I stare at her in disbelief, but she just purses those enticing lips and continues without missing a beat.

"And if you do have a problem, I can't and won't subject Parker to that."

"I do not have a problem." My voice sounds raw, gritty.

She slowly pulls my sunglasses from my face, her eyes hard as they blaze into mine. It's like she can see right into my soul. I blink back from the harshness of the light.

"Right. No problem at all," she scoffs and sets my sunglasses on the piano. She shakes her head, standing from the bench. "I'm sorry to have wasted your time. Maybe you could just sign a few posters or CDs for him. He'd be over the moon."

"But that's not his dream."

"As it turns out, his dream is a bit of a nightmare."

And that's it. She's dismissed me within a couple of minutes. I reach out for her arm, feeling her tense at my touch. "This isn't what it looks like. Half of San Francisco is probably hung over."

She doesn't seem to appreciate my attempt at humor. "Not at one in the afternoon on a Monday."

"Listen, I want to do this the right way. I just need some time, and I'll be okay."

Her eyes narrow, and then she lays into me. "*Time* is a luxury Parker doesn't have. I don't really think you understand what it's like for him. He's tired and exhausted from spending most of his childhood in a hospital when all of his friends were outside playing and just being kids." She yanks her arm from my grasp. "He's in pain most of time, but when he can find the energy to do something, it's always the guitar he picks up. And when he can't? When he's lying in bed or getting treatments? He listens to your songs, and he smiles when he does, because somehow you make it better for him. The only time he's really and truly happy is when he listens to you. So you'll forgive me if I don't want to ruin this idea he's built up of who you are with the sad reality."

"*Sad reality?*" I push up off the bench, towering over her. She doesn't flinch or back down.

"Yes, Kennedy. Sad."

♪ ♩ ♪ ♩

abigail

LOOKING UP INTO HIS OUTRAGED, but overly dilated and bloodshot eyes, a vast disappointment washes over me, making my heart ache. I had been counting on this working for Parker's sake. But I've seen this same look too often before.

I had deluded myself with my ex, Lucas, rationalized and ignored what was right in front of my nose; I won't make the same mistake now.

As devastatingly handsome as the man before me is, he looks like he's been dragged down a mile of rough road. Everything he's wearing, from his black jeans to his T-shirt under his misbuttoned shirt, is rumpled. Now that he's not sitting at the piano bench and hiding behind his sunglasses, he's swaying unsteadily on his feet and looks like he's having difficulty focusing on me. And he thinks this is just a regular hangover?

"My reality is far from sad, baby." He gestures to our opulent surroundings with a smirk.

I turn and take a few wandering steps, glancing around at the luxurious furnishings. I've never been in the Fairmont's penthouse before, and if the circumstances were different, I would be impressed. Now, however, the extravagance feels hollow. "How long have you been staying here? A week? Longer?" Facing him again, I shrug. "You know, a single night in this suite probably costs more than three of Parker's chemo treatments."

His mouth drops open at my matter-of-fact statement, and

he winces as if I'd slapped him. Maybe I did.

But, damn it; I just can't shut up. After hearing him at the piano, the once-in-a-lifetime glimpse of *Kennedy Lane* creating something, I know how incredible the experience would've been for Parker. It pisses me off that this guy just doesn't get it.

"You say the photos online lie. You say you don't have a problem," I continue, somehow managing to keep my voice even. "And yet you just woke up in the middle of the day after a night—*nights*, probably—of partying. Your pupils are the size of dinner plates, your nostrils are red, and you're sweating buckets in an air-conditioned room. I bet you're still wearing yesterday's clothes. And you're apparently thinking all of this is somehow acceptable because you're you. Did I get any of that wrong?"

Shock and even a little embarrassment flickers across his face; I definitely hit my mark. Then, his eyes narrow, and he stalks toward me, making me take a few steps back as he advances. "What gives you the right to judge me?" Those icy blue eyes harden. "Who the fuck do you think you are?"

I have to breathe deeply to keep my own anger at bay. "I'm not judging you; I only call it as I see it. I don't care if you throw your life away; your family and friends probably care, but I don't. You can drink, or snort, or inject whatever you want. You'll do it anyway, regardless of what I think. I will mourn the loss of your music, though, because frankly, I think your talent is amazing. You are incredibly gifted, Mr. Lane." It's the truth, and the thought of him so negligently throwing that gift away only makes me angrier. "My concern, my *only* concern, is with the children who come to me in the hope of having their dreams fulfilled, not dashed into a million pieces."

"Look at you; not a hair out of place, standing there in your uptight suit and wrapped in so much self-righteousness that your shoulders must bow from the weight." His voice drips with indignation and malice; a frisson of fear runs through me as he continues to advance. "I think your mother has a point. I bet you've never really let your hair down, have you? Really let loose and enjoyed life?"

"Who the . . . *My* private life isn't at issue here," I snap, my mortification he overheard my conversation burning brightly again. My back bumps against the wall and, before I know it, he takes two quick steps forward and effectively boxes me in. My eyes widen as he lowers his face to within inches of mine. He's taller than I expected, and his height right now, I'm sad to admit, is intimidating.

"Isn't it? Maybe if you took a walk on the wild side once in a while you'd be more tolerant." His voice drops to a raspy purr, and I stiffen at his proximity. Sucking in a breath, I freeze as he gently frees a tiny strand of hair, rubbing it between his fingers. Despite the stale smell of cigarettes that clings to him, I also sense something musky and earthy about him that strikes a chord deep inside me. I swallow thickly and frown, willing it away.

"I can't afford to be tolerant when one of our client's wishes is at stake. Step back, please." I push against his chest, but he doesn't move. Instead, he carefully tucks the strand he'd been toying with behind my ear. His lips curl in a sensual pout.

"Your mother asked a good question: *Are* you being satisfied? I bet you've never known what a man, a *real* man, can do to a woman. A man who can make your heart race, your toes curl, and your pussy clench . . . Have you ever felt that, *Abigail*?" I feel his hot breath on my neck. "Has a man ever done that from just a look?"

I gasp as everything in me does just that, but I'd rather die than admit it. Who the fuck does he think he is? "You'll never know. Oh, and Kennedy . . ." I brace myself and look directly into his blazing eyes. "A real man admits when he's wrong."

His eyes burn and he opens his mouth to retort when the door at the far side of the room begins to open. Kennedy shoves away from me and staggers back, just as Nadia, Brodie, and the record label rep, Janet, rejoin us. Janet and Brodie are oblivious; Janet has her face buried in her smartphone, and Brodie's staring at Nadia's ass. But my colleague purses her lips, her eyes darting between Kennedy and me. I straighten my shoulders and smile as if I wasn't just seconds away from either slugging or kissing him.

"Oh, Kennedy; you're awake." Brodie finally tears his eyes away from Nadia to smirk at his client. "This is Nadia Baskov, giving director of *What's Your Dream*. I see you've obviously already met Ms. Walker."

"Yes, we've already discussed Parker's case," I interject brightly. "Kennedy has graciously agreed to sign a few albums and, perhaps, a poster."

Nadia narrows her eyes in consternation. "That would be fantastic, of course, but I thought . . ."

I glance at Kennedy, but look away quickly when I see him glowering at me. At least he's not refuting my statement. "Unfortunately, the band's schedule won't allow anything more," I continue, letting my extreme disappointment seep into my voice. Everything about this situation is disappointing. I stroll over to the piano to retrieve Parker's file, stilling when I see the lyrics scrawled on the front in a strong hand.

If you let me take your hand, I'll wrap you in my arms . . .
Beautiful.

I open the manila folder and, bracing it against the piano lid, carefully tear it in two. With one last look at the lyrics, I place that half gently on the music rack. It also contains the label with Parker's name; maybe that will give the wayward genius brooding by the sofa something to think about.

"So that's it?" Brodie brightens considerably. He claps his hands and rubs his palms together, as if pleased with himself. "That's doable. Kennedy would be glad to—"

Janet pops up from her phone as I shove the remaining file contents into my leather tote and slip the thin straps over my shoulder. "Wait, what?" She looks between Brodie and Kennedy. "This isn't what we'd discussed."

"So? He could sign some CDs, enough for some of the kid's friends, too." Brodie nods his shaggy blond head, obviously warming to his idea. "And a few posters, and—oh, I know—how about a couple concert tees?"

"But we talked about this." The label rep glares at him. "It would be great press. And it's perfect timing for the album."

"Unfortunately, Parker's timing is my priority," I remind her.

The professional smile plastered on my lips masks my whirling emotions. I'm frustrated with Kennedy and appalled at myself for losing my cool and behaving so unprofessionally. Why did I goad him like that? My gaze lands on Parker's name taped to the ripped folder and my smile becomes wistful; most of all, I'm disheartened over not being able to fulfill Parker's dream properly. *Damn, damn, damn.*

I sigh quietly and look toward Kennedy, startling when a huge man with a black T-shirt and blacker hair steps into view from the curtains by the terrace doors. Shit, has he been here the whole time? Filing that embarrassing tidbit away, I focus on Kennedy who continues to stare at me stoically.

When he doesn't speak, I continue, "As I was explaining to Kennedy earlier, Parker doesn't have the luxury of waiting, I'm afraid." He squints at me from underneath the unruly mop of jet-black hair falling across his forehead, but I can't tell if it's in reaction to my words or his current "hangover".

"Well, Kennedy, if you've already agreed . . ." Brodie trails off, as both he and Janet look at their client with concern. He still hasn't spoken a word, seemingly content to let everyone talk about him as if he wasn't standing right here. I wonder if that happens a lot to him.

He nods, locking eyes with me. "Yes, certainly. Whatever *Abigail* deems acceptable." His voice is soft, but there's a dark undercurrent that I can tell his manager and the muscle-bound bodyguard guy immediately pick up on. The bodyguard moves a little closer to him, while Brodie looks like he's trying to solve an advanced math problem . . . and failing.

Nadia watches me carefully. She knows that if I'm taking this route, I have a good reason. I can see the dissatisfaction on her face as well. I busy myself by rooting around in my tote for my phone, half-listening to their conversation. I take a peek at Kennedy. He's moved back to the piano, standing stock-still with a hand on its smooth surface, his eyes closed with the same concentration etched on his face I'd seen earlier.

I'm struck with a sudden yearning, remembering those magical few minutes as his fingers danced over the keys. I'd give anything to know what's swirling around in his head right now.

"Are you sure we can't work something else out?" Janet asks again as we shake hands all around, except for Kennedy, who's still in a trance at the piano.

Brodie notices my look and shrugs. "Sorry. He doesn't mean to be rude. You know, musical genius and all that," he confides with a rough laugh. "They're on a different level."

I smile faintly. Apparently, entitlement is the rule, rather than the exception with this man.

How sad.

Brodie shows us out to the elevator in the foyer of the suite, but just before we exit, I remember. "Oh, the recording. Where should I send it?" I ask, holding out my phone.

"What recording?" Nadia murmurs in confusion, but Brodie's eyes light up in understanding.

"You can send it to me. Here's a number you can use—"

"Wait." Kennedy suddenly springs to life. He stomps across the room, and I hold my breath, bracing myself for . . . I'm not sure what. But, he merely snatches my phone from my hand and starts entering digits.

"Kennedy," Brodie groans quietly, looking displeased. Kennedy ignores him.

"I trust her." He stares down at me, searching my eyes, and I take my phone from him. Securing it in my purse, the thought hits me . . . *I have Kennedy Lane's phone number.* No one would believe me if I told them.

I turn quickly, ignoring Nadia, who gapes at me like a fish. She manages to compose herself as we enter the elevator and turn to face forward just before the doors close. The last thing I see is Kennedy, standing in the foyer with his hands shoved deep in his pockets, and staring at me with troubled eyes.

chapter three

kennedy

"HOW ABOUT INSTEAD OF HITTING the Jack, we hit the gym?" Tucker suggests. With the tension mounting in the suite, Tucker ushered Brodie and Janet away quickly after Abby and her team left. He always knows when I'm reaching my limit, when I need to just disappear for a while. This is one of those times.

I shake my head and twist the cap from the bottle, the familiar aroma drifting up and taunting me. "Tell me when we were in the gym last."

Tucker smirks, crossing his arms over his chest. "Sure, it's been a while, but I think I can still take you."

Lifting the bottle to my lips, my heart hammers against my ribs as I feel the first drops hit my tongue. It's like I've been in the desert for days with a thirst quenched by one thing and one thing only.

He forcibly lowers the bottle from my lips. "Come on, what do you say? We'll go a few rounds."

My eyes cut to his as I jerk my arm back, my grip tightening over the neck of the bottle. "The only rounds I want are coming from this bottle."

"Kennedy . . ." His voice is quiet and void of the usual smartass tone he uses. "I'm asking you to try. Please."

Holding his gaze, I lift the bottle back to my lips, tilt it up, and savor a few long, healthy sips. I welcome it all: the burn, the heat that radiates through my chest, the wave of calm that rolls through me.

Disappointment washes over his face. I'm pretty good at eliciting that particular reaction today. It's the same look Abby gave me, and with that thought, I take another pull from the bottle.

He lets out a frustrated huff, pacing across the room. Gone is the commanding presence he typically has, replaced with an air of defeat. I can't afford to lose Tucker. He's one of the only people left I truly trust.

I place the bottle down beside the others. The words leave my mouth in a rush. "Which gym?" He stops mid-stride, turning back to me. "I can't exactly just show up downstairs and hop on the treadmill. You'd have a riot on your hands."

He grins, and I see something I haven't in a long time. Hope. "I know a guy." He eyes me cautiously.

"Of course you do."

"COME ON, LANE!" TUCKER HAS barely broken a sweat and looms over me with that annoying grin I only wish I could wipe off his face. I'm the one sprawled out on the floor of an aged and stinking boxing ring for about the twentieth time.

If it's possible, I'm sweating alcohol, and while Tucker tells me it's a good thing, I feel like shit. My hands are clammy and wrapped in a protective lining of tape, and further, the leather boxing gloves he insisted I wear. "Can't have the musical genius injuring his most prized possession," I think were his exact words.

Tucker, of course, doesn't need gloves. He's doing just fine delivering kidney punches with his bare hands. I'm going to feel this for days. Bruises on top of my bruises. I also know he's going easy on me. Tucker could pulverize me if he wanted.

It's a bit shocking how weak I actually am. We used to work out quite a bit back in the day. A few times a week with weights, sparring, running. It's a good way to pass the time, and when I was first starting out, fuck knows there was a lot of time to pass. Everything was different then. I could go to the gym or out for a run, and no one really knew who I was. You don't realize the power of anonymity until you no longer have it.

I'm a lot slower in this area anyway. Give me a guitar, things are different, but trying to dodge Tucker? Forget it. I'm the picture of pathetic as he hauls me to my feet yet again.

I see two of him for a minute while I try to regain my balance. My legs feel like they did this morning—like Jell-O. And this is supposed to be an improvement over a hangover?

"Enough. You made your point," I say through a panted breath.

"Did I?" He's enjoying this way too much.

I surprise him with a right hook to his ribs. He winces only slightly before I hold my arms out to him. He starts to work on the laces of the gloves, tugging them from my hands before going to work on the tape.

"There may be hope for you yet, Kennedy."

LEANING AGAINST THE RAILING THAT lines the expansive terrace of the penthouse, I take in the night as it falls over San Fran. The private chef that is part of the price tag I now know could help fund at least one of Parker's treatments is busy preparing some masterpiece.

For the bulk of the day, Tucker has been intent on playing *Let's Keep Kennedy Busy*. He's pulled out all the stops. Challenged me to a couple rounds of pool in the billiard room, thrown on my brother Adam's latest NASCAR win on one of the televisions, tried to get me interested in the suite's library, even not so subtly left the file folder of lyrics next to my phone.

He means well, even if it does feel like I'm being treated like a child. I also know he's doing this because he doesn't trust me.

I'm restless, and while I should be relaxing and enjoying these last few days of freedom before embarking on this whirlwind of a tour, I'm keyed up and edgy. The sting of my meeting with Abby is fresh and raw.

My phone buzzes relentlessly from the table, and I scowl. Brodie doesn't know when to leave it alone. He's been texting all damn day. Sinking down to one of the lounge chairs, I see a message from an unknown number.

Mr. Lane.

I know it's from Abby. So formal, even via text.

Attached, please find the video of your song. I hope the quality meets with your requirements. Our team will be in touch to arrange for the signing of the items for Parker. Please acknowledge receipt of this message so that I can delete the video and your number.

Regards, Abigail Walker

Opening up the video of the song I played with her at the piano, I close my eyes and listen. Inspiration fires like it did when she was here, and I'm drawn inside quickly; sinking down to the bench at the piano. Picking up right where the video cuts off, the melody and adrenaline take me to where there are no expectations, no demands, no temptations.

Stopping mid-chorus, I return her text with one of my own.

Don't delete the video or my number. Don't give up on me yet.

♪ ♩ ♪ ♩

abigail

DON'T GIVE UP ON HIM?

What the hell is that supposed to mean? I blink at his message in disbelief, my finger hovering over the delete button. Why would he want me to keep his number? Is this some sort of test?

Carefully, as if I'm defusing a bomb, I put down my phone and slump back into my comfy armchair. I don't understand that man at all. Is he saying he's still interested in doing more for Parker? I can't let a drunkard around him. Besides, he made it *abundantly* clear he thought *I* was the one with the problem.

My blood boils again as I recall the arrogant tilt of his head, and the smirk on his lips when he asked if a man had ever made me . . . "What an asshole!" I mutter as I bring my wine glass to my lips. Who the fuck does he think he is? Setting my glass down again on the side table, I huff a wry laugh. He thinks he's an internationally known rock star who could probably get away with murder, that's what. Women line up around the block for this guy. Hell, probably a few men, too. The people surrounding him do nothing but tell him how great he is all the time. No wonder he doesn't think he has a problem.

To be fair, it would be difficult for anyone to say no for long when even the most forbidden temptations are constantly thrown in your face. And the sycophants who latch on to them . . . Well, they'd rather stick a fork in their eye than risk losing their plump, talented meal ticket by telling him or her the truth. At least until that ticket is spent, dried up, and on the skids. Then they move on to their next victim, er, *"client"*.

Restless, I brush a stray hair out of my face. Is there anyone in Kennedy's life who will tell it to him straight? Does he have anyone who, at the very least, might suggest a shower and a change of clothes before a business meeting with a charity, for God's sake? Apparently not.

Even as wrecked as he obviously was, he was one of the most alluring men I've ever met. How can that be? Closing my eyes, I recall the feel of his warm breath against my skin as he loomed over me, of his fingers tracing my ear. *Damn*. A shiver runs through me, and I shift uneasily in my chair. That sense of seductive danger I'd felt just by looking at his photos in a file magnified tenfold when I saw him in the flesh.

The man should come with a health warning.

Laughing weakly, I shake my head in wonder, the surrealism of the day catching up with me. Already on edge in anticipation of the meeting, when I first saw Kennedy emerge from behind the sofa, I was struck speechless for one of the few times in my life. He sauntered over to join me at the piano with an intensity that was captivating. Tall and lithe, his hips moved fluidly with each stride. And his hands! Those long fingers that floated over the keys, producing the most glorious sounds . . .

Groaning, I snatch up my wine glass and take another sip. He must have laughed his ass off when he saw the recording; I'd been so nervous, I could barely hold the phone steady. It was just so sudden. One minute, my mother was trying to set me up with a pastry chef, and the next, a fuck-hot musical genius was asking me to record something he's miraculously dreaming up at the piano.

I'm normally cool under pressure, but holy hell.

My phone weighs heavy in my hand, taunting me. Regardless of what he thought about my poor recording skills, he actually texted me back. But why? I'd expected only a resounding silence after our less than cordial exchange this afternoon. Is that how he thinks this works? He disrespects me, I insult him, and now we're text buddies or something? He must be high—again.

Or . . . Maybe he's saying he's willing to meet my terms. Perhaps he's willing to try to be what Parker needs? I snort and shake my head. It would take a miracle.

Instead of reopening his text, I tap my video app, and am instantly transported back to those few precious moments at the piano. I sink back into my chair, an unfamiliar longing coming over me as I watch the shaky image on the tiny screen. His commanding figure hunched over in concentration, his fingertips caressing the keys, his husky, smoky voice in the background promising to hold me under a sky of stars.

The ringing of my phone jolts me back to reality, and I'm surprised to find myself blinking back tears. What on earth is wrong with me? Fumbling with the phone, I answer automatically without looking to see who it is. "Hello, this is Abigail Walker."

I'm greeted with silence on the other end. Quickly checking the caller ID, my temper flares when I see it's an unknown number. "Who is this?" I demand. There's a muffled curse, but nothing else. Suddenly, I wonder . . ."Kennedy?" I whisper in disbelief, not sure what I'll do if it *is* him. The call ends abruptly.

Crap. I stare at the silent phone for a beat, resisting the urge to throw it across the room. It probably wasn't Kennedy, I decide. I have his real number, after all, and he doesn't seem shy about communicating. Which means my crank caller has my cell number. Damn it. I'll have to get a new number, which will be a major pain in the ass.

Shaking my head in irritation, I gather my glass and carry it back to the kitchen, before readying myself for bed. "No more wallowing and mooning over crappy videos and impossible dreams, Abigail," I tell myself sternly as I climb between the sheets. I don't know what game Lane is playing, but I don't play games.

♪ ♩ ♪ ♩

"HAVE A GOOD DAY, HANK," I call cheerfully to the gripman as I climb off the cable car.

"And to you, Abby. Go get 'em, girl," he responds with a wink, before pulling back on the lever and sending the car on its way. Hank is somewhere in his fifties, looks like a linebacker, and is one of my favorite people. He's always got a kind word and a friendly smile to send the morning commuters on the Powell-Mason line off on a good foot.

I love cable cars. They're one of the best things about living in San Francisco. Each weekday morning, I walk a few blocks to catch the California line at Van Ness, and then change to one of the Powell lines to get to Union Square. It's a great way to start the day.

After stopping for a latte, I finally make it to my office and am surprised to find April skulking by Tess's desk. "What's with the scowl? It's a little early to be in such a bad mood, isn't it?"

"What's with the Pollyanna smile this morning?" she counters as she follows me into my office and begins pacing in front of my desk with strides only as long as her pencil skirt will allow. "After blowing a dream fulfillment, I'm surprised to see you in such a *good* mood."

Grimacing, I set my latte on my desk and sit down to change out of my sneakers and into my pumps. "You've talked to Nadia, I see. What can I say, April? The guy isn't appropriate to be around a terminally sick child. That's it. Besides, it's not blown completely. He agreed to provide some signed gifts."

"That's it? Damn it. I wanted Redfall for a TV spot," she says, waving her hands in exasperation. "If Mrs. Jensen had given permission to use it, and I think she would have, it would have been perfect."

I sigh, knowing exactly what she's thinking: shots of Kennedy and Parker interacting with guitars, maybe giving a mini-concert at the hospital, Parker's face lighting up when he first sees his idol. Parker's well-being is first priority, of course, but April's job is to show the good work of the foundation to encourage more donations. Our ability to fulfill children's dreams is only as good as the donations we bring in. It's a never-ending cycle. I can't blame her for being frustrated. I'm frustrated, too.

"I have every confidence that you'll come up with something even better," I reply decisively and stand up, four inches taller than I was. Thank you, Jimmy Choo.

She raises her nose. "Of course I will." Turning to leave, she grumbles one last complaint, "But it'll be hard to find someone as hot as Kennedy Lane."

"Oh, for . . ." I roll my eyes. "Call the Patriots, for crying out loud. Surely, we need Tom Brady for something." I smile to myself, hearing her blasé acknowledgement drift back to me, and open my email.

chapter four

kennedy

"GOOD AFTERNOON, SUNSHINE." ADAM, MY older brother, equally an annoyance and an inspiration, glances at me from beside the elevator. He looks awake and alive—two things I know I'm struggling with.

"Fuck off, Adam. Sara, always a pleasure." Sara Grant, Adam's fiancée for the last million years or so, rolls her eyes at me as I limp my way over to them and lean against the wall beside the elevator. They both came to the standing room only acoustic session my band put on last night at The Fillmore. With Adam having another NASCAR race this weekend, they skipped the party last night.

I close my eyes, thankful the pounding in my head at least has been reduced to a dull, slow ache. The after party is a blur. Despite me telling the tempting Abigail Walker to not give up on me, I managed to put a dent into more than a few bottles last night. And now, not only do I feel hungover, I feel guilty. It's not something I'm used to.

"Rough night, bro?" Adam asks, with familiar concern

evident in his voice.

"You could say that."

"Well, we had a great night. Took full advantage of that Jacuzzi, if you know what I mean." I crack an eye open and laugh. Adam wags his brows and Sara hits him in the arm. "Ow! Babe, that hurt."

"What's with the limp?" Sara changes the subject, glancing down at my leg.

"Fuck if I know. The bottom of my foot is sliced. It hurts like a son of a bitch."

"I took a broken piece of glass out of your foot the other night, remember? I used some antibacterial spray on it if that helps, Sara," Tucker explains as he joins us.

"Huh." I struggle to try to remember when that happened. Despite my trending habit of indulging *after* a gig, I never do before one. I want to savor the adrenaline, the high that feeds me, the electricity of the crowd. It lets me get lost in a place where I can't feel the pain anymore. It's unlike any combination of drugs or alcohol you can find.

The problem is, inevitably, that high fades and I'm left with a gaping hole once more, one I've been trying desperately to fill since the accident two years ago that changed everything.

Sara frowns at me, running her fingers through her long dark hair. "As much as I don't want to look any part of your disgusting anatomy, I think you should get it looked at. It might be infected with God only knows what disease you brought home with you last night. Are your tetanus shots up to date?" She can't turn off the concern instinctual of being a nurse.

Adam met Sara when one of his early racing accidents sent him to the ER. A dislocated shoulder and a concussion led to a romance for the ages. She resisted him for a long time. But, if there's one thing Adam doesn't like, it's hearing the word no. A challenge only makes him try harder. "Probably not. But I'm sure it's fine."

"That's what they all say until a limb needs to be amputated."

The elevator dings and Tucker gives it a sweep before letting us in. "There's a couple of hundred fans outside. We can go out there and you can play nice before we go to the radio station for your interview, or I can get the driver to move the Hummer around to the service entrance."

He passes me my sunglasses, and I slide them on. Thank fuck. The lights feel like they're burning through my retinas.

"Service entrance."

"Dude, they would love to see you. Come on. Sign a few boobs and get some brownie points," Adam suggests as the elevator starts its descent.

"What are you, my fucking manager now?" I scowl at him as my stomach bottoms out with the movement of the elevator.

Adam is right, although, I would never admit to him. The album with my band, Redfall, is due to drop in a couple of weeks, and we've been relatively absent for almost two years until a few weeks ago when the marketing engine kicked into high gear.

I'm still not sure if I'm ready for the insanity that accompanies an album release and a world tour, but I also can't deny I miss the adrenaline and the rush. I miss the real fans who know every single lyric and belt them out as if they are a part of their soul. But right now, my body needs rest and caffeine.

I think I may collapse if I have to stand and sign autographs for any length of time. My schedule is absolutely insane for the foreseeable future, and there will be plenty of time for autographs, so I take the easy way out.

"Service. Entrance."

WITH THE REST OF MY band already safely inside the radio station, Tucker weaved me through the throngs of fans, held back by a metal barrier after we dropped Adam and Sara off at their sprawling home. The fans were satisfied with a passing glimpse and a few waves as I ducked through the back door. My hearing, which has taken a beating from years of touring, however may not survive. Their high-pitched screams are ear shattering, and after almost fifteen years of doing this, I don't think I'll ever get used to the reaction.

On impulse, I snapped a picture of the frenzied crowd, sending it to Abby, with a message: *Were you thinking something like this for Parker?* Maybe it will make her think twice about brushing me off.

Tucker tosses me a skeptical look while I blow across the top of the Styrofoam cup of cheap coffee. "I've got this. You know we always give good interviews. Stop worrying."

"I know. It's just you were pretty fucked up last night, man. I don't know how any of you are upright." His scowl is firmly in place as he takes in the rest of the band. Despite our collective haggard appearance this morning, I'm very lucky to have this talented, if not a little fucked-up group behind me. They're loyal, something that is a rarity in this industry, and they're the best in the business.

We're not without our fair share of in-fighting, but that's to be expected when you've logged a lifetime of hours together stuck on tour buses. There's now a balance between us all, a camaraderie that only comes from touring.

As Tucker debates our ability to function, I take a much-needed sip of coffee, the caffeine slowly working its way into my system. Fuck that tastes awful. Awful, but necessary.

A cute, young woman peeks her head into the room, motioning for us to join her. She's all flustered and wide-eyed, her gaze darting between each of us until she hones in on me and lowers the clipboard she clutches to her chest. *She must be an intern.* "We're ready for you." Her voice is timid and awestruck as she twirls a lock of her long dyed crimson hair, motioning for us to follow her.

I keep my eyes on the hot piece of ass sashaying in front of me as she leads us all down the hall to the broadcast booth. She's wearing the typical short miniskirt that leaves nothing to the imagination, a tight shirt revealing just about everything she owns, and blood-red high heels attached to her wobbly, long legs. It looks like a newborn foal trying to walk for the first time. It's amusing if nothing else.

Thoughts of Abby and her righteous indignation hit me hard. She's in stark contrast to this intern . . . to most of the women who linger around the fringes of a rock-and-roll band. Maybe that's why I can't get her out of my head. She's been there, haunting me, judging me, tempting me since we met at the Fairmont.

We wait in the hallway, and I try to focus on the interview. What I said to Tucker is true. I do eventually bounce back from a night of debauchery. It's always been that way for me since I started drinking in high school, and it's stuck with me.

Of course back then it was tame—a few shots of gin or rum stolen from my parents' liquor cabinet. If we were really feeling defiant, a shared bottle of vodka before a school dance. Real rebels.

The door to the studio opens, and my gaze falls to the beautiful creature that is Honey Hill. Of course, that's not her real name, but here at KICK-FM, one of the country's most influential rock stations, she becomes someone else for a while.

Her eyes widen as she leans out the door. She's gone casual today, her endlessly long legs encased in tight, dark-wash jeans a white blouse with the buttons open to her ample cleavage, her tousled highlighted hair hanging loose around her shoulders. She looks good enough to eat.

"Kennedy, you look . . ." She seems at a loss for words.

"Tired?" I help her out and grin as she opens the door to the studio wider, motioning for us to step through.

"Like shit," she clarifies without missing a beat, causing me to pause in front of her.

"It was a late night." The rest of the band mutters in agreement.

"Looks like you've had a few of those." Her assessment hits me harder than it should. I try to push away the nagging criticism as we cram into the studio.

"Have a seat." Turning to the sound of Honey's voice, she motions to the chairs situated around the announcer's table. "Are you guys okay to do this?"

"Of course we are. I may need more of this disgusting coffee, though," Cameron Chapman, our rhythm guitarist says.

Cam and I have been playing together the longest. I moved to LA when I was twenty, and Cam found me, playing one night at a bar just off Sunset.

He's probably the only person in the world who would've had the balls to join me on stage, unannounced and unrehearsed, but when he did, I knew I found my other musical half. Sometimes you get lucky in life; other times, fate has different plans.

Cameron comes from old Boston money. I'm talking private jets and a privileged upbringing. But, as soon as he picked up a guitar in music class and found his soul, that all took a backseat. Much to Mommy and Daddy's shock, he rebelled like a lot of rich kids often do, and he sought out anything that would distance him from the upper class monotony he had grown up with.

Honey watches him settle in as she places her headphones on. "The coffee is pretty terrible." She drops into her chair, rolling it to the desk that sits between us.

"So, you know the drill. We're live with about a ten-second delay, so try to keep the profanities to a minimum." Matt Logan, our bassist, can't hold back his laugh.

Matt answered an ad Cam and I had put out after we decided to try to make a go of it. It only took one song to hear his powerful, metal influenced, uniquely melodic sound to know he was our man.

Matt doesn't like to talk a lot about his past. But, on the bus during an overnight to some hick town in the middle of fucking nowhere Indiana, he came out with a bomb.

We knew he was adopted, but he said he didn't know his biological father—had never met him, and that his mother had killed herself when he was twelve. "It's an insult to the word 'mother' to use it for her." That's all we got, and we didn't push him for more. I know all about not wanting to talk about nightmares from the past.

"Honey . . ." The disembodied voice from the production room floats through my headphones. "We're back in twenty."

"You've seen some of the questions we've received over the past couple of days, so I'll ask you a few of those. By the way, the announcement you guys were coming here almost broke Twitter."

Sean Murphy, our drummer, barks out a loud laugh. "Did it?"

Sean was last to join us. An import from England, he's probably the most erratic of the bunch. He's a whirlwind of energy and essential to us as a band, as gifted drummers are. He's always playing around the edges of recklessness, but at the core, he's smart and soulful.

Sean and his twin sister, Sydney, have one of those unique relationships you often hear about with twins—connected even when thousands of miles apart. He's protective of her to a fault, and I know all about that feeling. Sean however, would never drive his sister away like I did.

Sean's had a few rough rounds with coke that have sent him to rehab in the past. He learned early on you can stay up and party longer if a bit of cocaine is involved. Unfortunately, he couldn't stop at *a bit*.

My thoughts drift again to Abby. She'd have a field day with this bunch.

"So, we'll talk about the album, I'll do the true-false quiz, and if you're okay with it, take a few calls." The producer cues Honey and she adjusts the microphone.

"That was Guns N' Roses with "Paradise City," and you're listing to Honey in the Hot Tub on 107.5 KICK-FM. And now, I know you've all been waiting for this. Over fifty million albums sold, seven Grammy awards, sold out concerts around the world, and finally back, after a two-year hiatus we've got Redfall up close and personal. Welcome to the studio, it's good to see you again."

"It's good to be seen. How's the hot tub been treating you?" Cameron asks.

"I think it just got a little hotter." We all laugh at her answer. "So, here we are on the eve of the release of your seventh studio album, *Crash*. I had a listen to it last night, and it's, well . . . the best work you've done to date in my opinion, but much darker than your previous albums."

I'm impressed by her assessment. Honey knows her music. It's one of the reasons she has the number-one rated show in the country. "That's a good way to look at it. Darker," Matt agrees.

"You collaborated with quite a few legends in the business on *Crash*. Tell us about that."

"It was an amazing experience, and we pushed the boundaries on this album. It brought a whole new flavor to our sound," I answer.

"Did that change the way you approached recording?" Honey asks, turning to Matt.

"It took us to places we hadn't really thought about. It's challenging, but we had a lot of fun, too," Matt replies, casting me a knowing glance. Some of our recording sessions this time around blew my mind. I think we all were a little star-struck at some point during the process.

"And we're lucky that Lane has his own recording studio at his house," Sean chimes in.

That studio cost me a small fortune, but I'll never regret putting it in. "It's pretty convenient," I admit. "I can just roll out of bed and go down there. I did a lot of that with this album. I'd just go into the studio and stay there for hours. Got lost in the process. It's what I needed to do."

"Let's talk about that a bit. Tell us about some of your early influences."

"I grew up around music," I start. "There was always a record player going in our house. My mom was a product of the sixties, you know? Hendrix, Joplin, The Who . . . Her and Dad would fight about it all the time. His taste is more along the lines of Chuck Berry and The Four Tops. I was lucky to have an eclectic mix of influences."

"Kennedy, you've been hiding away on us save for the odd picture of you looking like you're having . . . Well, let's just say a really good time."

"All work and no play . . . You know what they say? I do tend to keep to myself for the most part during recording."

"I've got a copy of *Star Life* here." Honey turns the gossip magazine around, pushing it in front of me. "This doesn't look like you're keeping to yourself. For our faithful listeners out there, I'm talking about a few pictures you might have seen. The members of Redfall living it up at the Pump House Bar a few weeks ago."

I scan the photos. I look trashed, my clothes are disheveled, and I have a glass of whiskey in my hand. There's an obligatory pair of groupies hanging off me in some dimly lit booth. It doesn't paint a good picture. I can see why Abby was worried about bringing a sick kid around me. An unexpected pang of guilt fires through me, and I push the cheap magazine back to Honey.

"Don't believe everything you see or read."

"Would you say it's getting harder to live in the limelight?" Honey settles her hand on the back of the mic.

"Lane has it worse than we do," Sean replies. "Pretty boy that he is. But if there's a negative about being successful, that's it. You lose a bit of yourself."

"Well, we have some questions that fans have been flooding us with." Honey searches the computer screen in front of her before continuing. "Here's one from Faller4Life on Twitter. Do you ever get nervous, and what's your advice for people who are shy about performing?"

"Every time," I answer. "But it's a good kind of nerves—more excitement, adrenaline, wanting to put on the best show you possibly can. And advice? The thing is, you have to just get out there and do it, or you'll never know. You don't want to live with 'what if.' What if I had just taken that chance?"

"And being scared isn't a bad thing," Cam adds. "It's good to scare yourself, push yourself out of your comfort zone. And you have to remember that in this industry, nothing comes easily. If it was easy, everyone would be doing it."

"You've all been pretty outspoken in the past about

streaming music. You always release vinyl versions of your albums a few weeks before they are available for streaming. Has that changed with this album? Will we ever see Redfall available online before you release on vinyl?"

Matt laughs at Honey's question. "Listen, we never said we're against streaming music. But the Internet is something that is both freeing and extremely dangerous. A blessing and a curse," he replies.

"And by that you mean?"

"It gives people access to music that they may have never thought about listening to," Matt continues. "But at the same time with piracy running rampant, you can get music for free. You tend not to value things you can get for free."

"Okay, it's time for the true or false questions." She rubs her hands together, beyond excited.

Sean taps out a relentless beat against the table. "Hit me!"

"Sean, you once put Cameron's head through a thirty-inch screen TV in a hotel room."

Cam snorts. "False. I think it was like fifty or sixty inches."

"Matt, you're a loner."

"False."

She doesn't look convinced. "You're hardly ever seen with anyone outside of the band. You don't seem to socialize much."

Matt levels her with a dark look. "Not that you see. Not everything is for public consumption."

Her smile falters as she reads the laptop screen, and she pauses before continuing. "Kennedy, we're coming up to the two-year anniversary of the tragic accident that killed your sister, Robin. What kind of influence did that have on this album?"

Silence fills the airwaves as what's left of my heart constricts and cracks. No radio station ever wants dead air, but she deserves it for asking me about something I have consistently said is off limits. "No comment."

She turns from the laptop, glancing at the producer's room. "Well, the phone lines have been lighting up all morning, so let's take some calls." She waits for the first call to click through to her. "You're live on KICK-FM with Redfall."

"Oh my God!" A shrill squeal pierces my ears, and I chuckle against the microphone as the caller practically hyperventilates. I may be pissed at Honey, but I won't let that ruin the experience of interacting with a fan.

"What's your name, sweetheart?" Sean asks.

"Tiffany! It's Tiffany! Oh my God! He just asked my name," she pants in a breathy voice to someone in the background who screams at the top of her lungs.

"Did you have a question, or did you just want to breathe heavily over the air?" Honey asks.

"Yes! Yes! I have a question. Kennedy, when did you get your first guitar? Like, how old were you?" Tiffany asks in a rush.

"Well, Tiffany, I was twelve, and it actually wasn't my guitar. My parents gave it to my brother for his birthday in hopes it would channel some of his hyperactivity. But Adam didn't give a sh . . ." I correct myself before I swear over the airwaves. "He didn't care about it. He was always focused on cars." I chuckle to myself. "So, he stuffed the guitar in his closet and never played it. Like any good younger brother would do, one day, I snuck into his room and stole it. It had an instruction tape and a book with it, so I took his ghetto blaster and went to the garage."

"You have to remember, it was winter in Minnesota, and it was cold as witch's t . . . Ah, it was feeling it all the way to your bones cold." I close my eyes, letting the memory flash back to me. "I had no idea what I was doing at first. I froze my ass off for hours. My fingers were bleeding by the time I stopped. I played until I had gone through the book so many times I had it memorized. That's where it started." My voice trails and I twist in the chair, needing to fuel the energy that's threatening to explode.

"That was a great question, Tiffany," Honey says. "We're going to take a short break, but when we come back, we'll all get to hear Redfall, live in the studio."

♪ ♩ ♪ ♩

abigail

"WELL, IT'S ABOUT TIME YOU emerged from that office. I was about to send out the Marines."

I turn to see my best friend standing at the end of the hallway. Our apartments are at the opposite ends of the same floor; mine looks out over Lafayette Park, while hers has a view of the Peace Pagoda. Frankly, I think I have the better view, but Maddie claims she can't think of a more inspiring sight to see from her bedroom window than a giant phallic symbol. Based on the amount of action her bedroom sees compared to mine, she may be right.

"If they were cute Marines, I might let you," I counter, a wry smirk on my face. She laughs, walking toward me.

"Are there any other kind?"

It's my turn to laugh as I fumble with my keys in the lock. "Marines aren't really my speed. Now, firemen on the other hand . . ."

"Ooh, I have just the guy!" she squeals as I finally get my door open. She trails behind me, babbling at full throttle. "His name is Wyatt, and he comes a couple of times a week, and orders a half-dozen tall Americanos for his shift. He's stationed at the firehouse a block down on California, and he has abs you could scrub clothes on."

I look at her sharply as I toss my bag and keys onto my small kitchen table. "When did you have the opportunity to see his abs?"

"He also happens to be Mr. July," she says with a huge grin, and I hum appreciatively. She'd purchased both of us copies of this year's San Francisco Firefighter Charity calendar, and we take turns salivating over the men-of-the-month. I don't know how they select the models, but they had done a stellar job choosing this year's crop.

"Well, if he looks as good in real life, I might consider it." I kick off my heels.

She wanders into my kitchen and roots around in my cupboard for a couple of wine glasses. "I'll get us set up while you change. Can't relax while you're looking like Corporate America."

"Thanks." Leaving Maddie to her own devices, I retreat to my bedroom and change into my comfiest pair of yoga pants and a stretchy T-shirt. I may rock a suit at work, but I can't get out of it fast enough at home.

Hearing Maddie call for me, I stroll back into the living area, rolling my shoulders as I walk.

"Tough day?" She hands me a glass of red wine.

"Just a complex day. And, thanks." I raise my glass to her as she makes herself comfortable on my couch. "What are we sampling this evening?"

"We're taking a trip north of the border tonight." She reaches for the bottle sitting on my coffee table.

I perk up. "Canada?"

"Not that far north; just Oregon. Not far from my old stomping grounds, in fact. This is a pinot noir from the Willamette Valley—*Domaine Drouhin*."

"Sounds pretentious." I wrinkle my nose and take another

sip. "But they can call themselves anything they want if they make wine this good."

I close my eyes and savor the rich flavors of cherry and cinnamon that roll over my tongue. Maddie and I started Wine Wednesdays as a ritual back when we were broke college students. The quality of the wines has improved markedly since then, for which our palates are thankful. It's a wonderful way to de-stress.

We chat about our respective days, and my spirits lift as my glass empties. Madeline Thomas and I met during our sophomore year at UC-Berkeley. Although I grew up in a little town not too far from here, Maddie hailed from wonderful and weird Portland. If there was ever a city that let you do your own thing, it's Portland, and Maddie had flourished there. But, when college came, she needed to fly the nest. Seattle was still too close to her parents, so San Francisco won. She now manages Screamin' Beans, a coffee shop two blocks away owned by one of our former professors. She's not only managed to keep it from being swallowed by Starbucks, but there are even plans for expansion in the works.

I lean my head against the back of the sofa. Maddie had turned on the radio to that Honey person's show while I was changing clothes, and it seems to have switched to an interview; the words are indistinct, but the man's voice is husky and sensuous, providing a soothing backdrop. "So, how is your campaign with that coffee bean supplier going?"

Maddie frowns as she reaches for the wine bottle and refills my glass. "It's not. Apparently, he's got a girlfriend. You'd think he might have mentioned it at least once."

"Well, maybe it's new." I nudge her playfully. "Not everyone likes to blab about their love life, you know."

"Yeah, yeah," she grumbles, giving me a wink. We both

know that she has virtually no filter regarding her own dating life. "We can't all be monks like you."

My mouth drops open. "I'm not a monk!" I sputter. "I'm just . . . choosy."

She laughs. "You know, Abby, you really should put yourself out there more. With that gorgeous brown hair and those big hazel eyes, you could have men lining up if you made yourself more accessible."

"I'm accessible enough." Jeez, what does she want from me? I went out last week with that Dante guy she set me up with from her yoga class. And I went to dinner three weeks ago—or was it four—with a nice guy I found all on my own. Okay, so it was kind of business related because he was a contributor, but still.

My head snaps toward the radio, the announcer's words grabbing my attention. "You're live with Redfall."

My eyebrows shoot up as an abrasive squealing from a fan who has called into the studio emits from the speakers. "What is this?" I ask as my heartbeat inexplicably increases.

"It's a replay of the interview from this afternoon with Redfall. I only caught a bit of it today and wanted to hear the rest. I didn't think you'd mind. They were actually there in the studio. I guess the place was mobbed."

I hum and take another sip of wine, my mind buzzing. I was hoping to put the raw encounter with Kennedy Lane out of my head, and now here he is—front and center in my own living room.

Maddie turns the volume up just as the man in question is finishing an answer about when he learned to play guitar. I can't help it; the image of a shy boy trying to play a guitar bigger than him, his fingers tipped in bandages, brings a fond smile to my lips. The tone of wonder and warmth in his voice begins to do odd things to me.

The phone rings just as they break for a commercial, so I rise and answer it in the kitchen, but it's just a dial tone. "Damn it," I grumble, hanging up with more force than necessary. "I think you're right. It's time to get rid of my land line."

"Another hang up?" Maddie calls from her spot on the sofa.

"Yeah." I snag another bottle of wine from the rack and un- cork it. "It's the fourth this week. I'm getting them on my cell, too. They are seriously beginning to get on my nerves."

I can hear the announcer's voice again, so I swiftly return to the sofa, where Maddie holds her glass up for a refill.

"Did you hear Redfall's last album? It was *incredible*! Can you imagine seeing Kennedy Lane in the flesh? God, I'd climb him like a tree!" I shift nervously in my seat. I haven't told Maddie about meeting Kennedy yet, or his text to me—it's still too fresh. *Don't give up on me yet.*

I hear a few tentative notes plucked on a guitar before his warm, husky voice begins to sing. His words are full of such poi- gnant sorrow and longing; it takes my breath away. The simplici- ty of the acoustic guitars fit the mood perfectly, and we sit stock- still, enraptured. I'm scarcely breathing by the time he finishes, and there's a profound silence after the last notes fade.

"Damn. That was incredible," Maddie moans beside me as they break for another commercial. I've never heard Redfall play an acoustic set before, and it's a completely different experience.

"Wow. He sounds so . . ." I'm not sure how to put it into words, but she nods, understanding me anyway.

"I know. I hope they play another one." But when the in- terview continues, we're treated only to some caller asking Kennedy to marry her amongst the giggles of seemingly dozens of girls in the background.

The announcer wraps it up and the station switches to the

Red Hot Chili Peppers, so I reach over and turn it down. "I can't believe that last person," I gripe. "She probably waited on hold for an hour, and God knows what she told the screener to get through, only to waste the one chance she'll ever have to ask someone like Kennedy Lane a question."

Maddie eyes me from her end of the sofa and smirks. "And what, pray tell, would you have asked him?"

I blink, momentarily thrown. Do I tell her? No. Not yet. "Maybe something about where he gets his inspiration? Does he have a muse? Shit, I don't know, but it sure as hell wouldn't have been about *marriage*."

Her smirk becomes a full-blown grin, so I flutter my eyelashes and clasp my hands to my chest while trilling in a breathy falsetto, "Oh, *Kennedy*, you're *so hot* . . . Do you like kittens and sunsets and long walks on the beach?" She cracks up, and I dodge the pillow she throws my way, managing to save the wine bottle in the process.

"You're so full of it." She chuckles. "Come on, I've got a meeting with a new distributor tomorrow morning. Let's clean up."

We recork the leftover wine—a rare occurrence in itself—and rinse out our glasses. Maddie gives me a hug and, with promises to talk tomorrow, she heads down the hall to her apartment.

Sometime after locking up, I lay in my bed listening to my Redfall playlist and mentally comparing his older songs with the new one he sang on air, and the snippet he played yesterday. It was raw and real, and just so damn sad. It's amazing how different he sounds without the growl of electric guitars behind him. His voice wraps around me, infusing me with warmth.

I stare at the ceiling, remembering those haunting blue eyes that seemed to reach into my soul at the Fairmont. I squirm beneath my sheets, wondering what it would be like to look into those eyes again, but immediately squelch those thoughts. What I *should* want to know is if he's still willing to sign a few things for Parker's dream. Disappointment washes over me again, because as much as I want to grant the boy's wish, I can't do it if it would do more harm than good.

With a huff, I roll over and punch my pillow. I need to stop thinking about this. It's settled. I'll let Nadia make the arrangements. Some posters, a few T-shirts and CDs, and Kennedy Lane will be out of my life and out of my head for good. With a deep sigh, I try to clear my mind, letting Lane's sultry growl lull me to sleep.

DAMN KENNEDY LANE.

I glare at my office clock and blow a stray hair out of my eyes with a huff. It's only three, but it feels like midnight. Between that damn radio interview, and his unexpected text, I tossed and turned all night. That voice . . . that sumptuous, rugged voice kept infiltrating my sleep, leaving me groggy and irritated.

I try to concentrate, but lack of sleep and frustration are killing my productivity. No matter how hard I try, I can't seem to stop thinking about him. Why is this bothering me so much?

Before I realize it, I Google his name. There are dozens of new pictures taken at the radio station. I shake my head at the crowd straining at the security line. It never fails to surprise me how normally rational adult women—and men, for that matter—become raving, hormonal teenagers in the face of celebrity. Not that I'm totally immune, of course. It's embarrassing what an English or Australian accent can do to me. But you'll never catch me—I peer at one photo more closely in disbelief—shoving *my boobs* at a perfect stranger to autograph. Does that woman have no shame?

Bemused, I examine the main subject of the photos. It's like he's channeling Johnny Cash. He's the man in black, from his sunglasses right down to his heavy boots. The simple jeans and T-shirt hug his long, lean physique perfectly and his unruly hair looks like he just rolled out of bed. He looks delicious.

Just before closing the page, I spy a couple photos that stop me in my tracks. Kennedy kneeling with his arm around an adorable little boy who's glowing with happiness. In fact, his enthusiasm reminds me of Parker. But it's the look of sincere gratitude and enjoyment in Kennedy's eyes that surprises me. His soft smile as he talks to the boy is poles apart from the cocky mask he sports when interacting with the other fans. Maybe he really gets it, I wonder. I click on another photo and can't help the squeak that escapes me. Kennedy Lane making some kind of pinky promise with the little guy. Good God, if that doesn't make someone's ovaries explode, I don't know what will.

If he can interact like that with a random fan, maybe we should give him another chance.

My heart twinges as I think of our dream candidate. Parker's mother, Joyce, says he isn't taking his latest round of chemo well, and she's understandably worried. Parker's doctor is trying different things to make it easier, but nothing seems to be helping so far. Joyce says the only thing that makes her little boy smile is his guitar.

I can only imagine the smile that would light his face if he were to be able to meet his idol.

There's a light rap on my door, and Nadia sticks her head inside my office. "Are you ready? I just have a couple of things."

"Sure, come on in." I wave her inside and come around my desk to join her on the small couch against the wall. She lays the files she brought on the low coffee table and peers over the top of her glasses as she selects one.

"We're having a little scheduling trouble with the Red Wings for the Simpson dream. I was hoping you could give their owner a call," she begins. We work through the half-dozen cases that need a little extra finagling, and I'm surprised to see it's past closing time when we finish.

Nadia restacks her files and rises gracefully to her feet. "Can we talk about what happened at the Fairmont?" she asks pointedly.

I take a deep breath. "I'm afraid our original fears may have been correct."

An uncharacteristic scowl takes over her face. "He seemed distracted from what I saw, but maybe it was just a bad day. Maybe he just needs a different approach," she says boldly.

My eyes widen in surprise at her bluntness. "And by that you mean what exactly?"

"Let me give it another shot, Abby. I'd hate for Parker to be disappointed just because you couldn't make it work."

I feel my face heat with anger. "Because *I* couldn't—"

"Abby," she interrupts, striding to the door. "This is what I do. I'm good at it. Just let me give it another try. For Parker's sake. I'll be talking to his management team about the signed donations anyway. It can't hurt."

I gape at her in disbelief. Nadia has never been so adamant about a dream fulfillment before, but I'm still conflicted. On the one hand, I see the photos of Kennedy with that little boy outside the studio, and I can feel the passion in his voice, see him at that piano. I can imagine Parker and the look on his face if he could meet his idol. I remember Kennedy's text telling me not to give up on him. And then I recall how he was at the Fairmont, and my heart sinks. It's too big of a risk. I can't subject Parker to the kind of behavior I witnessed.

"Let's just keep it to the signed items, Nadia," I say, and she purses her lips in disapproval. "Unless he cleans up his act, I don't want him anywhere near Parker."

"Fine." She glowers at me, her fingers tightening around the doorknob. "But you're making a mistake, Abby. Don't say I didn't warn you."

As I listen to her footsteps fade away down the hall, I can only hope she's wrong.

chapter five

kennedy

NO ONE PREPARES YOU FOR what this kind of fame brings along with it. The moments I'm on the stage make the sacrifice of a normal life, whatever that is, worth it. There is nothing like the rush of adrenaline that surges through you when the lights go up and an entire stadium explodes.

But it's a lethal mixture designed to test you at every turn. You indulge because you start to believe the hype. You believe you are invincible. You hurt and love in equal measure, taking no prisoners as the train you're on seems to be rocketing toward an unknown destination. You're a passenger to the most intense ride of your life, and no matter how hard you try to take control; sometimes the train veers off into a place that you never expected.

For me, it took something I can never get back. Robin's accident has left me trying to fill the empty void, *needing* to fill it, but no amount of whiskey can do that. I know this on some base level.

Robin was a constant in my life, the glue that held me

together when everything around me seemed like it was spinning out of control. And in this business, something *real*, something tangible, is hard to find. And, without her, I feel like I'm drifting off the track once more.

Writing this album has helped somewhat. In my studio, with the notes and chords that speak to me, is a place where I feel safe and in control. The problem is, that doesn't seem to last.

IT'S SATURDAY NIGHT, AND I'VE heard nothing back from Miss Abigail Walker after my text. It's like we're in some chess game, waiting each other out, seeing who will make the next move.

Tonight, I'm sitting behind the ropes of the VIP lounge at a nightclub in the heart of San Fran with rest of the band. Tucker has parked himself at the top of the stairs, ready as always to protect us should the need arise.

We're currently on round I forget, being served by a waitress whose tight, black boy shorts and tied off white T-shirt leave nothing to the imagination, much to our pleasure.

"Would you just go dance or something?" Cameron complains as Sean's leg bounces off nervous energy, causing the entire table to shake. "You're driving me fucking insane."

Sean looks horrified as he glances down to the pulsing dance floor below us. "I'll get mauled down there, Three." I laugh at his ridiculous nickname for Cam. He is after all, Cameron Louis Chapman, The Third. Cam claims he hates it when Sean calls him Three, although deep down, I think he actually loves it. He's always tried to distance himself from his overbearing family, and the nickname is just another fuck you to something he can't escape.

"And that's a problem because . . ." Cam starts.

"Just go get us another round," Sean fires back at him, kicking him hard in the shin.

"That fucking hurt!" Cam flips a coaster at Sean's head.

"I'll go," Matt says, his eyes roaming over our waitress as she leans over the side of the bar. She might as well be naked for everything those shorts cover.

"Just remember, she doesn't love you. She's just a good shag." Sean offers his sage advice, another one of his famous Murphy's laws, patting Matt on the shoulder.

"Her tits are pretty amazing," Cam adds.

"Well, with that glowing recommendation how can you refuse?" Sean nudges Matt off the bench. "Go now, grasshopper. Fuck and be free." Sean waves his hand in the direction of the bar.

"You're an asshole," Matt says, flipping Sean off before weaving his way to the bar.

"And another one bites the dust," I murmur, watching the impending train wreck with amusement.

"We should cover that on the tour." Cam turns his attention back to the dance floor below.

"That's a good idea."

"Of course it is. It's mine."

"A stripped down version?" Sean drums with his fingers a modified beat of the classic Queen hit against the tabletop.

"It's a bass heavy song. We should ask Matt what he thinks," I suggest, watching as Matt strikes up a conversation with the waitress.

"Too late. He's a goner." Sean raises his glass and shouts over the blare of the music, "Grasshopper! Drinks first, then fucking!" Matt ignores us, ushering the attentive waitress out the back of the lounge, away from prying eyes.

Over the course of the next several hours, we get well and

truly wasted. It feels like I've drank my weight in whiskey. Our glasses never empty more than a few minutes. I've completely lost track of time and space when I see Brodie moving to the table. He slides into the booth beside me, wedging me between him and a pair of sorority sisters from Alpha Gamma something or other. They claim to be political science majors, although what they're majoring in really doesn't interest me. I pretend it does, though. I'm getting very good at pretending.

"Looks like you're putting a dent in it tonight." Brodie stretches his arm across the back of the booth, and motions to the bottles of booze that cover the table.

I lift my glass to him, managing a grin. "That's why I pay you so much. You're a fucking genius, Brodie." This earns me a round of giggles from the sorority girls.

"Nice of you to join us at the radio station for the interview, by the way." I scowl at Brodie as he settles into the booth.

"I may have slept in," he says casually.

"No shit. I would've liked to sleep in, too, but I have commitments. In case you forgot, so do you. And she asked about the accident." I can barely even say those words without feeling another wave of pain rip through me. "If you would've been there . . ."

"She still would've asked it. What do you want me to do, Kennedy? People are curious. They're going to ask." He shrugs as if it's no big deal at all. As if the single most devastating event in my life can be swept away.

The room spins, and from somewhere far away, I hear Sean's distinctive howl. Life carries on regardless. "What's this one?" I turn to find the blond sorority girl sliding her fingers over the rose tat on my neck. Even as drunk as I am, I know what it is. Political science major, my ass.

"It's a rose," I say, although my voice sounds slower than

normal. I set my glass down on the table, feeling overheated and really needing some fucking air.

"It's really pretty," she says in awe.

"So are you, sweetheart," Brodie replies, leaning across me. "How about we get out of here? Take this back to the hotel? What do you say, gorgeous? You can bring your friend here."

It's like I'm watching the entire conversation from somewhere outside my body. Voices are echoes, my feet are suddenly moving, and Tucker is beside me. I slide my arm around the blond and somehow make it down the stairs and through the bar with Tucker cutting a path in front of us.

Flashes of light almost blind me when we step onto the street. My name is shouted from a group of fans or photographers, or both. I'm too fucking trashed to know. I feel Tucker push me into the back of the Hummer, and in the process, I climb clumsily across the seat, almost landing on my ass on the floorboards.

I hear Cameron crack up beside me, and then the Hummer takes off, leaving the flashes, the confusion, and the liquor behind. The only problem is, I think there's more where I'm headed.

abigail

"JEEZ, MADDIE, WHAT'S THE HURRY? You got a fire to put out or something?"

She fixes me with a classic Madeline Thomas Stink-Eye before flipping her blond hair over her shoulder. "Funny, Abby," she says. "Are you going to keep up with the fireman jokes all night? Because I guarantee they've heard them all."

She's currently hauling my ass down the street toward a popular tapas place to meet two of the firefighters from the station near her coffee shop. She has been flirting with one of them, Dylan, for weeks now, and after they had lunch yesterday, decided dinner was the next step. And, of course, Maddie decided she "needed her best wingwoman" with her. Although I don't understand her drive to keep setting me up on these random blind dates, I have to say I appreciate her efforts this weekend. This week has been so odd with its sleepless nights and pervading restlessness, that I welcome the chance to shake it off with an evening of fun that has nothing to do with my job or enigmatic rock stars.

"What time did you say we'd be there?" I struggle to keep up with her rapid strides. Maybe these sandals weren't the best choice for tonight. I tug nervously at the light blue peasant top I paired with my favorite jeans, holding it down so it doesn't fly up in the breeze.

"Ten minutes ago." She slows down minutely when she notices my fidgeting. "Relax. You look great. He won't know what hit him." She gives me an encouraging smile.

I roll my eyes, but can't deny the flutters of excitement I feel. Maddie's right—I need to get out more.

We round the corner and slow when we come in sight of the restaurant with two tall men standing outside. They're both easily over six foot and dressed casually in jeans and button-downs with the sleeves rolled up. They smile broadly as we approach, and I gasp in appreciation of the muscles I see flex in their strong forearms. Damn.

Madeline gives me a knowing smirk before giving blue-shirt dude a quick hug. "Sorry we're late," she chirps, and then steps back, waving her hand my way. "Abby, this is Dylan and his friend, Wyatt. Guys, this is my best friend, Abigail."

"Nice to meet you," Wyatt says with a warm smile, his eyes dancing over my form. His crisp white shirt contrasts nicely with his deep tan, and his kind eyes sparkle. He extends his hand politely and mine all but disappears in his much larger one as we shake.

"Shall we?" Dylan gestures grandly as he holds the door open, drawing a giggle from Maddie as she flits in front of me.

"Yes, let's," I breathe, smiling up into Wyatt's appreciative grin. "I'm starving!"

TWO HOURS LATER, WITH THE warm evening filtering around us, the four of us make our way leisurely down Fillmore toward one of our favorite bars. She and Dylan walk arm-in-arm ahead of where Wyatt and I are strolling casually side-by-side. I appreciate that he seems to be shortening his stride so I can keep up with him. With his height, he could easily leave me in the dust if he chose, something a lot of tall guys don't seem to understand. It's a little thing, but it shows how considerate he is, much like how he held my chair for me in the restaurant. He even stood when I left and returned from the ladies room. I didn't know politeness like that still existed.

Dinner was delicious, and I found myself relaxing as both the wine and conversation flowed. Dylan and Maddie did most of the talking, but that was fine. Wyatt hails from San Diego, but made the move to San Francisco three years ago to be with a girlfriend who broke up with him last year. Since then, he says he's been focusing on his work, and has only recently rejoined the dating pool.

I notice Maddie give me a quick grin over her shoulder before she whispers something to Dylan, who chuckles. They seem to be quite smug over their matchmaking success so far, which my companion also notices.

"I'm never going to live this down," Wyatt confides with

a chuckle. "He's been trying to set me up for weeks, and now that I've finally given in, I find myself wishing I hadn't wasted so much time."

"Oh?" I glance up to find his cheeks reddening in the glow of a streetlight.

"Um, yeah," he says, adorably flustered. "I mean, if I'd agreed when he first suggested it, I would've met you so much sooner."

It's my turn to blush and look away, and a small smile plays about my lips. "Oh, well, we're here now," I stammer with a little laugh, feeling my cheeks heat even more when a grin spreads across his face.

"Yes we are," he agrees, and with matching grins and glances at each other, we continue down the street, close enough that our hands brush occasionally. I like it.

Music from the jazz band playing gets louder as we approach the bar. We stand in line for only a few minutes until we make it inside. I let out a huff of frustration as I'm knocked from behind in the crowd as we make our way to a table on the far side.

"You're not much for clubbing, then?" Wyatt asks as we finally make it to the quieter area close to the back of the bar.

"Ah, no, not so much." I chuckle wryly. "I mean, once in a while is fine, but usually I prefer to hunker down with a good book or a movie."

He nods. "Yeah, me, too. This place is nice, though," he says, leaning closer to be heard over the music.

The next few hours fly by. We talk a lot and even dance a little. I sip my peartini and listen as Wyatt talks about life as a firefighter. He has an easy way about him I find appealing. Not as appealing as a certain blue-eyed musician, but certainly more accessible and—let's face it—realistic. He laughs often and isn't afraid to make fun of himself. He and Dylan have us giggling over stories of their cooking for the other guys on their shift, including one Thanksgiving when Wyatt accidentally used baking soda instead of cornstarch in the gravy, resulting in a foamy, fizzy mess.

"I honestly think the other guys try to switch shifts now on the weeks I pull kitchen duty, just to avoid my cooking!" He barks out a laugh as Dylan confirms his suspicion with a sheepish nod.

Maddie suggests another round, and I'm about to agree, but instead I quickly slip a hand over my mouth when a yawn threatens to break through. "I'm sorry," I apologize, but Wyatt shakes his head.

"Don't worry; it's late," he says quickly. "If you'd like to leave, I'd be glad to walk you home or get a cab."

Maddie smiles into her drink at his eager offer; she's no doubt congratulating herself again. I'm never going to hear the end of it. Ignoring her, I smile at him. "Yes, please."

After settling the bill and saying our good-byes—I roll my eyes at Maddie's whispered assurance that she'd slipped some condoms into my nightstand—we weave our way through the crowd. We catch each other heaving sighs of relief as we step outside, and share a chuckle. "I love Maddie, but I can only handle the bar scene for a few hours," I admit as we begin walking toward my apartment. He hums in agreement and politely steers me away from the line of people still waiting to get in.

We chat a bit more as we stroll down Fillmore. Wyatt seems genuinely interested in my work, and doesn't seem to mind when I get carried away talking about it. Most guys tune out after a few minutes.

"What do you like most about your job?" he asks after I finish describing a particularly complicated dream fulfillment.

"Without a doubt, it's the look on the faces of the recipients and their families," I answer immediately. "Whether it's a big wish or a small one, the joy and amazement on their faces when they get to meet their favorite race car driver or step on that plane to Hawaii make everything worthwhile. These kids go through so much. Hospital stays instead of vacations and draining medical treatments instead of birthday parties. Then there's the emotional and financial strain on the families . . ."

I take a deep breath to center myself, realizing I've stepped up onto my soapbox. "Sorry, I get carried away. Suffice it to say anything I can do to make their burdens lighter and provide a moment's respite is well worth the effort," I conclude, somewhat sheepishly. He gives me an encouraging smile.

"Please don't apologize. You're obviously passionate about what you do, and you *should* be. What you do, it's amazing, really."

I shrug, embarrassed by his praise. "I'm lucky I have such an amazing staff. They're the ones who do the heavy lifting. And you, that's *truly* amazing. I would never have the nerve to run into a burning building, and you do it every day. You save people's *lives*. You're a hero."

He chuckles self-consciously, and then gives me a grin. "Well, not *every* day. It's not all burning buildings. Usually, it's mundane stuff, like someone getting stuck while cleaning their chimney." After checking the traffic, we start across the street. "I love my job, but I'm beginning to think about the future, too," he says.

He tosses me more than a few admiring glances as we walk, and I can't help my grin when I feel the faint flutters of excitement stir in my stomach. I've forgotten what it feels like . . . the flush of exhilaration of being with an attractive man who genuinely seems to like you, and the anticipation of what may lie ahead.

I like it.

"Well, this is me," I say when we reach my apartment. For a second, I panic. Should I ask him to come up? I'm not a monk, no matter what Maddie thinks. But this feels different from the casual dates I've had these last few years. I haven't had a serious boyfriend since Lucas and I ended, and I don't want to screw this up before I have a chance to see where it may go.

He walks me up the steps and into our small foyer. "Abby, I've had a really good time." He steps closer and places one hand on my waist as he did when we were dancing. My heart races, and I look up as he cups my cheek.

"So have I," I whisper. I'm not going to ask him upstairs tonight, but a kiss . . . Oh yeah, I can definitely do a kiss.

He hesitates, looking adorably nervous, before leaning down, pressing his lips to mine, and . . .

Nothing. His lips are soft—too soft. There's no substance. I try to lean into the kiss, but there's no resistance, nothing to work with. It's like kissing a new sponge fresh out of the wrapper—pliable, but lifeless.

Ugh!

All the wonderful anticipation and excitement humming through my body abruptly fizzles. I pull away and bite back a snort because his eyes are still closed, and he's humming as if he's savoring the finest wine. Well, at least *he's* gotten something out of it. I manage to tamp down my disappointment and plaster a smile on my face just as he opens his eyes. He looks delighted.

"Wow," he breathes, and leans his forehead against mine. "You're amazing."

"Um, yeah, wow," I echo, somewhat listlessly. He steps back and releases me, looking at me hopefully.

"Do you have plans for Tuesday night? It's my night off. I know it's a workday, but maybe we can just get a quick bite somewhere for dinner or dessert?"

"Oh, um, Tuesday . . . let me think," I stammer. "Actually, I'm not sure if Tuesday will work. But let me have your number, and I'll let you know."

He beams at me and takes my offered phone, quickly punching in his number. He presses send, and his own phone rings. "There, now we're set." He leans down and, before I can react, I'm treated to a repeat performance of the Limp Lip-Lock. Determined to try to make something out of nothing, I redouble my efforts and pucker a little more, moving my lips against his. Nope—nada. A sense of helplessness swells within me when it becomes apparent there's nothing I can do to coax a more animated response from him. But I return his smile when we break apart, and I walk backward slowly toward the elevator.

"I'll call you about Tuesday," I manage brightly. "Good night, Wyatt, and thank you for a wonderful evening."

"G'night. Sweet dreams." He turns and steps back outside, smiling at me over his shoulder. Giving him a perky little wave through the glass door, I finally escape into the tiny elevator, letting out a vast sigh of relief as soon as the doors close.

"Damn, damn, damn," I groan, banging my head lightly against the doors. He's smart, polite, handsome, and a good dancer. So what if he's a crappy kisser? It's not the end of the world. It doesn't necessarily mean he'd be bad in the sack, does it?

Once I reach my floor, I trudge down the hall to my apartment. I dump my purse and keys on my kitchen table and immediately move to pour myself a glass of wine in the kitchen to give my mouth something to react to. Maybe it would've been better with a little tongue? On the other hand, tongue might have only made it limp *and* wet. I shudder.

I check my voice mail and scowl at the two hang ups. I

suppose they could have been wrong numbers, but . . . I really need to change my number. I take my glass and curl up in my ancient, plush wing chair. *There's more to life than passion, Abby*, I tell myself, toying with a loose thread on the chair arm. I had passion once upon a time and look what that got me. I shudder, pushing my last horrific memory of Lucas back. Yeah, passion is definitely overrated.

I frown out at the night beyond my window. Wyatt is a lovely man who seems genuinely interested in me. Don't I owe it to myself to give the guy a second date? For cripe's sake, he *saves lives* for a living. What more could I ask for?

So, why does a part of me feel like I'm settling?

THE NEXT AFTERNOON, AS APRIL and I return from lunch, I stop dead in my tracks. Standing like a stone sentry outside my office is the bodyguard I'd seen in Lane's suite at the hotel. From behind her desk, Tess ogles the biceps bulging out of his tight T-shirt and looks like she's about to expire. But my eyes are glued to my open office door and the vision standing just inside.

Looking tall, lean, and utterly edible, Kennedy leans with his back against my office windows, his arms crossed over his broad chest, the picture of nonchalance. He's wearing a beautifully tailored sapphire-blue suit with matching shirt, looking the exact opposite from the last time I saw him. His black hair is in artful disarray, falling over his forehead carelessly, and my fingers twitch involuntarily. He's stunning. A sly smirk spreads across his lips as our eyes meet; I'm suddenly aware I'm gaping at him.

"Holy shit. Is that who I think it is?" April asks in disbelief as I clamp my mouth shut. "Did you have a meeting scheduled with him?"

"I . . . No, I don't," I say, finally finding my voice. What on earth is he doing here? The smugness in his eyes infuriates me. It's like he's doing me a favor by gracing me with his presence.

"Well, you shouldn't keep him waiting. You can tell me all about it later," April murmurs, gently bumping her shoulder against mine and spurring me into motion.

Tess snaps out of her bodyguard-induced haze as I approach. "I'm sorry, Abby. I know he isn't on your schedule, but . . ." Waving off her apology, I give her an understanding nod before continuing into my office. Kennedy watches me like a hawk through his narrowed eyes, and I steel myself for what could be a prickly conversation.

"Mr. Lane," I greet him coolly as I close the door behind me. "What a pleasant surprise. What can I do for you?"

He takes a deep breath before the self-assured smile I remember slips into place. "I think it's what I can do for you, *Miss Walker.*"

I fight back a flash of annoyance. Arrogant bastard. "Oh? Did Nadia not speak with your management team?" I ask, confused. *What the hell is he doing here?*

"Oh, she talked to them all right. But, I wanted to talk more about that boy's dream with *you*—"

"Parker," I correct. "His name is Parker."

"Right. Parker." He purses his lips and shoves off from my window to take a seat on the couch opposite my desk. "You don't mind if I sit, do you?" He stretches his arm out along the back.

"Oh, excuse me. Please, make yourself comfortable." I take a seat behind my desk, feeling the need to have some kind of barrier between us. The buttons of his shirt collar are undone, allowing a few silky strands of his chest hair to catch the light streaming in my window. I clear my throat with difficulty. "You were saying?"

"It's just that a few signed albums, or even one of my old

guitars, isn't what that ki—Parker—wanted. The things you outlined, like a mini concert and whatever else, sound more reasonable. I could go along with that for you . . . for him. We could make it work."

I can't help the confusion that seeps into my voice. "Mr. Lane—"

"Kennedy. Call me Kennedy."

I ignore his interruption. "I believe we went over all the reasons this wouldn't work already. I understand, as your record label rep pointed out, that a full-on interaction with Parker would be very good publicity for you. But I promise you'll still get some benefit from the signed gifts. Surely you understand."

"Publicity?" The scowl I glimpsed earlier makes a reappearance. "You think I'm doing this just for publicity?"

"Why else?" I shrug. "Most of our donors do so because of an altruistic urge, of course, but they're also usually getting something out of it for themselves or for their business. I'm happy to receive help wherever I can get it."

He stares at me for a beat, frowning. "You'll take help where you can get it, just not from me?"

"Mr. Lane, you *are* helping, and I assure you that I *am* grateful for your donations," I begin, treading carefully. The last thing I want to do is piss him off again. If he changes his mind, we won't have anything at all for Parker.

He shakes his head gently and snorts in amusement. "Look, we clearly got off on the wrong foot. We'd had a party, and I obviously took a little longer than usual to bounce back. I apologize for my appearance. Believe me, I've looked a lot worse." He chuckles as if it's some kind of joke.

"I don't doubt it."

His smile falters. "Well, I just wanted to show you . . ." Uncertainty flashes in his eyes before his smug confidence returns.

"Since you seem to prefer a more *conventional* look. I can clean up pretty good."

I peer at him, trying to look beyond his handsome face and cocky smile. His eyes aren't as bloodshot as they were, true, and his pupils aren't hugely dilated anymore. His clothes are impeccable, although I suspect they're wildly out of character for him. The suit looks a little big on him, as if he's lost some weight since he last wore it.

However, his pasty pallor and the deep shadows under his eyes diminish the healthy façade he seems to want to portray. Even more telling is his almost constant movement, the tapping of his foot or fingers. It's more than simple nervousness. I wonder if he even realizes he's doing it.

It's a painfully familiar symptom that I'm not going to disregard again.

The acute disappointment I felt returns as I look at him, and I wish he'd just let this go. "Mr. Lane, as I was saying earlier—"

"And as *I* said earlier, call me Kennedy," he interrupts sharply, leaning forward and resting his elbows on his knees as he looks up at me. "All this 'Mr. Lane' crap is feeling suspiciously like a brush off."

I mash my lips together to still the sharp retort begging to escape. Does this guy really think a little window dressing would persuade me to change my mind? Swallowing my irritation, I manage a professional smile. "I assure you that isn't my intent. But I've already given you my reasons for why I don't believe your participation in a more extensive dream fulfillment for Parker would be advisable. I don't see anything today that changes that opinion. I'm sorry."

I quickly stand, trying to forestall any impending outburst. "Now, if you'll excuse me, I have a meeting starting in five minutes. Thank you so much for dropping by. I'll make sure our

Giving Team contacts your manager today." Giving him a winning smile, I move to open the door, but he rises swiftly, blocking my path.

"I can't believe this," he growls in frustration, raking his hand through his hair. "You'll really kill this kid's dream just because you caught me napping and hungover."

I'm barely able to hold on to my temper. "I'm not the one preventing his dream. And you weren't 'napping'. You were passed out on the couch in the middle of the day. Do you even remember how you got there?"

He looks away, the tips of his ears turning pink, before recovering his swagger. "You seem to be overly interested in where I sleep, Miss Walker." He steps closer, his spicy, musky scent surrounding me. "Why do you think that is, hmm?"

"I . . . I'm not," I stammer in barely restrained outrage. What is it about personal space that this guy doesn't understand? "My next appointment is waiting—"

"I don't get you," he bursts, startling me. He spreads his arms wide in supplication. "Most people would do anything to have me associated with their organization. Don't you know what I am?"

"I certainly do. You're the one in denial."

"I *don't* have a fucking problem." His eyes blaze, causing me to take a step back in spite of myself. But I stick my chin out and stare right back at him. I'm not about to let this pompous ass push me around in my own damn office.

"That remains to be seen," I say evenly. "But until I'm proven otherwise, I can't allow—"

"I can't believe this." He chuckles darkly, sending a shiver down my spine. "If I was a clean cut Boy Scout, you'd probably be falling all over yourself.

"What?" I blink, confused by his non sequitur. He takes

another step, crowding me.

"That's probably the kind of man who interests you. Mr. Boring Buzzcut. Solid, dependable, stable . . . *safe.*"

The breath catches in my throat as he trails one hand up my bare arm to my shoulder, setting my skin ablaze, before planting his palm on the wall beside me.

"You want the kind of man who's never colored outside the lines in his life. Isn't that right, *Abigail?*"

"You have no idea of what I want," I snap back, bristling.

"Don't be too sure." His voice drips with disdain. "You seem so eager to judge me that I feel it's only fair for me to do the same to you."

I feel my face heat. "Do you honestly think a fancy suit and a shave is all you need to do?" I glower at his beautiful and angry face. "Kennedy, you can do whatever you want when it comes to your own life. I don't care. But this kind of performance isn't going to fool me, and it won't fool Parker. Children are amazingly perceptive, and he's too fragile right now to be exposed to your bull—" I swallow my sentence just in time and continue, my firm tone becoming downright icy. "Furthermore, my personal life is none of your business. Now, if you'll excuse me."

He steps aside and gestures grandly toward the door, mocking me. I pause with my hand on the doorknob. "I'll make sure we work things out with your team quickly for those items. You'll be starting your tour soon, yes? I promise that we'll be out of your hair by then."

"Did you keep my number?" His eyes bore into mine, challenging me, and I'm immediately wary.

"Against my better judgment, yes, I did." I hesitate, suddenly afraid I've pushed him too far. "You haven't changed your mind about donating the signed items, have you?"

"Of course not. Despite what you obviously think of me, I

stand by my word." Relief surges through me, and I don't even mind as he reaches past me to open the door wide. Muscle Man snaps to attention as Kennedy steps out and pauses, obviously for Tess's benefit. "Text me when you're ready to talk about Parker. Oh, and Abigail," he says, tugging at the waistband of this trousers, as if to ensure it's fastened. "Thanks for letting me drop in. I hope it was as good for you as it was for me."

My mouth drops open. Then with a wink toward Tess, he saunters confidently toward the elevators with The Hulk, leaving me seething and exasperated in his wake.

chapter six

kennedy

"YOU WANT TO TALK ABOUT it?" Tucker sinks his colossal frame into the expensive leather seat across from me. We're currently flying somewhere over heartland USA, and the convenience of a private jet is not lost on me. I've worked my ass off to get to this point, where—finally—I don't have to fight the crowds, the paparazzi, and the ensuing mayhem that results when I've flown commercial.

Unfortunately, this time the flight, which usually serves to calm me, is doing anything but. I'm a fidgeting, edgy bundle of sheer energy. And I blame it all on Abigail Walker. I don't know when I've ever met anyone as stubborn as I am. I didn't think such a creature existed, but there she was today, testing me, throwing her opinions of my life in my face and daring me to prove her wrong. And the thing is, she doesn't think I'm capable of that. She really believes there's no hope for me.

I'm beginning to wonder if she's right. I've doubted a lot of things lately. Whether I'm getting too old for this entire scene, whether I've still got what it takes to be relevant in a business that is constantly changing. I can't seem to turn my mind off.

"Talk about what exactly?" I ask, desperate to stop the thoughts swirling relentlessly. Tucker darts his eyes to my bouncing leg.

"Do I really need to spell it out?"

"I need a fucking drink." Eyeing the lure of the bar, Brodie lifts a glass to me. I turn away, looking out the window to the endless blue sky. How many fucking hours do we have left?

"No. You don't need a drink. What you need is to talk."

"I've had a shrink, thanks. Wasn't much help, despite the shit-load of money I threw at him."

"Are you sure I can't get you anything, Mr. Lane?" The hired "attendant," handpicked no doubt by Brodie, leans down to get eye level with me once more. Her voice drips sex, and her outfit doesn't disappoint. Tight, low cut top, barely-there skirt, and cheap heels that have seen better days—standard groupie attire. She reeks of desperation. I doubt she's even a flight attendant. She's here for one reason and one reason only. She wants the experience, the certified mile-high rock star fantasy.

I give her my best attempt at a thankful smile. "I'm fine, thanks." If she's disappointed, it's short lived. She drifts over to join the rest of the band at the bar. I'm reminded once again of just how shallow my life is. It makes me think more about the woman I can't seem to get out of my head. Despite the general disdain for me, I don't think deep down that's who Abby is. You don't devote your life to a charity like *What's Your Dream* if you aren't a compassionate person.

Even fighting a hangover, I saw how invested she was the minute she started talking about Parker. I know all about that kind of passion, although mine is found with a guitar. We have more in common than she realizes. The big difference is she's doing work that actually changes people's lives.

"What did she say to you this afternoon, hmm?" Tucker asks. "You've been more of a pain-in-the-ass than normal since we left that office."

"Nothing I didn't already know."

"Come on then, mate. Party's just getting started over here." Sean's voice booms through the cabin, directed at me. My mouth waters as Sean waves a bottle of Jack at me, and my fingers tap relentlessly against my knee.

"I'll get your guitar," Tucker offers, his hand falling to my shoulder as he moves out of the seat and to the room at the back of the plane.

It doesn't take long for Brodie to find his way over, a full glass of temptation in his hand. "Looks like you could use this," he suggests.

I should've made him fly coach on some packed commercial flight. "I'm good. Thanks."

"Doesn't look like you're good at all."

I want to tell him to mind his own fucking business. I want to tell him he's the one that doesn't look good, but I can't seem to find the words. The ice clinking against the glass catches my attention, and my eyes fix on the condensation beading along the side. My hands are clammy, and I press my palms against my thighs, desperate to find a distraction. Fucking temptation is a bitch. But, if I'm going to stop drinking, I have to start somewhere.

Ignoring Brodie, I stare at my text message to Abby, asking her not to give up. An internal war rages in my head. If I go down this road, if, using her words, I try to prove otherwise, it's going to require total commitment. There is no halfway with her. It's all or nothing.

Tucker steps beside Brodie, shouldering him effortlessly out of the way. My Gibson acoustic, one of the few things I can actually count on in my life, appears in front of me, and my shaking hands know exactly what to do.

WE ARRIVE AT LAGUARDIA, AND I've had no messages from Abby. Stubborn little thing. Her biting words and those wide hazel eyes, and that air of defiance hint at something lying dormant, just waiting to be unleashed. It's all been consuming me.

The streets of New York are alive and pulsing, blurring by as we wind our way to the St. Regis. With Brodie riding shotgun, I look at the band of misfits surrounding me. They're feeling no pain, having demolished most of the alcohol onboard. I can smell it rolling off them in waves.

It's rather interesting to watch the train wreck when you're not on it. Tucker tries to tug Sean back into his seat. Typically, that would be easy given Tucker's sheer size; but when Sean is lit, it's almost impossible to divert him. He hangs his head out the window like a dog, letting out the occasional bark.

The "attendant" is perched firmly in Matt's lap, wrapping herself around him like ivy. Let's hope he hasn't proposed yet. Cam is passed out, sprawled across the entire back row and snoring away. And had this been any other day, if I had never met Abby, I'd probably be passed out with him.

Instead, I'm overthinking and weighing the pros and cons of actually trying to get my shit together. At the end of the day, it all comes back to the music. It's the thing that keeps me going when the world wants me to stop. Robin always used to say music was in my veins, that she couldn't imagine me doing anything else. She believed in me regardless of the fucked-up shit I would get into. I wish I could talk to her now. I wish—

"Was some good shit you were playing on the plane." This slur from Cam who, it turns out, isn't passed out after all.

I push his boots off the leather seat, and he groans a response. "You're loaded. I could've played Firehouse, and you'd think it was awesome."

He snorts, flipping me off, his arm landing with a thud on his forehead. His intense hate of second-rate eighties hair bands is legendary. "Don't get me started, man. Fuckin' bunch of . . ." The whiskey swimming in his veins wins the battle once more, and he's out cold again.

This is my normal, as fucked as is it. But sometimes it's good to change things up. No more excuses. I pull my sunglasses down, snap a picture of myself, and start typing a message to Abby.

You want me to prove something to you? Stay tuned.

abigail

SHUTTING MY APARTMENT DOOR BEHIND me, I heave a sigh of relief and sag gratefully against the doorframe, completely exhausted. I'm so friggin' glad this day is over. My feet are killing me. I drop my coat, kick off my shoes, and set my grocery sack in the kitchen before marching straight into my bedroom to strip. My most comfortable pair of stretchy, baby blue pajamas is like a whisper over my skin, and I instantly feel worlds better. The next step is predictable—a glass of wine. I leave the bottle open on the counter.

Jesus God, what a day. Taking large sips from my glass, I set about putting my few groceries away, reserving the salad and juicy red pear that is to be my dinner. And a box of Cracker Jacks for dessert. I'll feel guilty about the processed sugar later.

I wish Maddie were home so she could distract me with stories of compulsive coffee drinkers or shifty suppliers, but her fireman has the night off, so they are out painting the town. Since they'd reached the bedroom stage, with her usual alacrity, I only hear from her when he's working. But she's so stinkin' happy with him, I can't blame her.

Why did Lane come to the office today, really? Is it just that he's heard the word no so rarely that he simply can't believe me? Shaking my head, I refill my glass, gather my dinner and dessert, and retreat to my small dining table. This isn't the first time a dream hasn't worked out the way I wanted, far from it. I can't recall another prospective donor who has been so pigheaded. His manager was obviously relieved that Kennedy would only have to provide a few signed trinkets, so why is the man himself being so persistent? I growl in frustration and take a savage bite from my pear.

He says he keeps his word. *Well, he'd better,* I think with a grim smile. Nadia mentioned this evening that Lane's team hadn't yet returned her calls to organize the signed items. My stomach drops, my worry returning. If I've screwed this up . . . no. He'll follow through, if only to try to justify his anger with me.

Closing my eyes, I take another sip and savor the wine as I picture him standing in my office. God, the way that suit ghosted over his lean form and the devilish gleam in his blue eyes . . . Holy mother-of-pearl. If only the inside was as attractive as the outside.

I'm startled out of my brooding by the staccato trumpet notes of *Flight of the Bumblebee,* and I smile reflexively. It's the perfect herald for my mother, considering her frenetic energy and eclectic thought processes.

"Hi, Mom."

"Finally! I've been trying to get you all day," she bursts, and I roll my eyes.

"I hardly think one call in the morning constitutes all day," I say dryly, but with a smile.

"Well, it felt like it. How are you? Have you given any thought to my suggestion about Beau? When are you coming to visit?"

I laugh and feel some of the weight on my shoulders lift. "Fine. Not really—dating a pastry chef would make me gain twenty pounds. And I'm thinking of coming next weekend after I get back from my trip. How's that?"

"Really?" Her excitement is palpable. "That would be perfect! We'll have your room waiting for you. We just have to move a few things around, but I promise you'll have a bed to sleep in."

"Are you using it for storage again?" I tease, although I really can't blame her. It's been months since I've been to Napa and space in their bed and breakfast is at a premium this time of year.

"Just for a few cases of wine that couldn't fit in your father's cellar, and a few new quilts for the guestrooms. Really, the only thing I should probably move is our new tantric chair. It works best in your room since it's at the far end of the house so no one can hear us when we get kinda loud, but I suppose we could move it to our room—"

"Mom!" I squeal in protest. "God! Stop!"

Her merry laughter rings out over the phone. "Oh relax. You know I'm just kidding. Sheesh. Lighten up, sweetheart!"

Sighing, I rub a hand over my face. She says she's kidding, but with my mother, who knows? I wouldn't put it past her to talk my dad into getting a tantric chair, and . . . Good for them, I suppose. My parents have always had a very loving relationship that has lasted through thick and thin. But a tantric chair isn't exactly the type of thing I want to picture, especially in the bedroom they've reserved for me. Eww.

Her last words are uncomfortably similar to advice that someone else has given me lately. Someone who I wish I could stop thinking about. "Sorry, Mom. I've just had a really long day."

"Oh, sweetie, what happened?"

"An unusual situation has developed with a potential donor," I explain. I don't really want to talk about Lane, but there's a nagging part of me that really wants to hear my mom tell me it will all be okay. "He's a, ah, a celebrity who won't take no for an answer."

"Wait, you're telling him he *can't* donate? Aren't you usually trying to get people *to* donate?"

"Oh, he's going to, but not to the full extent that we were originally planning. I'm not sure I can trust him. I suspect he's like . . . Lucas."

She sucks in a sharp breath. "Then you made the right decision," she says finally, her voice full of quiet certainty. "Trust your instincts, honey. They won't steer you wrong."

I sigh pensively, reassured for the moment. "I just hope that he'll provide the items he promised. I was rather blunt, and he didn't take it well."

"Addicts rarely do," she says. "But, sweetie, you never have trouble with donors. I'm sure it's not as bad as all that. You're a professional down to your fingertips." The unmistakable pride in her voice warms me, until Lane's infuriating smirk dances in my mind again.

"He's just so *irritating*." I jump up to pace in front of my window. "I don't understand why he won't give it up. You'd think he'd be relieved that he's being let off the hook. You know how it is. So many celebrities are only interested in doing the bare minimum, just so they can brag about their involvement on Twitter. But he's being so obstinate. He showed up completely unannounced today to badger me. Apparently, he thinks because he's tall and hot and looks good in a suit that he can simply charm me into caving—"

"He's hot? I had envisioned some old crusty curmudgeon.

Who is he?"

"Um, well," I falter, caught off guard. "It doesn't matter. I'll just have Nadia deal with him from now on, that's all."

She hums, giving nothing away. "Well, sweetie, it is unusual to hear you so kerfuffled. What advice does Maddie have for you?"

"Oh, um, I haven't told her." I slump back down in my chair, feeling somewhat guilty. In truth, I've avoided talking to Maddie about the puzzling Mr. Lane.

She huffs in frustration. "You tell Maddie everything," she says carefully. She takes a deep breath. "If you're keeping this to yourself, there's something wrong."

I close my eyes. "Mom, there's nothing wrong," I reply not sure which one of us I'm trying to convince. "I'm sorry if I'm worrying you. Honestly, I'm okay. I simply haven't had time to tell Maddie anything lately since she's so wrapped up in her new man." It's not really a lie; Maddie *has* been scarce in the few days since I first met Kennedy. Luckily, it's enough to distract my mother.

"Ooh, that's right! Tell me all about the new man in her life."

I chuckle, glad to be on a safer topic. "There's not much to tell yet. Maddie and Dylan are spending a lot of time together lately, and she seems to be pretty happy so far. So, tell me what you guys have been up to lately. Has the tourist train slowed down yet this year?"

"Hardly! We just approved the final drafts for the ads about our "Live in the Vineyard" November specials," she gushes, referring to the biannual music festival held in Napa. "You should see the packages we're putting together!"

I listen as she prattles on about the coming season and the joys of being innkeepers, the sound of her voice soothing. It's heartwarming to know how happy they are.

My dad, Frank, had grown up in a small town called Burlington up in northern Washington State, not far from the Canadian border. My Grandpa Walker had been a policeman, and Dad followed in his footsteps. Sadly, Grandpa was killed on duty—a burglary arrest gone wrong—not too long after Dad joined the force, leaving him and Grandma alone. But a few months after the funeral, my free-spirited mother had wandered into the area on her way to a nature retreat in the San Juan Islands. Mom had dropped out of Berkeley in her senior year when a drunk driver had plowed into her parents' car, killing them instantly. Heartbroken, she turned to various spiritual remedies, searching for something. She hadn't known exactly what she'd been looking for. Whatever it was, she had found it in my dad.

For his part, Dad had been smitten. Love at first sight, they told me. Anyway, with Grandma's blessing, he followed Mom back to her hometown of Half Moon Bay, just south of San Francisco, and joined the police force there. It had been a nice place to grow up.

Everyone knew Grandma Walker was the Mary Kay queen of the region, but it wasn't until she'd passed away we'd discovered just how lucrative eye shadow and lipstick could be. The inheritance the dear woman had left to my parents fulfilled their dream of owning a bed-and-breakfast in Napa, and provided a tidy, not-so-little trust fund for me. It allowed me to live comfortably in San Francisco and still be able to donate a chunk of my salary back to the Foundation. I had loved my grandmother dearly and was thankful for her gifts every day.

"By the way, don't think I don't know what you did there, young lady," she starts sternly, but with affection. "I let you distract me. But I want the full details about your love life when you come to visit!"

"Yes, ma'am," I reply, giving a mock salute, before I let my voice soften. "Love you, Mom. Say hi to Dad for me."

"I love you, too, sweetie. Be safe."

I hit end and sink back into the chair, taking a long sip of my wine and feeling more relaxed than I have all day. I know I made the right decision regarding Lane. Besides, after today, I'll probably never see him again. Nadia can handle it from here. Problem solved.

I'm just settling back into my chair with a full glass in my hand and a financial report to read, when my phone chimes with a text. Expecting a note from Maddie, I take a big sip and swipe my thumb across the screen to reveal the message . . .

. . . And spit my mouthful of pinot noir all over the neat rows of numbers marching across the page.

Oh, for the love of . . . Cursing under my breath, I drop my phone and frantically dab at the stained papers with my napkin, my brain awhirl. I set the report aside with a groan over the mess I've made and retrieve my phone to stare again in shock at the sexy, determined sapphire eyes peering at me from over dark sunglasses, above the message, *"You want me to prove something to you? Stay tuned."*

After gaping at my phone, thunderstruck and infuriatingly intrigued by the challenge implicit in his words, I wearily slump in my chair and scrunch my eyes shut, my frustration escaping in a long, drawn out groan.

chapter seven

kennedy

THE PAVEMENT IS UNRELENTING UNDER my feet, jarring my bones and stealing my breath as New York greets the morning. I stop in the middle of the trail, surrounded by a lush green carpet of grass, skyscrapers stand tall in the distance as the sun starts to rise.

A group of runners blur past, with no hesitation, no curious glances at the pathetic, groaning idiot in their way. Somehow, I manage to stumble off the path, rip out my earbuds, and crumple into the cool grass.

Shutting my eyes, a vivid memory flashes of Robin, Adam, and me, collapsed in the snow in the backyard after one of our epic snowball fights. I can hear her laugh, infectious as it was, and the gaping hole in my heart opens a bit wider.

Feeling overheated and panting like a rabid dog, I sit up and check my phone for messages again. I would've thought by now, I'd have some sign of life from Abby, but there's nothing. I'm not known for my patience. I've always gone after what I wanted regardless of what stood in my way. I wouldn't be where I'm today if I had accepted rejection. You have to be driven. Breaking into this business, I got used to hearing the word no. I hate it as much now as I did then, maybe even more. So, Abigail Walker doesn't have a clue the lengths to which I'm willing to go.

I slide the phone to video mode, hold it at arm's length from me, and start recording. I don't care that I look like shit. That I probably have dark circles under my eyes from lack of sleep and sweat is literally dripping off me. I need her to see me—raw and unfiltered—so she realizes I'm serious about this.

"You'll be happy to know, I've just run—voluntarily. See the things I do for you?" I turn the phone to video the nondescript trees that line the path beside me. "It's early in the morning, my band is still asleep and usually I would be, too, but I want to do this for Parker." Flipping the phone back to me, I continue rambling, "I know I haven't actually met him yet, but I will. I want to help with his dream, and I don't mean just some posters and a couple of signed albums." I look up as a few birds make their presence known in the trees above, screeching through the silence of the morning. "I want you to know that I get why you don't think I can do this . . . That I shouldn't meet him. I'm not a saint. I'm the first person to admit that. But I want to do this right. I want to prove to you I can. So just trust me. Okay?"

I send the video to her without hesitation, and spend a few more minutes in the quiet of Central Park.

"GIVE US A BEAT, MR. Murphy. One that makes sense this time?" I glance at Sean from the microphone. He flips me off with a loud laugh from behind his drum kit before starting into *Shake Down* one more time.

We're currently rehearsing in an empty warehouse just off Broadway before our stripped down shows later this week. These pre-tour gigs are a great warm-up for the insanity that is about to descend upon us. It's more relaxed without the amped up light show and full throttle effects. Short of going fully acoustic, it's as subdued as we can get when we're playing together.

Roadies linger, checking and double-checking amps, adjusting sound levels, and replacing Cam's strings when he breaks them multiple times over. Brodie leans against the soundboard with a cigarette dangling from his lips, constantly checking his phone and giving us the occasional thumbs-up. It's organized chaos at its finest, fueling the adrenaline, and taking me to the only place in my life that seems to make sense.

Unfortunately, Sean is off this afternoon. I think I know why. The beat is more frenetic than it should be, and his timing slightly ahead. For anyone else listening, they probably wouldn't be able to hear it, but we all do.

We compensate for him, trying to find where Sean's insisting on taking us. The guitar comes to life under my fingers, and I close my eyes, belting out the lyrics into the mic.

"When the time comes, I'll remind you

Of all the things we didn't say."

"Fuck! Hold up." I step back, turning to face Sean. "What the hell are you doing?"

It takes him a few beats to recognize that the rest of us have stopped playing. "What?" He shrugs as sweat pours off him, soaking his T-shirt. His hair, freshly dyed crimson, is a wild mess, hanging down over one eye.

"Seriously? '*What?*' That's all you've got for me?"

"Mate, what are you on about?" He twirls his drumsticks between his fingers.

"I think that question is for you, *mate*. What is it this time, hmm? Coke again? Because this right here. This is how you were playing the last time."

Wiping the sweat from his brow, he glares back at me. "I'm not on anything."

"Whatever it is, get it the fuck together. We have a show later this week."

"Ah, orders from HRH himself," Sean bites back. "I'm truly honored to be in the presence of greatness."

"HR . . . What the hell are you talking about?"

"HRH. You know? His Royal Highness. I must have missed the official memo where you lot all became saints." He points his drumsticks at us. "Was it a nice ceremony? High tea and everything?" Typically, we'd all be howling at another one of Sean's epic rants, but there's nothing funny about it this time.

"Jesus, fuck. Can we just cut the shit and play already?" Cam hollers.

"I'm just trying something new," Sean counters with a shrug. "Didn't realize that was a crime."

"I'm all for pushing the boundaries, you know that; but you're not on even on the same map right now," I fire back at him.

A drumstick sails past my head, landing in the chaos of cords that snake around the floor of the warehouse. "Fuck this. I'm out." Sean upends his stool, and it crashes into his drum kit. He stalks to the metal side door, pushing it open with enough force that it slams against the side of the building.

Cam shakes his head, glancing back to me. "Whose turn is it this time?" While this group of dysfunctional misfits is like family, putting together four strong-willed and highly opinionated men for any length of time is going to result in a few arguments. Typically, we take turns talking each other off the proverbial edge, share a few drinks, and all is well again.

"Don't look at me. I got this one last time." Matt grins at me before starting into the bass line of the chorus again.

I pass my guitar off to one of the roadies, yanking out my earpieces before heading after Sean. "I got it."

"YOUR TURN, HMM?" SEAN SITS at the aged wooden bar inside a dingy pub, swirling amber liquid in his glass before draining back the contents. It was easy to find him; even in New York City, he tends to stand out.

"My lucky day." I slide onto the stool beside him, glancing back at Tucker who stands near the door, his expression grim.

Thankfully, the pub Sean has decided to grace with his presence for the afternoon is fairly empty. It's your standard watering hole: grunge classics crackling through a sub-par stereo system, dark wooden tables, sticky floor, back of the mirrored wall behind the bar lined with temptation. The smell of liquor is overpowering, my mouth waters as I try to focus on why I'm here.

"Indeed." He motions to the bartender, a bald, tatted, middle-aged man who looks like he spends too much time in the gym. "Just leave the bottle, yeah, mate? And another glass for my dear friend here."

Silently, a clear glass slides into my view. "You want to share your secret?" Sean fills up his glass.

"My secret?" I try to look anywhere but at the glass. A bar isn't a good place for me to be right now.

"Don't think I've missed that you've been avoiding the drink since we've been here." Sean's voice brings me out of my wandering thoughts.

"You noticed that?"

He nods and brings the glass back to his lips. "Hard not to when you're typically in the thick of things."

"Maybe I'm getting too old to party like I used to."

"Now, I'm going to have to call bullshit on that one. I'm

older than you," Sean says, swirling the liquid in the glass.

"Only by a couple of months, old man." He snorts before taking a long sip. "And take a look at you."

He leans back in the stool, turning to face me, waving his hands over his torso. "You only wish you looked this good."

"Whatever helps you sleep at night."

"So, spill it." His tired eyes meet mine, any trace of his usual humor gone. This is what he needs. Maybe it's a distraction, a way for him to cope, or maybe me talking about it will actually help, and that's why I'm here.

"You know that charity I was telling you guys about?"

"The one with the sick kid?"

I watch as he drains another glassful. "Parker, yeah."

"I thought you had that all sorted?"

"Everyone else thinks so," I reply. "Apparently, what I think doesn't matter." My gaze falls to the empty glass in front of me.

"And what do you think?"

"He deserves more than a couple of signed pictures." Sean refills his glass and turns to me. "He could've asked for anything, you know? And he wants to spend a day with me," I continue.

"I spend 24–7 with you. I could've saved him the trouble, told him what a treat you are." He laughs. "Well, that's as good a reason as any to lay off the booze for a while, I guess."

"Yeah . . ."

He narrows his eyes, studying me. "There's more, though."

"The woman who—"

"Aha! There's pussy involved," he shouts, shoving my shoulder. "I knew it."

"It's not like that."

He snorts and leans back in the stool. "Sure it's not."

"No, seriously. I think her feelings toward me lean to the side of general disapproval and revulsion." Not that I want it to stay that way.

"Ah, a challenge then. Good on you. It's been a while since you've had a steady girl. Since Michelle, yeah?" He tilts his head back dramatically, throwing back another shot.

"I could've lived the rest of my life without hearing you say her name again."

"Still stings, does it?" I glare at him in response, my hand itching to fill the glass. "Which band was that guy from again that you found her with?"

"Fuck, you are a pain in the ass, and it was Stomp the Faith, remember?" It's not a time in my life I like to revisit. Michelle and I were the real deal. At least, I thought we were. We had been together for over two years. Two years of turning down other women and flying home between gigs just to spend a few hours with her. Two years that came to a screeching halt when I found her with the drummer from a one-hit-wonder band.

"It's all coming back to me. Seems appropriate, the name of the band." I close my hand around the neck of the bottle, and fill up the glass in front of me.

"Anyway, we're not talking about me here; we're supposed to be talking about you." I refill his glass, setting the bottle out of my reach. "I need to know how bad it is. If we need to push out any concert dates or cancel appearances."

He looks surprised at my suggestion. "You'd do that for me?"

"The tour doesn't work without the four of us."

He claps my shoulder. "That means a lot," he says quietly.

"You'd do the same thing for me," I answer, shrugging him off.

He runs his hand over his face before staring blankly into the wall of bottles behind the bar. "It was just last night," he admits quietly.

"Something happen to set it off? You've been clean for almost a year."

He lets out a mock laugh. "Does it matter? It was a Tuesday? Broke a drumstick? You know how this works. There doesn't have to be some grand philosophical reason. Brodie said it was some of the best. I was curious. A moment of weakness."

I nod, gripping my hands firmly around the cool glass. Just one drink . . . "Do you want me to call somebody? Your sister?"

"Nah. You're here. Besides, Sydney would kill me." He touches his glass to the one cradled between my hands, and just like that, all is right in our fucked-up world once again. "I'm sorry about the drumstick to the head."

"No you're not." I chuckle. "And it missed me. Nice try, though. Your aim needs work."

"It won't happen again, Kennedy," he says seriously. "I know how important this is to you . . . to all of us. You have my word."

"That's all I need."

"Tell me something, though." He faces me. "When Parker's had his day, and you're done with the girl, what'll be your reason to stay sober then, hmm?"

"I don't know." The glass finds its way to my lips, and I hesitate before draining back the contents. "I don't know."

NO MATTER HOW MANY TIMES you tell yourself it's just one drink, the truth is, it's already too late. You've broken the promise you made to yourself, to the people around you, and those who aren't here anymore. You're a failure. The demon has taken over, grabbed hold of you, and you've got to decide to either fight or prepare for the inevitable.

Tonight, I'm trying to fight. I've locked myself away from the party well under way in another suite. I've shut the door on the band, and on Brodie. It's Tucker and me and a room full of guitars; I leave the demon lurking down the hall.

I had wanted to send Abby a video every day, but tonight, I just can't. If she sees me, she'll know. And she can't know about this. She can't know that less than a week after I told her to trust me that I screwed up.

But the phone is heavy in my hand, and I can't stop the overwhelming need to reach out. It's like she's calling to me without ever saying a word. I type out a message quickly.

I've been thinking . . .

Her answering text is a welcome surprise.

Dangerous for you . . .

♪ ♩ ♪ ♩

abigail

SMILING TIREDLY, I GAZE THROUGH the taxi window at the glorious art deco styling of the Chrysler Building. Although other skyscrapers may be more celebrated, I think it's still one of the most striking buildings in the country.

My flight from San Francisco was nonstop, but that also meant I had virtually no relief from the toddler sitting behind me who wouldn't stop kicking the back of my seat, no matter how many times I shot a look at his father, who was too busy playing with his phone to mind his son. All I'm thinking about now is room service and a nice long soak in a tub.

By the time I'm out of the cab, my luggage is out of the trunk and waiting for me with another helpful valet despite the late hour. Although a lot of people discount the New York St. Regis as being too old-fashioned, one thing that can't be argued about is its impeccable service.

I elect to haul my own bag and make my way into the

luxurious lobby. Starwood Hotels and Resorts is one of our largest corporate donors, and this year's annual meeting of its board of directors is being held all week at the St. Regis. One requirement of their continued participation is that I deliver a presentation on the fruits of their labor in person. It's a small price to pay considering all they do for us.

A tall man with hair dyed the most violent, unnatural shade of red I've ever seen and dressed like a designer version of Mad Max practically mows me down in his haste to embrace two scantily-dressed women who stare at him with such vapid adoration it makes me shudder. You can practically see the alcohol fumes clinging to all three of them. He slings an arm around each of their necks, crooning to them in a sexy British accent, and jauntily escorts the giggling pair toward the bank of elevators. They look like a disaster waiting to happen.

Shaking my head in amusement, I finally reach the desk to check in. "Ah, Miss Walker," the desk clerk says politely as he scans his computer screen. "You've been upgraded to one of our deluxe suites, compliments of Mr. Pavel Orlov. Complimentary butler service comes standard with those rooms. Your butler, Gregory, will escort you and see to your luggage."

My eyes widen in mild surprise. Pavel is Managing Director of the Starwood group, and he's become a good friend over the years, but an upgrade was unexpected.

"An upgrade isn't necessary, thank you. Please pass along my thanks to Mr. Orlov, but I'm perfectly fine in a regular guestroom." I'm scrupulously aware of my role and constantly guard my organization's reputation, especially when I travel. The last thing I want is for April to have to handle any bad press about me mishandling funds for my own benefit.

"I'm sorry, Miss Walker, but all our regular rooms are unavailable. The upgrade is an apology for your original reservation being unfortunately overbooked."

I look at him skeptically, but his face remains impassive. "Hmm, all right, then. Please thank Mr. Orlov for me." I sign the necessary papers and turn to find Gregory waiting patiently, my bag and laptop case in hand.

The Madison Suite is lovely, and I can't help but smile at this unexpected treat as I enter the well-appointed room. It's small as suites go, with only one bedroom, but that's much, much more than I usually allow myself. I decline Gregory's offer to help me unpack and place my dinner order instead. It's getting late, but my stomach is still on West Coast time. I'm just sitting down to put my feet up for a moment when my phone rings. With a sigh, I answer.

"Have you heard from Kennedy Lane or any of his representatives?" Nadia's irritated voice blares from the tiny speaker.

"Now, why would you think that?" I deflect, my shoulders tensing. My phone, containing today's video message from the man in question, is practically burning a hole in my hand.

"Because I know you still have his number, Abby," she snipes, and I bite my lip. "I haven't heard jack shit from his team since he was in your office. What the hell did you tell him?" Nadia was not happy that I hadn't called her when Lane had surprised me a week ago, and wasn't shy about telling me how she felt. Plus, she knew I wasn't telling her everything about why he'd entered his phone number into my cell. There was no way I'd tell her how I lost my cool with him that day. Besides, he'd trusted me with the video and his number, and despite my misgivings, I won't break that trust.

Beyond that, though, there was something *intimate* about experiencing his creative process that I selfishly want to keep to myself, which makes me exceedingly uncomfortable.

"Calm down. I told you what I told him." Well, essentially.

"I don't know why they haven't contacted you, but I'm sure they will. Nadia, it's Sunday night. Don't tell me you're working."

"Of course I'm working," she snaps and then takes a calming breath. "Sorry. I had some things to catch up on. The silence from the Lane camp is pissing me off, Abby. I want to get Parker's dream settled."

"Well, there's nothing to be done about it tonight. Tell me what else is going on." She gives me the rundown on a few other projects she's trying to finish up and I give her my input. "I have the Starwood meeting tomorrow, and then I've got the Yankees Tuesday. Anything else I need to know about that?"

"Nah. You've got that one in the bag," she says confidently. "Give me a call tomorrow night, okay?"

We say our good-byes just as my dinner arrives. After devouring a deliciously comforting butternut risotto, I sink gratefully into a hot bath and sigh in relief as I feel my tense muscles relax. But after soaking in silent bliss for a few moments, my thoughts begin to swirl.

I sink lower in the soothing water, annoyed that I can't stop thinking about him. I hate that I'm attracted to a man who seems to be such a train wreck. But is he? There have been other texts from him, little snippets of thoughts that are sometimes profound and sometimes prosaic. The picture they're painting is different from that of the arrogant, entitled man who had appeared in my office, and they've left me confused and even a little regretful. I still haven't responded to any of them, even the video he sent this morning after jogging. Snickering, I hope he has a medic on standby if he's going to keep up with his exercise kick. Then my smile dims. He says he's trying, or at least he thinks he is, despite my repeated efforts to let him off the hook. Why bother? I just don't get it. What does he—

My phone chimes with a text, and I mentally chide myself

for bringing it into the bathroom with me. I really need to learn how to unplug. "Yes, Nadia, what now?" I grumble, reaching over to the wide ledge to retrieve my instrument of torture.

What I see makes me almost drop the phone.

I've been thinking . . .

I suck in a breath, every inch of me suddenly on alert despite the lulling heat surrounding me. The fact that I'm naked makes me feel both vulnerable and slightly aroused. I quickly tap out a message before I can change my mind.

Dangerous for you . . .

Biting my lip, I don't have to wait long for a response.

Ah, so you are alive! I was beginning to wonder.

A dry smirk curls my lips. Maybe this won't be so difficult after all.

Alive and well. You were thinking?

I was wondering what I'd have to do to get you to respond. You don't make things easy, ya know?

No one ever said I was easy, Mr. Lane. You'd do well to remember that.

Don't I know it. Did you get my last video?

You looked a little out of shape. Did you survive?

Barely. It's been a while since I've been running. Do you run?

Almost every day.

Figures. What else do you do for fun?

My fingers freeze over the tiny keyboard. Sitting up, I pull my knees to my chest and take a calming breath. *Oh, a little of this, a little of that.*

Aw, come on . . . you must do something to relax.

Right now, I'm texting with a rock star. Just a typical Sunday night.

I bet. Well, I'm flattered that you consider this relaxing. What else?

The water sloshes as I shift uneasily, unsure of what I've

gotten myself into. With anyone else, it would be just a friendly question, but with him . . . Well, at least I've responded, so now he knows his messages haven't been floating aimlessly out on the ether. Besides, it really *is* getting late.

I'm sorry, but I need to go. I have an early meeting tomorrow.

Getting too personal for you?

His taunting voice from our last meeting floats in my mind, and my anger spikes as my fingers fly. Ass. You want personal?

No. But my bathwater is getting cold, and I need to get out of the tub. Goodnight.

I shut off my phone before he can respond and clamber out of the bathtub to dry myself. *There, I've shown him.* Stomping to the bedroom, I throw on my sleep shirt, plug my phone in to charge, and crawl into bed.

Sleep doesn't come easily.

THE NEXT MORNING, I TUCK a stray hair behind my ear as I make my way downstairs to the ballroom. It took forever to wrestle my hair into a French twist. The pot of coffee that was delivered to my door with breakfast hasn't done much to dispel my grogginess. Despite the softness of the plush hotel bed, my sleep was plagued with disturbing dreams of my ex, Lucas, and of intense ice blue eyes. Then when I finally turned my phone on this morning, it was to discover only texts from Maddie, work-related emails, and two more dead-air voice mails from my loyal assaholic crank caller. I blocked him the last time he called, but he must be using throwaway phones. I have *got* to remember to change my phone number when I get home. I received nothing from the cheeky rock god, which simultaneously irritates and relieves me.

I have no business being irritated. I never should've sent that final text last night. What the hell is wrong with me? What is it about this guy that keeps pushing me over the professional line into conversations that just aren't appropriate? I charge down my hallway and jab the elevator button repeatedly. He isn't my boyfriend. Hell, he isn't even my friend. He's simply a client, a means to an end. Frowning, I feel a twinge in my heart that tells me that isn't true. Okay, so he's a very hot and complicated client that I shouldn't be as attracted to as I am. Gah! Why can't he just leave me alone?

When I see the well-heeled crowd leisurely greeting each other as they enter the meeting room, I shake off my fatigue and moodiness and adopt my professional smile. I chose my wardrobe carefully for this audience; a navy suit with a blue silk blouse, paired with nondescript heels, should be appropriately conservative.

Before I can approach the doors, I'm stopped by a tall, slender, dark-haired man dressed impeccably in Armani and smiling confidently. "Abigail—it's a pleasure to see you this bleary Monday morning. Did you sleep well?"

"Well enough. Thank you for the upgrade; the suite is lovely."

Pavel smiles and adjusts one of his cufflinks. "It was the least I could do when your original booking was unfortunately squeezed. Is there anything else I can do for you?"

"You've done too much as it is," I respond with a dry smirk. "I'm scheduled to speak just after lunch, yes?"

"Yes. But I'm hoping you're still planning on being my guest for the morning session. There are some people you should meet." He takes my arm and I allow him to guide me into the room. It's a typical round table setup for approximately one hundred with a stage set up along one wall. But since it's the St. Regis, the chairs are comfortable, the linens are crisp, and the centerpieces are swallow crystal bowls filled with water and floating flowers that perfume the air with a delicate fragrance.

The morning proceeds as expected. The number of actual board members in the room is less than half the total of attendees; staffers and the odd bodyguard make up the rest. It's pretty easy to tell which is which, but I can't discriminate. The seconds and thirds-in-command are just as influential as their bosses, so everyone gets the Cordial Abigail Walker Treatment.

Finally, lunch is over, and it's time for my introduction. I listen attentively as Pavel goes through the financial aspects of Starwood's annual donation to *What's Your Dream*. He's all data and spreadsheets, and you can almost hear snores from the stuffed suits at the front tables. I hate presenting to these types of groups right after lunch. Between the monotony of the numbers and their full bellies, they're almost catatonic.

On the other hand, it's also a challenge I relish—to break through their lethargy and bring them back to life. Truly, these grim-looking men and women have made the difference in a multitude of children's lives. And it's time they knew it.

"And now, please welcome to the podium the executive director of *What's Your Dream*, Abigail Walker." I straighten my suit jacket and give the room my winningest smile in acknowledgement of the smattering of polite applause as I step up to the stage. Taking the clicker, I stand to the side of the screen behind me and take a deep breath.

"Thank you, Pavel." I give him a nod, before facing the sea of stoic faces. "You've heard the cold facts and figures, now let me show you the real story of your generous contributions." I click a button to lower the lights and another to begin my presentation. A huge close-up of a laughing, red- haired, freckle-faced boy with a missing front tooth dominates the screen. "Meet Paden. He's eight-years-old and plays second base for his little league team in

Barstow, California. He also has Burkitt lymphoma. His dream was to take batting practice with his favorite baseball team, the Red Sox."

With another click, a grinning Paden stands at home plate in Fenway Park with several members of the team lit up the screen. "Thanks to Starwood Hotels, Paden and his family were able to stay at the Westin Boston Waterfront for three days in fulfillment of his dream. He not only got to take batting practice and pose for photos with his heroes, but he also attended a game against the Yankees, and received the honor of leading the crowd in singing during the seventh inning. He was over the moon, as you can see." The last shot of a clearly enthusiastic and giggling Paden, sitting up in the press box with his father and the Red Sox announcing crew, draws a few appreciative chuckles from the crowd, and I grin to myself in satisfaction as they visibly begin to thaw.

I go through several other stories: Rebecca, a sixteen-year-old from Boise with Hodgkin lymphoma who studies French and wants to be an interpreter, so we sent her and her family to Paris. Bryant, a fourteen-year-old from Boulder with a brain tumor who dreamed of floating in zero-gravity, so we arranged for that and a personal meeting with Buzz Aldrin at the Kennedy Space Center in Florida. By now, my audience is sitting forward in their seats, and several eyes are gleaming with unshed tears. They are captivated by the faces on the screen and hopefully able to connect what they're seeing to the figures in their spreadsheets—and feeling good about it.

Finally, I move into my closer. "And last, this is ten-year-old Hailey from Medford, Oregon." Chuckles fill the room at the precocious, dimpled grin of the curly-haired brunette. "In spite of her brain tumor, she dreamed of seeing her favorite Disney characters, Belle and the Beast on a Broadway stage. *What's Your*

Dream, with your help, brought Hailey and her mom to New York, where they stayed right here at the St. Regis. Box seats at the theatre, stops at the Children's Museum and FAO Schwarz, and a hansom cab ride through Central Park, not to mention an enormous room-service hot fudge sundae, made her dream come true. And, I have it on good authority, she may have a *teensy* crush on her St. Regis butler, Fred." I wink, eliciting a round of laughter. "These are just a few of the dozens of dreams that came true through the generosity of Starwood Hotels. On behalf of my staff and the children whose lives you've touched through *What's Your Dream*, I thank you. Here's to another year of making a difference."

The applause is gratifying. I can tell from the looks on their faces that I've gotten through to them. During the break that follows my presentation, I shake several hands as Pavel escorts me out. Once in the hallway, he takes my hands in his, his eyes serious. "Thank you. It's good for them to connect with the real world once in a while."

"It's my pleasure," I assure him with a smile. "It's a small thing, really, compared to the joy their generosity brings."

"We're scheduled to go until five, and then I have to attend to a couple of the members. Would you be available to join me for dinner? Say at seven?"

"I'd love to, but I really need to prepare for my meeting with the Yankees tomorrow. But I'll be here until Wednesday. Perhaps tomorrow night?"

"I think I can arrange that. I'll call you tomorrow to confirm the time," he says, but then his attention shifts to the crowd preparing to return from their break. "I must go. Have a lovely afternoon, and don't work too hard."

We part and I make a beeline for my room and kick off my shoes with a sigh of relief. I love high heels, but damn if it doesn't feel good to take them off. I pop open a Diet Coke, sit down at my laptop, and lose myself in work.

chapter eight

kennedy

MY ARM FLAILS AS I swing and miss Tucker . . . again. His answering snort does nothing for my current mood. "Pretty sure you can do better than that."

I glare at him as he taunts me, bouncing on the balls of his feet in the middle of an aging boxing ring in a gym a few blocks away from the St. Regis. Of course, Tucker knows the guy who owns the gym. I think he's going to make it a mission to "know a guy" in every damn city we visit.

I really shouldn't complain about an hour of undisturbed time—a rare occurrence for me—but I've been dropped to my ass on the sweaty canvas floor of the ring more times than I can count, so I think I'm entitled.

He motions for me to come at him again. "Did I mention you're a royal pain in the ass?" I grunt as we circle each other.

"You love me, sunshine. Admit it." Sweat drips from my brow as my chest heaves with exertion; my ragged breaths fill the dingy room. He, of course, hasn't even broken a sweat, and I'm reminded once again as my stomach rolls of the glaring differences between us.

"Never."

His fist makes contact to my side and I wince. Pathetic, really, given that he's probably only got it dialed to just below light on the effort scale. "I've got some news that may be of interest to you."

"What's that?" I manage once I'm able to actually speak and regain my balance.

"I think I'll make you work for it."

The blood pumps wildly in my veins. It reminds me a bit of the feeling I get right before I go on stage, only this is sheer frustration and anger rather than euphoric anticipation.

"Tucker." I warn.

"Lips are sealed until you can land a punch, big guy." With my chest heaving, I scowl at him.

"You know I don't like it when you keep things from me."

"You'd have a heart attack if you knew about half the shit I keep from you. That's for your own good. This, however, you're going to like." He makes a show of leaning back against the ropes, craning his neck from side to side before coming at me again.

I manage to swerve away from him in an awkward and clumsy display. He looks only mildly impressed when I block his right jab. "Come on. You want to know? Hit me." His relentless torment continues, pushing and testing me over and over.

"My six-year-old cousin could do better." My weary body hits the floor under the force of another punch.

A few minutes later, it's, "You call that a punch?" And even better, "I thought you were supposed to be coordinated."

That last one strikes a nerve, and with the adrenaline coursing through me, I bury a right hook to his side, my head snapping up to meet his surprised face. Moments like these, where Tucker is vulnerable, are few and far between. I bounce away from him feeling more than a little smug even though every muscle in my body throbs in pain.

Lifting my glove-clad hand, I wipe the sweat from my forehead. "Okay. Out with it."

He grins, approaching me with his usual confident stride, still coiled to strike. "Abigail Walker is staying at our hotel."

I drop my arm, staring back at him dazed and unsure if I've heard him right. Maybe he's rattled too many brain cells this morning. "What?"

Out of nowhere, a swift jab makes impact with my stomach, sending me crashing to the floor in a heap as my world spins. "Fuck," I spit out as his face comes into view above me, and he lowers his hand to help me up.

"Rule number one: Don't ever let your guard down."

"HOW DID YOU FIND OUT she was here?"

Tucker leads me through a service entrance that opens to the back of a large ballroom at the hotel.

"You seriously want me to answer that question? Jesus, man. Give me some credit. I'm the head of your security detail. I get paid to know things."

He crosses his arms in front of me, blocking my view to the room. "I saw her in the lobby, talking to a group of people this morning, all right? It wasn't difficult to get the rest of the information." I step to the left and he moves with me, preventing any further forward motion.

"Stay to the back with me out of sight. If memory serves, the last time you two were in the same room together you just about took each other's heads off."

"Yes, *Dad*. And give me some credit this time. You honestly think I'm going to heckle her?"

He shifts to the side, and we step into the shadowed alcove of the back of the ballroom. I take in the detailed architecture and vaulted ceilings . . . I bet the acoustics would be fantastic in here.

The crowd, however, is another matter. I usually feed off the energy of a crowd, but this bunch feels lifeless and dull, lethargic even. They could use a serious pick-me-up.

I scan the sea of suits, looking for signs of life . . . looking for her. Finally, I see her, and it's more lethal than any punch Tucker could ever pack. Standing off to the side, a little nervous and slightly vulnerable. I'm treated to the sight of her moving across the stage. Her dark hair is up and away from her neck, exposing the smooth, unmarked flesh, just tempting me to taste it. The stilettos bring an immediate grin, and I wonder again if the impeccable suit is all a front. If she's hiding who she really is. If there's a slightly wilder and adventurous side hiding beneath this well-crafted facade.

She starts talking, and her voice wakes the dead audience up. Anyone can recognize passion when they hear it. It speaks to people on an emotional level, and she has it. This is her life, her mission, and I feel a twinge of pride as she gives a little insight into each precious face that flashes on the screen. I know she would move the earth for these kids. This kind of commitment isn't something you can fake.

My world narrows to her, and I'm fixated. Every single detail permanently etched in my brain. Without the hangover and freight train barreling through my head, I get to fully appreciate her unfiltered: her full lips, the gentle curve of her waist highlighted by the harsh glare of the projector.

I want her in ways I know I shouldn't. Beyond the instinct to pull her tight body against mine and keep her from every single set of male eyes. I want to lose myself in her. Take my time to find out what makes her tick, what she's like when the walls come down and I see her, really see her, for the first time.

As her speech comes to an end, Tucker guides me back into the kitchen. "Happy now?" he asks.

"Find out what room she's staying in, and I will be."

"I'm on it."

"And find me a piano."

He lets out a low chuckle. "Hang on, I have one right in my back pocket."

"You're an ass."

"I'll see what I can do. You need to play."

"Yeah, I do."

abigail

"HERE YOU GO, MISS WALKER." The ever-efficient Gregory sets the rest of my shopping bags down beside the sofa. After a successful meeting with the Yankees' charitable foundation, I celebrated at Saks and Barneys. My butler barely batted an eye at the plethora of bags he helped me carry up to my room. "I noticed that your supply of bottled water was running low. I have a lovely selection of beverages here that I hope will appeal to you," he continues politely, gesturing to a tray he must have set up earlier. "And I have a message from Mr. Orlov. He invites you to meet him in the King Cole lounge this evening at seven. Shall I tell him you'll join him?"

"Please do. Thank you, Gregory."

"My pleasure, Miss Walker."

A couple hours later, I walk across the lobby to the hotel's King Cole Bar. Most of the tables are taken, but I spy a couple of open seats at the end of the bar. I drape my short trench coat over the seat next to me, slide onto the high stool, and check my phone. I'm a little early. Eh, no matter. I take a deep breath and let my eyes roam over the whimsical mural behind the historic bar, feeling vastly contented. It's been a good trip. First, an excellent presentation to the Starwood group yesterday, then the Yankees today. It's been a job well done.

In celebration, I order a Grey Goose martini instead of my usual Pinot, and add it to my room tab. I glance around for Pavel. I'm probably going to shock him—he's never seen me in anything besides suits. I've left my hair long and flowing, and I'm wearing several of the items I purchased today: a red silk shirt over a black tank, and black leggings tucked inside a sensational pair of knee-high stiletto boots. I almost drooled over the butter-soft black leather at the store and couldn't hand over my money fast enough.

I love boots; what can I say?

"Here you go, miss." I nod my thanks at the bartender and take a sip of the ice-cold liquid. Ah, now that's good for the soul. Perfect. Wondering where Pavel is, I pull out my phone to text him. Almost instantly, I get a response.

I'm sorry Abigail, I can't make it. Duty calls. Perhaps next time you're in town?

Shoot. I was looking forward to getting out and seeing more of the city. I tap out a reply.

No worries. We'll do it next time.

Now that I'm on my own, I suppose I should grab a bite, go upstairs, and try to get some work done. I have an early flight tomorrow; it would be smart to get some good sleep.

First, though, I'm going to finish my It's-Been-A-Good-Day Martini.

My mind wanders, the alcohol and gentle buzz of the room

lulling me, until a few plinky notes on a piano draw my attention. I shift in my seat to see a grand piano in a room adjoining the lounge. A little boy wearing a Giants jersey climbs onto the piano bench and begins to pick out "Mary Had A Little Lamb" while a young woman smiles indulgently at him. The boy can't be more than five or six and is as cute as can be, with his blond hair sticking up in every direction. I'm instantly transported to the suite at the Fairmont, and the look of concentration on Lane's face as he hunched over the keyboard, pulling a tune out of thin air.

A shadow falls over me, and I turn my phone over in my hand. I haven't heard a peep from him since my rash text the other night. Not that I was expecting one really, but hardly a day has gone by in the last week that I haven't received either an obscure text or a video from him. I'll never forgive myself if I've pissed him off—or worse, embarrassed him—and endangered Parker's dream.

On impulse, I snap a photo of the little boy and text it to him.

Were you this old when you started playing?

I sip my drink and cast nervous glances at my phone. Shit, I really *have* pissed him off. Of course, he could just be busy. I'm sure he's not just sitting around waiting for me to call. I jump when my phone chimes; snatching it off the bar, I laugh.

Looks a bit young. I bet he's better than I was, though.

Relieved at his friendly tone, I can't help my grin, until another text arrives and I freeze.

I wouldn't have pegged you as a martini girl.

The hairs on the back of my neck stand up. Holy shit, he's here! I sit up slowly and cast a wary glance around the bar. My heart leaps the minute I spy him, a hooded figure standing tall and mysterious at the other end of the bar, staring right back at me with a devilish grin. My mouth drops open as he straightens and saunters toward me, his eyes locked with mine. He's dressed all in black again, from his heavy boots to the hoodie under his well-worn leather jacket. Reaching up nonchalantly, he pushes his hood back and runs his hand carelessly through his messy dark locks. He's magnificent, a lethal predator, and I can't look away even if I wanted to.

"What . . . What are you doing here?" I manage, my voice just above a whisper.

"I'll be glad to tell you all about it over dinner. Are you free?" He stands very close, close enough that I can smell the warm leather of his jacket mixed with some spicy scent. It's a delicious combination that makes my pulse race.

I take a steadying breath. "As it happens, yes."

"Shall we go?" He holds out his hand, his eyes almost daring me to take it. I stare at his offered hand, feeling that, somehow, this is more than just a simple dinner. Looking up at him cautiously, I slip my phone in my pocket, gather my purse and coat, and slowly put my hand in his. His warm fingers close over mine, the sensation igniting something deep within me.

"I hope I'm not going to regret this."

When he squeezes my hand, and draws my gaze to his, I'm trapped by those piercing sapphire eyes.

"You won't."

chapter nine

kennedy

"HOW FAST CAN YOU MOVE in those?" My gaze wanders down to her fantastic boots as we step onto the busy street. It won't be long before Tucker comes back to the suite and realizes I'm gone, and those boots, despite being my new favorite, are going to slow us down.

"I'm not sure. I just got them," she answers with a satisfied grin.

"I like them. Maybe not the best choice for what we're doing, but they'll do." I lift my eyes back to hers, and she arches a brow.

"I didn't realize I was meeting you and that we'd be going wherever it is we're going." There's no missing the sarcasm in her voice. It's obvious she's used to being in control. The fact that she's putting some trust in me is a big deal for her, and for me.

The feel of her beside me, the anticipation rolling off me in waves. The combination keys me up, while I lead her to the subway stairs, slowing as we descend into the underground station.

"Damn it," I hear her mutter under her breath, her boots clicking each step. "I wish I would've known about this."

"Now where's the fun in that?" My hand tightens around hers as she gingerly navigates below the bustling street.

"So, you don't want to have dinner at the hotel for fear of being seen, but you'll spend time on the New York subway?" She peeks up at me with an amused smile.

"I don't mind being seen. I'm used to it—as much as you ever can be. I did that for you."

"For me?"

"Pretty much everything I've been doing for the last few days has been for you." I want her to know I'm trying, that I'm taking this seriously even though temptation is around every curve. Like Sean said, Parker is as good a reason as any to lay off the drink for a while. The truth is, I think I'm holding hands with an even better reason. I know my time is limited to change to her mind about me, and I intend to take full advantage of whatever she's willing to give me.

Once we're underground and I finally find the right platform, I turn my back to the smattering of people waiting for the next train. "Is it always like this? You, skulking around?" she asks quietly, her eyes meeting mine with a look of concern I'm not used to seeing.

"Not all the time. Tucker will kill me when he finds out I did this without him."

"Is that the guy who was with you at the Fairmont and my office?" She tightens her purse against the curve of her waist. "He's protective of you," she comments.

"He's paid to be."

Tilting her head, she studies me carefully. "Do you have anyone in your life you think is there because they want to be and not because they have to be?"

"Other than my brother, probably not. And even he's a stretch."

I feel the train before I see it; the distinctive squeal, the tracks shaking under the platform. The cars blur past before it finally screeches to a stop.

A gust of air blows her hair in front of her face, and I can't stop myself from reaching over to tuck the wayward strands behind her ear. "I'm trying to decide if I like your hair up or down better."

Her eyes widen and meet mine, but she doesn't recoil from my touch. I drop my gaze to her plump lips, watching as they part slightly, begging me to taste them. She's so fucking tempting, and I can't remember the last time I actually wanted to get to know someone—really know them, and not just for a couple of hours that are soon forgotten.

I'm jostled from behind, bringing me back to reality and causing me to bump against her. I hear a quick gasp, and my arm instinctively curls around her waist as we're edged through the open doors from behind.

She laughs, and it's a nervous, sweet sound I want to hear again. Her hand flies up to the metal handrail, steadying herself, and I refuse to let her move any further away from me. Now that I've touched her I need more. I grip either side of the rail above her head, cocooning her right where I want her.

"Kennedy . . ."

My name is a whispered warning from her lips, sending red hot heat firing through my veins. "No turning back now."

"STAY RIGHT HERE." I LEAN casually against the wall of the subway station, waiting for the train to disappear down the track. To anyone looking on, we're just two people, hanging out and waiting for the next train. But, I'm on edge, literally vibrating with anticipation. I underestimated what having her close would do to me.

"What are we doing?" she hisses, her hair flying when the train speeds away, until it's only her and me, and the silence of the station.

"This way." I move along the length of wall, glancing back to see her following, stealing looks over her shoulder.

"Is this legal?" she whispers as I jump down to the shadow of the tracks, into the damp and dirty no man's land.

"Not even remotely."

I can see her hesitate, her eyes wide and excited. "Trust me."

My voice carries through the vastness of the cavernous tunnel, and with a grin, she puts her hand in mine and does just that.

"THIS IS INCREDIBLE," SHE WHISPERS in awe as I shine the small flashlight onto another mural—this one more cryptic than the last. It's a dark piece, splashed with only intermittent streaks of scarlet red, and hints of something sinister and forbidden.

We're in an abandoned, uncompleted subway station that houses a street art exhibition few people even know exists. To some, it's an urban legend, an elusive conquest. To the police and subway security, it's an annoyance.

"How did you find out about this place?"

"One of the artists did our last album cover. He told me about it. And you don't have to whisper. No one is going to find us." I lead us slowly down the darkened gallery.

"Why are you doing this? Bringing me here?"

I look down at her as she takes a step away. "I'm trying to—"

"But see? Here's what I don't get. You don't have to try. You're already off the hook. It would be so much easier for you if you just signed some CDs, maybe a T-shirt or two. No one is holding you accountable for Parker."

"What if I don't want to be off the hook? What if I *want* to be accountable? Parker deserves more than a few signed posters."

"Yes. He does, but he'll be thrilled with that."

"Would you believe me if I said it's not just for Parker? I'd like to tell you that this is a selfless act. But the truth is it's not. I need to do this."

"This is about your image, isn't it?"

"No. That's not what this is about, at least not for me. When we lost Robin . . ." I take a deep breath, trying to find the words she deserves to hear. "My sister died in a car accident."

I see what I don't want to in her expression—she feels sorry for me. "Kennedy, I'm so sorry. I can't imag—"

I don't let her finish. This has been gnawing at me for so long, just begging me to release it, so I push on. "When we lost her, it was . . ." I feel my heart tighten.

"You don't need to say anything," she says quietly.

"Fuck, I probably shouldn't be telling you this, but maybe you'll understand if I do." Those devastating hazel eyes search mine, and I push on. "Robin always thought I should do more. I've donated to charities and played at functions for different things over the years, but for her, I wasn't doing enough." I swallow back the lump in my throat. "The night of the accident, we were supposed to meet with a group of people she had gotten together to discuss setting up a charity. I had put her off for weeks. My schedule was nuts, and I was a lot like you saw me at the Fairmont."

"I should apologize for that, for my behavior."

"No. I should be the one apologizing. You were right. Everything you said to me that day was right. I was hung over, and the truth? Probably still high when you saw me. I deserved everything you said and more. Trust me."

I take her hand with a gentle squeeze, feeling the warmth of her skin against mine. She offers me a ghost of a smile, a little encouragement that spurs me on. "Before the accident, I was drinking everything in sight when I wasn't performing. Robin and I used to fight about it all the time." I give a half laugh, remembering how we used to go rounds on it. "Anyway, I had totally blown her off that day, didn't even call her, and she showed up at the hotel, demanding for me to get my shit together. We just screamed at each other, and I said some awful things. Shit."

"People say things when they're mad. It happens all the time." Gently, her hand slides to my shoulder. "You can't beat yourself up for it."

"I told her to get the fuck out of my life. It's the last thing I ever said to her. The next time I saw her we were putting her in the ground." Her eyes brim with tears, her grip tightening against my shoulder. "I'm not telling you this for you to feel sorry for me. Fuck, I don't want your sympathy. I just want to do something she would be proud of."

A lone tear streaks down her cheek, and I can't resist brushing it away. Her skin is tempting against the rough pads of my fingers, and my eyes drop to her soft lips. She's right there, sharing this intense pull that sparks between us, her eyes searching mine, and for a second, I think maybe, just maybe . . . "She's proud of you," she says quietly. "Look at everything you've done."

"Like treating you like I did the first time we met? Drinking my way through bottle after bottle? Yeah—she'd be real proud of that."

"What about everything else? Your awards? Your success? The way you are with your fans? You can't always look at the bad."

"Awards don't mean shit. In this business, you're only as

good as your next hit, your next tour. They always want more no matter how many awards you get."

"But you love that, don't you? Isn't that why you got into music in the first place? Because you love it. You can't imagine doing anything else?"

Smiling, I lean against her, feeling the tempting curve of her body against mine. "Someone's been doing a little research. Maybe some late-night reading when you can't get to sleep?" I tease, shining the light onto her face. She turns away with a chuckle, shielding her eyes from the glare.

"Put that thing away," she manages to say through a laugh.

"Haven't heard that one before." I turn to the opposite wall to cast the light over the next mural. "What do you think of this one?" I grin down at her as she takes in the chaotic design before she meets my gaze.

"I think there's a lot to it. More than people think. And it's worth spending time getting to know more about it."

abigail

HIS SMILE BROADENS FOR A brief moment, before his perma-smirk returns, and he looks away shyly. It's another display of that devastating blend of drop-dead sex appeal and coyness that has almost brought me to my knees several times this evening. The fact that he seems completely unaware of what he's doing makes it even more appealing.

"Good to know." He aims his flashlight back down the gallery and gives my hand a gentle tug. "Well, we've come to the end of the line. Are you hungry?"

"I could eat," I say, hoping he doesn't hear my belly growling.

"Good. Me, too." He leads me back down the tunnel and

past the amazing artwork. This evening has been a revelation in ways that I'm still trying to grasp.

"Don't tell me—you know of an underground café run by renegade gnomes or something?" I return his teasing smile as he laughs.

"No, but I do have a destination in mind," he assures me with a wink. "I hope you haven't reached your quota of adventure yet."

A soft chuckle escapes me. "No, not yet."

WE NAVIGATE OUR WAY IN silence down the dark, lonely tunnel and back to a regular platform. Everything about this evening so far has been incredible.

I notice, with a degree of sadness, that he's pulled his hood up again and angled himself away from the drunken couple at the other end of the platform. I don't think they even noticed when we climbed up from the tracks, but it seems he's taking no chances. I'm not sure I could stand living such a public life and having to take such precautions just to maintain a modicum of privacy. I'm never going to take my anonymity for granted again.

With a rush of noise and air, the train arrives and he ushers me on. I take hold of one of the poles and find myself encircled from behind by a strong pair of arms. He places his hands over mine on the cold metal and presses his hard chest against my back. "Wouldn't want to fall, now, would we?" he murmurs in my ear, his warm breath caressing my neck. Words fail me, so I simply nod and try not to shiver as his chuckle vibrates through me. No, I don't want to fall . . . in more ways than one.

My heart feels like it's about to burst out of my chest as I melt into his warmth. No man has ever provoked this kind of reaction or this kind of unbridled exhilaration from me before.

I'm not sure what to do with this much pure giddiness coursing through my body, but I'd better get a handle on it quickly.

Because now it's obvious why he's trying so hard; I must remind him of his sister. It doesn't really have anything to do with me personally, but only with the foundation and my desire to help the kids. His anguished expression as he told his story almost broke my heart. He feels guilty about Robin; he shouldn't, but he obviously does. This is something I understand. How many years did I beat myself up over what happened with Lucas? I close my eyes and savor the warmth surrounding me, my emotions warring. It would be so easy to let this silly infatuation bubbling inside of me take over, but I know I can't. Not when he's simply reacting to his guilt and remorse.

It's admirable that he wants to prove to me, or at least to the memory of his sister, that he can *reform himself* somehow for the greater good. And, for reasons I can't quite explain, I need to help him if I can. Parker is the main reason, of course. But now there's also . . .

The train lurches to a squealing stop, jarring me out of my thoughts. When the doors slide open, my human cage releases me and takes my hand securely to lead me off the train and up the station steps to emerge once again on the streets of New York.

"Where are we?" I look around, but nothing is familiar.

"Not far from the hotel. Come on." He gives me a devilish smile. I appreciate that he shortens his stride to allow me to keep up in my not-made-for-walking boots.

After a few minutes, we come upon a row of food carts. Based on the crowd milling around, they must be popular. Kennedy pulls me to a stop in front of one shiny trailer, and we join the short line. The tantalizing aromas of cinnamon, cumin, and turmeric swirl heavy in the air. "Do you like lamb?" He glances down at me, and I nod. "Good. Still trust me?"

"It's worked out so far tonight."

His lips quirk in amusement, and he turns and places our orders at the window. Minutes later, we're strolling down the street with cardboard containers of succulent grilled, marinated lamb and vegetables over fluffy rice. I have to force myself not to inhale it.

"Wow. This is delicious," I comment. "Thank you."

"You're welcome. I did promise you dinner, after all." He nudges me playfully with his elbow, and I laugh.

"Yes, you did."

I have no idea where we are, but I find myself not caring. Kennedy clears his throat and looks at me nervously. "So, what's next? You know, with Parker. What do I need to do?"

"Well, it depends on your schedule," I say between bites. "You're right when you say Parker deserves more than a few signed posters. What do you have in mind?"

"I'm thinking about a benefit concert?"

I nod thoughtfully. "That sounds wonderful. But when? Doesn't your tour start soon?"

"I could work it in."

"But your schedule isn't the only one at stake here," I remind him, my voice sterner than I intend. "Parker's been having a hard time of it. His last chemo treatment really took a lot out of him. I need to be careful about what he's exposed to."

He purses his lips and shoots me an irritated glare. Snatching my empty container from my hands, he stalks to a nearby garbage can and chucks our trash in. "You know, Abby—I'm trying here," he says defensively. "I'm obviously not a saint, but damn it, ease up, would you?"

My gaze darts to his and remorse washes over me when I look beyond his scowl to the hurt in his eyes. He is trying. He's revealing the side of himself that lives beyond the flashbulbs, and he's confided in me. I don't know what will come of it yet, but he *is* trying.

"I didn't mean it like that." I place my hand on his arm. "Parker's medically fragile and needs to be stronger if you plan on holding an event outside the hospital. Whatever happens will ultimately depend on his condition." He huffs in frustration and looks down at my hand, but doesn't shake me off. Instead, he looks back up at me contritely, his eyes searching mine.

"Sorry. I'd thought we were past . . . Well, past your initial reservations. I apologized for my behavior in San Francisco. Please don't hold it against me."

"I'm not. I'm simply . . ." Withdrawing my hand quickly, I glance down, debating with myself. I've only told a few people my story, but maybe if he hears it, he'll understand my hesitations concerning Parker. Although Kennedy keeps asking me to trust him, he's shown how much *he* trusts *me* tonight. In fact, he's shown me since that day he gave me his phone number. It's time I repaid it.

"Lucas and I met in high school," I begin quietly, and he looks at me cautiously, no doubt wondering what the hell I'm talking about now. I resume walking, and he falls in step beside me, our hands brushing occasionally. "He was the star running back on the football team, and our dads were friends. My dad was the police chief, and his owned the local grocery store. Lucas was smart, but he'd never been the best student. My dad asked if I'd be willing to tutor him in English."

"It was probably just a convenient excuse to get to know you," Kennedy teases, one eyebrow cocked.

"Doubtful." I chuckle, remembering my awkward teenaged self. "I wasn't on many people's radar. I was more often studying at home than sitting in the stands at a game. I liked football, but I had other priorities."

"I bet you were on more people's radar than you realize," he murmurs, so quietly that I'm not sure I was supposed to hear. He clears his throat before continuing in a normal tone, "So, you started dating?"

"Not until that summer. He was funny and charismatic, and I fell head over heels. Our fathers were pleased; Lucas's dad thought I'd be a good influence on him." I laugh, but the sound is hollow. "We both ended up getting into Cal. Lucas went on a football scholarship, but he wasn't the only star on the team anymore. He really had to work to become a starter. Then, in the last game of the season, this huge defensive lineman flattened him and separated his shoulder. He was given a prescription for Percocet for pain."

Kennedy shifts uncomfortably, but remains silent, so I continue, "He worked on rehabbing his shoulder during the rest of the school year, and recovered fairly quickly. I remember finding a half-full bottle of his prescription that spring, which was surprising because I'd thought he was done with it, but he said it was old, and that he'd forgotten he had it. He took it from me, threw it away, and that was that."

"However, in our sophomore year, a couple of his teammates caught him using OxyContin at a party, and he was suspended for one game. The team made him go to counseling. He swore to me it was just a one-time thing, that a couple other guys had tried it, too, except they didn't get caught. And I believed him. I knew a couple of his teammates, and I could see how that could happen. More importantly, I *couldn't* imagine that he would lie to me.

"We didn't go home that summer; I was taking extra classes so I could complete my double major, as well as working. Lucas stayed with me and got a job doing yard work. He'd been after me to leave the dorms and move into an apartment with him, and I finally agreed to do it that summer."

"Don't tell me that you actually lived in sin with a boy?" He places a hand against his chest in mock horror, and I roll my eyes.

"Don't look so shocked," I reply dryly. "I've probably done plenty of things that would raise even *your* eyebrows." At his eager grin, I laugh. "But that's another story for another day."

"I'll hold you to that."

"Anyway, that's when things changed. Fast." I'm quiet for a moment, gathering my thoughts. "Our junior year began, but Lucas was . . . different. Distracted. The occasional late practice became more of a constant, and sometimes he wouldn't come home until really late. And he wasn't eating—his coaches started riding him because he was losing weight. I started worrying. So I showed up to surprise him with some dinner one night at practice, but he wasn't there."

"Oh, no," Kennedy groans, squeezing his eyes shut. "Don't tell me the asshole cheated on you?"

"No. Well, at least, not with a woman." At his startled glance, I continue, "I finally found him at some guy's place completely wasted. The place was a trashed. I didn't know what he was high on, but he could barely keep his eyes open."

"Ah." He shoves his hands in his pockets and stares at the pavement, a troubled look on his face.

"I was shocked. And hurt and furious." The image of Lucas's uncaring grin and slurring speech still rankles. "He was risking his spot on the team, his scholarship, his degree . . . everything. But I was also mad at myself. There had been other signs all along, but I either rationalized them away or blindly believed his lies. He begged me not to leave him. He promised he didn't have a problem. That it wasn't his Oxy—that one of his friends had the pills, and he only indulged after particularly tough practices.

The guys were expected to play through the pain, so I could kind of understand, but . . ." I grit my teeth at the memory. I had been so fucking naïve. "I demanded that he get into counseling, and he agreed."

I swallow down the lump that has appeared in my throat, a chill coming over me. "The next several weeks were awful. In trying to cope, I became someone I didn't recognize. I started going through his drawers and his pockets checking for drugs. I watched him like a hawk, convinced that he would give into temptation. I threatened to tell his parents, but he begged me—*begged me*—not to. He promised he was going to therapy and would never touch another drug. "Just before the last game of the season, though, everything came to a head. There had been a string of thefts since the season began—money from teammates' lockers, team equipment, things like that. They discovered Lucas was the culprit at the same time he failed a surprise drug test. He was dismissed from the team and lost his scholarship. I was heartbroken, and our parents were horrified."

We pause at a corner, and I realize I've been gripping my elbows, my arms rigidly crossed in front of me. "My parents were just as upset as his were. Plus, they were disappointed in *me*." Kennedy glances at me sharply, but I keep walking. The sting of my parents' disappointment is still sharp even after all these years. "I don't know why I agreed not to tell them. I was just so in love with him . . . I was young and inexperienced. Lucas had been my only real boyfriend, and it felt *disloyal* to rat him out. I didn't know what addiction could do to a person. How insidious it is, how deep a hold it can have on a person. Or the lengths an addict will go to appear normal in order to maintain the façade."

"I was a cop's daughter, for Christ's sake," I continue with an angry shake of my head. "I thought I knew a few things. But addiction . . . Well, it's a like being the proverbial frog in slowly heating water. You don't realize you're cooked until it's too late."

Kennedy is silent, a tall, brooding presence keeping pace at my side. His hands are still deep in his pockets, and his jaw is clenched so tightly I expect to hear it pop. He clears his throat with difficulty. "What happened next?"

"His parents put him in rehab, and I moved back into the dorms with my best friend. When Lucas got out about a month later, he came back to school, but I refused to see him. He kept begging me to forgive him. But it hurt too much to see him. Plus, there was also a part of me that felt I'd failed him somehow."

Kennedy huffs derisively. "That's ridiculous. It was his own fault."

"It's how I felt at the time, and a long time afterward. Anyway, I finally decided that I owed it to him to end it in person. I went to the place he'd been staying, but when he opened the door, he looked panicked. He hauled me inside and began rushing around, throwing clothes in a duffle bag like a mad man. He yelled at me that we needed to leave. I started crying and begging him to tell me what was going on and accusing him of using again. I turned to leave, but he grabbed me and kept saying he was sorry, so sorry, that he'd never meant to get me involved—"

My voice has become an almost robotic monotone, but I can't help it; it's the only way I can get through the rest. "Before we could leave, the door was kicked open and this guy burst in. He was Lucas's dealer. Oxy wasn't giving him the same high as before, and he'd graduated to heroin. Lucas owed the guy a lot of money. It's why he'd been stealing before. The guy grabbed me by the throat. Said that if Lucas didn't pay up, he'd take his payment out of me. He had a gun."

Kennedy spits out a curse and gapes at me, but I keep going. "I was terrified. I didn't know if the guy wanted me to pay him the money, or if he'd meant something else." I swallow thickly, remembering the feel of hard metal against my temple.

"It was horrific. Lucas was screaming, the guy was screaming back. He kept pressing the gun in my cheek."

"Holy fuck." He takes my arm to bring me to a stop and pulls at my shoulders so I'm facing him, but I can't look him in the eye.

"The same day, my dad was transferring a prisoner to Oakland. Lucas's dad asked him to stop by and check on Lucas," I whisper, my throat feeling like a desert. "It was a perfect storm of coincidence. He heard the yelling and saw the open door, so he called it in. It wasn't his jurisdiction. But he had the feeling he couldn't wait, so he entered, gun drawn. The dealer panicked. He shot Dad in the left shoulder. I can still see it."

I squeeze my eyes shut, trying to block out the horrifying image of my father's blood soaking his shirt as he fell to the floor. "I freaked out. I bit the asshole's arm, the one he was holding the gun with, and he pushed me away; he aimed at me. My dad shot him in the head."

I'm shaking as Kennedy pulls me close and wraps his arms around me tightly. The scent of warm leather and spice envelops me; it's intoxicating. "I'm sorry," I whisper against his chest. "It's still hard to talk about, even though it happened years ago."

His lips brush my ear, sending a shiver down my spine. "Don't apologize. I can't even begin to imagine." One of his hands finds its way inside my trench coat and slides smoothly over the silk shirt at my waist. His other hand moves up to sink into my hair, cupping the back of my neck and gently compelling me to look up at him. His blue eyes have darkened, and I can't look away. He's mesmerizing. My heart pounds, drowning out the sounds of the street. His face lowers toward mine, and I can't breathe . . .

"Holy shit, man! You're Kennedy Lane!"

The coarse voice is like a bucket of ice water over my head, and I instantly jump away from my safe haven. A small group has gathered, armed with excited grins and camera phones. My nerves are still raw from the emotions of my story, and I anxiously pull my coat closed and cinch the belt, as if donning my armor.

Kennedy fights a scowl and settles on a tight smile as he nods to the group. He automatically takes the pen and scrap of paper a woman thrusts at him to sign as the phones click around them. I instinctively try to step out of the way so he can do whatever it is he does with his fans, but find myself boxed in.

"Hey! Is this your girlfriend? Sweet!"

"Can I have a picture?"

The suddenness of the encounter is confounding, and I'm beginning to feel claustrophobic with the bodies hemming us in. But then Kennedy slips his strong arm around my waist and purposefully steers me toward the curb. "Sorry, man, but we need to go," he says with a practiced smile before placing two fingers between his lips and letting out a piercing whistle. I wince, but it does its job—a cab screeches to a halt in front of us. The crowd follows, with yells of support or pleas for a photo, as Kennedy wrenches the back door open and practically shoves me inside. I barely have time to scoot over before he climbs in behind me and slams the door.

"The St. Regis," he barks at the driver. The silence of the cab is almost eerie after the clamor that preceded it. Kennedy glances over and gives me a sheepish smile as he hesitantly takes my hand.

"Sorry about that. It's times like that when I remember Tucker is really worth his weight in gold. Are you okay?"

"I'm fine. Is it always like that?"

"They're not always so demanding, but yeah." He shrugs, but looks at me intently. "I'm sorry they interrupted, though."

A fluttering in my stomach threatens to break my composure. There's something about his eyes that draw me in, to the point I almost feel like I'm drowning. Abruptly, he shifts and looks down at our joined hands, and I can't decide if I'm relieved or bereft. "What happened next?" he asks quietly. "To your father and your boyfriend."

"My dad was ultimately okay. He'd lost a lot of blood, and it took him a while to rehab his shoulder," I say softly, mindful of the cabbie. "My mother had dreaded for years that Dad would be injured in the line of duty. About a year later, they came into an inheritance when my grandmother died, and Mom was able to convince him to retire from the force. Now they have a bed-and-breakfast in Napa."

I sigh softly. "Lucas was arrested for theft and possession. He's been in and out of jail ever since." Kennedy is gazing at our hands with a pained expression, so I squeeze his fingers to draw his attention. "I didn't tell you all that to badger you or piss you off, but in the hope that you'd see where I'm coming from." I shake my head, not wanting to make this personal. "So you'd understand why I'm so vigilant concerning the kids."

The pain in his eyes diminishes somewhat, so I continue quietly, "Addictions like Lucas's are devastating, and not only to the addicts themselves. They wreak havoc on everyone they touch. Celebrities will likely never be confronted with a violent situation like that. But I guarantee you that someone somewhere up the supply chain has. The people who deal this shit aren't exactly understanding." I glance over at him.

"And then there are the innocents, people like my dad, who was only looking out for his daughter and a friend. Two inches to the right, and I would've lost my father that day."

He shakes his head dejectedly. "Abby, I swear that—"

"You don't have to swear anything to me," I whisper quickly, seeing the St. Regis up ahead. "I'm not judging you, Kennedy, although I know it may feel like I am. Nor do I need to know exactly what your situation is. There are a million reasons why people fall prey to substance abuse or addiction. But as I think you already know . . ." I look at him searchingly. "Habits are hard to break until you resolve the root problem."

Sorrow flashes in his eyes, and I steel myself for a rebuke, but he shocks the hell out of me. "I know that, but fuck, now I just need to play. Come with me."

I'm stunned speechless for a beat. He needs to play? *Now?* But I find myself nodding as his hand clutches mine like a life rope. Before we can say anymore, the eager hotel valets open our door. Kennedy tosses a few bills to the driver and hauls me out like his ass is on fire. However, we only make it a few steps toward the doors when an insane flashing erupts all around us. This is nothing like the group of fans earlier—this is the paparazzi in all their intrusive, offensive glory. A pair of strong, protective arms hustle me into the lobby, where Kennedy's irate manager and angry bodyguard immediately confront us.

Out of the pot and into the fire.

"Where the fuck have you been?" the manager—Brodie—demands. "Why haven't you answered your phone?" He's completely in Kennedy's suddenly angry face, while the bodyguard glowers in the background next to a tall, blond man decked out completely in black leather and observing everything with mixture of concern and suspicion. He looks familiar, but I can't quite place him.

"Let's take this somewhere else," the bodyguard advises, trying to herd all of us out of sight of the photographers outside, who are still snapping away through the glass doors and ignoring the valets' directives to leave.

"Jesus Christ—I don't have to answer to you!" Kennedy

looks like he's five seconds from blowing, and I know this is my cue. Whatever else he has planned isn't happening now. Placing my hand on his forearm, I give him a sympathetic smile.

"Thank you for tonight," I whisper, ignoring our audience. "I think I'd better head back to my room. I'm flying out in the morning. I'll talk to you later to start on Parker's dream, okay? And don't give up, Kennedy."

He rakes his hand through his hair, frustration etched on his face. I level a scathing look at Brodie, who's eyeing me with equal distaste as I turn and quickly make my way across the spacious lobby to the bank of elevators. A hissed war of words erupts in my wake and tears spring to my eyes unbidden. I hate leaving him like this, but he's obviously got other things right now that take precedence. His manager may be a paid flunky, but his bodyguard—Tucker—seems genuinely to care about him. It's obvious, whether Kennedy wants to acknowledge it or not. He's not as alone as he thinks he is.

I can't resist a quick peek back over my shoulder, needing to see him one last time, but they've vanished, leaving only a few random hotel guests whispering and watching me with curiosity. Mustering as much dignity as I can, I march into the steel box and wait for the doors to close with a blasé expression belying the tumult raging inside me.

chapter ten

kennedy

"YOU NEED SLEEP." TUCKER'S VOICE echoes through the warehouse as I sit at the piano, feverishly writing lyrics. The floodgates have opened, brought on by some explosive combination of frustration, longing, and anger.

I keep hearing her words, her story, over and over in my head. *It's insidious . . . He promised he didn't have a problem . . . collateral damage . . . two inches to the left and I would've lost my father . . .* and maybe most importantly . . . *Don't give up.*

"What time is it?" Looking up from the keys, I see moonlight spilling into the warehouse through the windows, casting an eerie shadow over his form. His chair is backed up against the steel door, his legs outstretched in front of him, keeping watch over me.

"After three."

"Fuck." It's typical for me to lose track of time, although lately that's been due to indulgence rather than creativity. I have no idea how it got to be this late, or when the rest of the band left. It's all a blur of swirling notes, and what Matt has taken to calling, "acoustic experiments."

While we've traditionally been firmly based in hard rock, over the last few weeks, our sound has begun to morph into something else. Not quite completely unplugged and acoustic, but it's going to cause a stir.

"Tell me about it. You have *The Tonight Show* tomorrow or today, whatever. You'll need sleep for that."

"Yeah. I know."

Tucker moves from his perch by the door to join me. "Finally, someone has gotten to you."

"It's not just her—"

"Mhmm. You just keep telling yourself that, my friend." He leans against the side of the piano.

"It's not. You think I want that? All a musician is good for is drinking and partying? Talk about feeding into a stereotype."

"There's places that can help with that, you know."

Glancing up at him, I lean back on the bench. "Tucker not again."

"All I'm saying is that AA meetings are everywhere. It could help."

I trail my fingers along the keys, feeling the tension of the day start to take over. "Rehab didn't help, why would AA?"

"You didn't want help before," he fires back at me.

The thought of baring my soul in random dingy community centers doesn't sit well. "I don't know, man."

I can hear the disappointment in Tucker's voice. "Just think about it."

IT'S ALMOST FOUR WHEN WE drag ourselves back to the suite. I haven't gotten a text from Abby, and I'm not sure if I expected to or not given the way the night ended. There're so many things I wanted to say, things I wanted to tell her tonight. Hearing what she went through with her ex-boyfriend was like a kick to the gut. A dose of reality I was totally unprepared to hear. Having gone through a stint in rehab, they tell you about the kind of effect your indulgence of choice has, but I've never heard anyone tell me a story like that.

Part of me—a part I'm just starting to recognize—knows that level of self-indulgence and debauchery is part of the path I was on. I also know that in her telling me her story that she's letting me in. I don't think it's something she does often. It's a huge step for her, and I hope for us. But then, I think the whole night was.

"I'm going to catch a few hours of sleep. You okay, or do I need to put a GPS on you?" Tucker asks, looking exhausted.

I toss a pillow from the couch at him before picking up one of my acoustic guitars. "Go to sleep, idiot. I'm not going anywhere."

"Text me if you change your mind." He levels me a look of warning. "I mean it."

"Yes, Dad."

"Try to get some sleep, too. You don't want to be looking like death warmed over on national television."

"I thought that was the latest look? You know, zombie style?"

He snorts, moving down the hall, quietly shutting himself in the bedroom. Time to enjoy a few moments of quiet and solitude before the insane cycle starts all over again.

I lean back against the cushions of the couch, feeling the weight of the world start to overtake me. My gaze automatically goes to the bar in the corner, to the full liquor bottles left by Brodie gleaming in the muted light spilling in through windows.

It would be so easy to numb the sting of emotions rolling through me. Take the edge off, disappear for a while. The real problem lies in the fact that I'm not very good at resisting temptation. If I was, I never would've texted Abby, never would've touched her, never would've let her in this far.

Leaning forward, I scan over my scrawled lyrics. The song will sound different played on the acoustic, but I hope she likes it. I pull my phone from the pocket of my jacket and flip it to video mode, pressing record.

"I'm sorry about how tonight ended. I didn't want it to. I wish . . ." I shake my head. "I wish a lot of things, but mostly that you'll like this. Do whatever you want with it. Use it as your ringtone or delete it if you want, but this is me not giving up." Propping the phone up against the bowl in the middle of the table, I focus on the music and start strumming, the melody raw and a little haunting. Letting the last chords fade out, I look into the camera. "Travel safe, Abby."

There's a wave of relief as send it off and set the guitar to rest against the side of the couch. I'm spent—emotionally and physically. My body begs me for a break, my eyes fighting to stay open. Stretching out on the cushions, I glance over at the familiar outline of a bottle of Jack. It can taunt me all it wants. Tonight, I'm just too fucking exhausted to care.

♪ ♩ ♪ ♩

abigail

"OOH, THIS ONE'S A LITTLE clearer!" Maddie's excited voice floats to me from the passenger seat. "It's a clearer shot of your hair, which looks fabulous, by the way. The side of your face is still blurry."

Frowning, I glance over to see her eagerly flipping through the photos on her tablet. She's been at it for days now. It began as soon as I'd stepped off the plane, when she'd called and almost punctured my eardrum with her squealed news that I'd almost broken Twitter. I finally caved and told her what happened, right from our inauspicious first meeting.

"Give it a rest, Maddie." I return my gaze to the road ahead of us and tighten my grip on the steering wheel.

"Are you kidding? I'm living vicariously through you. This is the most exciting thing that's happened to either of us in years."

I roll my eyes. "More exciting than Dylan?" I taunt innocently. She pauses for a moment, considering, and shrugs.

"Of course not. But he and I both have our celebrity crushes, and he's confident enough in our relationship to let me have my little rock star fantasies."

"Dylan has a celebrity crush?" He seems too down-to-earth for that.

She shrugs and resumes tapping on the screen in her lap. "Emma Stone. He's got a thing for that whole naughty-nice vibe she's got going. We've used it in role-play. It's hot."

I wince, not wanting that image in my head. "I'll take your word for it. But seriously, haven't you seen everything that is out there to be seen?"

"*This* time." She slips her tablet in its sleeve. "You two make such a lovely couple; it makes me feel better about poor Wyatt."

A pang of guilt hits me. After dodging a few of his calls, I finally sucked it up yesterday and let him down as easily as I could. He took my "just friends" request well, better than I probably deserve.

"But *next* time," she continues and flips her hair over her shoulder, "I expect you to hold your head high and smile at the cameras."

Scoffing, I shoot her a look. "Next time? It was sheer coincidence that there was *this time*. A complete fluke."

"You say coincidence, I say fate." I groan at her proclamation.

"You've been reading those sappy romance novels again, haven't you?" I ask dryly, making her laugh again.

"Don't change the subject. Of course it was fate!" She tosses her head, ignoring my question. "And he took full advantage of it. My God, the whole evening, sounds awesome."

I glance at her, but see no reproach in her statement. She knows, as only a best friend can, that I haven't told her everything that happened; only that he'd taken me to an off-the-beaten-path gallery and dinner at a food cart. A wistful smile spreads across my face as I recall the murals, illuminated only by the wavering flashlight. But more importantly, I remember the feel of his strong hand engulfing mine. How he could impart both comforting warmth and an electric sense of adventure at the same time.

But those pictures . . . I've been in paparazzi shots before; the inadvertent shot of me as part of a group at a symphony fundraiser or some such event, but never like this. Never as the "lucky bitch du jour," as one dubious blog dubbed me. Thank God they didn't know my name, and my face had either been obscured by my hair, or only caught in a blurry profile.

That hadn't stopped those closest to me from figuring it out. Before I'd even checked into my hotel in LA, I'd had Maddie's squealing phone call, excited texts from April and Tess, and an almost hostile voice mail from Nadia. I cringe, remembering my discussion when I'd called her back.

She had gotten right to the point. "I thought you said there wasn't anything going on between you and Lane."

"There isn't. Nadia, it was an accident; a complete fluke that we were staying in the same hotel. He ran into me and asked me to dinner to talk about Parker." Okay, so it was a little more than that, but anything else that happened is private. "It turned out to be a lucky break. It gave us a chance to discuss the issues I've been concerned about. After we talked, I'm comfortable going ahead and starting the planning process. Let's talk when I get back in the office next week, okay?" I had smiled, sure that would put her in a better mood.

It didn't.

"Great. I've been busting my ass to get this arranged and getting nowhere, and you just 'happen' to run into him out of town? You certainly looked cozy enough when you got back to the hotel," she spat. I frowned into the phone, taken aback. I understood her irritation, but the near-outrage in her voice confused me.

"Trust me, it wasn't. What on earth is the problem?"

She snorted. "Seriously? The problem is that it looks like your personal relationship is taking precedence over Parker Jensen's dream. You're using Parker to get close to Lane."

My mouth dropped open. "Nadia, I don't have a *personal relationship* with him. You know you can't take anything from a bunch of photos. They're always used out of context."

"Out of context. Right." Her sarcasm was seriously beginning to piss me off. "Well, our other donors may not care about 'context.' Some of them may even wonder if you slept with him to get his donation."

"Nadia!" I was dumbfounded; I couldn't believe she said that. Then my eyes narrowed as my blood boiled. "I'm going to hang up now, so I can prepare for my meeting with Mattel," I stated coldly, my temper getting the better of me. "But I promise—we *will* be discussing this again later."

There was a nervous silence from her end, as she finally realized that she pushed me too far. "Abby, I'm sorry," she backpedaled quickly. "It's just that, after you *direct* me not to try to fix your blunder at the Fairmont, his team stonewalls me for days, I see pictures of you holding hands during some clandestine date."

"There was no 'blunder' and it wasn't a date," I snapped.

Angry adrenaline surged through my veins, but I wasn't sure who I was more upset with—Nadia or myself. "He was merely helping me past the photographers. That's it. I was networking with a client, as we *both* do with clients. I'll talk to you when I get back."

Shaking off the memory of her angry words, I hit my signal to turn onto Sonoma Boulevard and point my black Audi convertible north to Napa. I bought it used almost eight years ago, but it's my baby. Driving it usually puts me in a good mood, but it's not helping today.

God, even the mere thought I would exploit Parker to get to Kennedy brings a sour taste in my mouth. I grit my teeth as my outrage rises again.

I may find him attractive—who wouldn't? That's not a crime. To suggest more is just plain insulting. A twinge of guilt hits me as I remember the feel of his arms around me, and the intensity of those blue eyes burning into mine as his face came closer, closer . . .

I shake my head slightly to clear my mind. I'm being ridiculous. There's no reason to feel guilty. I simply remind him of his sister. It had been a good conversation, we cleared the air, and I gave him something to think about, hopefully. His intentions are good. I believe that now. The next step is to introduce him to Parker. I feel a surge of excitement at the thought. Parker is going to be speechless.

"Stop that." Maddie startles me, and I glance over to see her stern look.

"What?"

"You were thinking about Nadia, weren't you?"

I purse my lips. "How did you know?"

"You looked like you wanted to slap someone, and I was fairly certain it wasn't me." She reaches over and gently tucks my scarf back into my collar, preventing it from flapping around in the breeze. "Don't worry about it, Abby. No one who knows you would ever think you were taking advantage of your position simply to bone some guy." She gives me a wink. "Even if the guy is a total sex god like Kennedy Lane."

I snort. "Sex god?"

"He must be! Hello! You've seen those pics of him from the show at the Hollywood Bowl, wearing those tight jeans. The man is packing some serious heat!" We burst out laughing even as I feel my heart skip a beat. There was a moment on the subway where I felt a hint of *something* when he brushed against me, but I can't think about that. Ever again.

"Maddie," I scold when I can breathe again, but she simply grins at me, having succeeded in raising my mood. Then her look becomes mischievous, and I brace myself.

"Have you heard from him again? Since you had your non-romantic non-date?"

My breath catches with the thought of his latest video message flooding my mind. His song is so poignant, so pensive and honest, it brought tears to my eyes the first few times I watched it. *This is me, not giving up*, he'd said. The sound of his voice filled me with warmth that I haven't felt in a long time.

"He sent me another song."

"Wow." Her eyes grow big, and she's obviously struggling to rein in a grin the size of California. "Abby, that's so . . ." She shakes her head, her hands flailing in front of her, and I roll my eyes.

"It's okay. Let it out before you hurt yourself." The words are barely out of my mouth before she bursts, "That is so freakin' awesome! You know he doesn't send things like that to just any-body. He obviously trusts you. Say what you want about what he's feeling, but this is big."

I zip past a semi and smoothly rejoin my lane. "I remind him of someone he used to know, is all." I wouldn't break his confidence by talking about Robin, but I need to nip this in the bud. "Yes, it's pretty cool, but don't make it into something it's not. And don't tell anyone about it. Please."

She shoots me a hurt look. "As if I'd tell anyone your business. Give me a little credit."

"I know. Sorry." We smile at each other, and I turn up the music to allow Ed Sheeran's lively patter swirl around us in the open air.

EVENTUALLY, I LET MYSELF RELAX as we're surrounded by California's lush wine country. I love it out here, and it's been too long since my last visit. When we reach Napa, Maddie is full of ideas for what we "absolutely must" do during the two days we're here, despite my plea for rest and relaxation. Fortunately, we can both agree on hitting the outlet mall. I head for the outskirts of town and soon pull up in front of a charming white building that boasts elegant black trim and a dark red front door.

The Walker Inn is my parents' pride and joy. It had been a large farmhouse back in the day, and my parents have turned it into one of the most popular lodgings in the area. It's beautiful, peaceful, and has been a refuge to me when I need to unwind.

Before we've even pulled our bags out of the trunk, my mother is skipping down the porch steps, a smile eclipsing her face. She's wearing a floaty skirt in beiges and burgundies with a simple cream top and looks like she could be in a House Beautiful ad. "Abby! Oh, sweetie, I'm so glad to see you! And, Maddie. You're looking wonderful!" She envelops us in hugs that only a mother can give, full of warmth and comfort, and smelling like home.

"Hey, Terri. Thanks so much for letting me tag along." Maddie grins at my mother.

"You know you're always welcome. And maybe you can give me some insight as to why my daughter has been so moody lately." She eyes me, but laughs again and flips her reddish hair over her shoulder when I roll my eyes. "I'm just kidding, Abby."

"Well, it's about time you've come for a visit." I whirl around to lay eyes on my dad, standing with his hands on his hips. Sometimes I think that he's never quite adjusted to not wearing a gunbelt during the day.

"Hi, Dad." I give him a hug, giggling a little when his beard tickles my cheek. I pull back and look at him in confusion. Dad is strictly a jeans and T-shirt man, and yet he's standing before me wearing a neat black button down and pressed khakis, looking supremely uncomfortable. "You look good, Dad, but what's going on?"

He scowls, but before he can open his mouth, my mother chirps, "It's our new look. It's good for business to dress up a little. Raphael highly recommends it."

"Who's Raphael?"

"He's the consultant we hired last month to spruce up our image a bit. He's done wonders with just a few small suggestions. I can't wait for you to meet him!" She's bubbling with excitement, and I smile reflexively. Dad turns, and I swear I can hear him grumble something along the lines of, "pretentious bull-shit," before he grabs our bags. "I'll take these inside. We're full up, so you girls are bunking together this weekend, all right?"

"No problem. I brought earplugs," I deadpan, while Maddie gasps and pushes my shoulder.

"I do *not* snore!" With a huff of mock indignation, she grabs her bag and stalks into the house, leaving my dad and me chuckling behind.

After Mom happily shows us the changes Raphael the Consultant has suggested, we help her prepare the evening meal. Mom's cooking skills have improved markedly since I was a kid, when mac and cheese out of a box was the standard fare. Tonight she's serving grilled venison with a port wine reduction and roasted root vegetables. It smells fantastic. She's coaxed me into making my chocolate cheesecake for dessert—assuming I can keep Maddie from eating the Oreos before I can make my crust.

A few hours later, the guests have eaten, Dad is camped out watching football in the den, and Mom has corralled us with a bottle of wine in the abandoned dining room. The room is all dark wood and mocha walls with comfortable chairs surrounding round oak tables. The sconces high on the walls illuminate it with a soft glow. I'm relaxed and thoroughly enjoying listening to my mother chattering away. This is what I've needed—a little time away from bitchy coworkers, tragic stories of childhood illness, and intense rock stars.

Mom is eating up Maddie's stories of Dylan and shooting me inquisitive looks. Finally, she can't stand it anymore and turns to me fully. "Okay, Abby, tell me what's up with you. You've been very quiet tonight. I get the feeling that something is bothering you. Whatever happened with that obstinate-but-hot celebrity donor who was giving you trouble? Did that work out?"

Maddie coughs into her wineglass as she stifles a laugh, and I shoot her a look. Mom thumps her on the back a few times, before turning back to me expectantly. "Things are looking up there," I say vaguely and quickly pour her some more wine.

"Well, there is nothing you can't handle." Her obvious confidence in my abilities warms me. "But why do I get the feeling there's more?"

"I've just been thinking about Lucas a lot lately," I admit.

Their expressions sober immediately.

"Ah. Did I tell you that . . ." She pauses, biting her lip. "I talked to his mother last week. Did you know he's out of jail?"

"Again?" Lucas had been in and out of rehab and jail a few times over the past few years. I didn't know the details. I no longer cared.

"He has to attend court-ordered therapy as part of his probation." She sighs. "Maybe it will stick this time."

"Maybe." Maddie sounds doubtful and watches me carefully. I know she's worrying he'll try to contact me again, like he did the last time he was released. I doubt he knows where I'm living now.

"Well, I don't know about you ladies, but I need to get some sleep," Mom says brightly, diverting me. "I want to take you to a new shoe store tomorrow after the breakfast rush. Okay?"

We eagerly agree and stand to give goodnight hugs all around. Maddie and I make our way to my bedroom at the far end of the manor, moving aside a few boxes of wine to act as suitcase stands. After we've pulled out the sofa bed and made it up for Maddie, we snuggle in for the night. However, after a while of listening to Maddie's soft snoring while I toss and turn, I sit up and throw back the covers. My mind won't stop churning. Maybe a walk will help.

I pull a fleece throw over my shoulders and wander out the back kitchen door to the porch in my pajamas. Taking a deep breath of the cool night air, I instantly feel myself relax. I walk along the trimmed path down past the small parking lot, with no real destination in mind, but my body seems to know what it needs. I end up at my favorite spot and sit down. It's a flat area on the backside of a slope so that when I sit, I'm hidden from the house. In front of me is the edge of one of the vineyards, row upon row of neat vines coming to stop just feet away. Something breaks from the row closest to my spot, startling me; it's only a rabbit, which darts across the lawn toward my mother's kitchen garden. I sit in the quiet, looking up at the moon. I can barely hear the cars in town. Much more peaceful than the constant traffic noise in New York.

Pulling my knees up to my chest, I prop my chin on my forearm. New York. I can't regret anything that happened there. Kennedy is, without a doubt, one of the most complicated people I've ever met . . . complicated, sad, alluring, exasperating. Closing my eyes, I can almost feel his arms around me and smell his spicy scent. It's an intoxicating combination. I smile wryly; I'm sure plenty of women have succumbed to that particular brand of intoxication over the years. He's probably lost count.

Even though Kennedy could never be the man for me, the feeling he evokes tells me what I should be looking for in a man. I know I made the right decision with Wyatt. I shouldn't settle for limp and listless, no matter how nice and safe the package. The fire and smoldering emotion that flare in me whenever Kennedy is near are what I want . . . what I need. I just have to find it in the right man.

I pull my phone out of my pocket and play Kennedy's latest video again. I haven't responded to him yet, partly because of the paparazzi photos, and partly because of Nadia's accusations. I know I have nothing to hide, but it pisses me off that anyone would question my ethics. Standing up, I look out over the vineyard, the sound of Kennedy's guitar blending with the rustling of the vines in the light breeze.

The last notes of his song fade away, and I look into his eyes on the tiny screen as he tells me to travel safe. I quickly switch over to record my own message before I chicken out.

"Hi, Kennedy. Thank you for that. Your song is beautiful. Sorry I haven't responded sooner. I wanted you to know that I loved it. And I like that you aren't giving up. Please know that I'm not giving up, either. I'd like to start with a call to Parker. He'd love it, and we can start the planning on the concert from there. I guess I'll talk to you later."

I hit end, feeling rather foolish to be recording myself, and quickly send it before I change my mind. Taking a deep breath, I can't help the smile that spreads across my face. I head back to the house and my own bed, feeling like a weight has lifted from my shoulders.

chapter eleven

kennedy

"I'M NOT SURE ABOUT THAT Jimmy Fallon." My dad's voice echoes through the phone as I sit in the back of another SUV, this time enroute to the airport. I love New York, but the West Coast is home for me, and its call seems stronger than ever.

The timing of this tour couldn't be worse. So many things I want to do . . . *need* to do and to say. Many of them revolving around the one woman who seems to have taken up residence in my thoughts. The fact that we're moving ahead with Parker's dream has stirred something deep inside me that's been dormant for a long time. Hope.

The blaring horn from some frustrated commuter beside us stirs me out of my wandering thoughts. "I thought you liked *The Tonight Show*."

"There's no one like Carson," Dad notes almost wistfully.

"Truer words were never spoken."

"You and the band sounded good. Playing is sharp."

I smile at his assessment. "I was going for sharp, so that's good." I watch out the darkened windows, the rain starting to fall after a few solid days of soul-sucking humidity. We sit in deadlocked traffic, yellow cabs jammed together as far as the eye can see.

I miss the California coast and Bodega Bay. Of all the homes I've had over the years, the one just outside of Bodega is probably my favorite. There's a rugged beauty about the coast—soaring rocky bluffs, miles of hidden coves and sandy beaches, churning surf crashing relentlessly, and sea-weathered surf shacks. "Did Mom see . . ." I don't need to finish that particular thought. I already know the answer.

"I recorded it for her." His voice is quiet. "She's getting there, Kennedy," he adds after a long beat. "You have to give her time."

"I know. How is she?" My voice trails as I shake my head. "Forget it. I know how she is."

"Yes. I suppose you do. One day at a time and all that."

"Easier said than done."

"Staying away from the bottle helps." Dad's voice is stoic as always. This is about as judgmental as he gets. Through everything—including my stint in rehab that obviously was of little to no value—he's kept his opinions to himself. He's let Mom do the talking, or in her case, the ranting. It was deserved, and fuck knows if I had listened to her, and to Robin, maybe things would be different.

"Easier said than done," I manage, my leg bouncing with pent up energy and frustration.

"Saw a few pictures of you with a young lady on that Twitter." I'm surprised he knows anything about Twitter or anything else online. Maybe it's his way of checking up on Adam and me. The thought is a sobering one. I've never been son of the year, but he shouldn't have to find out about what's happening in my life that way. It slams home that the distance I've deliberately put between us has had ramifications that I'm only just starting to realize.

"Looked a little cozy," he says, amusement in his voice.

"Hmm . . ."

"That's all I'm getting?"

I smile out the window. "You told me to never kiss and tell."

"Fair enough. I had a listen to the album. It was delivered the other night." Always a pro on changing the subject.

"I was going to ask if it got there. You got one of the first copies. What did you think?" From beside me, Tucker huffs out a sigh of relief as the SUV finally starts to move.

"It's edgy. Lots of emotion in there. Did it help? Writing it, I mean?"

"Jury is still out on that."

"I'm proud of you. I know I probably don't say it enough, but I am. Your mother is, too." I let out a half snort. Proud isn't a word I'd associate with how my mother feels about me. "Whether you believe it or not, she is," he continues. "A lot of other people would've packed it in after everything, but you're still out there."

I chuckle, my mouth dry and my patience waning from the chaos of the last few days. "Guess that stubborn streak you always complained about came in handy."

"And who do you think you get that from? You're your mother's son through and through."

If only.

"YOU ALL RIGHT THERE?" TUCKER'S voice is laced with worry as I roll my neck, waking up from a less than restful sleep.

"Fuck. It's supposed to be more comfortable to fly this way." I rub my hand over my shoulder, feeling the muscles complain, and my head pounds.

"I don't think it really matters when you've passed out like you did."

"I was exhausted." I unfold myself from the leather seat and glance out the window. Endless clear sky stretches out around the plane. "How much longer?"

"Maybe an hour." I feel his scrutinizing gaze on me as I turn to the bar area.

"Ah, Sleeping Beauty has risen from the dead. Praise be! Join us, mate." Sean lifts his glass in my direction with a grin. He's half in the bag. Judging by the look of them, they all are.

A commotion at the back of the plane diverts my attention. A flash of blond Mohawk—Matt's new haircut courtesy of an ill-timed bet with Cam yesterday—spills out of the bathroom, followed by giggling. Lots of giggling. His latest true love.

His arm snakes around the girl's waist, holding her up as she fights to tug her white skirt down. She giggles the entire time, trying to smooth her tangled, messed-up hair. "Thanks, baby," she gushes, running her fingers through what's left of Matt's hair. "This is super cute."

I let out a laugh. "You look like an idiot."

"You only wish you had this hair, Lane." Matt coaxes his latest conquest to the bar. She's been hanging off his arm for the last few days, but I'm not even sure he knows her name, not that it matters.

"I can't believe I'm on a plane with you guys." Her eyes widen at me again, and then she squeals—a sound I'm sure is meant only for wild animals. "My friends are going to, like, freak out."

I glance at Tucker who just rolls his eyes. "Jesus," he mumbles under his breath.

"Where are these friends anyway, sweetheart? It's rather unfair to leave the rest of us out of the fun, don't you think?" Brodie leers at the girl, taking his time in getting the full length of her in. "Not bad, Matty. Not bad at all."

"Hands off, man. She's mine." Matt takes a seat on one of the stools, pulling the girl into his lap in the process.

"Oh, I don't mind." She looks way too excited than she should. "At all."

"Of course you don't," Cam chimes in from his seat opposite the bar and strums away on his acoustic. "They never do."

"Would you get your sorry ass over here? Fuck, it's like herding feral cats with you. Sit. Have a drink," Sean shouts at the top of his lungs, shaking the ice in an empty glass. "What's your poison?"

I wet my bottom lip as I scan the bar. "Just some water, man. I'm not feeling great."

"Water?" Sean snorts with a shake of his head. "Would you like me to bring 'round tea with crumpets for you, too?" I laugh even though I shouldn't. There's nothing funny about this situation. "The tour's sold out, and the presales of the album are flying. You can have one drink. It's not going to kill you, and what's more, you deserve it. We worked our bloody arses off to get here. Sit."

I feel the weight of Tucker's gaze on me—of all of them, actually, and I'm tired. Tired of fighting, tired of resisting, tired of feeling like I'm not in control. I should be able to do this. I should be able to have a drink without feeling guilty. "All right, all right. Jesus, you're a pain in the ass."

"And he's back!" The Brit lets out one of his signature howls, pounding the top of the bar like the lunatic he is.

Tucker's quiet, and I can't meet his eyes. I can't see that look of disappointment.

"Just one."

DESPITE THE CELEBRATORY MOOD ON the plane, I did stick to just one drink. I'm not going to lie; it was hard as hell. The rest of the flight was torturous as I danced with the temptation around me. But once the plane landed in San Fran, the band dispersed quickly, some of them catching other flights. A few days away from each other is a good thing before we set out on this tour.

Today, I'm using the free time to do something I should have done a long time ago. Under an overcast and darkened sky, I glance over my shoulder at Tucker as he leans against the rental car. His arms are crossed, concern evident in his face. With my heart hammering, I knock on the door of the Minnesota home I grew up in. I haven't been back since Robin's funeral, the single worst day in my life.

Everything looks exactly the same. The walkway lined with perfectly groomed flowers, the front porch with the beat-up wooden chair in the corner that dad would read the paper in every day, the crack still in the front bay window from an ill-timed football throw by Adam. Despite the fact that they could live anywhere they want, they've never wanted to move. It's like this place is frozen in time, and maybe that's part of the reason why they can't or won't leave.

Memories come flashing back, making my head spin. Adam and I tormenting Robin as her and her friends tried to skip in the driveway. Robin sticking the garden hose through the open window of Adam's beloved Trans Am and flooding the front seat. The virtual sea of friends and neighbors congregating in the backyard after Robin's funeral.

My throat is dry as I reach for the door handle, unsure of whether I'm actually welcome to just walk in. The heavy door whips open, ending my concern, and my eyes fall on my father for the first time in over two years.

He stares at me in disbelief, his normally vibrant blue eyes troubled behind his black reading glasses and emphasized by deep, dark circles. A few more wisps of gray pepper his hair, and his expression is beyond grim, as if he's carrying the weight of the world on his shoulders. He looks like he's aged ten years instead of two.

"Dad," I manage.

"You're . . . you're here," he stammers, his voice strained as he drops the jacket in his hand and pulls me against his chest, his arms tightening around my shoulders.

"Yeah. I am."

He pats my back and releases me, looking me over like he can't quite believe I'm here. "Aren't you supposed to be in Europe?"

Rubbing the back of my neck, I nod. "Yeah. We have a bit of a break before we head out. You should come out for a concert when we're back. You haven't seen one since before—" I catch myself before I finish that sentence. His face falls, darkness clouding his features once more.

"Maybe, son. We'll see," he mutters cryptically.

"I could send a plane for you. You can stay with me." He lifts a brow at my suggestion. I think it's the first time I've invited them to my place in Bodega Bay.

"You don't want your old man cramping your style," he hedges, eyeing me warily.

"Well, I'm trying a new style on. You know? Taking it down a notch."

He pats his palm against my shoulder before picking up his jacket. "It's about time." He opens the door wider, easing me into the entryway, the door falling shut behind us.

An eerie quiet descends as my heart thunders in my chest. The house was always so vibrant and full of life, with music spilling from open windows out into the yard while we caused havoc in the neighborhood. But now? All the windows are shut and the blinds closed, encasing us in a tomb.

Faintly, I can hear the sounds of a blender die down in the kitchen, and I'm unable to stop myself from looking at the framed photos that line the darkened hallway as Dad leads the way. Adam winning his first NASCAR race, the band's platinum records arranged artfully on the wall, and finally, Robin, glowing in her graduation cap and gown, and hugging me by one of the red sandstone buildings at the University of Minnesota.

"You're back already?" Mom's voice is quiet, but manages to seep into my soul and stop me in my tracks. The kitchen is a whirlwind of chaos, every available surface covered; pans, flour, open packages of various mixes. And then, I see her hunched over the sink, steam rising, water blasting, and scrubbing furiously at some glass bowl. She looks frail with her hair twisted back into a bun and clothes hanging off her. My heart shudders at the sight.

"Found a little something outside," Dad begins, clearing his throat.

"Not another one of those damn leeches looking for a picture?" she hisses.

Dad grimaces, shaking his head to her turned back. "We haven't seen them in a while."

My jaw clenches, and I level Dad a look of concern. "What leeches?" The bowl slips from her hand at the sound of my voice, shattering into pieces on the floor. She grips the edge of the sink, her body tensing before she whirls around to face me.

"Mom . . ." She's glaring at me, her eyes troubled and cloudy, brimming almost immediately with unshed tears. Her chin quivers as she lifts a shaking, soapy hand to brush away a few wayward strands of her dull, lifeless hair from her face.

"What are you doing here?" she seethes as Dad hurries to her side, taking her hand and steering her away from the broken glass on the floor.

"Thought it was time."

Her brows descend. "How big of you, taking time out of your schedule to grace us with your presence," she bites out.

"You said you didn't want to see me . . ." I begin, knowing that no matter what I say, it will never be enough. Nothing I can ever do or say will ever bring back Robin, and an ocean of unspoken words and accusations seem to float between us as we stare at each other in a silent standoff.

"What makes you think I do now?" she finally fires back at me.

I take a tentative step toward her. "I just wanted to . . ." I watch as her grip tightens around Dad's hand like a lifeline. He slides his arm around her thin waist, beginning to steer her to one of the stools at the counter.

"Let's get you sitting down—" Dad suggests, his words fading as her voice raises above his.

"You wanted to what, exactly?"

"I don't know . . . apologize, talk to you, and see how you're doing." Her features soften slightly at my words, and she reaches out to grip the back of the stool.

"How does it look like I'm doing?" she asks, her voice harsh.

"You're surviving. Just like I am. Just like we all are." I go for the cold, hard truth.

"I'm not . . . I lost everything that day, Kennedy. Everything." Her voice breaks and tears spill over onto her cheeks as Dad begins rubbing her back in an attempt to calm her.

"No, Mom. You didn't. We're still here. Your friends, Dad and Adam . . . me."

"You were supposed to protect her!" she screeches, the knife in my heart twisting just a little bit more. "You were supposed to . . ." She squeezes her eyes shut, trembling as Dad tightens his arm around her. "Where's my Ativan?" she asks abruptly, pushing against Dad's chest. His stricken gaze meets mine for a moment before he addresses her like she's a child.

"It's in the medicine cabinet. You're not due for another until—"

"I need it, Graham. Look at me!" He shakes his head at her. Clearly, this isn't the first time they've had this type of conversation.

A sense of dread washes over me. "Mom. No."

"Look at what he's done to me." Her voice trails to a whisper, my stomach threatening to unleash the stale airline coffee from this morning.

He lets out a defeated sigh, his shoulders hunching over. "Okay," he manages, glancing between us nervously.

"Go. I'm fine," she urges, giving his hand a squeeze, and with my heart in my throat, there's no more hesitation. I cross the room and wrap my arms around her, meeting her resistance immediately. Her fists pound against my chest, but she's so weak, it hardly registers.

"I've got you, Mom." My arms tighten around her delicate shoulders, feeling the sharp angles of her bones as she melts against me, her sobs muffled against my jean jacket. "I'm sorry. I'm so sorry." My face falls against her shoulder as her hands fist the fabric of my jacket, her body rocking with grief. Her knees buckle, and my grip tightens around her as we sink to the kitchen floor.

"HOW LONG HAS THIS BEEN going on?" I ask Dad as Mom sits beside me on the same living room couch that Adam and I used to chase each other around.

"Don't talk about me like I'm not here," she chides, her voice calmer. A good hour-long cry and a dose of Ativan will do that to you.

"I'm sorry. It's just . . ."

"Don't you start. You're not exactly an expert at handling stress, Kennedy," she scolds. If she only knew what I've been doing to numb the pain. I realize that me having an opinion about how she or anyone else handles a situation like this is wildly hypocritical. Even now, the temptation of the bar looms in the corner of the room. Something to take the edge off, to numb the pain that rarely seems to fade.

My thoughts immediately go to Abby and Parker. The reasons I want to change this vicious cycle my life has become, and the main reason why I'm not currently plowing through a bottle of twenty-year-old scotch I know is lurking in that liquor cabinet.

Tucker glances at me from his perch at the piano bench at Mom's words, digging into another brownie from the tray Dad put out. Once our initial confrontation and subsequent meltdown was over, Dad had urged Tucker inside. He was appalled that he had been left to wait outside. Tucker, of course, took it all in stride.

"I haven't been. That's true. But I'm trying," I admit.

Mom's hand shakes slightly as she sets her teacup down to the saucer. "The doctor gave me the prescription just before the funeral," she offers calmly as if she's just commenting on the weather. "It helps when things get . . . hard."

I'm in no position to judge her, even though it's taking everything in me not to. "I know what that's like."

She glances at me, her half-smile forced. "I know you do. I haven't been . . . I haven't been fair about this . . . About what happened," she starts slowly, her red-rimmed eyes searching mine.

I give her a tentative smile. "Let's not do this now, okay? We have lots of time to talk about it."

She glances at Dad, looking for some sort of acknowledgement it seems. "Yes we do, son," he says, taking her hand with a squeeze.

"YOU HAVEN'T CHANGED ANYTHING?" I linger by my childhood dresser, glancing at the framed photo on top. Adam, Robin, and me dressed up like the Three Musketeers for Halloween. No girly princesses or ballerinas for Robin. She demanded to be a Musketeer, much to the horror of every single one of her friends.

I catch Mom's eye in the mirror, and she frowns. "I thought about it." She looks away, scanning the room. "It felt wrong to change it." She sinks down to the edge of my double bed, her shoulders slumped. She looks so defeated it breaks my heart. She nervously picks at the frayed edge of her sweater. "And I wanted you all to have a place to come home to."

Taking a seat beside her on the bed, she leans against my shoulder. "I wish I could—" I start, but she interrupts me quickly.

"So do I. But we can't. We can't go back," she whispers.

"We can't just stay in limbo either," I answer gently, knowing that whatever progress we've made is raw and tenuous at best.

She lifts her head from my shoulder, looking up at me. "Isn't that what you've been doing?"

"I don't really know what I've been doing," I admit. "Hiding. Trying to numb the pain."

"In a way, it feels like I've lost both of you. And I know that's my fault." Her voice is strained, cracking under the weight of what she's been carrying around for the last few years.

"No, Mom. It's not your fault. I could have called, visited."

"And I could have, too," she cuts me off. "We're more alike than you might want to admit."

Her tired eyes search mine as she takes my hand, and I try not to lose it completely. "Maybe we can, I don't know. Start over?"

My words hang in the air. A simple suggestion, a promise, a hope for something that will start to take us both out of this misery. She smiles slightly, squeezing my hand. "We can try."

IN THE DISTANCE THE THUNDER rumbles as I grip the cool marble headstone. Slowly, I trace the etched R over and over with my fingertip. My boots sink into the soft, wet grass as I crouch down at Robin's grave. My throat is parched, and my heart hammers in my chest.

"Fuck, I miss you. I don't know what I'm doing. This is where you would tell me to suck it up." I stare blankly at the black marble.

Beloved daughter, sister, friend.

Four words summing up someone's life.

"I met someone." I shake my head, trying to get a grip on the whirling emotions. "She's . . . making me question everything. You would love her. She doesn't put up with my shit either. Dark and light. Good and evil." Another round of thunder rolls, the first drops of rain hitting my face. "Okay, I get it. Maybe I'm not evil. Misguided? Is that better?" I glance up at the threatening clouds, silence greeting me. "Thought so."

The wind picks up; it's uncharacteristically warm for the impending storm. "I'm sorry I haven't been by. Doesn't mean I haven't thought about you every day. Every single day, Robin."

I rearrange the bright pink Gerbera daisies I brought her, pressing my lips to my palm before resting it over her name. "I'll be back soon. I'm going to make you proud of me."

Standing up, I slide my sunglasses back on, shove my hands into the pockets of my jacket, and make my way back to Tucker. The sky opens up with another crack of thunder, the rain softly falling as I haul open the door and slip inside.

"Where are we going?" He wastes no time in starting the engine.

"Back home." My leg bounces with nervous, pent-up energy. I can't even begin to process the roller coaster of emotions I've been riding today.

"To your parent's place?" He starts down the gravel road as I stare out the window, the black marble of the headstone fading while we move down the path towards the gates of the cemetery.

"No. To California."

♪ ♩ ♪ ♩

abigail

"MY GOODNESS, WHAT'S GOT YOU so happy this morning?" Tess takes my latte while I divest myself of my coat and hang it up on the hook behind my door, and then hands the steaming cup back to me.

I can't help the smile that stretches across my face. "Oh, I just had a nice weekend."

"Oh, me, too." She sighs and holds the stack of files in her arms against her chest. "I met this guy last weekend down at the Wharf, and he asked me out. Six-foot-plus, dreamy green eyes, and a package that makes me see stars, I swear."

I bark out a laugh, shaking my head at her oversharing. "But enough about me," she continues, eyeing me mischievously. "Spill, boss lady. What happened with the rock god last week?"

"Nothing happened." I ignore her skeptical huff. "I ran into him in the hotel, and we talked about the Jensen dream." It's the truth, as far as it goes. Anything else that happened is private.

"Humph. That's it? How can I live vicariously through you if you're not going to give me more than that to work with?" She plops the stack of files on my desk.

"Guess you'll just have to deal with it. What's all this?" I wave a hand at the mountain of paperwork.

"Duane's office finally worked through some of the post-dream financial reports." She smiles sympathetically at my sigh, before turning to her notes to read off my packed schedule for the day. I'm barely going to have time to breathe. But I can't concentrate on the list, knowing what's coming next. "And you made a last minute addition at two. Something for the Jensen dream?"

"Yes. It's a little unorthodox, because the final details of the dream fulfillment haven't been fleshed out yet, but Kennedy Lane is coming in to make a Skype call to Parker. I arranged it with his mother yesterday." I grimace internally. Not only haven't the details been fleshed out, but I haven't even gotten a signed fulfillment contract yet.

I brace myself for her reaction, and I'm not disappointed. Her mouth drops open for a second, then a brilliant smile emerges.

"Parker will love that!" She makes a few notes, humming softly to herself. "I'll get conference room one ready for you, okay?"

"Great. So, anything else I need to know for now?"

She squirms a little. "Nadia asked for a few minutes. Um, did something happen between you two last week? She was hell on wheels while you were gone." I grimace. I know I still have to deal with her today, but she can wait.

"Nothing I can't handle. I'll call her later. Is that it?" She nods and finally leaves me in peace. Not that I feel very peaceful. My stomach flutters with excitement in anticipation. There is some-thing about him beyond his larger-than-life persona and tragic problems that calls to me. The glimpse of the man I saw in New York. That, I think, is the real Kennedy. At least I hope it is. That man was as shy as he was cocky, as introspective as he was glib, and talented in ways I can't comprehend. He made me laugh, he made me think, and . . .

A shiver runs through me as I remember, yet again, the feel of his arms around me. Okay . . . I'll admit it. He's also one of the sexiest men I've ever had the pleasure to meet.

Leaning back in my chair, I shake my head at myself. I need to calm down. It's just another dream fulfillment. Besides, he would never . . . I let out a soft grunt. Sister—remember? I'll just keep my private thoughts private, and after this is all said and done, I'll take them out of their box every once in a while to fan-tasize over until I find someone else who makes my heart pound and my blood race.

Right? Of course, right.

I'M STEAMING THROUGH A PILE of publicity ideas April has sent me when I hear a light tap at my door. Expecting Tess, I barely manage to keep my sour grunt inside when the door opens and I see Nadia instead.

"I have a few proposals for you to review." She steps into my office and sets a small stack of folders on my desk, as if it's just a regular day. I have to say I admire her chutzpah.

"Fine. Please sit down, Nadia. I'd like to discuss your behav-ior last week."

Keeping her expression neutral, she ignores my request and remains standing. "I'm not sure what there is to discuss." She looks down her nose at me. "I suppose the timing could have been better, but someone needed to point out how your little 'meeting' last week could affect our image. I'm not going to shy away from that simply because you're my boss."

She sticks her chin out, the picture of confidence. "There's a difference between candor and slander. You were out of line last week, Nadia," I retort with quiet seriousness. Her self-assured smile falters, as if she hadn't expected me to stand my ground. "You went beyond advising me about our image. You practically accused me of sleeping with a client, either for personal gain or to secure a donation. So, based on a few blurry photos, I'm either a skank or a whore, is that right?"

Her eyes shoot open. "No! I just thought . . ." she stammers, looking uncharacteristically nervous. "Abby, I'm sorry, but—"

"Fine. Apology accepted." I let her squirm for a beat. "For the record, my private life is just that—private. It will never interfere with the work of this foundation, nor would I *ever* do anything to jeopardize the good work that we do." I lean forward in my chair as my eyes drill into her. "And I expect the same from every member of my staff. Got it?"

Her lips mash into a straight line. "Got it," she says flatly. "Anything else?"

"As a matter of fact, there is." I take a sip of my latte, using the moment to calm myself. Nadia is good at her job, and until now, we've never had any problems. She can be standoffish at times, but it's only because she cares so deeply for the kids; she has to distance herself to maintain her objectivity. We all work seamlessly together—usually—and I don't want to jeopardize our team by wallowing or rehashing her careless words any more.

"What are you doing at two? I'm meeting with Lane today, and I thought you might like to join us."

"He's coming *here*? Today?" She looks shocked. "Why?"

"We're going to have an initial call with Parker." I let some of my excitement seep into my voice. "This is one of the things I wanted to discuss with you today. Parker is going to be thrilled. You've been working so hard on this, I thought you'd like to be there, too." There's no reason why she shouldn't be there. She's our giving director, after all. Plus, it's a way to get things back on track between us.

"I can't today," she mutters in consternation, frowning at her feet. I can practically see her trying to reshuffle her schedule in her head. "I'm leaving for LA after lunch to meet with Lucas Films. It took weeks to set this meeting up; I can't reschedule."

"Well, this is just the first step; we have a lot of work ahead of us. Maybe April can join us today instead." I shrug, and then gesture to the files she set on my desk. "Did you have something in particular you wanted to discuss in any of these cases now?"

She shakes her head, coming out of her thoughts. "What? Oh, no. I'll see you at the morning huddle, okay?"

"No problem. See you." She looks almost constipated as she turns and heads out the door. With a satisfied smile, I turn back to my work. That should put all that ridiculousness to rest.

FINALLY, THE HOUR ARRIVES. I pace around my office and try to pretend I'm not excited. I nervously smooth down the burgundy wrap dress I've paired with my New York boots. I love these boots, and I seem to remember that Kennedy did, too. That's not why I'm wearing them, of course.

Tess buzzes, startling me, and I jerk the door open. I hear an amused snort, and there he is. All smiles and tousled hair, and carrying a guitar case. I struggle to keep my grin at bay. "Mr. Lane, how nice to see you again." My voice is a tad too breathy to be professional. "Won't you come in?"

His eyes twinkle with mirth. "Thank you, Abby. And I'm pretty sure we're past the Mr. Lane phase."

Tess gives me a surreptitious wink as he saunters past me, before turning her attention to Lane's ever-present bodyguard, who has planted himself in a chair next to her desk.

"Won't you sit down?" I offer as I close the door, but turn to find he's already situated on my sofa. He grins impishly at me, making me laugh. He's traded in his hoodie and leather coat for a black crewneck sweater and a canvas jacket the color of cognac. He looks casual but neat, with three or four days' stubble on his chiseled jaw, and his color is good. A great improvement over the first time we met. I sit opposite him in one of my low chairs, and we sit there grinning like fools, until we both try to speak.

"I liked your song—"

"I'm glad you texted me—"

With a laugh, I wave for him to go first. "I'm glad you texted me," he begins again. "I was beginning to think you were pissed off with me for the paparazzi shots, even though they were pretty fuzzy."

I shrug. "I've been in photos before, for events and things. I've never had paparazzi swarm me like that, but the photos didn't bother me. I had to do a little damage control here, though." He looks at me with concern, and I quickly change the subject. "I really liked the song," I blurt and try not to squirm under his intense gaze. God, why am I so nervous?

"Yeah?" His voice is almost shy. "I was sorry about how that night ended. I thought that might make up for it."

"It was beautiful. Raw and edgy, but beautiful." I pause, searching for a way to lighten the suddenly intimate mood. "I hope you didn't get in too much trouble with your team that night."

He laughs. "Nah. I've been in worse trouble, believe me.

Tucker knows that sometimes I just have to get away, although it makes him nervous. And Brodie . . ." A shadow passes over his face. "Well, Brodie needs to back the fuck off. He frequently has trouble remembering he's only running the tour, not my entire life."

"I could see that." I remember the scathing look Brodie gave me that night.

"Hey, what did you mean about damage control?" I tense, not really wanting to go down this road with him, but his expression is so earnest, I find myself explaining.

"One of my colleagues read a little too much into the fact that we were together," I say delicately. "She's spent quite a bit of time on Parker's dream, and then I'm suddenly seen ducking out of a taxi with you. I tried to explain it was completely innocent, of course, but she was worried by how it might look to our Board." He looks confused for a second, and then his eyebrows shoot up.

"You're kidding, right?"

"I wish I was," I grumble, embarrassed. "It's been taken care of. No worries."

"It was that blond chick, the one who came with you to the Fairmont, wasn't it? She gave you shit about being with me?"

How does he know? "Nadia—" I begin, but his laugh cuts me off.

"Well, you know what they say," he mutters sardonically. "A good offense is a good defense." He chuckles, a wry smile curving his lips.

"What do you mean?" I look at him in confusion, but he ignores my question.

"Don't worry about it. No one in their right mind would ever seriously accuse *you* of doing anything improper." His teasing makes my face heat.

"But I do want you to see how serious I am about fulfilling Parker's dream, to see if you'd agree to something more."

"More?"

He fixes me with a look that virtually liquefies my insides. "More."

My mouth dries instantly as we stare at each other, the room crackling with tension. But before I can say anything, there's a quick knock and the door opens. I blink in surprise and scramble to my feet.

"Nadia! I didn't think you—" I don't get any further before she strides confidently in the room and holds her hand out to Kennedy.

"Nadia Baskov, Mr. Lane. It's so nice to see you again. Abigail invited me to your meeting, and I was fortunately able to move a few things around to accommodate her. I'm sorry I'm late." She smiles at him as if he's the answer to the mysteries of life. She's still wearing her crisp navy suit, but I swear she's undone one of the buttons on her silk blouse. What the hell?

Kennedy looks at her with an indecipherable expression before rising with the grace of a panther and reluctantly shakes her hand, releasing it almost instantly. She moves to sit next to him on the sofa, but instead of retaking his seat, he abruptly steps over and takes the chair next to mine. Nadia's smile wavers for a split-second, but she recovers and gracefully sinks to the sofa.

The door is still open a fraction, and I can just see Tess hovering outside. I wonder what Nadia said to her before she came in. I also wonder how she managed to reschedule with Lucas Films; she better not have canceled on them outright.

"I'm surprised to see you, Nadia." I manage to keep a conversational tone. "We were just going to talk about the call with Parker."

"Actually, if you don't mind, I have several other ideas of my own that I'd like to discuss with you, Kennedy," she purrs, flipping open her leather notebook.

"Mr. Lane." His voice is silky smooth, but the underlying steeliness is unmistakable. At her startled look, he elaborates, "I prefer Mr. Lane, if you don't mind."

I manage not to gape at him. It was all "we're past Mr. Lane" a few minutes ago.

"Oh, of course," she stammers, momentarily flustered. "Mr. Lane, if I may continue?" Kennedy simply listens quietly, a secret smile playing about his lips, but I get the feeling it's not directed at anything she's saying. His legs are casually crossed, and he absently rubs the tip of one long finger back and forth over his knee. My attention jerks back to her when I suddenly realize what she's suggesting.

"So why don't we just step down to my office, and I can show you the preliminary drawings." She delicately tucks her pale blond hair behind her right ear. "You don't mind, do you, Abigail? I know you have a full schedule today." Her eyes glow with anticipation, and she leans forward, no doubt giving him a good view of her ample cleavage. I'm appalled.

"Nadia, may I have a word." I begin, but Kennedy overrides me.

"Ms Baskov, is it? I'm sorry, but that's not possible. In fact, I would prefer conducting any arrangements for my involvement with Parker's dream with Miss Walker directly. I realize it's an imposition on her part, given all she has on her plate, but I'm just not comfortable working with you in any capacity."

"I beg your pardon?" Nadia looks like she can't believe her ears, and honestly, I can't blame her. I have no idea where he's going with this.

"Well, I hadn't wanted to bring this up in front of your boss." He smiles, but it's not reflected in his eyes. "But the way you were eye-fucking me the last time we met was completely inappropriate. And your blatant display today hasn't done anything to improve your standing. You're lucky your boss is so generous; if you worked for me, you'd be out the door already."

Nadia's mouth drops open as she stares at him in disbelief. "What? I've never . . . I assure you that . . ."

Kennedy rises to his feet, prompting me to do the same. "Don't even try. You think I don't know when a woman is hitting on me? Not exactly the behavior I'd expect from a charity." He looks at her scathingly. "Now, if you don't mind, Miss Walker and I have an important call to make."

"ARE YOU SURE YOU'RE READY for this?" I ask as we sit at my laptop, Skype blazing on the screen. My heart pounds with a sudden burst of nerves. Kennedy's blistering lecture had put Nadia's complaints about me in a different light. She disappeared with her tail between her legs quickly, but I know I haven't heard the end of this. Trying to shake off the confrontation, I focus on what's really important. I know how much this is going to mean to Parker, but I have no idea what kind of impact it may have on Kennedy.

"Yeah, sure. Why wouldn't I be?" Kennedy asks with a confidence that impresses me.

"Reactions can be very intense when you first meet these children, and you're well . . . you." He glances at me, those icy blue eyes hard. "Kids are very perceptive if they sense you're freaking out, or feel sorry for them. Let's just say I've seen something that could be a wonderful moment ruined."

"Have a little faith in me. I know how much this means to him."

"I know you do," I say gently. "But, Kennedy, seeing a picture and reading about him is very different than actually talking to him and hearing his voice. It's an emotional experience for most people." I run my finger along the edge of the laptop. "He thinks he's having a call with his uncle. He'll be in his room at the hospital, and his mom will be there. You might see some equipment around him, an IV for example."

"I'll try not to focus on that." Kennedy lifts an acoustic guitar out of its case and places it in his lap.

I click on the call button and wait, smiling as Parker comes into view on the screen. Nothing can really prepare you for seeing a child this way. Parker's blond hair is gone, his bald head covered by a dark green Redfall bandana, his bright blue eyes cloudy and tired. Those haunting eyes blink at the screen, and then blink again, as if he can't quite believe what he's seeing.

Kennedy pauses, his eyes darting around the screen. Despite my earlier warning, it's hard to miss the IV stretching to his bed, disappearing under a Redfall T-shirt that hangs off his frail little frame. I smile and give a wave to Parker before Kennedy speaks, his voice strong and sure.

"Hey, Parker. How's it going?"

Parker's cracked lips widen into a smile that lights up his face before he turns away from the screen. "Mom! Come here!" His voice sounds strained, a bit labored. He turns back to focus on the screen, and I see a bit of life creep back into his eyes. "Holy . . . wow. Is that really you?"

"Yeah, bud. It is."

"I'm supposed to be talking to Uncle Tim."

Kennedy laughs, his eyes widening. "Well, if you want, I can go and you can call Uncle—"

"No! I just can't believe it's really you. Mom! Come see. Kennedy Lane is on the computer!"

I see Parker's mother, Joyce, with a beaming smile come into view. She gives a wave, mouthing, "Thank you," before wiping a stray tear from her cheek.

"Hey, aren't you supposed to be on tour?" Parker asks.

"It's starting soon. We'll be doing some shows in London first." Parker smiles, his eyes wide and excited. "So, tell me about your day."

"Well, I had a chemo treatment earlier." He says the words as if we're just talking about the weather.

"Shi . . . I'm sorry, bud."

"I'm used to it. And anyway, I listen to you when I have them, so it not's so bad."

I feel my heart stutter at how brave Parker is in the face of such an intense struggle. "I'm glad it helps. Hey, I hear you're learning to play the guitar," Kennedy comments, lifting his own so Parker can see it.

"Yeah. When I can." He nods enthusiastically, reaching up to tug the bandana down on his head. I can see a series of red marks along his arm, a bandage around his wrist. "I get tired fast though, so I'm not very good."

"I doubt that's true. Do you want to play something with me now?"

"Really? Mom! Can I?"

Behind him, Joyce nods, disappearing from view. "This is so cool. Ben will never believe it," he gushes.

"Who's Ben?" Kennedy asks, slipping the guitar strap around his shoulder. His hand squeezes the neck of the guitar, as if it's holding him in place, grounding him.

"He's another kid down the hall. He has CF. We hang out sometimes."

Kennedy seems thrown for a bit, but recovers quickly. "What have you learned so far?"

"Just a couple of songs. Mom wanted me to learn 'You Are

My Sunshine' because she sings it to me every night. And the start of 'Sweet Home Alabama,' " he says, leaning back as Joyce sets a well-used guitar in his lap.

"Nice guitar."

"Mom got it at a garage sale. It's okay," Parker says, dropping his eyes from the screen to study his fingers as he carefully positions them on the strings.

"Hey, no Gibson is ever just 'okay.' That's your first lesson, Parker."

He lets out a laugh that splits my heart open, followed quickly by a cough. Joyce appears, placing a clear straw to his lips, and I watch him take a sip. Kennedy turns away from the screen, glancing at me, and I offer him an encouraging smile. "Okay. Let's go with 'Sweet Home Alabama'. It's a good one to learn when you're first starting out. "I'll count you in, okay?" Parker nods, singularly focused on the guitar. "Three, two, one."

The chords of the familiar song fill my office, and I find myself holding my breath as I hear Parker join in. The fact that he's able to do this at all, despite the pain he must be in, is nothing short of a miracle.

"That's it. You're doing great, Parker."

He lifts his face to the screen with a smile, his fingers faltering. "Oh, sorry." He shakes his head, looking disappointed.

"Hey." Kennedy presses the guitar against his chest. "Never apologize. You know how many times I had to practice before I got this song right? I lost count. And I still practice every day. You're really good at this, Parker. Don't ever doubt that, okay?"

"That was so cool," he says with a tired smile.

"You want to know something else that's cool?" Kennedy asks, glancing over at me before focusing back on the screen. "I'm coming to visit you soon."

"You are?" Parker's eyes grow wide, and I suck in a breath.

We didn't discuss a visit before the concert. I guess this is what they mean by unpredictable rock stars.

"Yeah. If that's okay. Would you like that?"

"That would be great! Mom!" He turns away from the screen. "He's coming to see me. Do you know when?"

"I have to get through the next couple of weeks of the tour, and then I'll be there. As soon as I know the date, I'll let you know. How about that?"

Parker clears his throat. "That would be so awesome."

"Hey, thanks for playing with me. Get some rest now, okay?"

He places his palm up on the screen, and Kennedy doesn't hesitate, covering it with his own. "Thanks, Kennedy."

"You're welcome. I'll talk to you soon." Joyce gives a wave from behind him, before pulling Parker into her arms, and the connection is broken.

Kennedy stares at the blank screen, and slowly, I reach around him to exit out of the app. He blinks up at me, and I can see his blue eyes gleam with unshed tears. With my heart pounding, I gently set my hand on his shoulder. "It'll be okay." I hope I'm right.

I'M MUNCHING ON A HUM bao as we stroll through the heart of Chinatown. I hum in pleasure, savoring the succulent combination of savory pork and lighter-than-air sweet bread.

Once the call with Parker was over, Tucker whisked us out to a waiting SUV. After a heated conversation about boundaries and rabid fans, Kennedy managed to convince him that we wouldn't get mauled in Chinatown. I wonder if Kennedy is ever left alone. Does he ever get downtime?

"That happens to be my favorite Chinese bakery." I gesture behind us, as I continue to enjoy my treat.

He swallows and grins at me. "Mine, too. See, we *do* have something in common."

"I never doubted it. It was just a matter of finding it." Although the streets are as busy as usual for a weekday, the locals here don't pay much attention to us. He tosses our wrappers in a trashcan and glances at me while we walk.

We pass an elderly woman gesticulating and arguing loudly with a street vendor over a bushel basket of some vegetables, and I can't help but giggle—I don't understand the words sizzling through the air, but I bet they wouldn't pass a censor. Kennedy shoots me an amused smile and then clears his throat.

"So, tell me, why do you do what you do? I've shared some of my thing. But I want to know how you got here. How long have you been with *What's Your Dream?*"

"A little more than three years." I pull the strap of my tote bag higher on my shoulder.

"You've always wanted to help kids?"

"And their parents. It's kind of a passion of mine." I glance up to see him watching me with interest. "When I was sixteen, one of my good friends began having migraines. They were affecting her vision and balance and would make her terribly sick. She thought they were just something she'd grow out of, but she was diagnosed with an inoperable brain tumor."

He sucks in a breath. "Holy shit. She was sixteen, too?"

"Yes. It was hideous. Her family wasn't poor, but they weren't rolling in money, either. Just a normal family. They didn't have the greatest health insurance. It covered some things, but not nearly enough. They had to take out a second mortgage to pay for the treatments. They worked for a while, but it made Beth even sicker than the headaches did. The town and their church held fundraisers for them, and the hospital charity helped some, but they ended up losing almost everything.

"Beth was the oldest of three girls. Her younger sisters were twelve and ten, and I felt especially sorry for them. They were not only terrified of Beth dying, but they also felt resentful toward her for sucking up all their parents' time and the family's resources. It's a tough dynamic that many families in that position experience."

"I can imagine," he says, frowning.

"My mom and I helped as much as we could. Little things, like cleaning the house so Beth's mom didn't have to do it, or making them dinner for the week. After watching everything she and her family went through, I always wished there was something more that I could do to make their lives easier. But I was just a kid.

"Beth was an amazing cellist. She dreamed of playing in a symphony someday, but she never got that chance. She died just before we were to graduate high school." My voice catches, my heart aching with old sorrow for my friend. "Before she died, Beth told me that she would've given anything to have her dream, even for one day. That's why my job is so important to me."

Startling me, he takes my arm and quickly pulls us into an alley. His searches my face, his hands resting on my hips pressing me to the brick wall. "Abby . . . Fuck it . . ."

My heart feels like it's going to burst out of my chest as he lowers his face, his eyes flashing pure sapphire fire. And when his lips touch mine . . . It's sheer perfection. My knees buckle, and I cling to his jacket as hugs me closer. I've never been kissed like this. His lips are smooth, warm and supple, but with firmness I feel all the way to my toes. He owns this kiss, taking as much as he's giving, and I'm lost. Absolutely lost to the sensations coursing through me. The stubble on his chin gently scrapes against my skin, but I don't care. It's not important. The fact that someone could discover us at any second isn't important. Breathing isn't important. But this kiss is *everything*.

"Jesus, Abby," he mutters when we finally break apart. We're both panting as if we've run a marathon, and maybe we have. I feel light-years beyond where we were when we'd left my office. His eyes are wide, giving him a lost and vulnerable look I haven't seen before on him. "What are you doing to me?"

"I . . . I was about to say the same." I can only manage a hoarse whisper, the shockwaves still reverberating in my heart. But then a thought pierces me, making me gasp.

Oh my God—what am I doing?

After all my indignation over what Nadia said and did. I'm no better than she is.

"Stop." His voice is just above a whisper, but it's as if he screamed it. An inarticulate noise escapes me, and I try to pull away, but he holds me fast. "No, I mean stop thinking whatever you're thinking," he says more forcefully. "Right now. This isn't wrong."

I try not to cringe in embarrassment. "Isn't it? I'm so sorry." I can't finish; I squeeze my eyes shut, wishing I could will the last few minutes away. But if I could, would I really want to? I'm not sure. I feel split open. More exposed than I've ever been, and I try again to step away. He lets me, but keeps a firm grip on my hand.

"Come on," he commands, pulling me along. I manage to move with more grace than I think I'm capable of at the moment, considering my legs feel like jelly.

"Wait—" I try to protest, but he surprises me by stopping again and placing his hand against my cheek.

"No more waiting." He gives me a searing look. "We need to talk."

chapter twelve

kennedy

"MY MOUTH IS ON FIRE!" Abby fans her hand in front of her mouth, and I pass her the bottle of water once more. "Holy God, that's hot!"

My gaze fixed on her lips, plump and full from the searing heat of the meal. "Heard that one before."

We're sitting together on a bench in one of the parks in Chinatown as she tries not to laugh, not to give anything away. It's hard to know what she's really thinking. But that kiss says more than words ever could. Even as we sit here, the subtle glances, the brush of her fingers against mine as we both reach for the next taste off our shared plate, the tension thick and heavy, swirls between us.

Despite all of this, she's been a pro at trying to ignore this pull between us. We've talked about the weather, my tour, her family, everything essentially, except what we need to.

"So, are we going to talk about this?" I motion between us, leaning back on the bench.

Her eyes widen, glancing down nervously at the dragon

design on the napkin in her lap. "We can't . . . I can't do this with you, Kennedy." Her voice is quiet and laced with doubt. A sea of doubt that I need to wade through or drown in.

"Can't or won't?" She's killing me with the intensity in those eyes.

"Do you know how it would look? If we . . . you know."

"I don't give a fuck how it would look." My voice is gritty, and I can feel the anger rise.

"But I do. I have to. This is more than just you and me. It's the reputation of the charity, and every single child's dream."

"Bullshit."

"It's not bullshit," she counters, righteous indignation blazing. "If something happened before everything was finished with Parker, it could look like I . . ."

I lean forward, my jaw clenched as I try to rein in my frustration. "Are you saying that no one would believe I'd want to be part of Parker's dream on my own? That somehow if we're together, that's the only reason I want to help? Some low expectations you've got there."

"You of all people know how the tabloids are . . . the rumors." She pauses, struggling to find the right words. "You're *you*. Not some no-name. I can't be splashed across the cover of some gossip rag." She quiets, but I can still hear the struggle there, and it gives me a glimmer of hope.

"You're allowed to be happy. Your life shouldn't be dictated by your job."

She lets out a huff. "Look who's talking."

"What's that supposed to mean?" I raise my voice.

"Rock star, your groupies, drinking, who knows what else. Are you telling me your life doesn't revolve around your job?" she asks pointedly.

"Just looping me in with all the clichés now, are you?" I bite back.

"I'm telling you like it is. It's what I saw that first day we met, and I don't think I need to remind you that *you're* the one who said you wanted to change."

"Yeah? Well, maybe I'm not the only one who needs to change." That shuts her up quickly. It looks like she's been slapped across the face with a reality check. I didn't think I'd ever see her at a loss for words, and I seize the rare moment, reaching for her hand. "Look at me and tell me you don't feel something. That you don't feel this."

Her scrutinizing gaze falters, and her eyes drop to linger on the path my thumb is tracing over her wrist. "I do feel something, but . . ."

"No buts. Don't think."

"I have to think. Everything that the charity has done, it could all go away because of a mistake." I can hear the passion in her words, but it stings to hear her say I'm a mistake.

"A mistake? Is that what you'd think this would be? You're allowed to have a life."

"Maybe it's not with you." Children squeal in excitement as they race around in the park, a reminder that we're not alone, and I can almost see her guard slam back into place.

"You're right. Maybe it's not, but you're not even going to give it a chance to find out? There's something here. I know it, and you're lying to yourself and to me if you say there isn't. And I'm not willing to walk away from you. I owe it to myself and to you."

She squints as if she's trying to read me and extracts her hand from mine. "How does this work exactly? I mean . . . with what happens when you're on the road? Are you going to try to tell me that the partying and groupies aren't part of this . . . part of what comes with you?"

"No. A lot of shit comes with me and the truth is that will

be there whether I'm with someone or not. But you are able to have a relationship in this business. I know, because I had one—a serious one for a couple of years. I was committed to her, and I never cheated on her. She's the one in the end who couldn't keep her legs shut."

Her pretty mouth drops open in disbelief or shock—it's hard to tell which. "All I'm saying is give me a chance. Give *us* a chance to see where this takes us. Walking away isn't an option."

She pauses, her big hazel eyes searching mine. "So, we're just going to skulk around the streets of San Francisco."

"Skulking gets a bad rap." She laughs, and I brush a strand of her hair behind her ear. "There's advantages to skulking. Back alleyways, hidden places to get lost together." Her eyes widen. "I can promise you one thing. When I'm with you, I'm with you. There won't be anyone else." She opens her mouth to speak, but I cut her off. "I get that you're scared. Hell, even without Parker and the charity in the mix, it's a risk. But no matter what happens with us, I promise you that I'll do the concert for him."

"Maybe we should talk about that before we make any other decisions."

She's an expert at deflecting, but I'm all too eager to indulge her. "I thought we could bring all sorts of bands in, satellite feeds for the ones on tour." She eyes me skeptically. "We can raise a lot of money, Abby. I know a ton of people in the industry, and most of them either owe me a favor, or would want to help. I want to treat him like a rock star. Pick him up in a limo, have a press conference. I want it to be something he'll never forget."

Any trace of tension from our earlier conversation is gone from her face, and she's practically beaming at me. "I love that you've thought about this, but it would take an enormous amount of work," she says tentatively, and I know she's testing me. It's one thing to throw around big ideas like this; it's quite another follow through with them.

"I have people. A whole team of them sitting around waiting for me to give them something to do." She grins, and I can feel our matched anticipation about the possibilities growing. "Let me do this for him. Please."

She's quiet for a minute. What I wouldn't give to be able to get inside her head. "Nadia isn't going to like this," she says finally.

"I'm pretty sure her ideas had less to do with Parker and more to do with getting me into bed." She shakes her head and grimaces. "But you know what? I don't really want to talk about her anymore."

♪ ♩ ♪ ♩

TURNING AWAY FROM A DISPLAY window of kitschy plastic Buddhas, I watch as Abby emerges from the Golden Gate Fortune Cookie shop. There's no shortage of places to get fortune cookies in Chinatown, but these are, hands down, the best.

We've been lucky today, and I haven't been noticed. A rarity for me. We're navigating a very precarious line, and that's actually fired the adrenaline of us both, not that I think she'd admit to it. There's something raw and edgy about the day, an undercurrent sparked by electric energy and heady anticipation.

She makes her way toward me, holding a bag high in the air like a victory flag, swaying it back and forth, beaming a smile. She has no idea what she does to me. She's real—hardly any makeup, her hair loosely framing her beautiful face, her guard down.

"How many did you eat before you came out of there?" I ask as she stops in front of me.

"I reserve the right to remain silent."

"They are damn good. Hand them over."

"Nope." This she says with a firm shake of her head. Little

tease.

"Nope? Did you just say nope?" She swallows hard, trying to bite back a laugh, her heated gaze locked to mine as I stalk toward her. The playfulness fades quickly from her eyes, morphing to something else entirely, something raw, and heated, and laced with desire.

Her tongue darts out to sweep along her lower lip, her back hitting the exterior brick wall of one of the small shops as I tower over her. I trace along her tempting bottom lip with my thumb. "Kennedy—" Her voice is breathy, and there's no way I'm letting her finish this lame protest.

I cup her cheek as my lips crush down to hers with a ferocity I don't recognize. I feel her grip my side, urging me closer, as I stoke her tongue with mine and press my torso against her soft curves. The muted activity from the street fades, and it's just her and me, and the deepening kiss that sets my body on fire. While I'm definitely leading, she's meeting me, answering each stroke of my tongue and sweep of my lips with her own, driving me out of my mind.

I slide my hand around her waist, squeezing her hip and pulling her flush against me, needing more—always more. Any restraint is gone. This is pure unadulterated desperation and desire. Her fingers twist through my hair, tugging feverishly. I can't stop the groan that vibrates through my chest as I claim her lower lip, pulling it roughly between my teeth.

Our ragged breaths mingle as I rest my forehead to hers, and she leans back against the unforgiving wall. With her heated gaze locked to mine, I can only manage three words. "Take me home."

"I DON'T USUALLY DO THIS," she says, not for the first time.

She's trying hard to maintain her composure, but I know it's slipping. Mine may be gone altogether as her hands shake trying to fit her key into the lock.

"I'd never judge you, you know." I can't seem to stop touching her, and this time my hand skims across her lower back, feeling the rich fabric of the trench coat beneath my fingers.

"I just don't want you to think that I do this all the time."

I lean forward, sliding my arm around her waist from behind, lowering my mouth under her ear. "Do what exactly?" I breathe her in, trying to keep myself in check, knowing the clock is ticking. This fucking tour couldn't come at a worse time. I'm due to fly to London in the morning. The thought of leaving her makes my chest tighten. This is all moving too slow and too fast at the same time. It's the constant dichotomy of my life.

She lets out a soft laugh, pushing the door open, and we stumble through, my grip faltering on the fortune cookie bag, causing the baked goodness to spread across her floor. "No!" she wails dramatically. "Anything but the fortune cookies."

With a laugh, I shut the door, effectively closing out the rest of the world. Finally. I have her to myself. "Ten second rule." I watch with a grin as she crouches down to rescue the cookies, placing them carefully back in the bag.

"I think I managed to save them." She folds the top of the bag over, offering me a nervous laugh before retreating to the direction of her kitchen. "Shit," she mumbles under her breath, and I watch as she swipes a wine bottle from her counter, stowing it under her sink.

Following her to the kitchen, I lean against the counter, amused at her change in demeanor. She's usually so sure of herself, so in control. "Why are you nervous all of a sudden?"

She turns to face me and toys with the belt on her coat. "Because it's been a while."

I make my way around the counter, stopping in front of her to cup her jaw and tilt her face to mine. "Hey. I don't care what we do. I just want to spend time with you, as long as we have. We can watch some mindless movie or listen to music. Just don't shut me out."

She swallows hard. "I know you're probably used to—"

I place my fingers over her tempting lips. "I'm not used to anything. So stop comparing yourself to people that don't exist."

She leans back slightly, trying to protest. "But . . ."

I press my thumb against her lower lip. "I think I have a solution to these wild ideas you have about me." She narrows her eyes at me. "Come with me to London."

abigail

"LONDON?" I MANAGE TO SQUEAK. "When?"

"Our plane leaves tomorrow morning. It's the first leg of the tour. We're spending a week there to rehearse more before the opener. Then it's Paris and Madrid. Oh, and I think we're squeezing Cologne in there somewhere before we head to Australia."

I shake my head, relieved he removes his thumb; I can't think straight with the taste of him on my lips. "Kennedy, I can't just up and fly to London on a whim." He can't be serious, can he? "Do you have any idea what my schedule is like right now? I just got back from New York. Tess is probably having a fit right now trying to reschedule the stuff I had this afternoon that I blew off to be with you." I feel a pang of guilt at that. It's so unlike me. It's small potatoes compared to abandoning everything to fly to another continent for an indeterminate period.

"It's not a whim," he argues. The feel of his hands as they grip my hips and pull me against his hard frame again is almost my undoing. "You need to know I'm serious about my plans for Parker, as well as my hopes for you, and for us. The best way to do that is for you to see it with your own eyes. *Come with me.*"

His voice lowers to a husky purr that reverberates inside my heart, knocking down my defenses and taking up residence. I suck in a ragged breath at the feel of his scruff brushing across my cheek. He tugs at the belt of my coat, letting out a small grunt of triumph when the stubborn fabric comes loose. Although he releases my waist to work on the buttons, he keeps contact between us by pressing his forehead to mine. In an instant, he's slipping the coat off my shoulders and fisting the supple wool jersey of my dress.

"I like this," he hums softly. "It's almost as soft as your skin." I cling to his jacket as if I'll collapse without it, and I'm not sure that's far from the truth. In just a couple of hours, this man has completely rattled me. I don't know which way is up. All afternoon, every touch of his hand against mine, every searing look has stoked the fire he lit within me with that kiss.

That *kiss*.

Never have I been kissed like that before. First in the alley, and then again outside the bakery. The exquisite blend of strength and softness, of passion and restraint, almost brought me to my knees. The nerves I felt when we walked in my apartment disappear, but my sense of propriety makes one last stand. "It's not that I don't want to go with you. I just—"

"Just nothing," he interrupts huskily, his lips brushing my cheek and sending a shiver down my spine. "You deserve a life, and I'll keep reminding you of that." He abruptly pushes me away from his body, but holds my waist in a firm grip.

"Unless there's someone else. Tell me now if there is." He gives me a hard look. "I've already told you I won't go down that road again if you're playing both sides against the middle."

My heart twinges at the vulnerability lurking beneath the wariness in his eyes. It's inconceivable to me that someone would ever cheat on him. His former girlfriend is clearly an idiot. "No! I would never do that." I hope he hears the sincerity in my words. "There's no one else." I whisper before his lips claim mine again.

My heart beats a rapid tattoo to accompany the struggle in my head. All my clear-cut ethical boundaries have become blurry. Would it really be so wrong to let myself have this? He's said he's serious about me and his desire to help Parker. The two things don't need to be mutually exclusive, do they?

I deserve a life.

Suddenly, I don't care about should dos or could dos. I dig my fingers into his thick hair to pull him closer and am rewarded when he lets out a guttural moan. Grabbing the collar of his jacket, I force him back a pace and peel it off him, letting it join my coat on the floor. His light sweater stretches enticingly over his chest and biceps. But my scrutiny is interrupted when he grabs my ass and lifts, forcing me to wrap my arms and legs around him. I gasp at the hardness of his erection pressed between us.

"Are you sure?" he mutters against my lips. "I meant what I said; we can just watch crap TV or—"

"I'm sure."

"Thank fuck." He spins us and carries me out of the kitchen, not giving me a chance to change my mind. "Bedroom?"

"Down there . . ." I wave in the direction of the hallway, but my mumble cuts off when he squeezes my ass hard. I frantically try to remember if I'd picked up at all this morning before leaving for work. It's bad enough that my wine bottle from yesterday was still sitting out in the kitchen—I'll die if my vibrator isn't tucked away in its drawer. After tossing me on my bed, he pauses only to kick off his Doc Martens before he's on me, giving me no chance to worry further.

His lips meander from my ear to the base of my throat,

driving me wild. My hands can't decide where they want to be—I want to touch everything at once—his soft hair that curls deliciously around my fingers, his broad shoulders, and the scruff on his face. I can't believe this is happening; that he's here with me. That he *wants* to be here with me, and not some hot model somewhere. Whatever—it's their loss.

"I really like these boots." He runs his hands over the buttery-soft leather, from my ankles to my knees. He toys with the zipper for a second, and then he decisively unzips one, and then the other.

"But . . ." I'm trying not to pout as he slips each boot off and tosses them on the floor. I had delightful visions of those heels digging into his. But then his strong hands caress my feet, shins, and higher, causing a yearning moan to escape me.

A low chuckle rumbles in his chest. "We'll leave them on next time." He carefully rolls my thigh highs down each of my legs in a slow, sensuous tease. Holy shit. I'm on fire with anticipation.

When I feel his hands at the belt of my dress, I eagerly tug at his sweater to pull it off, but he gently bats my hands away. Then he leans down and kisses my confused pout.

"Now, now, Miss Walker." His lips brush mine. "I bet you're one of those people who rips their presents open the minute they get them, aren't you? No patience for the big reveal." His husky tone, full of promise, makes me shiver. "Me, on the other hand. I'm all about savoring my gifts. I like to unwrap them slowly and enjoy the build up."

Is he kidding me? He's the one who was all "I want to try," and "Come to London with me," and now he puts on the brakes? "Seriously? You seem like more of an in-the-moment guy," I complain, although my breathy tone ruins the snark. He huffs a laugh.

"Not gonna lie, there's a time and place for hard fucking."

My heart stops for a beat, and I can't help my gasp. "But right now? All I want to do is take my time with you."

Dead. Honestly—how am I still breathing right now? All my snappy comebacks fail me as I lay there, gripping his hard thighs desperately and panting with eagerness, as he leisurely unties my belt and pulls open my dress, exposing my black lacy bra. "Fuck," he groans in appreciation, drawing his fingertip across the top of each of my breasts, leaving a fiery trail in his wake.

"See, it wasn't all business for me in New York. You should see the other things I bought."

He huffs a laugh. "I want to, believe me." He cups and massages me over the lace, making my blood race. Suddenly reaching around me, he abruptly pulls me up against his chest.

He kisses me possessively, as if his lips are trying to brand themselves on my skin. Slipping my dress off my shoulders, he unclasps my bra and flings it across the room. My giggle dies in my throat when he drops me back down and takes my nipple in his mouth. It's like there's a live wire connecting it to my clit, and I arch off the mattress. His hands join in the fun, kneading and pinching. Suddenly, I don't care about his "savor the gift" plan. I just want to *feel* him.

I grab the hem of his sweater and tug hard. He gets the message and leaves his worship of my chest long enough to sit back on his heels and pull the fabric up over his head. And what I see renders me speechless.

The hint of ink I saw on his wrist when I first met him has tantalized me for weeks. But now that it's finally revealed, I know nothing could've prepared me for the sheer perfection that is a shirtless Kennedy Lane. He's leanly muscled, with well-defined pecs, a flat belly, and strong arms that show the long hours of wielding his guitar. But my eyes are drawn to the intricate lines of ink that trail down his left arm. Beginning with a few strands curling up over his shoulder near the rose on his neck, before twisting down and around his forearm to the edge of his wrist, is a piece of music, complete with treble and bass clefs, and notes scattered along a set of whimsical staves. It's beautiful work, with precise shading that makes it resemble a grayscale photo rather than a tattoo. Woven between the lines are a few stylized red roses that provide bursts of color amongst the black and gray. Reaching up, I tentatively trace a few notes, my eyes roving over his arm in wonder.

"Amazing."

He snorts, as if disputing my opinion, and covers me with his body again. What follows is sheer bliss . . . hands, lips, and limbs moving together to create a perfect symphony of sensations. Murmured words of appreciation blend with the faint noise of the traffic down on the street below. Kissing his shoulder, I savor the salty taste of his skin, and I fear I'll never get enough of him. His lips travel from my throat to my chest, my belly, and beyond, leaving me quaking. He helps me slide my lace underwear off, and then shucks his jeans. Oh. Oh my. He's gone commando and . . . wow.

Everything down south clenches in delicious anticipation.

He kneels over me and deftly rolls a condom over his impressive length. When I look back at his face, the intensity of his gaze leaves me mute. He teases my swollen clit with his fingers, making me squirm, and his eyes darken. "Kennedy . . ." His name slipping from my lips seems to trigger him. With no further warning, thrusts deep inside me.

"Fuck, yeah," he growls as I gasp. My God . . . He feels incredible. It's been so long since I last . . . but it's so, so good. With a long, drawn out groan, he slowly slides out, leaving me panting, before slamming back into me. I cry out in surprise, and he looks at me with alarm.

"Are you okay?" His eyes show his relief as I nod quickly, a beatific smile blooming on my face.

"God, yes, yes. Please . . . don't stop." My whimpered plea is cut off by a searing kiss. Pinning my hand against the mattress, he clutches my opposite hip and sets a driving pace; plunging into me again and again. He's hitting spots that haven't been touched in forever, and my body responds with fervor. It's like being awakened from a deep, deep sleep to the most glorious of sunrises.

He nuzzles my neck, and I groan at the sensual feel of his stubble grazing my skin. "You feel so fucking good," he rumbles. He hooks a hand under my knee and abruptly pushes it up almost to my shoulder, making me yelp in surprise at how much deeper it feels. "That's right, baby. Let me hear it. I need to hear you."

"Oh my God . . . Kennedy, I . . ." I have no idea what I'm saying. My heart is pounding a mile a minute, and I'm rising, higher and higher . . . and then I shatter, a strangled groan erupting from me.

"Oh, thank Christ" he breathes in anguished relief, before his tone changes, sounding almost panicked. Abruptly, he stiffens, his fingers digging into my flesh almost painfully, as he comes with a loud cry. He is stunning in his release: eyes squeezed shut, jaw clenched, the tendons standing out on his neck. Even in my dazed state, his primal beauty is magnificent.

His breath comes in short, hard pants, and he's practically quivering beneath my fingertips. "You are so fucking beautiful." His voice is raw, which matches the feelings surging within me. He collapses on me for a moment while we both catch our breaths before he rolls to the side to remove the condom. Blearily, I notice that there's a short strip of them lying next to us on the bed; he must have come prepared. I frown with the realization that he has much more occasion to use them than I do. It's part of the rock star mantra, right? After all, it's not *chastity*, drugs, and rock 'n roll.

Rolling back to gather me in his arms, he smooths my hair away from my face. "What? Are you okay?" Am I okay? Physically, I'm much more than okay. Ecstatic is closer to the mark. I smile, wanting to ease his worried expression, and snuggle into his embrace. I shut out all thoughts of the inevitable other women. I knew whom and what he was when I took him to my bed. I have no regrets.

"I was just wondering if you always are prepared," I joke, gesturing to the strip lying not so innocently next to us. He smirks, looking uncomfortable, and I'm surprised to see a faint flush on his cheeks as he pulls me closer.

"I promise I didn't have any expectations. Since I met you, I've had no expectations for anyone else, either. But before that... Well, let's just say they've been standard equipment for me since I broke into the business. It, uh, kind of goes with the territory. I always use a glove." He actually looks a little embarrassed for a moment, until I lean up and kiss him.

"You don't have to explain yourself to me. It's not my business. I'm sorry, I was just teasing." I smile wryly. "I should actually thank you. I wasn't thinking about protection, which is *really* out of character for me."

"From what I've seen so far, you seem to be extraordinarily skilled in protecting yourself from all things." A crease forms between his brows as he tucks a strand of hair behind my ear. "Until now, at least."

"I don't need to be protected from you." I pause, hoping against hope that my statement is true. "But I need to keep some separation in my head between my working relationship with you and my other relationship with you. Or friendship. Or whatever we're going to call this." I bite my lips to stop blather-ing and look away, feeling incredibly awkward.

"Hey," He cups my cheek, drawing my attention. "You can call it a relationship, because that's what it is or what it can be. But if it's easier for you, don't label it at all. We can just be. I want to try with you. If all you want is this one time . . ." A frown flickers across his face. "All I'm saying is that I want more, howev-er you need it to be. I can't be plainer than that."

I can't help my shy smile; he's right. He's been incredibly up-front about what he wants, and what he's willing to do. Whether it's for me, or Parker, or for himself, it doesn't really matter. He says he'll be faithful—I simply have to believe him. "I know. I'm sorry I sound so conflicted. I just have to work a few things out in my head." I reach up and brush my fingers lightly through the smattering of his chest hair. "But I'm not sorry for this, Kennedy. Not sorry at all."

I can see more than a little relief in his eyes before his con-fident grin returns. He dips his head and I feel his lips brush my ear. "Good. Because I'm hoping we can use up a few more of those suckers before I leave."

WHEN I OPEN MY EYES, it's dark in the room and the traffic sounds like it's picked up outside. I have no idea what time it is. Kennedy sits on the edge of the bed, muttering into his phone. "Calm the fuck down, Tucker. Yeah, okay. Fine. I know. I'm not going to the meeting. Fuck, they can email me. It's not like I ha-ven't heard it all before." His shoulders tense as he listens for a moment. "Thanks, man . . . Yeah, bright and early. See you then."

He tosses the phone onto my bedside table as his shoulders slump in defeat. Sitting up, I wrap my arms around him, pressing my front to his back, and place a soft kiss to his neck. He hums contentedly and reaches back to weave his fingers into my hair.

"Hey," he greets me softly. "Sorry, I didn't want to wake you."

"S'okay." We're quiet for a few moments, simply enjoying the feel of sitting wrapped up in each other amongst the rumpled sheets. "Is everything okay with the call?"

He leans back against me. "Yeah. I'm supposed to have a meeting tonight, since we're leaving at the crack of dawn tomorrow."

"I don't want to keep you," I lie, my nerves suddenly making an appearance.

"Don't worry about it. It's not a big deal." He kisses me on the cheek, and then turns sharply to bury his face into my neck and pull me into a fierce hug. Tears spring to my eyes, but I'm not sure why.

"Are you all right? Kennedy?"

"I'm fine." He pulls back and smiles at me shyly. "I'm perfect, actually. You?"

With a happy little sigh, I pull him close again. I can't remember feeling as thoroughly satisfied, more content, or more . . . "Better than perfect."

He chuckles quietly. "Yes, you are." With another soft kiss, he eases me down to the bed once more, and I'm able to appreciate the tattoos that wrap around his arm.

"What is it? The music." I trail my fingers along his decorated arm.

He looks away for a moment, his lips pursed. "It's one of my first compositions. It was one of Robin's favorites."

The pain I saw when he spoke of his sister in New York flashes in his eyes, and my heart aches for him. "It's beautiful. I'd love to hear it sometime." He gives me a soft smile, and brushes a strand of my hair behind my ear.

"I'd love to play it for you sometime."

Suddenly, he grabs me by the waist and pulls me on top of him, looking at me with anxious eyes. "Come with me," he pleads. I melt against him, but he must see the hesitation in my face.

"Kennedy . . ." My mind is a jumble of my upcoming schedule and the obligations I have. Plus, there's still Nadia to deal with.

"Never mind. It was just an idea." His voice is cool, detached, but before I can say anything, his hand drifts down my back to palm over my ass, squeezing tightly. "I knew there was a wild side lurking beneath that demure demeanor," he says, effectively changing the subject. I let him.

"What made you so sure?" I shoot back, pushing against the heat of his palm.

His lips linger on the curve of my neck, and I close my eyes, savoring the feeling. "Call it a hunch. Let's explore that some more, hmm?"

"I DIDN'T MEAN TO WAKE you." Kennedy's sleepy, warm voice drifts to me, and I tighten my arm around his waist, snuggling closer to the warmth of his body. A girl could get used to waking up like this. His fingers lazily trail up my back, and I feel the goose bumps rise, my mind spinning with the events of last night.

"Okay, so I did mean to wake you," he mumbles, gripping my chin, tilting my face up, and lowers his lips to mine. His lips are supple and warm, and my pulse quickens. My hands close around his wrists and we hold each other in place, locked in a sweet kiss, until his phone starts to buzz from the nightstand. Slowly, he breaks the kiss, but gives me three short pecks, as if he can't quite bring himself to finish.

Reaching over to quiet the phone, he groans, setting it back down to the nightstand. "That's Tucker. He's here." He glances up at the ceiling, a frown pulling at his lips.

My heart twinges and I grip his bicep reflexively. "Morning came too quickly," I whisper, and finally release him. His gaze softens.

"I'm not saying good-bye," he says, his voice sure. "I'll be gone for a while, but there's always Skype, right? The time differences will be a bitch, but we'll figure it out."

I swallow thickly as he traces his fingers over my lips. "Of course we will." This is for the best . . . So why am I feeling so desolate?

"You sure I can't convince you to come with me?" His warm breath covers my skin, his lips skimming over my neck making me dizzy as they did so many times last night.

"I can't go to London with you," I whisper, the weight of my responsibilities pressing down on me.

His phone buzzes again as he takes a playful swat of my ass, surprising me. "I really have to go. The jet is waiting."

"If I had a dime for every time I heard that one."

Laughing, he slips from the bed, searching the floor for his clothes. Now that I'm finally able to check out my bedroom, I'm relieved to see nothing incriminating lying around. Pulling on a pair of sweatpants and a Cal Bears hoodie, I turn in time to see him pull his jeans on.

He smiles at me, and jams his feet in his boots. I follow him as he saunters out and down the hall to the kitchen. Retrieving our coats from the kitchen floor, he hands me mine with a smug smile. It's clear evidence of my impetuous need from last night, and my cheeks heat at the reminder. He's probably had scores of women throw themselves at him. Thankfully, he doesn't belabor the point.

I toss my coat on my sofa, and when I get back to the front door, I see he's ready to go. He's looking at his phone with a pensive expression on his face. With a sigh, he tucks his phone into the pocket of his jeans. "Fuck this timing sucks." He steps closer, framing my face between his hands. My heart hammers as he lowers his lips to mine for one last kiss.

"Do me a favor . . ." he whispers, his fingers brushing over my cheeks.

"Mmmm?"

"Miss me just a little."

I'm reeling, dazed from the kiss, from the thought of him leaving, but before I can respond, he opens my door and moves toward the elevator. "Don't come down with me, just in case. You never know if the paparazzi are following the SUV or not." He looks down at his boots. "Call me if you change your mind."

"I can't go with you," I whisper. He nods; his face is impassive, but I can see the disappointment in his eyes. The bell dings and he instantly releases me to step into the steel chamber. And as the doors begin to slide shut, my heart lurches. Because everything he was saying earlier is right. I *do* deserve a life.

I grab the doors to stop them and look into his startled face as the words tumble out of me impulsively. "But, I'll meet you there."

chapter thirteen

kennedy

"YOU'RE REALLY NOT STAYING WITH us?" Cam complains as he stretches his legs out against one of the sofas in the Extreme Wow suite at the W. That's the actual name of the suite—Extreme Wow. Not pretentious at all.

"I'm really not."

"You are a killjoy, man. Jesus, what are you, seventy?" Cam tilts his head back against the cushions, staring up at the recessed silver disco ball in the ceiling.

"You'll never even miss me."

"Who will be my wingman?" Cam asks.

"Matty here seems more than capable."

Matt shuffles his way through the suite, depositing himself into the hanging bubble chair facing the picture window.

"I claim this for the week," he announces, curling up against the red cushions.

"What happens when you find the love of your life again, hmm, grasshopper?" asks Sean as he peers out the window to the bustling square below.

Matt opens one eye with a snort. "What's your point?"

"Don't you want a room? That thing is out here in the open for everyone to see," Cam chimes in.

Matt shrugs his shoulders, relaxing in the chair. "That's never stopped me before."

"And you wonder why I want to stay away from this train wreck." I snap off a picture of Cam sprawled out on the couch.

"Must be some fantastic pussy, man." Cam turns his attention back to me.

I narrow my eyes at him in warning. "Don't."

He lifts his hands up in mock surrender. "Just sayin'."

"There's a DJ station," Sean hollers from across the room. "You should've brought your vinyls, Lane."

"I think he's more concerned about rubbers." Cam chucks a pillow at my head.

"Is that why you're ditching us?" Sean moves to check out the bar area.

"We're not in high school, asshole." I toss the pillow back at Cam. "And I'm not ditching you. I just want a change of scenery."

"Yeah. Scenery involving one hot chick." Matt spins around in the bubble chair to grin at me.

"She's not just some chick."

"She's going to have to meet us at some point, mate. We're your family, after all." Sean appears at my side, draping his arm around my shoulder.

"I know. It's just . . . It's complicated." I shrug him off, desperate to get away from this whole scene.

"Isn't it always?" Sean muses, dropping to the couch beside Cam.

"Like I said, she's the director of the charity I was telling you guys about. So, you need to be discreet. If you can."

"A little pleasure mixed with business, yeah? Good on you,"

Sean says.

"She's different."

"Meaning what? A magical pussy? Three tits?" Cam teases.

"I dated a girl with three tits once back in the day. Interesting. I should give her a ring, actually." Sean pulls his phone from the back pocket of his jeans, scrolling through his endless list of contacts.

"Must be something magical to take you away from the brilliance of us," Brodie adds, glancing at me from the side of the bar.

"I'm not even sure when she's coming."

"So, stay here tonight at least then! Come on, it'll be like old times. Remember the '01 tour?" Cam asks.

The memory bank is relatively empty for '01. "Some of it. Parts are . . . missing of that one."

"I'm not surprised. We were shitfaced for most of it. Fuck, that was awesome," Cam says through a laugh.

"Brodie? We need entertainment, my good man. Lots of it," Sean hollers from the sofa.

"No. We really don't. At least I don't. You guys are welcome to it." I wander over to the windows, glancing down to the bustling square below. London is always alive, pulsing with energy no matter what time of day.

"Two words for you—pussywhipped," Cam states, and I flip him off.

"Is that actually two words or one word with a hyphen, Three?" Sean asks. Abby is going to have a field day with these two.

"I'm not sure if there is a hyphen. We should look it up. You got Wi-Fi working on that thing?" Cam hops up from the couch and darts for my phone.

I tug it out of his reach. "Use your own damn phone. And

we don't need to look up anything. Jesus."

"Why is she even coming?" Brodie asks pointedly.

I scowl at Brodie. "It's none of your fucking business. Why do you care?"

"I care about you, idiot. I've seen you go through this before. You think she's any different than any of the other whores you've been with? That she's different from Michelle?"

"You don't know a goddamn thing about Michelle."

"You'd be surprised what I know." He leers, narrowing his eyes.

"Nothing surprises me anymore, particularly where you're concerned."

"Who was there to pick up the pieces when you two broke up?" he asks, his voice gritty. I'm not much taller than Brodie, but right now, he looks weak and small, like a punk kid who doesn't know when to shut up. "Or how about after Robin? Who was there for you then?"

The thin thread I've been holding onto snaps, and I grip his leather jacket, pushing him back against the table. "You didn't know a thing about—" I feel my heart shudder at the mention of Robin, my fists tightening against the leather. "Don't you dare say her name."

"Kennedy." I hear Cam's voice drift to me. "Come on, man. We're here to celebrate the start of the tour." He moves beside me, trying ineffectively to push his arm between us.

"Look at you, you still can't even talk about her," Brodie sneers. "I can see what's going to happen here. Fuck, if you want a piece of ass, there's plenty to go around."

His flippant comment just about sends me over the edge, and I try to shoulder Cam out of the way. "You don't know the first thing about what I want. Do your job and keep your mouth shut. I'm not going to warn you again."

"Everybody just relax. We're exhausted, and more importantly, we need the group photo for the Instagram account. The world awaits our glorious presence in my homeland," Sean orders steering me away from Brodie.

"How did you get access to the Instagram account, anyway?" Cameron asks.

Sean nudges him in the ribs. "Because I'm a ray of sunshine, unlike you."

"Grasshopper, make room!" Sean yells, crawling into Matt's lap and causing the hanging bubble chair to swing.

"Will that hold you both?" Tucker asks.

"It had better if Matty plans on enjoying quality time in it. Gather 'round."

Cam snorts out a laugh, leaning against one side of the chair while I take the front. Always the frontman. The burden, the spotlight, the criticisms, the accolades, they all fall to me first. Sean passes his phone to Cam, and he holds it out. Trying to frame us in the shot is easier said than done, with the chair constantly swaying. "Jesus. It's like we're drunk already. Say mother-fucking cheese," Cam instructs.

We all yell the words in tandem, the flash blinding me slightly in the dimly lit room.

"Now, time to celebrate selling out this first leg of the tour in style!" Sean yells, pushing off Matt and moving to the bar.

Tucker drifts beside me. "Ready to go? Remember that thing for Abby?" Tucker asks while I try to ignore the questioning glances of my bandmates. I know exactly what Tucker's plan is: get me away from temptation.

"See? Pussywhipped!" Sean shouts, but I glance at my phone regardless.

It's been hours since I texted Abby when we landed, and I shouldn't be disappointed about the delay in her response, but I am. I scowl, reading her message.

Glad you made it safe. I'm just heading out for the night.

In other words, don't bother me? A wave of unease rolls through me. Heading out for the night can mean a million different things. Some other guy? Or maybe it's just with friends or her family. It's hard not to jump to conclusions when you've been burned and have the lingering scars to prove it.

I try to tame the rising annoyance, typing out a reply.

Enjoy it.

Lifting my gaze to Tucker, I turn away quickly from the bar. "We should go." Before I do something I'll regret.

I STARE UP AT THE intimidating century-old church, my heart in my throat. Ivy climbs the walls, massive wooden double doors wait to be opened. There's a marble statue of an angel beckoning me inside. "You really think this is going to help?" I ask Tucker, as we sit in the back of the SUV. A new phase in Tucker's plan that he's been on me about—AA meetings—is about to begin.

"I think you don't want go to rehab." He pauses, frowning a bit. "You were right about that actually. It didn't help the last time."

"I'm sorry, what was that? Did you just say I was right?" I tease him, if only to delay the inevitable.

"It's an open meeting. Anyone can attend, and I can go with you this time. You don't have to do this alone."

Raking my hand through my hair, I stare back at him, feeling my jaw tense. "You really think I'm an alcoholic?"

"It doesn't matter what I think. It matters what you think."

"You've been reading the AA website again, haven't you?"

"You must remember the questions they ask," he challenges. "Have you ever have blackouts? Have you told yourself you can stop drinking but keep getting trashed anyway? Have you tried to stop drinking but plowed through a bottle of Jack the next day?"

"Fuck! Enough, all right? You've made your point." I peer out the window, taking a shaky breath. "And yes, I've read the website. Repeatedly."

"Look, Kennedy, I can pick you up and bring you home as many damn times as it takes. I can tell you not to take a drink. I can run you ragged on a treadmill until you're too tired to do anything but collapse into bed. But, I can't help you with this. I have no idea what it's like for you." He nods his head at the massive church. "They do. They've all been there."

"One step at a time they say, right?"

"Right."

I push open the door to the SUV and take that first step.

"YOU WANT TO TALK ABOUT tonight?" Tucker asks as we cruise the streets.

"Nope."

"All right, then." He turns to gaze out the darkened window of the SUV. I know he wants to go over the AA meeting and what it means, but I'm totally drained. I didn't say a word in that church. Just sat and listened, and what I heard is going to stick with me for a long time. The words run on a loop in my head. *"I lost everything . . . It destroyed my family . . . I thought I knew what rock bottom was."*

Given what I've read, and the articles Tucker insists on leaving me nearly every day, I know this road is a long one. A lifetime commitment. Tonight was just the beginning.

We stop in front of the hotel, and Tucker scans the area before pushing open the door and letting me out. I take a much-needed breath as we head into the lobby. "It's going to change things, me not staying with the band."

He turns back to me. "Change can be a good thing."

"Sean's right, though. We are family. I'm not going to be able to just shut them out. I don't want to."

Tucker studies me for a moment as we wait at the check in desk. "You know what I've found over the years? Sometimes family isn't good for you."

♪ ♩ ♪ ♩

abigail

I HAVE TROUBLE KEEPING THE grin off my face as I peer out my office window. Even Hank the gripman commented on my chipper mood. I actually managed to beat Tessa into the office—a rarity. However, after my early, but oh-so-welcome wake-up call, I'd decided to just come in and face the day. I'll have to get my game face on before she gets here and begins her inquisition.

With a blissful sigh, I close my eyes and think about yesterday. The feel of his hands gliding over my skin, his warm, spicy scent, and the sound of his voice whispering and panting in my ear. Nothing could've prepared me for him. It was like being consumed, possessed even, but also *treasured*, like I was a rare treat he was honored to have. He was breathtaking.

A shiver of desire, mixed with a bit of fear, runs through me, and I take a deep, steadying breath. God, I hope I'm not making a mistake.

I hear Tess's purse drop on her desk, and I know my respite is over. "What the heck happened to you yesterday?" She stands in my doorway with her hands on her hips. "The rock god shows up, Nadia makes an ass of herself, you leave with said rock god, and all I get is a text later saying to cancel the rest of your appointments for the day?" Her exasperated voice is climbing through her upper registers.

"Yes; what the hell, Abby?" April chimes in as she brushes past Tess and seats herself on my sofa with an expectant look on her face.

"Erm, well . . ." All my prepared explanations evaporate, leaving me struggling to maintain my usual placid demeanor. Based on their shocked and eager expressions, I'm sucking at it.

"Oh, my God," April breathes, her eyes lighting up behind her chic glasses. "It's true, isn't it? You and Lane have a thing."

Tess's eyes practically bug out of her head as I scramble to find words.

"No—I mean, we didn't, at least not until yesterday after-noon. It was purely business until—"

"Until it wasn't," April finishes for me. Shaking her head, a small, amused smile on her lips, she sits back and crosses her legs, smoothing her immaculate trousers. "Okay, let's have it. Not *everything*," she cautions, seeing my alarmed expression. "But I need to know the basics so I can prepare in case we need a state-ment of some kind."

I tuck a stray hair that has escaped behind my ear with a sigh. She's right. I don't know where Kennedy and I are headed, but I'm pretty sure we'll be exposed in the press eventually, prob-ably sooner than later. It's always better to be prepared.

"It's as I've explained previously. All my interactions with Kennedy, up until yesterday afternoon, were business-relat-ed. We discussed my earlier concerns about his involvement, Parker's health and his dream, and—oh, April, he's got some fan-tastic ideas," I blurt, my grin escaping. "In addition to his person-al interaction with Parker, he wants to pull some other names together for a benefit concert. I mean big names—Bono, the Foo Fighters. Even Ed Sheeran. It could be incredible—one of the biggest things we've ever done. If he can pull it off, it'll give

Parker the thrill of a lifetime." My voice rings with excitement; I can't wait to see Parker's face when he actually meets Kennedy, and I'm hoping that he'll be well enough to enjoy it.

She blinks in surprise, and I can almost see the wheels turning in her head. "Holy . . . That would be amazing, for Parker and for the foundation. Sheeran and the Foo would be a great draw among the millennials." But then she cocks her head and looks at my slyly. "Stop distracting me. We were talking about *you* and Lane."

"Well, you see, we just . . ." I flounder, while watching their matching grins grow with every passing second. "We were talking about all his ideas, and then . . ." I can feel my face heating to thermonuclear levels.

"Holy shit." Tess looks like she's about to pass out. "Did you—"

"Not our business," April cuts in, giving me a wink, and my shoulders slump in relief. "Is there anything else we *do* need to know?"

"Um, yes, actually. I'm going to take a few days off to go to London for a few days." My voice drops to a mumble while I squirm under their scrutiny.

"He's asked you to go on tour?" Tess squeaks, and I frown at her.

"No, of course not. It's just a few days, no more than a week—"

"But, Abby," she practically whines. "If you're only going for a few days, why go at all then?"

"Because he invited her, obviously," April sums up. "And that's all we really need to know right now, right?" I smile at her gratefully and feel some of my anxiety wane.

"Right," I say, trying to get back to business. "So, Tess, can you please get my appointment list so we can start deciding how to reschedule the next few days?"

She immediately disappears back to her desk where I can hear her firing up her computer. Casting a glance out my still-open office door, April quickly rises and shuts it before turning back to me. I tense, worrying what is going on behind her intense gaze. But then, she chuckles. "Nadia is going to lose her shit."

I smile grimly at the reminder. "What happened after we left?" I sit on the edge of my desk, facing her. My consternation increased as she rolls her eyes.

"You mean, after she had her ass handed to her by a client?" April's dry tone crackles. "What do you expect? She walked out with her face flaming redder than yours is now, completely ignoring Tess and me, and stalked back to her office. She left for the rest of the day, probably so she could start working on her resume."

"She quit?" I ask with surprise. Shit, if she quit, there would be no way I could go to London. *Not that my schedule was the most important consideration*, I quickly scold myself.

"Hell, no," she retorts with a derisive snort. "But I wouldn't be surprised if she thinks her term here is tenuous at best. You know Nadia—she'd rather leave on her own than be fired for cause."

"What are you going to do?" April looked at me seriously. "I mean, Nadia was totally out of line, but she's . . ."

"I know. She's incredible at her job." Besides this one instance, I've never known Nadia to step over the line with a client. We've all acknowledged how handsome various donors have been over the years, but none of us has ever acted like that. It was completely out of character for her. I feel a twinge of guilt—how is what I've done any different? I skipped right over eyefucking and cleavage flashing to jump right into bed with a client.

Except . . . It *is* different, damn it, even though I'm not sure I really want to examine the reasons why right now.

"You obviously have to address it. I still can't believe she was that stupid." April shakes her head. "What else do you have planned?"

"I asked for an appointment with Ralph for today."

She nods in approval. "Good move. If you have him behind you, she won't get any traction, in case she hasn't come to her senses yet."

"That was my thought, too."

April moves back to my door, pausing with her hand on the knob. "Have Tess assign whatever meetings to me that you need to move. Just be careful," she says quietly, her dark eyes concerned. "I'm happy for you, truly. Despite whatever seeds of doubt Nadia was trying to sow out of jealousy, no one is going to question your motives. But the kind of crazy that surrounds Lane and Redfall is on a whole different level than the usual celebrity bullshit. Not that you can't handle it, but just be careful."

"MR. SHEPHERD WILL SEE YOU now, Ms. Walker." I smile my thanks at the middle-aged receptionist and stand, tugging my suit jacket down. This conversation could be beyond awkward, but it needs to be done. I won't have anything hanging over my head.

Straightening my shoulders, I steel myself and swing open the heavy office door. Ralph Shepherd, CEO of one of California's largest financial brokers and the president of *What's Your Dream*'s board of directors, greets me with a cordial smile. "Abigail. So nice to see you. What was so urgent? How can I help?"

I smile automatically, but don't allow myself to relax. Ralph has always been one of my biggest supporters, but I have no idea how he's going to react to my news. "Thank you for making time for me on such short notice, Ralph. I'm heading overseas for a few days, but need to apprise you of a certain situation before I leave."

"In person?" He raises his bushy, iron-gray eyebrows in mild surprise. "All right. Please, sit down." He gestures to the small grouping of chairs gathered around a low table at one end of his spacious office. Once we're comfortably arranged across from each other, I take a deep breath and dive in.

"You may recall from our last meeting that we went over the most recent list of dreams in progress. One of those dreams is for a boy named Parker Jensen." I pause as Ralph glances up at the ceiling thoughtfully.

"Oh, yes," he comments, remembering. "The boy with the rock-and-roll dream, right?"

I nod. "Yes. His dream is to meet his idol, Kennedy Lane, the lead singer for Redfall. As I think I mentioned during the meeting, I wasn't sure at first if Mr. Lane would be the most suitable candidate. However, Mr. Lane assures me that our trust in him won't be misplaced, and he's working on several things that I think would be fantastic for Parker." I quickly outline some of Kennedy's ideas, and am pleased to see Ralph's impressed expression.

"Sounds wonderful. I won't pretend to understand all the ins and outs of the music industry, but it sounds great." He gives me an appraising look. "Why do I think there's more to the story?"

"Yes." I swallow down my sudden nerves. "Well, during the course of discussions regarding Parker's dream, Kennedy and I, um . . ."

"*Kennedy?*" Ralph's eyes narrow. My palms start sweating, but I keep on going.

"Um, yes. We've become, um, quite friendly and I feel that, in the spirit of transparency and full disclosure, I need to let you know about our, um, friendship. You see, he's the reason I'm taking a vacation—an unscheduled vacation—for a few days."

He braces his elbows on the arms of his chair and steeples his fingertips in front of him. "I see," he rumbles, his face impassive.

"I assure you, Ralph, that my personal relationships will not have any bearing on the foundation's work. Regardless of what happens, Parker's dream will be fulfilled," I declare earnestly, trying to keep the assertiveness that's been bubbling up within me since Kennedy's "you deserve a life" speech in check. It's not easy.

Ralph grunts and shifts in his chair, crossing one leg over the other. "How did this start, if you don't mind my asking. Who pursued who?"

I can't help my tiny smile as I remember the feel of his chest pressed against mine during our subway trip back in New York. "He's very tenacious."

He purses his lips. "Are you sure he isn't just using the foundation to get to you? Will he still follow through with the dream fulfillment if your friendship goes south?"

My stomach twists as his question sinks in. Is it a possibility? On paper, I suppose so. I could just be a challenge to him. He could be laughing his ass off right now with his band about how I finally caved. He could be . . .

I sit straighter and return his penetrating gaze. "Yes, I believe he will follow through, regardless."

Silence reigns for a beat, and then his eyes crinkle in wry amusement. "Oh, Abby," he says with a chuckle. "You've been really worried about this, haven't you?"

"Well . . ." I trail off, surprised by his response. "I realize how it might look, and I don't want you to think—"

"I think that you're one of the hardest working people I know. *What's Your Dream* has flourished under your direction, and the entire board recognizes that." He smiles kindly. "People form attachments through their work all the time. It's been what? Two years since you've taken a real vacation? Go and have fun. I'm sure Nadia and April can muddle through without you for a week or so."

My smile falls at the mention of Nadia. "Actually, that's one of the reasons I wanted to make sure you were aware of my situation. One member of my senior staff has expressed concern about the appropriateness of my date—I mean, being friendly with—a client we're negotiating with for a dream."

He looks surprised for a moment, and then frowns. "I see." After a beat, he shrugs and looks at me directly. "You'll keep work and play separate?"

"I can't guarantee that everyone will see it that way," I say, tapping my finger on the table. "But yes. I promise."

"That's good enough for me." Leaning forward, he gives me a sly smile. "You're really dating Kennedy Lane?"

I feel my face light up like a stop sign. "Well, no, not really, I mean, I wouldn't say dating. I just . . . um, we're friends." My stammering dies out as his chuckles fill the room. Oh, God, shoot me now.

"Friends, huh?" He leans back in his chair, his amusement written on his face, and I finally feel my shoulders relax. "Well, whatever it is, I hope it works out for you. Just . . ." He pauses, searching for the words. "Getting your picture taken leaving a nightclub at midnight is one thing. Just don't end up splashed across the Internet naked in front of Buckingham Palace with a goat or something. Okay?"

A snort escapes me, and I clap a hand over my mouth as he laughs again, making his moustache quiver. My relief is almost tangible, and I give him a wry smirk. "Well, that certainly gives me some room to maneuver."

"SO WHAT'S THIS BIG NEWS you have for me? You aren't switching to Make-A-Wish, are you?" Maddie raises her wineglass to her lips. We're sitting at the bar in one of our favorite restaurants near Fisherman's Wharf in jeans and T-shirts. At least I'd grabbed a stretchy, flowing cardigan on my way out the door, so I didn't look too sloppy. Maddie had shown up at my apartment for wine Wednesday, only to say she was taking me out for some much-needed girl time. She couldn't have been more right.

"No, nothing like that." I take a sip from my own glass, stalling. My confidence has surged since my meeting with Ralph. Knowing I have him in my corner has laid my last worries to rest. But I have no idea how Maddie will react.

"Moving to Maui?"

"Of course not."

"Dying your hair blue?"

"Not this week."

"Won the lottery?"

"No!"

"Well, spit it out, then!"

The words tumble out. "I'm going to London to meet Kennedy Lane."

An instant later, I'm thumping her back with a fist as she coughs and snorts a mouthful of merlot. "What the fuck?" she squeaks, after finally catching her breath. "Are you shitting me? What happened?"

In a low voice, I give her a quick synopsis of everything that happened with Kennedy yesterday, from our meeting, to the trip to Chinatown, and what happened afterward. I gloss over the more intimate details, but can feel my blush almost become a living thing, as her eyes get wider and wider.

I gape at her in surprise when her shocked expression gives way to a triumphant laugh. "I knew it! I knew there was more between you than you claimed!" she crows, throwing in a fist pump for good measure.

"Maddie—no, there wasn't!" I hurriedly correct. "There wasn't, until yesterday. It's been strictly business." But she merely chuckles and looks at me fondly.

"Oh, please. The man has been wooing you for weeks." She rolls her eyes at my dumbfounded expression. "What do you think all those texts, videos, and songs were about? And the night in New York? He may have an army of groupies fighting to be with him, but do you *honestly* think he spends that kind of time and attention on *them*?"

My mind quickly flits over all of his messages, his playful banter, and those songs . . . snippets of the most beautiful, soulful, and poignant songs . . .

"And you!" she barrels on. "Your eyes light up like it's Christmas every time you talk about him."

I gape at her. "They do not! You're exaggerating." She rolls her eyes and waves over the bartender. After ordering something I can't hear over the laughter of the man behind me, she looks back at me with a satisfied smirk.

"Deny it all you want, sweetie, but you know I'm right."

I huff in frustration. April said almost the same thing this morning. Which, after yesterday, makes sense, I guess. But not before! We were just networking, and he was trying to convince me to . . . to . . .

Oh, for the love of . . .

I pinch the bridge of my nose, feeling like a Class A idiot. How could I be so dense? Okay, so I finally realized yesterday that he wasn't thinking of me like his sister. But did that really mean that he'd felt more than that the entire time? Certainly not the first time we met—that was awful. When did it change?

I'm a strong, independent woman with above average intelligence, and I pride myself on my ability to see to the heart of an issue and perceive the intentions of those around me. It's an invaluable skill that's never failed me, except that once with Lucas. And again now, apparently—doubly so, in fact, because I didn't see my attraction for him turning into something else, either.

Closing my eyes, I easily recall the intoxicating feel of him wrapped around me in my bed, the air smelling of his delicious spicy scent and sex. With a shiver, I groan in frustration.

"Okay, I like him. Happy?"

She snickers. "Fine. I'll take 'like' for now. It's enough to win me that bottle of wine from Terri."

"You made a bet with my mother?" I shriek in indignation, before wincing and shooting a look around. Fortunately, no one seems interested in my outburst. "Did you tell her who he was?"

She rolls her eyes. "Of course not. You needed to figure out how you felt first. We simply had a feeling that there was more going on than you wanted to admit or were aware of, that's all. She thought it was going to take you months yet."

Awesome. "Her faith in me is touching," I comment dryly.

"Oh, suck it up, Walker. She just knows you—better than you know yourself, sometimes." The bartender reappears, setting a small tray of shots before us. I eye them suspiciously, to which she huffs an exasperated sigh.

"Come on. I thought we needed something more substantial than wine to celebrate your epiphany." Without preamble, she grabs a glass and downs it with only a slight flinch. "When are you leaving?"

"Tomorrow night. I'm taking the day off to do laundry and

pack." The thought lifts my spirits, and I mimic her, although I can't repress my violent shudder as the fiery cinnamon liquid slides down my throat. "Good God, what the hell is that?" I cough and fan my flaming mouth.

"Fireball," she says, unconcerned. "Don't worry—you said you have tomorrow off. You'll recover before you have to deal with packing, I promise. Speaking of old baggage, what did Nadia say when you told her?"

Scowling, I take another shot—I need it to deal with the thought of Nadia. "I didn't have a chance. She called in sick today," I growl, smacking the empty shot glass on the table. I didn't want to leave that situation unresolved, but there wasn't much I could do about it.

"Coward," Maddie notes. "Oh well. Don't let her weigh on you while you're gone."

"Oh, I won't. I'm hoping she's licking her wounds and remembering what her job is really about. If she hasn't pulled her head out of her ass by the time she gets back to work, she'll discover I've put a little kink in her game." I describe my meeting with Ralph, and the sense of relief I felt earlier returns.

Maddie laughs at Ralph's final words of advice. "That's brilliant! What else did he say?"

"He made me promise to bring him some mustard from Fortnum and Mason."

"Well, if a personal condiment delivery is his biggest concern, I'd say you're off scot-free. Cheers!" We clink glasses and slurp another shot. I notice vaguely that it's not burning as much now as it goes down. In fact, it's rather tasty.

"So, what does Mr. Rock Star have planned for you in London?" She wiggles her eyebrows, making me laugh.

"I have no idea." A sudden panic hits me, and I clasp her hand tightly on the table. "God, Maddie, am I doing the right thing? Tell me this isn't going to be the biggest mistake of my life."

She tuts softly and covers our joined hands with her other hand. "Of course you're doing the right thing. You like him, yes? I mean, *really* like him."

"Yes. More than anyone in a long time," I say softly, her reassuring smile lessening my anxiety.

"Then don't worry. You're the hardest working person I know. You deserve a little fun," she urges, giving our hands a little squeeze. "Trust yourself, and do your best to trust *him*, too. You've said he's working on his problems, right? Give the guy a break. And give yourself one while you're at it."

Looking into her sparkling blue eyes, I feel the weight on my shoulders lift. She's right. Kennedy and I both deserve a break.

"Thanks, Maddie." I wrap my arms around her in thanks.

"So . . ." She smiles devilishly at me—always a bad sign. "Do photos lie? Is he as *gifted* as he seems?" She wiggles her eyebrows, and I gasp, my face instantly heating. "Come on," she pleads. "Tell me! Does he live up to the image?"

"Maddie!" I look around to make sure no one is hearing us. Then, with Fireball-assisted courage, I fix her with my own smirk and deliberately cock an eyebrow.

"I knew it!" She lifts our last two shots and hands me one.

"To fuck-hot rock stars and firemen!" she offers, and we knock back the last of the lethal brew.

I HATE FIREBALL WITH THE heat of a thousand suns. As Maddie promised, I have recovered enough to board my plane, although it took me most of the morning to bring my killer headache into submission. What possessed me to think shots were a good idea? Oh, wait—it was my realization that I'd been a complete idiot. That I've fallen in *deep like* with someone and had absolutely no clue. Brilliant.

The flight attendant gives me a perky smile, and I plop down into my business class pod. Thank God for air-mile upgrades. I'll be able to sleep most of the flight. In due course, I feel the surge from the engines that make me sink back into my seat, and then the sudden shift in vibration as we leave the earth and steadily begin to climb.

Watching the clouds rushing past my window, my thoughts automatically turn to the complex man awaiting me. There will be no alcohol for me this trip. If he's not drinking, I won't either. I don't want to make things uncomfortable for either of us. I certainly won't miss it; more importantly, I don't want to waste any time dealing with even a mild whiskey headache. My heart races as I think again about what I'm doing. I've never taken a leap of faith like this. Kennedy's shy smile and the light in his eyes when I told him I'd meet him tells me that maybe, just maybe, I should've leapt sooner.

After the inflight meal and doing a little work on my laptop, I recline my seat and snuggle under the lightweight duvet. Seriously, whoever invented these sleeping pods deserves a medal. Popping in my earbuds, I replay the new song snippet he sent me this morning. Well, last night, really, but I wasn't in any shape to notice then. It's beautiful, seeming to fit his deep voice perfectly.

Come on, baby all we got is time
But how long you gonna wait 'till I can call you mine

How long until he can call me his? A thrill runs through me as I tuck my phone away, his soulful voice echoing in my mind. Something tells me it might not be too long.

IT TAKES FOREVER TO GET through passport control. By the time I exit, I realize I'll barely have time to get to the hotel to shower before I meet him at the arena. I slept most of my flight, so I'm feeling pretty alert. Searching for my name in the sea of signs, I finally locate my escort. He's tall with a blond buzz-cut and is built similarly to Kennedy's bodyguard, Tucker.

"Miss Walker?" he asks politely when I stop in front of him. "My name is Colin. I'm sorry, but due to the delays in passport control, I will need to take you directly to the arena after we've fetched your bags."

"Oh, all right," I concede. Dismally, I look down at my hood-ie and tennis shoes. "Can I make a quick stop in the restroom af-ter I pick up my bag?"

"Certainly."

Twenty minutes later, I'm brushing out my hair and pulling it up into a loose bun. I've freshened up as much as I'm able to in an airport bathroom, and changed into black skinny jeans tucked into my favorite tall boots, a white V-neck T-shirt, and a black blazer. Quickly looping a long, silk red scarf loosely around my neck, I'm as ready as I can be.

I'VE NEVER BEEN TO THE O2 before, and my nerves are at an all-time high. The entire band will be there. What will they think of me? Do any of them have girlfriends, or will I be the only non-groupie there? I toy with the ends of my scarf anx-iously. I have no idea what to expect, and I'm chastising myself for not quizzing Kennedy earlier. Since when have I been this unprepared?

The lights in town are already coming on as the daylight fades. I eagerly watch the familiar sights fly by my rain-streaked window. Colin isn't wasting any time. He doesn't talk much, and the silence is feeding my nervous energy. Soon the huge round building looms before us, and I smile to see the band's name up in lights. The place is a massive hive of activity. Minutes later, Colin and I are at the artist's entrance, and I'm being escorted deep into the bowels of the arena. Finally, we reach a door at the end of a series of hallways. There's a guard standing outside, and I nervously finger the VIP credentials hanging around my neck that Colin provided.

"Mr. Lane is waiting, Miss Walker," Colin announces and my heart rate skyrockets. I square my shoulders and nod to him.

Time to face the music.

chapter fourteen

kennedy

BACKSTAGE AT THE O2 HAS been a whirlwind of chaos. At the meet-and-greet, we see everything from diehard, devoted fans who have us signing everything in sight, to the typical groupies wearing next to nothing who not so subtly slip their phone numbers into the back pocket of my jeans.

We can feel the electricity of the crowd as the arena fills, while the best crew in the business rushes around with last minute equipment adjustments. To put on a show like ours, takes an army of people, and that's not counting Tucker's amped up security detail.

Brodie has kept busy for the majority of the day, orchestrating the entire setup including the addition of the baby grand piano I threw at him a couple of days ago. We typically don't incorporate one, but we decided on a few acoustic versions of some of our biggest hits. People don't expect me to play the piano, and it's going to cause a stir, shake things up by taking things down a notch.

"Any word on Abby?" I ask Tucker as he leads me to the

dressing room, stopping in front of the door.

"I think I'll keep you in suspense. I like seeing you sweat."

"Did I mention you're an asshole?"

"Several times today. But you love me, sunshine." He pauses, setting his hand on the door handle. "You've got twenty minutes. Use them wisely." With a smirk, he pushes the door open and ushers me inside, closing it quickly, to take his place outside.

Furrowing my brow at his weird behavior, I turn to scan the dressing room, and when I spot her, it feels like the breath has been knocked out of me. Just the sight of her reflection in the mirror across the room, wide-eyed and obviously nervous, does things to me I can't understand.

My heart hammers, every inch of my skin buzzing with intensity, the energy pulsing raw and electric between us. It feels like months since I've seen her, touched her, heard her voice, and now she's here, all mine in my dressing room.

Her plump lips part slightly as we stare at each other in the mirror, and I take an appreciative sweep of her outfit. I can't help the smirk when I see the boots, my gaze traveling over her tempting curves poured into black jeans, her hair piled up under one of my tattered cowboy hats. She's been in here a while if she's managed to rummage through my wardrobe, and I could kill Tucker for keeping me from her. Not wanting to waste a minute, I close the distance between us, striding across the room to her.

She takes a deep breath and starts to turn, but I stop her. "Don't you dare turn around. I want you to watch." My gaze lingers on the swell of her breasts, rising and falling quickly under her simple white shirt. "I've been thinking about you all fucking day." I brush my fingers along the exposed nape of her neck, her gaze dark and hooded, locked to mine in the mirror. She's so soft, so fucking perfect.

"Yeah?" It's a breathless whisper from her lips as she

shudders at my touch.

"Mhmm. I want you naked and aching for me." I slide my palm along the column of her neck, watching her eyes widen as I bend to press my lips against the sliver of exposed skin at her shoulder.

"Right now?" She swallows loudly before wetting her lips.

"Right fucking now," I mumble against her skin. It's a full-on assault to my senses, breathing her in like she's the air I need, my eyes sliding shut to savor her. I feel her tight body tense against me, and I open my eyes to find hers trained on the door. "No one's coming in."

She seems to relax, but I can still feel her pulse beating wildly as my tongue glides against her neck. I slowly peel her blazer down her arms, dropping it to the floor. "Watch," I whisper under her ear, and her eyes follow the path of my hand as I gradually lift her shirt up, splaying my palm over her stomach, feeling her muscles shudder at the contact.

The lines of ink on my hand are in sharp contrast to her creamy unmarked skin. Tipping the cowboy hat from her head, she lets out a hitched laugh as it falls to the small countertop in front of the mirror. "Something funny?" I lift a brow, catching her gaze in the mirror. Fuck, I love seeing her like this, open and laughing, exposed and vulnerable.

"This is crazy," she whispers as my fingers trace the red scarf draped around her neck.

"Want me to stop?"

"No." She shakes her head as I tug the scarf from her, feeling the smooth silk against my calloused fingers.

"I really want to cover your eyes with this, but I want you to watch me fuck you more."

Her breath catches, and she watches me set the scarf on the countertop. I lift her shirt over her head and trace the thin, white lace of her bra before unhooking the clasps at the back. With a sweep of my hand over her shoulder, I tug it from her. It joins the growing pile on the counter.

"Touch yourself." There's a gritty edge to voice as my lips trail across her skin, grazing my teeth against her neck. I can see her hesitation, and I wrap my arms around her from behind, sliding both hands up her torso to palm her perfect breasts. "You are so fucking beautiful. Show me what you like, baby."

Her eyes drop to my hands, and she watches my fingers tease and tug her hardened nipples. I can feel her heart hammering. She grinds her hips slowly back against me, driving me out of my mind. She grips the edge of the counter as if she's fighting some internal battle, and I waste no time, covering them with my own and lifting them to close over her breasts.

My fingers tighten over hers, the weight of her breasts heavy in our joined hands, and the stubble on my chin scraping her neck. I drop my hands away to let hers take over, and I curl my fingers around her hips, tugging her ass back against me. One of her hands flies from her breast to reach back between us, palming me through my jeans, her mouth dropping open as she feels my cock hard and aching.

Tracing the band of her jeans, I pop open the button and tug the fabric down her creamy thighs. I'm unable to look away from our reflection as I slip my hand under the enticing lace between her legs, my breath warm and ragged against her skin.

Slowly stroking two fingers into her, she squirms against me. Her palm tightens against my cock, threatening to snap the last bit of control I have. "You like that, don't you?" I mutter against her shoulder blade, feeling her shiver.

She's so warm, wet, and ready, and she teases her nipple with each pass of my fingers. It's a visual overload to see her like this, the muted, chanting crowd pulsating behind the wall a few feet away only adding to the desire that bounces thick and heavy between us.

Pushing back from her, I frantically work to remove her boots, stopping when I hear a soft whimper above me. I lift my gaze to hers. Her face is flushed, and her lips are parted. "One day, we'll keep these on," I mumble, and tug one boot off, followed quickly by the other, hearing her giggle as she tries to balance, leaning against the edge of the counter.

She shimmies the rest of the way out of her jeans, and then she's standing before me, in just a patch of simple white lace, a few wayward strands of hair escaping from where it's piled on her head. She holds my gaze in the mirror as she rolls her thumb over her peaked nipple. "Touch me," she urges, her voice soft and wanting.

Reaching around her for my wallet on the counter, I flip it open and tug a condom out. "You said you're always safe, right?" My hand slides along the delicious curve of her ass, squeezing as my thigh pushes her legs apart.

"Always, I promise, but are you . . ." She nods quickly.

"I've had the shot for a couple of years n—" I crash my lips to hers stealing her breath and quieting her words. My hips roll against her, letting her feel the rigid outline of my cock.

"Is this what you want, hmm?"

"You're wearing too many clothes," she manages, dropping her free hand beneath the lace between her legs. The red scarf taunts me from the counter, and I lift it to trail the luxurious fabric across her torso, up between her breasts.

Her eyes flash, wild and hungry. She watches as I loop the scarf around her neck, and cross the fabric between her breasts. pulling it taut underneath them before knotting the ends tightly around her back. The deep, rich color of the scarf against her skin draws even more attention to her full tits, and I can't resist cupping them in my hands as I stand behind her, her nipples tightening further under the rough pads of my fingers.

It's tempting just to watch her like this, her fingers moving desperately over her clit to get herself off, and one day I will. But right now, the need to take her is overwhelming every other thought in my head. Nothing else matters—not the concert, not the fans screaming for me, not the fact that the rest of the band is waiting for me. Only her and me, and this insane energy between us.

I yank my shirt over my head and go to work on my belt. Then I kick off my shoes and tug my jeans down, the sound of the heavy buckle echoing through the room as it hits the floor. She never stops stroking between her legs as she watches me in the mirror. "No boxers?" It's such an innocent question at a moment like this, and I can't resist smacking her perfect, round ass as I press against her with deep laugh.

"No." Sliding one hand up her neck, I coax her lips to meet mine, feeling her grind against me. Kissing Abby is something I should be doing every fucking hour of the day. She lets out a soft moan, my tongue gliding against hers as we devour each other. "Fuck, you taste so good."

She answers with a nip to my bottom lip, slowly turning her head back to the mirror, her eyes wide as she watches me rip the lace at her hip away, and my fingers moving with hers to tease her swollen clit.

"Spread your legs and hold on."

Her head drops forward with a groan, and she grips the rough edge of the counter as she bends over. I try to bite back a moan at the sight of her ass, her hips circling back as I push inside. She mumbles something I can't understand, and I feel her stretch around me, both my hands tightening around her hips as I drive forward.

Flattening one hand up her spine, over the knot in the scarf in the middle of her back, I push my fingers through the messy twist of her hair and tug her head back, seeing her eyes finding mine in the mirror once more. "Watch us, baby."

The intensity of the sheer desire in her eyes is more than I can take. There's nothing gentle about what I'm doing. I'm taking exactly what I want, and she's right there meeting me, each thrust deeper and more powerful than the last, her gaze darting around the mirror as if she can't quite decide where to look first.

It's a harsh, fast, and jarring pace. The ink on my skin snakes out to touch her silky skin as I wrap my arm around her waist, urging her back against me. Our movements are highlighted in the glare of the bulbs that line either side of the mirror, her tits bouncing against the fabric of the scarf with each punch of my hips, and I know it's going to be over much too soon.

"Kennedy." My name is a cry from her lips, and I feel her shudder around me. I roughly tug her back, the slap of our skin drowning out the rumbling outside the door. I can feel the white heat building, humming up my spine and spiking through my veins.

Her hands push against the counter as she throws her head back against my shoulder, a thin sheen of sweat breaking over my skin. "You're so fucking tight. Christ." My hips buck forward with the intensity of my release, my cock swelling and throbbing as my heated gaze locks to hers in the mirror.

"Holy God," she mumbles, collapsing forward. Her breasts press to the countertop as she rests her cheek on the surface. Her panted breaths fog the mirror in pulses, and I palm the sweet swell of her perfect ass. My heart hammers as I try to gain some sense of control, not wanting to move. I should be buried inside her every second of the fucking day.

I gently trace my fingers up her spine as I reluctantly ease from her with a rumbling groan. Releasing the knot of the scarf at her back, I pull her to lean against my chest, unbinding her breasts. "I think I'll keep this," I whisper into her ear, trailing the scarf over her collarbone. "Maybe put it on my microphone." She blinks at me in disbelief, her chest rising and falling rapidly. "Mmm. Fucked speechless looks good on you. Welcome to London, Abby."

♪ ♩ ♪ ♩

abigail

HOLY HELL. EVERY INCH OF me is tingling, and I barely have the strength to stand. I stare at his smirk in the mirror for what feels like eternity while I'm desperately waiting for speech to return.

"That was quite a welcome," I manage weakly, as his smug smirk grows into a full-fledged grin.

"I want nothing more right now than to throw you on that couch and take you again, but we don't have time." He drops a kiss to my bare shoulder, making me quiver. "They'll be coming for me any minute, and I don't want anyone else seeing you like this."

"Now?" I squeak, instinctively covering my breasts with my arms. He nods and gives me a playful slap on my ass, spurring me into motion. I quickly grab my bra from the pile of clothing on the counter and slip it on, as he pulls up his jeans behind me.

My head is spinning. After waiting for about fifteen minutes in the expansive green room while staffers set up tables of booze and snack food, I was shuttled to this smaller dressing room to wait another half hour. My nerves were stretched so tightly I thought they'd snap. To distract myself, I'd poked around the clothes hanging from the rolling rack. Then he was there and everything happened so fast. One minute, I'm laughing at how I look with a cowboy hat, and the next I'm naked and getting roundly fucked.

"I can't believe you did that right before going on stage," I mutter, pulling my T-shirt over my head.

He snorts in amusement. "Are you kidding? Getting you naked again has been the only thing I've thought about since I left your apartment." My eyes meet his in the mirror, and I can see that he's serious. I feel my blush, so I hastily look away and retrieve the scrap of lace that used to be my panties from the floor. Damn it—I liked that pair.

"Was this really necessary?" I demand in exasperation, shaking the pieces at him. Going commando might work for him, but not me. And after he dropped me off, the driver took my luggage to wherever we're staying, so I can't get a new pair.

Kennedy barks a laugh, roughly pulls me to his chest, and kisses me soundly. "Definitely," he growls, the sound making me melt against him. "It was in my way." I can't hide my smile; maybe going commando isn't so bad, after all. Then his arms tighten around me and his mood shifts again, his cocky demeanor slipping a bit.

"I'm serious—you're practically all I've been able to think about for days," he murmurs, his eyes boring into mine. "Not just the naked part, as sweet as it is. You need to know that." I feel like I'm drowning in that sapphire gaze, and I nod, speech escaping me again. So instead, I reach up and pull his lips to mine, allowing myself to get lost in the sweet sensation. He moans softly, and the sound kick-starts my libido. He starts to move us toward the couch when a sharp knock at the door startles us apart. "Damn it," he swears, his breathing heavy. "Come on, babe. Hurry."

I scramble to pull on my jeans, as he steps over to the rolling wardrobe and plucks a black shirt from a hanger. Distracted by the sight of his lean, muscular frame, I gape at his back for a second before turning again to the mirror. I frown at the state of my hair. Just-fucked doesn't even come close to describing it. I pull out the clip and use a brush sitting on the counter to start working out the tangles. I'm about to sweep it up again, when Kennedy stops me with a touch to my elbow. "Leave it." The hungry look in his eyes almost undoes me, but instead he hands me one of my boots. He holds me steady while I step into them and raise the zippers, just as there's another knock. This time the door opens slightly, and I can hear the rush of noise in the hallway beyond.

"All ready in here?" Tucker asks, before poking his head into the room. His eyes flicker between us, and he quickly stifles a smile, his lips twitching with the effort. Kennedy runs a hand through his disheveled hair and grins like a fool. I feel a flash of embarrassment and pray no one could hear us in here over the sounds of the crowd filtering in from the arena. With as much dignity as I can muster, I pull on my blazer, pick up my red scarf from the chair where Kennedy had draped it, and take a deep breath.

Taking my hand, Kennedy looks down at me, his blue eyes flashing. "Ready?" he asks softly, and I nod.

"For anything," I assure him, and my spirit lifts when I see the relief in his eyes.

"Let's hope so," he murmurs and pulls me gently to the door, where he addresses Tucker. "Do you have someone to take her?"

"She's all set." He opens the door wider and gestures to where Colin is waiting behind him to escort me somewhere. "Colin will seat you, Miss Walker."

I move to follow, but Kennedy doesn't let go of my hand.

He leans down and kisses me deeply, obviously not caring about our audience, and making my heart skip a beat. I have to blink a few times to clear my head, and when it does, I realize he's now holding my scarf.

"I told you I was going to keep this," he teases, and then tilts his chin toward the door. "Stay close to Tucker's guy; he'll take care of you. Enjoy the show, baby."

I lift an eyebrow in challenge. "I thought I already did." His eyes shoot open in surprise, and then he laughs.

"Good to know. Act two, then." Tucker clears his throat to draw our attention, and I obediently step away from Kennedy. He lets me this time and follows Tucker down the hall in the opposite direction. I start to follow Colin, casting one last glance over my shoulder; I manage to catch a glimpse of Kennedy's roguish smile as he looks back at me, and then he disappears around a corner.

♪ ♩ ♪ ♩

"THIS WAY," COLIN SAYS POLITELY, and I fall into step with him. The pace of the people in the hallway increases, and I can feel the energy surge as show time nears. It's exciting to be behind the scenes, and I can't help my grin when I suddenly find myself backstage.

"Do I get to watch from here?" I ask, my eyes taking in the frenetic waltz of stagehands and roadies behind the curtains.

"Mr. Lane thought you'd have a better view from out front," Colin explains. "This way, please. Mind your step." We turn a corner and come face-to-face with a sneering Brodie Dixon. His expression makes my skin crawl.

"Jesus Fucking Christ."

"It's Abby, actually," I correct him. "I believe Mr. Christ is busy elsewhere tonight." Colin coughs into his fist, and I think

I see a ghost of a smile behind his hand before he straightens. Brodie ignores him.

"What are you doing here?" he demands, scowling at me with disgust.

I purse my lips, trying to keep my temper in check. "Not that I have to explain myself to you, but I was invited. Didn't you get the memo?"

"Your seat is this way, Miss," Colin interjects, placing a hand at my elbow and guiding me away. I toss a quick glance over my shoulder; Brodie stares darkly after us, fists clenched.

"What the hell is that guy's problem?" I mutter, turning again to follow Colin. He opens another door and leads me to a stairway that's dimly glowing with light built into each step. Shaking off the last few minutes, I gasp as we step through another door into the vast arena, pulsing with noise and light, and filled with enthusiastic fans. Colin escorts me to a small section situated stage right, above the sea of people milling in front of the apron. I'm guessing it's the O2's version of box seats. Colin sees me to a spot in the front row, nearest the stage.

"Can I get you anything, Miss Walker?" he asks politely, and I give him a thankful smile.

"No, thank you, Colin."

"I'll be just over here if you need me."

The anticipation in the arena is palpable. I quickly pull out my phone, snap a photo of the packed audience and waiting stage, and send it to Maddie with the caption, "Guess where I am?" Her answer only takes two minutes—I love how she manages to squeal like a banshee using only exclamation points and emojis. I promise to call her tomorrow, and then tuck my phone away.

There are a few other people already seated; two dark-haired men who look like media-types and three blond women dressed in tight Redfall tank tops. Based on their accents, I appear to be the only American in the box. The women eye the biceps peeking out from Colin's black shirt appreciatively as he retreats to the box opening, and then their curious eyes turn to me.

"You missed the opening act!" one of them chirps helpfully, and I barely suppress my smirk. The opening act was rather spectacular, I think.

"I saw it from back there," I say, pointing vaguely behind me. She nods, and then goes back to chattering with her friends. If they only knew.

I close my eyes, savoring the memory of his hands on my skin, the force of his thrusts, and the burning hunger in those intense blue eyes staring at me in the mirror as he took me. I can't believe that he *did* that . . . even more, that I *let* him just walk in and fuck me with barely a hello.

Oh, who am I trying to kid? That was, hands down, the most erotic moment of my life so far. A shiver runs through me. I don't know what this man is doing to me, but I'd be lying if I said I didn't want more. And that scares the living hell out of me.

Suddenly, the lights go out, plunging the arena in near darkness, and the crowd gives a deafening roar in response. The energy in the room is amazing. Then the stage is illuminated by four white spots, and noise in the hall increases exponentially as the band takes the stage. The drummer—Sean—is cloaked in the Union Jack and appears to be howling as he prances around his drum kit like a maniac. The other two guitarists are more low-key, simply sauntering into the light and raising their instruments high over their heads to the joy of the crowd.

And then, Kennedy appears from the darkness, triggering a spike in the cheering. He confidently struts to center stage, looking like sex incarnate and triumphantly holding my scarf aloft in his clenched fist. He punches the air over his head in rapid succession, the red silk looking like a ribbon of fire in the spotlight. The crowd goes nuts, and I'm on my feet with the rest of them, cheering like crazy.

Stalking to his mic stand, he's in complete command of the crowd. With a deliberate glance in my direction that almost stops my heart, he grins lasciviously as he carefully ties my scarf around his microphone. The women sitting next to me go wild, while a disbelieving laugh bubbles up from my throat. I can't believe that, barely twenty minutes ago, he was inside me. The licentious thought makes my cheeks heat and my thighs clench, and I laugh again, this time in sheer delight.

A familiar driving bass guitar riff begins and the excitement increases tenfold, as the crowd recognizes one of the group's most famous songs. Kennedy picks up his waiting guitar, slings the strap over his head, and begins belting out the lyrics.

The lights pulse and swirl, and the crowd sways and surges. Song after song, the energy never flags. If I thought I'd had a hard time fighting Kennedy's allure before, it's nowhere near the pull I'm fighting now. He prowls around the stage as if it's his personal property. There are no lavish set pieces, no choreographed teams of half-clad dancers, and no showy costume changes, unless you count Sean taking his shirt off halfway through the first set. It's sheer musical talent—genius, actually—and I can't remember when I've been this captivated by a show. Or by a man.

Even when they move into a couple acoustic pieces and the pace slows, the audience remains riveted. An excited buzz rushes through the crowd when a gorgeous concert grand is illuminated on stage, and Kennedy strolls over and takes a seat.

"I realize that this isn't part of our standard fare," he explains in a throaty purr, giving the audience a smirk. "But I've recently found myself drawn more and more to my roots, so I beg your *indulgence*." The buzz becomes an enthusiastic roar of approval. I'm mesmerized as Kennedy's fingers dance over the keys, his powerful voice soaring through the air, singing about a sky full of stars.

It's my song! Okay, not *my* song, but the one he sent me after I met him for the first time in San Francisco. I rub absently at the sudden ache in my chest, regret flooding me over the words I'd hurled at him then. The music surrounds me, filling me with a deep longing that I can't explain. Then he looks up from the keys—almost straight at me—and it's as if he can feel it, too. This intense, poignant craving for something more. More than lust, more than a physical connection. A craving for the kind of security, confidence, and serenity that only comes with the absolute knowledge that someone *would* be there to catch me, who would *never* let me fall, and who would keep me, and my heart, *safe*.

I suck in a ragged breath, shaken by the intensity of my emotions. Sinking back into my seat, I'm almost relieved when the band resumes its hard-driving electric rhythms, exhorting the crowd to join in. *Don't get carried away, Abby*. It's just a beautiful song, not a personal manifesto. Keep it light and fun.

Enjoy the moment. Right.

Equilibrium restored, I stand and let myself go. I am one with the crowd as I clap, sing, and stomp my way through the rest of the show and two encores. It's one of those perfect moments where the artists and the audience are in sync, feeding off each other's energy, and urging each other on. When the lights finally come up, I feel drained, but elated. I can't wait to see Kennedy—all I want is to throw my arms around him and never let go. And for once, I'm not questioning it.

chapter fifteen

kennedy

I'M BLINDED BY ANOTHER SERIES of flashes as we pose for more photos in the green room. Mayhem is a good word to describe the circus that greeted us once Tucker led us through the winding hallways to the interview space.

Our latest album blares through the speakers as I scan the undulating line of fans with VIP passes that wind through the room, snaking into the hallway.

These meet-and-greets are grueling, particularly this one where I'm amped up more than normal with just the thought of Abby waiting for me. Still, there is a science to it all, according to Brodie. Try not to get into an actual conversation with anyone; you'll end up off schedule. Sign whatever is put in front of you, and always agree to the photo. There's no such thing as too much publicity in Brodie's world.

There's a difference however, between real fans, die-hards like the ones I'm currently taking a picture with, and the women dressed in next to nothing who just want a chance to fuck a rock star.

There's way too much skin showing in the next group. Tight, fake leather scraps of material and sky-high stilettos make up the groupie Fashion 101. I wouldn't have cared about it, in fact, I would have welcomed it in the not-too-distant past, but everything is different now.

Brodie shoots me a grin as he ushers forward the giggling pair of women as if they're some prize he's personally hand-picked for us. The leer he offers them doesn't escape me. Tucker looks on, menacing and steadfast as ever. If given the opportunity, I think he'd love to take Brodie down.

There's something simmering just under the surface between Brodie and I that I don't like. We've managed to keep a lid on it, but I have a feeling it won't be long until it boils over. With a smirk in my direction, Brodie turns back to the crowd, disappearing into the fold.

"I got a special pass," the vapid dyed-blonde wearing way too much makeup breathes against my ear. She reeks of cheap perfume and desperation. She swings the Redfall lanyard around her neck, waving the gold pass in front of my face.

"Did you, now? Lucky you."

"You were brilliant!" she squeals, practically vibrating beside me. "That last song was amazing," her tag-along friend chimes in, and while I appreciate her purchasing one of our concert tanks, I think this one came from the children's section.

"It's a classic."

"I love when you play your new songs just for us. You know, like before anyone else hears them." She bats her eyes at me, pushing her tits forward and pressing against my arm. I take a step back.

"It's not a new song." I wait for some glimmer of recognition of the 'Live and Let Die' cover we did, but she looks at me like I have six heads. "Never mind."

Cam slides in beside her, casting his gaze down her outfit, lingering over her too-tight top. "Did you have something you wanted us to sign, sweetheart?" he croons.

She giggles, sticking her chest out, pointing to her tits.

"Maybe something that will last longer?" I suggest.

Cam snorts, uncapping his marker, and scrawling his signature across the ample swell of her left breast.

"Did you get a picture of that?" she shrieks at her blond partner in crime.

The blonde titters a response. "It looks so good!" She feels the need to tug the fabric of the tank away from her chest, revealing a black push-up bra.

I shake my head, looking away as Cameron grins at me. "You know what else would look good?" He slides his hand down her back. "You on top of me." Her eyes widen to about the size of dinner plates, and she nods so fast I think she might do some damage.

"Can Jade come?" the brunette blinks up at Cam in an attempt to appear innocent. I wonder how many times they've done this. It's probably not a question I want to explore too much. Hits a little too close to home. "Sweetheart, I thought you'd never ask." Cam slides his arm around her waist, and she melts into his side.

A round of squeals just about does my eardrums in, and the blonde, Jade, tugs on my arm. "Come on, handsome."

"Nah, I'm good. I have a few more people to see. But you go have fun." She's disappointed for about a nanosecond, and then Cam pulls her against his other side, aiming a smirk in my direction.

"You're missing out, man."

"I'm not missing a damn thing."

♪ ♩ ♪ ♩

TUCKER'S ARMS HAVE TAKEN A beating getting us through the worst of the crowd. Arms flailing, ear-shattering screams, hands reaching out to grab at my T-shirt. It reminds me of the outdoor concert we played in Minnesota after our first Grammy win. Sheer insanity that only serves to fuel my amped-up state.

The anticipation of seeing Abby again is tangible. The way she looked at me during our last set is burned in my memory. Desire, hot and thick, but something deeper too. Something I never really thought I'd find. It feels like she truly cares about me, that we're connected. That this isn't just some fling with a rock star she wants to get out of her system. I need to keep reminding myself to take it slow. Someone like Abby can't and shouldn't be rushed, and I intend on savoring every single minute I get with her.

"Thanks, man," I say once we're clear of the crowd, and winding down a back hallway.

"These Brits are a rowdy bunch tonight." He laughs, slowing the pace slightly, checking over his shoulder once more. "Looks like we're clear."

The sound of footfalls echoing ahead wipes the grin off his face quickly, and he immediately resumes the all-consuming, protective gait I'm used to. "Shit," he mutters under his breath as Colin comes into view.

My stomach takes an immediate dive when I don't see Abby with him. I feel my jaw clench. "Why aren't you with her?" Tucker asks, his voice edgy.

"Brodie said you wanted help with the crowd," Colin explains hesitantly. "I tried to get you." He motions to his earpiece. "I think we're in a dead zone."

"You were told to stay with her," Tucker grinds out.

"He said you needed me. I'm sorry, I didn't—"

I don't wait to hear the rest of the explanation. Panic has set in, washing over me and igniting something dangerously raw. I trust Brodie about as far as I can throw him right now. Fuck knows what bullshit he'll try to fill her head with. With a muttered, "Fuck," I bolt down the hallway, hearing Tucker following on my heels.

"Kennedy, wait!" I feel Tucker fist my shirt, tugging me from the door. "Brodie's an idiot, but he'd never—"

"Take a step back." Even through the door, I can hear the disdain in Abby's voice. It chills me to the bone, and I'm reminded of our first meeting at the Fairmont. Tucker frowns, glancing at Colin, his expression grim.

I try the door, meeting resistance, and slam my fist against the surface over and over. "Open up, Brodie!" Tucker moves in front of me and twists the handle. "Why is the fucking door locked?"

"You really think he gives a shit about you?" Brodie's voice is loud and laced with irritation. I wouldn't be surprised if he's high already, jacked up on some lethal cocktail.

In a blur, Tucker is shouldering his sheer muscle into the door with brute force. The man is a machine, bursting into the room; the door swings open, and I take a step around him, autopilot engaged, my one and only thought to get to her.

I scan the room, frantically seeking them out, until my eyes land on Abby, backed up against the counter in front of the mirror and staring Brodie down in defiance. His hand is wrapped firmly around her arm in a way that can only be aggressive, and that's all I need to see. I'm launching across the room, both hands gripping his shoulders, hauling him away from her.

"You son of a bitch." I slam him against a nearby table, sending the glasses that line it shattering across the surface and down to the floor. Brodie's back hits the table, a rough grunt escaping him as he takes a swing at me, his fist landing squarely on my chin.

The table buckles under the force of our impact, and we crash to the floor as pain radiates against my jaw, blurring my vision slightly, but it only serves to spur me on. I'm firing on instinct alone, sheer protective mode the likes of which I've never experienced before driving me forward.

"Kennedy, no!" Through the haze of rage, I register Tucker's booming voice from across the room, but it's too late. I'm past the point of no return, my fist pounding against Brodie's face over and over until blood oozes between my fingers.

"Your hand . . . Tucker stop him!" I blink at the sound of sheer terror in Abby's voice, and Brodie seizes the moment of hesitation, pushing his arm up in an attempt to block his face. A cut splits open above his bloodshot, sunken right eye, the distinct scent of whiskey heavy through his ragged breaths.

With a sneer, and powered by his own rage, Brodie juts his arm forward, his hand clawing at my throat before Tucker's muscular arm drives between us. With my chest heaving, I push back as Brodie closes his hand around a stray shard of glass. "Don't even think about it," Tucker hisses, lifting me away as Colin heaves Brodie up from the floor and wrenches his arms behind his back.

The glass in his hand falls to the floor. His face is blotchy red with blood dripping from his temple, the coppery scent lingering in the air. I open and close my hand, aware of the searing pain that shoots through me. "Get the fuck out."

"This is me, man," Brodie starts, a look of panic on his face, his nostrils flaring. "Come on . . ."

"You don't deserve to breathe the same air as her."

"Let me explain," Brodie pants, trying to break from Colin's firm hold. Colin, while not as big as Tucker, has the advantage here. Brodie's not going anywhere.

"You're fired, and if you so much as look in her direction, so help me, I'll—"

"Don't finish that sentence," Tucker says, his voice calm as his arm tightens around my shoulder, pulling me further away from Brodie.

"You can't fire me. I have a contract!"

"Fuck the contract!"

"She slapped me." He lifts his chin in Abby's direction. "Across the face," he adds, sounding like a petulant child. I turn to take her in finally, my heart thundering as her worried gaze cuts to mine.

"He said some things . . ." Her voice shakes. "I know how to take care of myself." Her chin juts out in defiance.

"Isn't that interesting? I know some things too, Kennedy," Brodie sputters, contempt dripping in his voice. "Things the media would love to get their hands on." That smug look I'm so used to seeing makes a reappearance, and Tucker's arms tightens around my torso as I lunge toward him.

"Don't you dare threaten me. You have a confidentiality agreement, so try me. I'll look forward to suing your sorry ass."

The tension hangs thick and heavy in the air, and I see the moment Brodie knows he's lost this round. His haggard frame sags back against Colin.

"This isn't over," he growls.

"Get him out of my sight." Colin drags Brodie to the door that's hanging off its hinges, out to the hallway.

Taking a shaky breath in, I try to get a grip as Tucker turns me around to face him. "Get him out of here. I mean it, Tucker."

He holds my gaze, his expression worried as he nods slowly. "I'll take care of it. You stay put until I'm back. Colin will be here."

"Like he was supposed to be, you mean? Before he left her?" I snap.

"It's not his fault." Abby's voice is quiet, but douses my anger quickly, and Tucker takes a step back, giving us some room.

I slowly step toward her, and she gently cradles my face between her hands, the soft pads of her fingers tracing my jaw. I can feel her tremble as I slide my hand down her back, resting my forehead to hers.

"I'm so sorry, baby. So sorry." I lean into her touch, closing my eyes, the blood still rushing violently in my veins.

"It's not your fault either," she whispers. "Don't blame yourself. Please."

The look of worry and fear in her eyes when I lean back just about brings me to my knees. "Did he . . ." I can barely handle the thought of something happening to her. "Did he hurt you?" I finally manage.

She shakes her head. "No." Gently, I press my lips to her forehead.

"Did you really slap him across the face?"

She lets out a half-laugh. "I really did."

"Badass." She offers me a hint of smile, shaking her head.

I ignore the steady throb in my knuckles. She lifts my bloody hand. "We need to get you to a hospital. It might be broken," she says softly.

I shake my head, my free hand pressing her against me, needing to feel she's safe. "It's not. I'm fine."

"When did you become a doctor, hmm?" She leans back with a forced grin.

She's putting on a good front for my benefit, but I can see right through her. "Please tell me, you're okay. No bullshit."

Her eyes search mine and gloss over with unshed tears. "He

scared me, but I'm okay, really."

"I could kill him for touching you like that."

She places her fingers over my lips. "Don't. Don't say that."

"If I had just . . ." Her fingers press harder over my lips.

"Don't go there either. If I had just done this or I should have done that. Believe me; it's not going to help."

I can see the torment as she lightly traces the bruise on my jaw. "This brought it all back, didn't it? What happened with your ex?"

Her eyes widen at my question, her lips parting slightly. "Let's just get out of here. I want to take care of you."

Right now, that's all I want her to do.

♪ ♩ ♪ ♩

abigail

"FUCK! WATCH IT, WILL YOU?"

With a soft sigh, I watch the doctor gingerly examine Kennedy's hand. Tucker made a call on our way back to the Corinthia Hotel, and the bespeckled gentleman met us here. He'd first cleaned the scraped knuckles and rinsed the blood off, and was now gently probing and flexing those long, talented fingers that I love. Although Kennedy winces several times, the doctor seems satisfied.

"Well, it's not broken," he proclaims, and I let out a relieved breath. "But you'll have some bruising, as well as pain for a while."

"No shit," Kennedy mutters, and I shoot him a reproachful look. "Uh, sorry, Doc," he continues, chastened. "Thanks for coming."

"It's my pleasure," the doctor assures him. "Although you'll have to pay attention now, if you want to be playing that thing anytime soon." He nods toward one of Kennedy's guitar cases sitting by the door.

A rueful smile creeps across Kennedy's face. "Yeah, okay. Lay it on me."

The doctor cracks open a cold pack from his bag and hands it to Kennedy, instructing him to keep his hand elevated and to use the ice for twenty minutes off and on for the next couple of hours. Although Kennedy refuses the doctor's offer of a prescription painkiller, he does accept the ibuprofen. With the promise of an autograph for the doctor's daughter once Kennedy can write again, I show the man out with our thanks.

Returning to the living room, I ignore Kennedy's silent plea to join him on the sofa, and instead elect to lean against the piano, facing him. We stare at each other for a beat, the uncomfortable silence growing until Tucker clears his throat.

"I, uh, think I'm going downstairs for something to eat," he announces, glancing between us as he pushes off from his spot against the wall. "Let me know if you need me to bring up some more ice or whatever."

"Thanks, Tucker. For before, too," I say with a grateful smile. He flashes me a small smile in reply and closes the door softly behind him, leaving just Kennedy and I in the opulent suite.

"I'm sorry—"

"How bad does it fee—"

We stop and smile tiredly at each other; he gestures for me to continue. "Do you think you'll be okay in time for the next show?"

"Sure. I've had worse," he says with a snort and gives me a cheeky grin, but I can only manage a wan smile in return.

"Why doesn't that surprise me?"

He pats the sofa next to him with his good hand. "Come

'ere, please."

I force a brighter smile this time and walk over to sit on the ottoman in front of his knees. But he frowns and fiddles with his icepack as he observes me.

"What's wrong?"

"Nothing," I try to assure him, but I'm not sure it's entirely true. My nerves are still jangled from what happened; Brodie's ugly words, the sudden violence, the *blood*, and especially the look on Kennedy's face when he saw us. His expression held a disturbing combination of sheer rage and naked fear, and it struck a chord deep within me.

"Then why won't you sit with me?" His voice is soft, but his eyes burn with that intensity that never fails to move me.

"Because we need to talk, and I can't think when I'm too close to you," I admit, looking down at my feet. I kind of hate and love that he has that effect on me, but I'd promised myself I wasn't going to hide from my feelings anymore. I've done that for long enough.

"Then don't think." Before I know it, he pulls me into his lap and wraps both arms around me securely. I automatically melt into his embrace, until he grunts in pain.

"Kennedy, your hand!" I make to stand, but he gives me a warning look and grabs the fallen ice pack.

"Don't move and I promise I'll ice my hand." I nod obediently and wriggle slightly on his lap, a tiny smirk on my lips when he lets out a low groan. "Careful, woman," he growls. "Or I'll show you what I can do, injured hand or no."

"Sorry," I murmur, taking his hurt hand as it rests on my knee and positioning the ice over his swollen knuckles. I lean over and press a few soft kisses against the skin that isn't covered. He sighs, a sound of contentment and regret.

"Baby . . ." His whisper floats over my head as I feel his hand gently stroke my hair.

"I'm all right, honest."

Swallowing my sudden emotion down, I press my cheek against his arm. His hand feels so good in my hair, and I can feel my tense shoulders begin to relax. "Tell me what he said to you before we got in there."

"It doesn't matter," I mumble against his skin. "It was all lies. I know that." I sit up with a sigh and try to give him a bright smile. I'd been so happy when Colin had escorted me to the small dressing room after the concert. That third encore had almost done me in. They'd been on fire, the four of them seeming to employ a hive brain as they played, they were that tight. And every time Kennedy's eyes had swept over the crowd, they seemed to home in on mine with an intensity that made my knees weak. I couldn't wait to throw my arms around him and kiss the ever-loving crap out of that mouth that had been taunting and teasing me all night.

But Brodie had come in instead.

"Lies or not, it couldn't have been easy to hear. He had no right to speak to you like that." His voice is tight, anger bubbling just beneath the surface. "And he never will again. I promise."

"You can't make that promise," I argue gently. "Even though you fired him, you can't stop him from walking up to me on the street sometime to spout random bullshit." The notion was ridiculous.

"Watch me." The determination in his tone sends a shiver of desire down my spine despite the circumstances.

"Well, it won't be necessary. He had his chance and it didn't work. He won't try again—I'm not worth the effort." I shrug dismissively and search around for a quick change of topic.

"What did he say?" Kennedy asks again, emphasizing each word. He's not going to let this go, so I give in.

Slowly, I begin to replay the conversation for Kennedy's benefit, although I know it's just going to piss him off further. My anger surges as I picture Brodie as he stood back in the dressing room—his sneer and narrowed bloodshot eyes as I stared him down.

"Tucker didn't really need Colin, did he?" I had asked him, crossing my arms and standing straighter. He'd merely laughed, the sound more hollow than amused.

"You're pretty bright for just being a hot piece of ass." Brodie sniffed and wiped his nose with his hand. It was then I noticed how red his nostrils were, and his pupils were the size of dinner plates. Shit. Not good.

"And you're supposed to be working," I shot back, trying to mask my apprehension. "What are you on right now—coke or something else? Besides the alcohol, of course. I can smell the whiskey from here."

"None of your fucking business, princess." He paced closer. I stepped back reflexively, but found myself trapped by the make-up counter. "In fact, none of this is your fucking business. So just run along back to your boardrooms and stuffed suits, and leave this to me, okay? You've got no fucking business being here."

"Except that I was invited, of course," I reminded him, a cold smile on my lips. I glanced around the room, trying to see another way out, to no avail.

"Fuck that," he spat, his eyes narrowing to slits. "Kennedy only wanted to get in your pants, and now that he has, you're yesterday's news, sweetheart. You should see the groupie he just took into a room for a private autograph session. Blonde, stacked, wearing fuck-me heels and a smile. He'll be by to pick you up after he's done, I'm sure. You don't mind sloppy seconds, right?"

"Get the hell out of here," I hissed and clenched my fists. I was equally enraged and fearful—not of anything Kennedy might do with a groupie, but because whatever control Brodie had when he walked in was obviously slipping. I've seen what anger mixed with drugs and alcohol can do, and I didn't want to experience it again.

I stepped to the side, but he moved with me, an evil smirk on his face. "The truth hurts, doesn't it? Guess you aren't as smart as I thought."

It was my turn to laugh. "You wouldn't know the truth if it slapped you in the face," I retorted. "I'm smart enough to see that whatever relationship you had with Kennedy is changing, and if you don't smarten up, you'll be the one to find yourself out in the cold."

"Bitch," he'd snarled, taking a quick step to tower over me, ignoring my demand for him to back up. "I've known him for fucking years! You think you know so much, just because you've spread your legs for him a couple of times?" The door rattled—I could hear someone pounding on it, but I couldn't get around Brodie. "He can't do this without me!" he yelled, his eyes wild. "You really think he gives a shit about you? Get your ass on a goddamn plane and go the fuck home, you stupid cunt."

I'm shivering as I finish describing the scene, but Kennedy is sitting still as a stone beneath me. "I didn't think. I slapped him so hard my hand stung. Then he grabbed me, just as the door burst open and you charged in." I shake my head, trying to dispel the image. "He was crazy, Kennedy."

He tries to move me, tightening his fingers against my waist and wincing with pain.

I cup his face and look him in the eyes, willing him to relax. "You aren't going anywhere right now, Lane, so calm down. You've already fired him; that's enough. He won't bother me again."

After a beat, he huffs and relaxes slightly, so I release his face. He lets me fiddle with the ice pack on his knuckles for a moment, and then presses his forehead to mine. "I'm sorry he had a chance to get to you like that," he murmurs. "You don't believe any of that bullshit he spewed, do you?"

"No." He looks at me as if he can't quite believe me. "As bad as his words were, it was more upsetting to see you go after him like that. God, I was so scared you were going to get hurt. When he grabbed that broken glass . . ." I shiver and close my eyes, trying to block out the image; Kennedy's free arm tightens around me and I sink into his comfort. "You were right; the yelling and then your *fight*. It reminded me of when my dad was shot."

"I'm sorry," he says, his voice penitent. "I saw his hands on you and I saw red." He squeezes my waist to draw my attention from his wounded hand to his face. "What he said, it couldn't be further from the truth . . . now. I'm not proud of it, but I can't pretend it didn't used to happen. A lot. But I meant what I told you in your apartment. You're all I want now. It doesn't matter how many fake tits in Spandex parade around in front of me. What's more, Brodie knows it." His jaw tightens, his eyes snapping with temper. "It was pure desperation that made him fuck up tonight. Desperation and whatever he was jacked up on."

"That's why I was scared for you," I admit quietly. "It's a frightening recipe." I give myself a mental shake and press a soft kiss on his lips before continuing more certainly, "It's over now. We have almost two whole days before I go home and you go off to set the European Union on fire. Let's enjoy them."

He kisses me, his free hand secured in my hair while his lips move smoothly over mine. I hum softly, feeling the leftover tension drain from my body. Eventually, he flips the ice pack off his hand and wraps both arms around me. "Hey," I object, but he simply chuckles.

"My twenty minutes is well past," he assures me. "I'll let you ice my knuckles again later. Right now, it's almost two a.m., and it's time for bed, gorgeous girl."

At the reminder of the time, exhaustion sweeps over me. "Oh. Okay." Apparently, my higher vocabulary has already called it a night. I heave myself up, but before I can step away from him, he stands and scoops me up in his arms.

"Kennedy," I protest through a laugh. "Put me down, you idiot. You'll hurt your hand again!"

"I'm indestructible, baby, dontcha know?" he croons, leering at me outrageously, making me laugh again. It's cathartic, and I appreciate that he's trying to lighten my spirits. I cling to his shoulders and curl up against his chest as he walks us up the stairs to our room. The bed beckons, the silky blue duvet gleaming in the moonlight that streams in the French doors.

Kennedy tells me about some biker-dude at the meet-and-greet who brought a rare album for them to sign, and the spark in his eyes warms my heart. He's so appreciative of his fans and seems in almost in awe of their dedication and the lengths they sometimes go to out of love for his music. I know that it embarrasses him sometimes, but it makes perfect sense to me that someone would scour the Internet looking for one of his albums in vinyl. His talent is worth it. *He's* worth it.

"It made me think it would be cool to make sure Parker gets a few of our old albums as well as the newer stuff. I need to re-member to tell Brodie—" He breaks off, his bright eyes dimming and a frustrated scowl marring his perfect lips. He sets me on my feet next to the bed, his hands sliding along my upper arms as my hand rests on his chest. "Sorry. I didn't mean to bring that shit up again," he mumbles, his broad shoulders slumping a little.

"Don't worry about it." Then an unwelcome thought occurs to me. "Are you able to fire him by yourself or does everyone need to agree?"

"I'm not sure," he admits with a grimace. "He's been

managing our tours forever, and he's damn good at it. He was tight with us for the first couple of years, but he's different now." He tests his hand, scowling as he makes a fist. "Fuck, the number of times Tucker's warned me about his partying." He lets out a huff of frustration. "That fucker's number is up. The guys will understand."

I'm not sure about that, but keep it to myself. Reaching up, I take his face between my hands. "Don't think about him now," I instruct gently. "Brodie doesn't matter.

He wraps his arms around me tightly. Our lips meet, first gently, and then with increasing vigor. My fatigue vanishes, and I gladly let him maneuver us down onto the soft bed. I lock my hands in his soft hair and feel like my heart is about to burst out of my chest. Being with him feels as natural as breathing. The feeling no longer worries me. In fact, I embrace it.

"I believe I owe you for letting that fucker ruin your night," he murmurs, kissing his way up my neck to my ear.

"Wasn't your fault." My reply is garbled as he pulls my shirt over my head. "Nothing is ruined," I say more clearly and give his shoulder a nip, making him grunt, a low, sexy sound that makes my blood race. "And I believe I told you to stop talking about the fucker tonight."

He snorts in amusement. "So you did." The rest of our clothes come off at a leisurely pace. Hands and lips glide over smooth skin as we worship each other. Kennedy seems intent on taking his time, no matter how many times I try to move things along. My emotions have been all over the place tonight—for obvious reasons—and they've all coalesced to make me one big ball of smoldering need.

Rolling him onto his back, I kiss my way down his chest and belly, enjoying the way his breathing becomes choppier the lower I go.

He lets out a whimper that turns into a raspy groan when I lick up his length. *"Fuck."*

I've wanted to wrap my lips around him like this since our first time. It's been a while since I did this, but based on his enthusiastic grunts, muffled curses, and pleas of encouragement, I seem to have retained my skills. He is steel encased in satin . . . salty and earthy and all things delicious man. His long fingers wind themselves in my hair and the rhythmic tugging matches my own.

Before I can finish, however, he reaches and pulls me up. "I want you on top," he rasps as I scramble into position and lower myself onto him. His soft curse of surprise is covered by my gasp; he feels so good with no barrier between us that my eyes roll back in my head. Thank god for the depo shot. I think that I could be with Kennedy for a hundred years, and I would always feel this rush, this indescribable thrill that flies through my veins when we're joined.

"Damn, woman," he growls. In a heart-stopping, smooth move, he manages to roll us so that he's now above me without losing our connection. The air fills with murmured endearments, muttered curses, and the faint chimes of Big Ben that float to us from across the Thames. His lips claim mine without breaking his stride, our breaths mingling, and our hearts pounding as one. It's an electrifying ride that I never want to end.

My climax hits me without warning. I cry out and arch off the mattress, digging my nails into his biceps. And, not a moment too soon, apparently; he releases a strangled expletive and comes like a freight train immediately after me.

Collapsing on me, he automatically draws me into a tender embrace as he rolls to the side. His warmth is addictive, and I snuggle against him, focusing on his labored, steady heartbeat. Despite my boneless state, I can't help the sudden tears that spring to my eyes. The thought is jarring: I could have lost this tonight. If Brodie had managed to cut Kennedy, maybe hit something vital . . . I blink, trying to shove the ill-timed thought away, but it's too late. I shudder and gasp out a near-sob, causing him to pull back and look at me with alarm.

"Baby, what is it? Did I crush you?"

I shake my head, all my stupid emotions crashing to the forefront. "No, no, of course not. I'm sorry—it's just that I was remembering tonight and how afraid I was of what he could do to you . . ." I take a deep breath. My voice quivers as I continue, "Kennedy, I never want to see you hurt."

In the bright moonlight, I can see his eyes soften, and he holds me more closely. "Why?" he asks simply, his eyes searching mine.

The words escape me before I can think, my whisper hanging in the air between us. "Because I'm falling in love with you."

chapter sixteen

kennedy

THERE'S FEW TIMES IN MY life that I've been stunned speech-less. While my heart wants to believe those words, I've heard them before and they've meant nothing.

But I know Abby isn't someone who just blurts out things she doesn't mean. Most of the time she's so careful about what she says and how she says it. And right now, she looks up at me with those big, hazel eyes filled with longing and searching for something she hopes to find in me. Her guard is down, and she's never been more real, more open and vulnerable, or more beautiful.

I trace the path of the moonlight across her jaw, gently brushing her tangled hair back with the fingers of my stinging hand. "It's the adrenaline," I whisper with a grin, giving her a chance to take it all back, allowing myself to hope she won't.

She shakes her head slowly, reaching up to skim her fingers over my raw knuckles. I try again. "Florence Nightingale syndrome?"

She skims her lips over the back of my hand, soothing the

steady ache and lets out a half laugh, but she pushes back against the mattress to put some distance between us. Her expression turns serious. "It's okay if you don't feel the same. I know it might take you a while to catch up. I'll never regret saying it, no matter how you feel."

I let my gaze wander down over her exposed body, drinking in the tempting swell of her breasts and the luscious curve of her hips against the disheveled sheets. Pushing both her hands up and over her head, I straddle her waist, pressing her hands into the pillow and lowering my full weight over her. "I don't feel the same way," I whisper, and her eyes widen. "I'm not falling in love with you; I'm already there."

"You are?" The wary look of disbelief on her face overwhelms me. I never want her to doubt me, to doubt this. Not when it's so real to me. The fact is, I'll never have what people tend to define as a normal relationship. It takes a strong person to deal with the insanity that comes with me, and finally, I think I've found her. She's the calm to my chaos, and right now, her eyes search mine, waiting.

"You still don't get it, do you?" She furrows her brow at my words as they tumble out. "I've tried to show you. I've been drowning in everything for so long . . . booze, bad decisions, the partying . . . I knew there was something missing." I let go of one of her hands and gently trace my thumb over her bottom lip. "It was you. And you just came out of nowhere—you saved me." I lace our fingers together above her head, feeling hers tighten against mine, ignoring the pain that radiates through my fingers.

"You're in love with me." I'm not sure if it's a question, or if she's just trying the words on for size.

"And it terrifies me. I'm afraid I'll screw up, or you'll realize what a chore this all is, but I can't deny it. So it's you who needs to do the catching up, baby." Her lips curve into that smile that slays me, and I lean forward to taste her, throwing every-thing into the kiss. All the spoken and unspoken words floating between us and every last amped-up emotion of the chaotic day.

My tongue sweeps over her swollen bottom lip, stealing her breath and making it mine. I feel her arch from the mattress, her warm breasts pressing against my chest, and I focus all of my attention on her.

It's just about feeling her, worshipping her, trying to make her realize how deep I'm in. The more I taste, the hungrier I become. More urgency at a time when I just want to savor her. She's more intoxicating than any cocktail ever could be. My lips trail the curve of her neck, close over her hardened nipple, and then skim down her torso. I'll never get enough of her. That's the thought in my head as my tongue flattens across her navel, and I lift both her legs over my shoulders.

Every whispered breath she has fills me, pushes me higher. Every stroke of my tongue against her heated skin imprints itself in my brain. The feel of her fingers tugging in my hair as I push her thighs wider only serves to intensify the constant ache I seem to have for her.

Turning my head to suck against the smooth skin of her in-ner thigh, I press my thumb in hard circles against her sensitive clit, just the way I now know she likes.

When she's like this, when that mask she's built up is stripped away, it feels like she's really mine, like she's letting me see something no one else gets to. I push her legs back, teasing and tasting her with my tongue. Nothing else matters, not the constant demands, or the drama, only her; warm, sated and shat-tering because of me.

Her palms roam across my shoulders, her nails digs in to mark me, and I do the same, biting against her hip before I claim her as mine once more.

♪ ♩ ♪ ♩

"ARE YOU FUCKING KIDDING ME?" Cameron pushes off the plush sofa in the suite at the W hotel. "You can't just make decisions like this without talking to us."

"He had her backed into a corner with his hands on her. I wasn't stopping to get permission," I fire back at him.

"Fuck's sake. Who is going to handle this shit now? You really think we can find someone who knows us? Who knows our schedule, the industry, the people he does?" Cam asks.

"We'll find someone. I'm not having him anywhere near her. He was jacked up on something. I haven't seen him like that in a long time. If we hadn't been there . . ."

Cam throws his hands up in the air in frustration. "Like you're a saint all the time when you've been partying a little too hard." His words sting, but even at my worst, I've never been as out of control as Brodie was last night.

"I've never threatened a woman."

Cam glances at Tucker, looking for his assessment. Tucker just grimaces. "It was bad," Tucker offers from the familiar position he's taken up beside me. "I wouldn't want him around any of you, actually. He's been getting worse over the last few months. I think we've all seen that."

"I'd say think about how you would feel if it was one your girlfriends, but I can't even say that."

"I get it, mate," Sean chimes in. "The timing sucks, I'm not going to lie, but I understand."

Cam huffs, turning from the wall of windows to face us. "You do realize this shit all started when you two hooked up, right? You're staying somewhere else; you're distracted, pretending you're a prizefighter. What if you had broken your hand? What then, hmm? What about the tour?" He fires off the questions in rapid succession.

I unclench my fist, trying to ignore the radiating dull ache. "I didn't break it. It'll be fine in a couple of days."

"Where's Brodie now?" Matt asks from his perch in the hanging chair.

"He's in his suite here. At least that's where I sent him last night. I'm hiring some more security," Tucker adds.

"Seriously? This is *Brodie* we're talking about. He's not exactly a threat. If he turns sideways, he almost disappears," Cam argues, crossing the room to stop directly in front of me.

"And why do you think that is?" I counter.

"Maybe you should ask yourself that."

I return his blistering glare. "I haven't done anything in a while, and you know it."

"Define *a while*. And what happens when she goes back to the States? Old habits die hard, my friend."

I can feel my anger spike. Sure, we've been at each other's throats before. It's bound to happen when you've logged as many miles on the road as we have together. But, this feels different. It feels like Cam's challenging me. "We're not talking about me."

"The hell we're not. This is only about you," Cam yells and Tucker shifts, ready to step between us. "That's your problem. You only think about yourself. To hell with the rest of us."

"Cam, relax, let's all just take a deep breath, hmm?" Sean suggests, clapping his palm against Cam's shoulder. "It's an epic cluster fuck, but we'll figure it out. It's what we do."

"Is that really the kind of the person you want around? Someone who would threaten a woman and take so much shit that he doesn't even sound like himself?"

"How come you're just complaining about him now, hmm? Didn't seem to bother you a few months ago when you were snorting up half a bag and downing a bottle of Jack a night." I may not want to admit it, but he's right. That's been my cycle. A cycle I know was enabled by Brodie. I can't change anything that's happened in my fucked-up past, but now, I have a reason to change. Maybe more importantly, I want to change.

"We weren't on tour a couple of months ago, and—"

"I'd like to rip his fucking head off for touching her," Matt practically growls as he interrupts, pushing up from the chair.

An unnatural silence stretches between us all. There's been enough drama amongst us during the years we've been together, that I recognize this as one of the more intense situations we've had. This lifestyle—the demands of it all and the temptation that lurks around every corner—is an unpredictable force that can result in either explosive genius or total disaster. And, for the first time in a long time, I'm not sure which way we're headed.

"I'll find somebody to manage the rest of tour, all right? I'll get Nicole on it."

Nicole Hays, our PR manager will kill me for springing this cluster fuck on her, but I really don't have a choice.

"This is bullshit. You should have told us so we could make a decision together, as a group, if that's what we even are anymore," Cam grinds out.

"So vote now," I challenge.

"Would it make a difference? You've already decided."

"I gotta say, Cam, I'm with Kennedy on this one," Matt announces.

Sean slings his arm around my shoulder. "We'll figure it out. How hard can planning this shit be, really? I mean come on. We're Redfall for Christ's sake. We just need to show up and play."

"Maybe we should name the tour that. Show up and play," Matt muses, ambling over to us.

"I need some air," Cameron grumbles, stalking to the door.

It slams shut behind him with a brutal force, sounding very final.

"I HAVE NEWS," I MUMBLE under Abby's ear as she sits with her back pressed to my chest in the sea of a tub in the ensuite. We're ignoring the fact that she's leaving soon and making the most of our time together. With the exception of a few conference calls she had, and me trying to track down Cam, we've been inseparable and insatiable. She leans back to press her warm, wet lips to mine. "Tell me."

"Ravine is going to do the concert," I whisper under her ear. She turns around quickly to face me, the water splashing over the sides of the tub as she straddles me.

"Landon Ravine? As in lead singer of The Vandels?"

I narrow my eyes, my hands sliding over her perfect tits, around her hips, settling to palm her ass. "The very one."

"That's huge, Kennedy!" she says enthusiastically.

"Mmm. I've heard that before," I tease, earning me a splash of water to my face. "You're a fan then, I take it? It's his tats, right? You know, I have those too."

She leans forward to trace her finger against the notes that line my shoulder. It's something I've found she enjoys doing, and I'll never complain about her hands being on me. If it were up to me, it would always be that way.

"Really? Is that what these are?"

"There's a condition, though. There always is with him."

She frowns. "What condition?"

I let out a huff, still not quite believing I'm even considering this. "He's been trying to get me to be a guest mentor on his reality show pretty much since it began." Her eyes widen at my words.

"And you didn't want to?"

"I wasn't really in any condition to be a mentor to anyone."

She holds my gaze, her fingers tracing gently against the lines of ink on my chest. "And now you are?"

"I'm getting there. Because of you." She smiles, a blush covering her face. "I wanted to check with you, and see what you thought about it."

A look of confusion clouds her face. "Why does it matter what I think?"

I shift my hips, my length hardening against her sensitive skin. "I care about what you think. Also, they might joke around like they always do, and ask about my love life. I wanted to see what I was allowed to say on national TV. What you're comfortable with."

She lets out a soft groan as her hips roll back, her sweet pussy teasing over my cock. "I'm comfortable with anything," she murmurs.

"That's a very dangerous thing to say, Miss Walker." Her answering giggle dies quickly as I show her why.

"KENNEDY! OH MY GOD! TUCKER! Stop him," Abby practically hisses at Tucker who's too busy trying to stop traffic.

"Come on!" I shout back to her as I sink down to the famed Abbey Road zebra crossing and lie down over it.

"You can't lie down there. You're going to get hit, you crazy man!" she half laughs-squeals.

"I can and I am. Get over here, you." I lean up to motion her over as horns blast from either side of the street. Annoyed yells from impatient drivers and a round of applause from the other tourists float around us. I can see her hesitation and that internal battle I know she's fighting.

"Clock's ticking, Abby," Tucker offers, as he jumps into the role of pseudo traffic cop. "I can't hold them off forever."

She laughs, shaking her head before running over to me and taking my outstretched hand. I tug her down as she giggles away, another series of horns exploding down the street. My fingers tighten around hers, and I glance over at her. "Now close your eyes and tell me what you hear."

"You're nuts," she mutters, but closes her eyes. "You know most people just walk across here?"

I smile at her amused expression. The temptation to kiss her is running wild through me. "Where's the fun in that? What do you hear?"

"I hear people who are going to run us down," she says through a laugh.

"No." I shut my eyes, feeling the pulse of the street seep into me. "It's a song . . . it's history . . . a rhythm . . . it's alive."

"Hey, fuckwit! Sometime today!" a deep, booming voice shouts to us.

I hear Tucker try to calm the masses, and then his concerned voice rumbles over to us, "Got about a minute before they lose it, sunshine."

"Kennedy . . ." Abby whispers, her grip tightening around my hand.

"Shhh. Just listen."

abigail

QUELLING MY NERVES, I TAKE a deep breath and focus, trying to feel what he's feeling. At first, there's nothing. And then . . .

"A dance," I whisper tentatively, as a strange sensation fills me. "Stately, but impatient."

"Good." I peek at him to see his encouraging smile. "Go on."

"Perpetual movement, but with sweeping grandeur, like a waltz." A blaring of horns interrupts, and I hear Tucker curse behind me as I spring to my feet in alarm. Kennedy laughs at me, but concedes and gracefully rises to his feet. Tucker ushers us off the road, but before he steps onto the safety of the curb again, Kennedy turns back toward the street and the impatient traffic flying by and makes a sweeping bow, as if he's a courtier. The tourists across the street break out into applause and laughter, and I can't help but join them. I'm grinning like a fool, my spirit feeling lighter than it has in years.

"One of these days, man," Tucker grumbles, but I catch a hint of smile lurking on his lips.

"Oh, come on. Live a little." Kennedy grins and slings an arm around my shoulders, pulling me close. He presses a kiss to my temple and then releases me to take my hand as we continue down the street. "So, a waltz, eh?"

Feeling foolish, I straighten my back and jut my chin out in challenge. "You're making fun of me?"

"Not at all." He brings our joined hands up and kisses my fingers, a move that makes my heart skip a beat and my pique evaporate. "Everything has its own energy, its own story just waiting to be told. All it takes is for someone to hear it. And everyone hears a different thing, so there's no wrong answer."

A throat clearing behind me is an abrupt reminder that we're not alone and I wince. How can I keep forgetting a six-foot walking wall of muscle? Tucker has shadowed us everywhere we've gone today, but only speaks when needed. I can only imagine the things he's seen since he's been with this crazy bunch.

Kennedy glances over his shoulder at Tucker, and gives my hand a squeeze in reassurance. "Don't worry, baby. Tucker tells

272 B.B. MILLER AND LESLIE CARSON

no tales."

"Lucky for you," I mutter, casting around for a change of subject. "Hey, are you hungry? I think my stomach is finally acclimating to the time zone."

"Yeah, I could eat. I know of a great—" He's interrupted by the ringing of his phone in his pocket. With a scowl, he pulls it out and looks at the screen; his scowl deepens as he silences the cell and puts it away.

"Don't you have to get that? They might need you."

He releases my hand and pulls me closer, dropping a kiss to the top of my head. "It's my day off. Today is about us."

My spirits soar at his declaration. He's been like this all day; warm and openly affectionate regardless of the people around us. This onslaught of intimacy has completely torn down all my defenses, rendering all my previous worries moot. And I can't remember being so happy.

"Okay, then. How about we go to a little place *I* know this time?" He's led the tour today so far, and I want to share a bit of what I know about the city.

"Lead on, MacDuff," he agrees, seemingly delighted at my offer.

"Sure. There's a tube station over there." I begin to lead us toward the entrance, but Tucker interrupts.

"Let's take a cab instead," he asserts, giving Kennedy a look. "You've been lucky today, but let's not push it." Kennedy looks like he's about to argue, but Tucker stalks to the curb and immediately flags down one of the city's charming black cabs. Truth be told, I love taking taxis in London, so I head off a potential argument by climbing inside. As I rattle off our destination to the obliging cabbie and quickly find myself squished between the two hard-bodied men. Not a bad place to be.

♪ ♩ ♪ ♩

AFTER A QUIET LUNCH AT an unassuming pub, we mumble good-byes to the smirking bodyguard as we close the door to the suite, and then we're an awkward mass of limbs struggling to pull off jackets and sweaters and jeans between kisses. We fall down on one of the luxurious sofas, and he grunts softly as I run my hands over his firm chest. His skin feels like velvet to my touch, and I can't keep my hands off him.

It's sweet, sweet torture when he lowers his head between my thighs, sending my senses spinning. I push up to meet his unrelenting tongue. My breath comes in soft pants; it's the only sound in the room besides his soft grunts of encouragement. In minutes he has me falling apart, my cries echoing off the walls.

He crawls up my body while I'm still coming down from my high and kisses me deeply.

"You're next," I promise, my voice still breathy, and he smiles. Over the next few hours, we move from the sofa, to the floor, and finally make our way upstairs to claim the bed. I've never been so insatiable, but he meets me every step of the way. When I finally collapse against his firm thighs, every inch of me feels spent. Jesus.

"Holy fuck," he pants from behind me. "I think you've broken me, woman."

A giggle bubbles up as I rest my forehead on his knee. "I think you'll recover." I feel his hands gliding over my ass.

"What a view, though." He still sounds winded. Maybe I did break him.

"Speak for yourself," I tease. "I'm staring at your knobby knees." I give one of the knees in question a playful nip and he laughs, slapping my ass in return.

"Turn around, wench, so I can kiss those sassy lips."

I lift and let him slip out of me, and roll off to the side before I scramble into his arms. I snuggle in and give him a sweet kiss. Humming contentedly against my lips, he lets me settle with my head resting on his shoulder.

"Jesus. I have no fucking control around you." He sighs happily, but chuckles when his belly rumbles again. "I think I'd better order something. Unless you'd rather get dressed and go out?"

I shake my head, perfectly content where I am. "Ordering in is great." We untangle ourselves, and he pulls on some jeans while I wander into the bathroom for a few moments. When I emerge, I hear a few notes from the piano drift up to me, and a grin blossoms on my face. The notes become a line, and then a flowing torrent. I don't recognize the song, but I don't want to interrupt him by going downstairs to ask. Whatever it is, it's beautiful and complex, just like him.

I lie back down and drift for a few minutes, the music lulling me, and my eyes wander to the terrace outside the French doors. A sudden urge has me rising to my feet. I wrap the blue coverlet from the bed around my shoulders to protect me from the chill and go outside. The large terrace has a lovely view of the city, and I wander past the outdoor dining set to sink down onto one of the large chaises that dot the space. I can see the famous Eye as it turns, the lights winking at me in the darkness.

I take a deep breath, letting the early autumn air fill my lungs. A cloud floats in front of the moon, making it look like cotton candy, lit from within. It looks like I feel—every inch of me feels alight and alive in a way I've never felt before. And it's not just because of the amazing sex. It's him, in all his multi-layered, brilliantly-talented glory.

A sound distracts me, and I look over to see him depositing a tray of food on the table before he walks over to join me. "Hey, baby," he whispers, looking at me with concern. "Are you okay?"

I nod and give him a reassuring smile before pressing my lips to his. Our kiss quickly becomes heated, and I open my wrap to allow him to snuggle against me. He manages to rid himself of his jeans and leans me back against the cushions, whispering sweet encouragement in my ear. I know I'll be sore in the morning, but I can't bring myself to care.

As he slowly fills me, the clouds disappear, unveiling a blanket of stars above us, and I beam. Because I am safe in his arms. Just like his song.

RELENTLESS POUNDING ON THE DOOR and muttered voices in the hall show no signs of letting up despite Kennedy's insistence we just ignore the racket. Having made our way down to the main floor the next morning, he spent some more time trying to find Cameron while I got caught up on email. I was surprised how comfortable it was to just be together, an easy companionship I wasn't expecting as we both worked away. Well, no longer. Kennedy is up and hauling the door open, his jaw rigid.

"Do you have nothing better to do?" Kennedy scowls and I can't help but laugh as his bandmates and Tucker push past him and into the suite.

"I tried to stop him," Tucker says. "You know how he gets."

"Fuck's sake," Kennedy mutters, letting the door shut behind the group.

"Bloody hell! Look at him blush!" a British voice bellows. "She really must have a MP!"

Kennedy glares, and I see the drummer, Sean, grinning at me maniacally. His dyed hair is wild and unruly. It's disconcerting. "Come on, mate, aren't you going to finally introduce me?"

"Abby, this is Sean." Kennedy's voice is a warning growl, but it's not directed at me.

Sean ignores him and slips a conspiratorial arm around my shoulders. "Come with me, my beautiful MP, and tell me all your secrets," he sings, while I smile at him in confusion. "You can meet my sister, Sydney. She's gracing us with her presence today." He waves over at a tall redhead standing near the door who simply laughs at him before he ducks back down close to my ear. "I'm the better-looking twin, but don't tell her that."

"Twin?" I say. Kennedy tries to take hold of my hand, despite Sean tugging me toward the seating area near the piano. "And sorry, but I don't have any secrets." I playing along. At least, none that I'm going to share with him.

He waves a hand dismissively. "I'll tell you my secrets, then. Mine are probably more interesting anyway." He stops in front of our destination and throws his free hand in the air victoriously before sinking to one of the couches. "Boys! Behold, the MP!"

"Oh, fuck," Kennedy groans softly, and pulls me from Sean's grasp, securing me to his side. "Keep your fucking paws off her, asshole." He shoots me an apologetic smile, and I lean closer.

"MP?" I ask quietly. The only MPs I've heard of are Members of Parliament or Military Police. Embarrassment flashes on his face for an instant.

"Never mind. He doesn't even know what the hell he's talking about most of the time."

"Sit, HRH. Tell us all about the lady who has managed to tame the savage beast," Sean coaxes gleefully, patting the cushion beside him. The bass player with the ridiculous Mohawk, Matt, leans against the side of the couch, but Cameron is nowhere to be seen.

Kennedy sandwiches himself between Sean and me, pushing him out of the way with a frustrated huff. "Jesus you're a pain in the ass." Sean just laughs as his sister Sydney drifts in to join the fold.

I smile when Kennedy leans in for a soft kiss that I can feel down to my toes. It's like he's my anchor to reality amongst these larger-than-life characters, and I take comfort in the feel of his arm slung around my shoulders and his steady gaze. But when I look back to the group, I see them examining me with a mixture of curiosity, shock, and wariness.

Alrighty, then . . . Here we go.

chapter seventeen

kennedy

"AND THAT'S WHEN OUR MAN here stood right up to the guy and told him to step aside," Sean explains as he perches on the back of the couch across from us. He's holding court as only he can. The presence of Sean's twin sister, Sydney, doesn't seem to have had any impact on his behavior, and nothing he says or does seem to faze her. I think she's just accepted the fact that her brother is who is. Something tells me he's given her a lifetime's worth of ammunition to tease him with.

Sean and Sydney are polar opposites. Syd with her short, always perfectly styled red hair, dressed like she's just got off a *J.Crew* photoshoot, and Sean with a new color of hair every week and a personality that needs its own zip code. If they didn't finish each other's sentences half the time you'd never know they were related.

We've been indulging on takeout from a Chinese restaurant Sean claims is the best in London. The table is strewn with just about every dish on the menu. I pass Abby another fortune cookie before trailing the pad of my thumb over the back of her hand.

She offers me a hesitant smile. It's probably been a bit like an episode of the *Twilight Zone* for her. Sean alone is a trip at the best of times; couple that with the incident with Brodie, and she must feel like she's stepped to the other side of the looking glass.

Sean continues on, and I shake my head at him and his ridiculous telling of yet another embarrassing moment. At least I remember this one. "Thought the brute was going to level him right then and there. He was a badass. The size of a Redwood." He flails his arms, almost toppling off the back of the couch.

Matt steadies him with a laugh. "But no. Kennedy here wasn't having it. Wanted the kids to get their swag and autographs first. Almost a saint your man here is, MP."

"Stop calling her that," I growl.

Sean gives me a smirk and a salute as Abby's hand tightens against my thigh. "I like that story," she whispers under my ear, leaning into my side. I can feel her breath against my neck and smell her warm, inviting scent, her tight little body pressed up against mine, making me just want to kick my annoying bandmates out.

"Yeah?" My fingers find their way to the back of her neck and into her hair, and I feel her shiver slightly. It's good to know I'm not the only one affected.

"Then there was that time in Singapore when were at that bathhouse," Sean starts.

I almost spit my mouthful of water across the table. "And that's your cue. Time to for you all to go."

"They're leaving?" Abby asks, those big hazel eyes blinking up at me, making my heart clench.

"Please tell me you're not enjoying listening to this idiot's ramblings."

"Actually, it's very revealing," she teases.

"Lies. It's all lies. Don't believe a thing any of them tell you."

A balled-up napkin clocks me in the back of the head, and I level a glare at Sean.

"Every word is true and you know it, mate. Actually, you might not remember some of it, and I may have embellished that bit 'bout the bet with the roadies that landed us in questioning at the border crossing in Vancouver, but everything else? True." Sean opens up another fortune cookie from the bag. "Kind of."

"See?" I wrap my arm around her shoulder, bringing her into my side right where she belongs. "Here's an example of those reliable sources close to the action you always read about. Believe nothing unless you hear it from me, baby."

"Grasshopper!" Sean shouts. "Time for us to go—."

"Just no," Sydney starts, hitting him on the shoulder. Sean pouts at her. "You're only here for a few days, and I've hardly seen you. No more clubs or groupies."

Abby leans against my shoulder, whispering under my ear. "I really like her."

"You're no fun at all," Sean complains, nudging her in the shoulder.

Sydney shakes her head at him. "You'll thank me in the morning."

"No word from Cam yet?" Matt asks, putting the elephant in the room front and center. Cameron's MIA stunt is starting to worry all of us. None of us have ever gone this long without at least checking in.

Sean shakes his head. "I've checked the usual haunts . . . No one's seen him, man. It's like he's up and vanished." He reaches for another takeout box, collecting the noodles with his chopsticks.

"I know. Fucker hasn't returned any of my texts or calls either," Tucker adds as he looks up from his phone, a familiar look of concern firmly in place.

"He'll turn up. You know that. He lives for touring." Sean's trying to sound convincing.

"Think he might have been living for something else lately." Matt's voice echoes through the room. I feel my jaw tense, and both Sean and I turn to face him.

"What are you on about now, Matty?" There's a strain in Sean's voice, a concern we don't hear very often.

Matt rubs the back of his neck before leaning back against the leather chair. "Ah, fuck, man. Ignore me. I'm exhausted." He stretches his legs out in front of him, settling in.

"You don't get to say shit like that and then brush it off. Not with us. What do you know?" I bite out.

"It's probably nothing." He tries to wave us off, but Sean pushes off the couch, moving to get in his face. Sydney tries unsuccessfully to hold him back.

He plants his hands on either side of the chair, his brow furrowed. "This is Cameron we're talking about. He's saved your ass more times than I can count. He's like our fucking brother. If you know something, you damn well better spit it out."

"He's been drinking," Matt starts after a long beat, causing Sean to scoff. He pushes away from the chair, and the pacing starts.

"Tell me something I don't know."

"A lot," Matt adds, looking between us.

"Define a lot." My words are clipped, and the dark unease that's been lingering around us seems to close in. I feel Abby squeeze my hand in silent support.

"I guess I started noticing before we left the States. And then after the show at the O2, it was just different." He shrugs and pauses before he continues, "I mean, we always party, but, you were both MIA, along with Brodie, and he seemed pissed about where everyone was. Got it in his head that we had to go to one of the late night clubs in Soho." I hear a muttered curse from Tucker as he moves closer. "It was like he was on a mission or something. Started doing rounds of the Seven Deadly Sins and chasing them with fishbowl martinis that just kept showing up. I practically had to drag him back to the hotel. He's usually a happy drunk, you know? This was something else."

I frown as I listen to Matt. It's rare when he shares anything, and it's a bit of jolt to hear the worry in his voice. "He didn't seem that wrecked when we met the next day at the W," Tucker remarks. I've partied enough with Cam to know that he recovers like I do. We're always able to function after a blowout—it's a blessing and, I'm starting to realize, a curse.

I rake my hand through my hair in frustration. This entire situation is, in Sean's words, a cluster fuck. "Fucking hell."

"Why didn't you say anything?" Sean barks out, turning back to Matt.

"Why didn't *you* say anything a few weeks back when you decided to snort whatever he put in front of you?" Matt fires back at him, pushing out of the chair. "Why don't any of us say anything about half the shit we do? We just take a few days and figure it out. That's probably what he's doing."

"And what if it's not, hmm? What if he's dead in a ditch somewhere?" Sean rants, his arms flailing wildly.

Tucker grips Sean's shoulder, steering him back a few paces. "Everybody just calm down. He's not dead in a ditch." Tucker's voice rises as he levels us all with a knowing look. "I'll make some calls. See if Brodie has heard from him too."

"Fuck. I don't want you to get him involved."

"Kennedy." Tucker cuts me off before I can finish my violent objection. "We need to find him, and Brodie might know where he is. I wouldn't be doing my job if I didn't check it out."

The tension riots through me, but I know he's right. "All

right. I'll get in touch with a few more people, too. Let's regroup in the morning. Text if you hear anything. I don't care what time it is."

♪ ♩ ♪ ♩

abigail

TIME HASN'T STOPPED, NO MATTER how much I wish it could. I secure my hair into a ponytail as our butler carries my luggage to the main floor of the suite. I cast one last look at the opulent bedroom swathed in blue silk and the lovely terrace that witnessed some of the most passionate moments of my life. I wonder if I'll ever be back.

I find Kennedy at the piano downstairs, his eyes troubled as his fingers float effortlessly over the keys. I don't recognize the tune, but it's sweet and sad, and makes me want to curl up on one of the sofas to listen to him all afternoon. Unfortunately, that's not to be.

"So, you have everything?" he asks quietly, stopping to swing his legs over the bench and stand.

"Not everything."

He returns my sad gaze and walks over to pull me into his arms. "I know," he whispers. "How am I going to make it through this fucking tour without you?"

I chuckle weakly. "I was asking myself the same thing—how I was going to make it through the next few weeks."

"You'll be fine," he says with a wistful sigh. "You've got all those kids whose dreams you're making come true. You're strong like that, baby. I've seen it."

"You'll be fine, too. Stick close to Tucker." My whisper is garbled against his chest, but he seems to hear me anyway. "I'm going to miss you so much."

"Oh, fuck, me, too," he blurts, his breath coming rougher. "You have no fucking idea." His arms are like steel bands around me, and I cling to him just as strongly. Burying his face in my hair, he inhales deeply, as if I'm the very air he breathes.

There's a discreet cough behind us at the door, and I suddenly remember that Tucker is waiting with Colin and the butler. I force myself to release him and step back a pace, his arms still loosely holding my shoulders. "We've got to go, or I'll miss my flight."

He smiles sadly. "I'm not going to the airport." My protest dies on my lips as he explains, "If I go to see you off, I'll end up on that plane with you back to San Francisco, and then I'll really be in the shit with the guys."

"Well, I wouldn't want to be responsible for that," I try to joke, but it falls a little flat. Oh, this is ridiculous—it's only for a few weeks. I nod to myself, and manage to smile a bit brighter. "I'll call or text you when I land."

"Call me. I'll want to hear your voice." My eyes dart back to his, but he doesn't meet my gaze. Instead, he steers me toward the door and our waiting entourage with his hand at my waist. "Guys, can you wait outside for a second?"

Tucker's concerned eyes belie his impassive expression as he escorts the other two out to the hallway. "I'll take your luggage downstairs, Miss," the butler informs us crisply, as the door closes. Before it even latches, Kennedy swings me around, his lips descending for one last, devastating kiss. I'm panting and blinking away tears when he finally pulls away, because—this is it.

"I love you, Abigail Walker. Never forget it." His eyes bore into mine with an intensity that takes my breath away.

"I won't," I promise. "I love you, too. And I'll tell you every day until I can do this again." I pull his lips back to mine, surprising him, but he moans into my mouth and clings to me. The desire is overwhelming, but I wrench myself away, my eyes welling. "See you soon," I mumble and yank open the door to leave while I still can.

"Not soon enough." His whisper draws my eyes to his, and I think I manage to return his lopsided grin as I let Colin lead me to the elevator. The last thing I see as the doors close is his bleak half-smile, and Tucker's hand clapped on his shoulder.

IT'S THE IMAGE THAT STAYS with me as I sink into the plush leather of the waiting SUV with Colin, and later in my first-class cocoon. Staring out the tiny window, I wallow like a champ, clinging to the dull ache in my heart like a badge of honor, at least until I feel the thump when we touch down in San Francisco.

Taking a deep breath, I wipe my tired eyes. I'm being ridiculous. I know this. I'll see him again in a few weeks. He'll be back for a break before beginning the North American leg of his tour, and he promised we'd spend some time at his house in Bodega Bay. In the meantime, I have work to do.

I join the stream of other people trudging through the airport to collect luggage and try to tuck the bliss of the last few days away. A chime alerts me to a text, so I drag my phone out of my pocket—the words bring an instant smile to my face and a skip to my step.

I love you, beautiful girl. I can't see you soon enough.

chapter eighteen

kennedy

"HOLD UP." I TURN AROUND from the microphone, glancing at Sean and finally drop my hands from my faithful Les Paul. My knuckles throb with an ache that still lingers, but I welcome the pain. I'd do it all over again to protect Abby.

Sweat pours off Sean, soaking his ridiculous white mesh shirt under his leather vest. His drumsticks are poised in the air, ready to play more, but thick tension radiates between us and we need some air. "Let's take a break."

Sean tilts his head up to the exposed rafters in the rehearsal hall we've commandeered for the rest of the week. "Thank fuck. Thought you were going for a world record there for a while."

"We need the practice," I note, not that they need reminding.

"Because we're not ready?" Matt tries to ease the gnawing tension that's been building, passing his bass to one of the roadies with a roll of his neck. Unfortunately, we're missing the one thing that will bring balance back to the group. Cameron has yet to surface.

Calling the police would be a PR nightmare, as Nicole Hays,

my PR manager wisely pointed out. The last thing we need is bad press at the start of this tour. Tucker is doing his job, chasing down every lead he can find, but so far, he's come up empty. To say we all are walking a precariously thin line is an epic understatement.

"Not even remotely," I mumble, leaning my guitar on one of the stands by the stack of amps. Tucker shoves a bottle of water into my hand.

"A little hard to be ready when one of us isn't here," Sean mutters, twirling one of the drum sticks through his fingers the way he always does after we play. He's a bundle of frenetic energy, always in perpetual motion, but it's even more pronounced today.

Twisting the cap off the water I take a long sip.

"What if—"

"Don't go there," I cut Sean off. "There's not a 'what if.' It's like I told you, this tour doesn't work without all of us. We'll find him." And even though my voice sounds confident, for the first time with this group, I'm anything but.

"Don't you think we need to at least talk about a backup plan?" Matt lifts the strap of his bass over his head as we enter into hour four of rehearsals.

"It's not an option." I wait while a couple of roadies make yet another adjustment to the amps.

"We could get some guest guitarists," Sean suggests. "Shit, between the three of us we know everyone worth playing with." He wipes his brow with the back of his hand, looking exhausted. We're all sharing that familiar look these last few days.

I turn to face them both. "How many times do we have to have this conversation? We're in this together. This is our album, *our* tour."

"Yeah and in case you missed it, we sound like shit without

him," Sean adds quietly.

"How would you feel if you went off the radar for a while, and we just replaced you with some other drummer without even having a conversation with you?"

"That would never happen. I'd never just disappear like this," he counters defiantly.

"Well, we never thought he would either, and look where we are," Matt adds.

"I'm not going to do that to him. I wouldn't do it to any of you. Think about everything we've been through. You honestly think he's not going to show?" I ask, feeling the frustration boil over.

Matt and Sean exchange a look that makes me think they've been talking about this behind my back. Vaguely, from across the room, I hear the thick wooden door to the room shut, but I'm past the point of caring who hears me unleash on them. "Then give me a name!" My voice fills the hall. "Tell me someone who knows the material the way he does. Who can play it like he can. Who is even half as good as he is."

Slowly, a grin appears on Sean's face as he focuses his attention to the door, pointing his drumsticks across the room as he bounces on his stool. Matt and I follow his gaze and a wave of relief washes over me, followed quickly by an unexpected shot of alarm.

Flanked by Colin and Tucker, Cameron takes a tentative step toward us. His clothes are disheveled, and he's gripping his guitar case to his chest like a lifeline. Under the glare of the overhead lights, he looks haggard, like he hasn't slept in a week. He approaches cautiously, and I take in his bloodshot eyes. He's a little worse for the wear, but he's here, and to me, that's everything.

He looks between the three of us, his mouth curving into a smile before he finally speaks. "I hear you're looking for a guitarist."

♪ ♩ ♪ ♩

"PLEASE TELL ME YOU'VE FOUND a replacement for Brodie." I lean forward on the couch in the suite at the Corinthia in London, glancing at the computer screen as Nicole's face comes into view. I'm going to have to give her a raise for dealing with the chaos that seems to follow me. These last few days have been particularly challenging, and she's been working all hours handling the madness.

Rumors are big business, and right now, they're flying. It started with grainy photos of Abby and me in various locations around London. Twitter blew up, and I'm sure Nic has said, "No comment," a thousand times in the past couple of days.

Rumblings that we had lost our tour manager have been making the rounds. The sharks are circling. Redfall, according to every single media outlet, is on the verge of breaking up.

"You're so bossy. Good morning to you, too," Nicole teases, taking a long, loud, exaggerated sip of coffee from a black Redfall mug. She lifts the mug to the screen. "These are in high demand these days, what with you guys breaking up tomorrow and everything." She smirks from behind the cup, and I can't help but laugh. "And would it kill you to shave?"

"You don't like the scruff?" I brush my hand over the stubble on my jaw.

"Doesn't matter what I like. Your fans will probably love it. So, I've been working on a few leads," she starts, sliding on her bright red glasses. "Dawson Hampton. He ran point on the Foo Fighters tour last time around. He's coming in today." I'm impressed with Nic again. Dawson is a legend in the business.

"I'm surprised he's even free."

"He took some time off. His wife had a heart attack earlier this year. Puts things in perspective, if you know what I mean.

He's only doing selective shows now," she adds. "He won't be cheap."

"I know. It's worth it, though. I can't deal with the logistics of this shit anymore." Between rehearsals, we've all been pitching in, trying to navigate the insane touring schedule, but despite our best efforts, the well-oiled machine shows signs of breaking down.

"The lawyers have Brodie's release ready to be signed," Nicole states, bringing my attention back to where it should be. She looks up from the tablet, hesitating for a moment. Despite her attempts to hide it, I can see the worry etched on her face.

"Spit it out, Nic."

"I got a tip today. Brodie's making the rounds with the media, gauging interest in a tell-all interview."

I feel my jaw clench with aggravation. "I'd like to see him try. He's signed a confidentiality agreement."

"Doesn't matter what he signed," she interrupts. "If he doesn't use your name, he's probably free and clear."

"Everyone knows he's worked for us for the last decade."

"Exactly. You might want to think about beating him to it. I'm sure I don't even want to know some of the stories he could share. Talk about a PR nightmare."

My shoulders slump, and I hang my head in my hands. "I should have gotten rid of him a long time ago."

"Should have, could have, my friend. It's too late now. The lawyers have tried to put a gag on him in the release, but this is Brodie we're talking about. You know that saying about keeping your friends close and your enemies closer?"

"Tell me what to do, Nic, because honestly, I'm at a loss on this one."

"Brodie thinks he has the upper hand right now, throwing around the threat of releasing any skeletons you may have lurking around in the closet." I feel a wave of panic roll through me. He could ruin everything with a single interview. "But exposing you means exposing him. Honestly, I think he's full of shit. I think it's a tactic to get you to call him, beg him to come back. My advice? Show him you don't care. Brodie's news will be a fading memory as soon as the next story breaks." I let out a heavy breath. "I'm sorry," she adds quickly. "That sounded really shitty. Just focus on the tour, the concert for Parker."

"How's the planning going?" I ask, feeling the overwhelming need to steer the conversation away from Brodie. The less I have to think or talk about him, the better.

"We've got the venue secured. AT&T Park." I grin as she continues, "The website is set up and already taking donations." I can hear the excitement in her voice, her words coming faster than normal. "Media outlets have received the primer and are already talking about what a saint you are." She takes a much-needed breath.

"And we have a Twitter hashtag that's started trending—*Rock the Dream.*"

"I know I probably don't say it enough, but—"

"I'm a genius and you love me. I know. Save the praise for when we're through these next few weeks. Besides, I want to go over the agenda for the morning of the concert."

"Bring it on."

"As long as the doctors give the okay on Parker being released the morning of, we'll have a press conference at the hospital." She gives me a pointed look. "It's good publicity for them, as long as we can keep Sean under control, of course."

"Good luck with that."

"I swear to God that man gives me more gray hair than you do, and that's saying something."

"He's harmless."

"I'll remind you that you said that one day." She laughs before pushing on through the agenda. "We've already had our camera crews in to film some footage of the hospital, and we've done a few interviews with some of the kids who received the swag I sent over." She pauses, taking her glasses off, her expression taking an immediate downturn. "Some of these kids are so sick, Kennedy. It's just heartbreaking to see. What you've done so far has made such a difference, and I'm not just saying that because you pay me to."

"That's all I want out of this. For them to feel a little better, you know? Give them a bit of happiness, even if it's just for a little while."

Nic's eyes gloss over, and it stirs up my own rioting emotions. I don't ever think I've seen the woman cry, unless it was at some ridiculous stunt Sean has pulled over the years. She clears her throat and soldiers on.

"You'll do a walkthrough of the wing Parker is in after the press conference. Meet a few of the kids, maybe do an acoustic session?" She waits, gauging my reaction. "I like the sound of that."

"Good. Then the limos will take you and Parker, his mom and dad, and his nurse."

"Wait, his nurse?" I interrupt.

"It was a condition of the hospital, and his mom insisted, too."

"Is she a hot nurse?" I tease.

She scowls with an exaggerated shudder. "Jesus. Get your mind out of the gutter. You have Abby for that, remember?"

"Oh, how I do remember. Pick me up one of those sexy nurse uniforms in your travels, will you?"

"Only if hell freezes over, pervert. Do your role-playing kinky shopping on your own time. No amount of money could get me to do that. Just ew." She scans her tablet before continuing, "The limo will take you to your place for a photo shoot. Keep in mind, and I need to repeat this to the other guys, the media is going to be following you along with our own camera crew. You'll need to take it down a few notches, try to keep the swearing to a minimum."

"Obviously." I scowl at her, and she rolls her eyes.

"Please how long have we worked together? I know you four better than anyone needs to. Just try to keep it PG-13." I chuckle with a salute.

She grins, her gaze dropping from the screen to her tablet. "I've got a meeting with Landon's team in fifteen. Apparently, he wants to make sure his name is highlighted in the billing because he's the center of the universe and all." She rolls her eyes.

"Of course he does."

"Fucking rock stars. Why do I put up with all of you?"

abigail

"WHAT TIME DOES YOUR MEETING start?" Maddie asks. I prop the phone between my chin and shoulder so I can use two hands to rummage around my desk for a file.

"At ten. Most of them are here already; Ralph likes to have a little pre-meeting pep talk with the officers beforehand. How's Dylan?" He suffered some bruised ribs during a training exercise last week, which pulled him off duty until they heal. The inactivity is driving him nuts.

"He hates sitting around," she sighs tiredly. "He's still really sore, so the most we can do now are blowjobs."

I bark out a laugh. "Not sure I needed that little detail," I comment, rolling my eyes. Her answering giggle is infectious.

"Who said anything about little?" she shoots back playfully. "By the way, what's the news from over the pond?"

I glance at the clock with a beaming smile, my automatic response lately whenever I think about Kennedy. "He should be taking the stage in Madrid in about two hours." The text from him that awaited me this morning made me swoon. "I didn't know I was going to miss him this much."

"That's love, sweetie," she coos. "Oh, I need to go. Dylan can't find his pain meds. Call me tonight? How about joining us for Thai food?"

"Sounds good," I agree, and we part ways. Finally locating the file I need, I add it to my stack for the meeting and check the time—I'm fifteen minutes early. Good. It wouldn't do to be late today.

I'm halfway to the large conference room when April intercepts. "Hey, Abby. I wanted to let you know Nicole Hays called me again—she has some great ideas for the hospital visit," she says, matching her steps to mine.

"Great. How do you find working with Nic?" I ask curiously. I clicked with Nicole instantly, but was a little worried that I was reacting to the fact that she was Kennedy's employee. I seem to click with all things Kennedy these days.

"She's fantastic. She's also right on-point with the PR side of things. I kind of want to assimilate her."

"How very Borg-ish of you."

She laughs and tucks her shiny black hair behind her ear. "By the way, she said something about The Vandels joining the show, too."

"Yes! Apparently, Landon Ravine has wanted Kennedy to work on his TV show for a while, and he's agreed to do it in exchange for their participation," I explain quickly, still shocked that Kennedy would be willing to do something like that.

April eyes me skeptically. "Really? You've got him agreeing to do his show?"

"I didn't ask him to do anything," I protest. "It was all his idea. In fact, I think he did it before even telling me."

"But you hate reality shows." She stares at me in puzzled amusement. "You always call them . . . What is it? Oh, yeah, 'disingenuous drivel designed to provoke people's baser side'," she quotes meticulously.

I wish for once that April didn't have such a good memory. It's true, I do hate reality shows. But, I love Kennedy, which apparently means I'll follow him even into reality show hell for a good cause. "The Vandels will be a good addition, however it comes about. What I think personally doesn't matter."

Her eyes crinkle with amusement. "Fine. I won't tell anyone." We reach the boardroom and she swings the door wide. But upon walking in, we both stop in our tracks.

Nadia is smiling at me smugly from her seat next to Ralph at the head of the table.

"Abigail, April," Ralph greets us politely. "Please sit down. Nadia requested permission to join us early." He looks at me directly. "She's been telling us an interesting tale."

chapter nineteen

kennedy

"YOU'RE DOING GREAT, BUD." I smile at the screen as Parker flows into the last notes of the chorus of "Sweet Home Alabama." It's far from perfect, but he's come a long way in a couple of weeks, and given everything that he's going through, it's a miracle he can sit upright and hold a guitar at all.

He lifts his angelic face and smiles. He's got more color in his face today, his eyes a little brighter, and the bandage on his arm gone. It's progress. Baby steps, as Abby tells me. It's much more than that for me. It's hope.

"That was awesome," he gushes, sliding his hand to rest over the strings of the guitar. "When this came the other day, everybody on the floor freaked out." He lifts the new Gibson I had delivered to his hospital room last week. "They totally didn't believe me when I told them about you."

"Guess you showed them, hmm?" I laugh and take a long sip of much-needed caffeine. A good night's sleep has been elusive on this tour so far, and that shows no signs of changing any time soon.

"I still can't believe you're going to be doing a whole concert!"

"Well, *I'm* not. *We're* doing a whole concert." A smile fills his face. "And some other things too, but I want those to be a surprise."

"Aww." He pouts at me—a look that I'm sure gets him whatever he wants whenever he wants it. "Just a hint? Pleeease, Kennedy? Pleease?"

I groan, shaking my head. "Man. You're killing me here, Park." His pout slips a bit as he lets out a half-laugh, and then it's back, along with the big, blue eyes, pleading with me from half a world away. I do the only thing I can. I cave. "All right. Just one hint, but you have to promise me you'll go to sleep right after this and rest." I narrow my eyes, pointing at the screen.

"But—"

"No buts," I interrupt his objection. "Part of being a musician is being prepared and getting lots of rest. You don't want to disappoint your fans."

He nods excitedly. "Okay. I promise I'll rest."

"Good. We'll be driving in a limo for part of the day. That's your hint."

His eyes widen, and he bounces a little on the bed. "A limo! Like with a sunroof and everything?"

I laugh at his enthusiasm. "Parker, my friend, is there any other kind of limo?"

POUNDING ON THE SUITE DOOR invades my much-needed sleep.

"Kennedy!" Tucker's familiar voice seeps through the door once more, and I whip the covers off the extremely large and empty bed. Each day that goes by makes me miss Abby more than the last. The texts and Skype sessions only go so far to fill the void. Time isn't exactly on our side these days, but we're both making the effort. Although I'd much rather have her spent and breathless beside me, over the phone will have to do for now.

I haul open the door. Tucker's large frame filling the space. "What the fuck? It's not even dawn," I complain.

"You look like shit." It's too fucking early for this.

"You're not exactly GQ-worthy there either, asshole. What's going on?" He pushes his way past me and into the suite, radiating nervous energy. I let the door shut behind him. "By all means, come on in."

In an uncharacteristic move, Tucker sinks to one of the leather chairs, leaning forward to rest his elbows on his knees. "It's Brodie." The tone in his voice is like sends an ice-cold shiver through me.

I eye him warily, a wide range of worst-case scenarios flashing through my head. What if he's gotten to Abby? I should have sent security with her. I feel my jaw tense, the anger spiking dangerously. "What about him?"

"Cops picked him up late yesterday afternoon."

"Fuck no." A wave of panic rolls through me.

"It's bad. He's in the hospital. OD'd on heroin." I stare back at him in disbelief, my mouth dropping open.

"They found him behind a club. Mugged, beaten up, arms shot to shit." He shakes his head.

"But he's going to be okay, right?"

His angry gaze meets mine. "Did you even hear a single word I just said? That could have been you, idiot."

"It's not like that now. I'm going to the meetings. I'm reading every single thing you shove in my face."

He takes a step back, his anger fading slightly. "Fuck, I know you are. I'm sorry. It's just . . ." He hesitates, struggling it seems to find his voice. "I don't have any brothers or sisters. You know the story about my mom. She passed when I was in high school. My dad is a sorry sack of shit," he continues, his frown intensifying for a moment before he recovers. "So, whether you like it or not, you, the guys, you're my family."

I can see the worry in Tucker's eyes. How many times did I let him down? How many times has he had my back? He's been in my corner when most people would have left me to rot. And if he's this worried about Brodie, it must be bad.

"Where is he? London?" I ask finally.

"No. He's here."

"Why is he here?"

"Why do you think?" he asks pointedly. "He came to find you."

A NURSE'S SHOES SQUEAK ALONG the freshly cleaned linoleum floor of the hospital as she heads down the long hallway, back to her station under the harsh glare of fluorescent lights. The hospital is eerily quiet at this time of the morning. Visiting hours haven't started yet, but here we are. My name is worth something on a morning like this. Sign your soul away to visit, and I did it. I did it for him, and I did it for me, but mostly, I'm doing it for her. Because this ends right here, right now.

I pause in front of the door to room 819 and exchange a glance with Tucker. The fact that Brodie is lying just beyond the door, having survived a brush with death, has hit me hard.

"This has disaster written all over it," Tucker mumbles.

"Hey, I didn't just sign virtually every single body part that's legal on that nurse for you to pussy out on me right now."

He smirks, crossing his arms over his chest. "Actually, I don't think you signed *that* particular body part, but if you like, I'm sure she'd be more than willing."

A chill rolls through me. "Don't give me a visual like that. God, you're an asshole."

"You love me, sunshine."

I push the door open, and he takes a step with me. "I'm going in with you," he says emphatically, his eyes blazing with determination.

"I'm not going to be long."

"The last time you two saw each other, you just about beat the shit out of him, and he would have cut you with a piece of glass if I hadn't been there."

"But you *were* there." I grin.

His eyes narrow in warning. "You know what you said at the hotel, about family?" He gives me a quick nod. "This is me as your brother telling you I need to do this. Trust me, please."

Reluctantly, he steps to the side, issuing me a warning glance before taking up his position outside the door. "You've got five minutes, and then I'm coming in to get you."

"Wouldn't expect anything less."

Stepping into the room, I scan the depressing beige room, taking a sharp breath in when I see Brodie. He's beyond pale, under the thin sheet, his eyes closed, his breathing deep and uneven.

An IV is shoved into the back of his hand and my eyes travel up the tubing to the pole that holds whatever they're filling his veins with. Swapping one drug for another. It seems like madness.

I take in his haggard appearance: hair matted and dirty, a fresh black eye, his jaw purple with a few new bruises, and cuts that have opened up on his forehead. And then, my heart stops as I find the track marks up his arms where he's been injecting fuck knows what into his system. If there's a more hopeless visual, I'm not sure I want to know about it.

Snippets of the years we've shared together come flashing back to me, and it's not all bad. Brodie was there for our first performance at Madison Square Garden and the first Grammy win. He was on the tour bus the first time we had a song hit number one. He was also there the first time I tried coke, the first time I took a handful pills he offered, and he was there the first time I woke up in a room and didn't remember what happened the night before. I sink into the stiff chair, my hand dropping to his. It's lifeless, cold as ice.

"Fuck. What did you do yourself?" I hang my head and try to get a grip on the raging emotions rioting through me. Could I have done something to stop him?

A low grumble from deep within his chest causes me to glance back up to his face. One eye blinks slowly open, the other swollen shut from whatever beating he's taken. A look of sheer death stares back at me and jars me back to reality. "My hero come to spring me? You look like shit," he rasps, his tongue snaking out to wet his dried, cracked lips.

"Right back at you."

He laughs through a hacking cough, his body bowing in on itself. "Would have gotten sent to the hospital sooner if it meant you'd come talk to me," he manages, sinking back to the pillow.

"What the hell were you thinking?"

"I just wanted to get lost . . . take the pain away, you know?"

"Heroin, Brodie? Come on. And it looks like someone did a number on your face."

"Just the wrong place, wrong time." That sums up a lot of the experiences we've had together.

I shake my head. "You could have died."

"We all have to go sometime. It's inevitable. It's that one thing we can't get out of. That a snake?" he mumbles, making a feeble attempt to lift his arm. Jesus fuck. The nurse said he's been hallucinating as he tries to come off of whatever he's injected over the last few days. This is fucking bad.

"Robin was good," he stammers, his voice slower than normal. "So good, Kennedy. She's an angel, you know? She visits me sometimes."

My jaw clenches, my heart constricting at the sound of her name. "Don't talk about her," I grind out.

"We used to talk, you know? Your sister and me. Not all the time. Just sometimes. Concerts, hotels . . . places. She was good in all this." He tries to lift his hand unsuccessfully. It flops lifelessly back to the bed. "I hated you. You had everything, and you just ignored her. You pushed her away."

"Brodie . . . Jesus. You don't know what you're talking about right now."

"I know." He tries to grip my arm, failing quickly. "I know you'll come crawling back, begging me to help you." He tries to laugh, but ends up hacking again. "I'll be out soon, and I'll hook you up. Remember that time in Amsterdam? Fuck that was . . ." His eye shuts again, his body racking with a shiver under the sheet. "It's so fucking cold in here. Why is it so cold?"

I stand, pushing the chair across the floor. I can feel the tenuous hold I have slipping; the walls are closing in, threatening to suffocate me.

"This is what's going to happen." My voice is tense, bordering on menacing. "You're going to sign your release. You're going to forget about any ridiculous ideas you have about going to the press. And then, you're going to get some help."

He tries to flash me a grin, grimacing with pain in the process. "Thirty-day wonder program. And when I'm all better, it'll be just like it used to be. I'll come look you up, right?" There's a glimmer of hope in his eye that cuts me to the core.

My mouth goes dry, the words bubbling to the surface. "No.

When you're better, you stay the hell away from me."

♪ ♩ ♪ ♩

abigail

"PLEASE, TAKE A SEAT, LADIES."

April and I exchange a glance before taking seats at the other end of the table from Ralph and the board members. Out of the corner of my eye, I notice Tess rising to prevent other staff members from entering, and then closing the door behind her. Knowing her, she's probably going to stand guard to keep anyone else from entering for the time being, which is just as well. The last thing I want is to add more fodder to the gossip mill.

Ralph steeples his fingers in front of him and gives me a troubled look. "Abigail, Ms. Baskov has provided us with some information, which I must say is very concerning, about the Parker Jensen dream. She claims that you've failed to maintain appropriate boundaries with a celebrity donor; in fact, you've used Parker and the Foundation to achieve a, ah, *closeness* with the donor in question."

I glance at the tiny, triumphant smirk on Nadia's lips, and narrow my eyes. Seriously?

Game on, sweet pea.

"Really? And, just to be clear, which donor would that be?" I ask coolly.

"Kennedy Lane," the Board's Vice President supplies helpfully, and Ralph rolls his eyes at the woman's breathy tone. I'll have to explain to him later that Kennedy just has that effect on people. I should know.

"I see." I purse my lips thoughtfully. "Well, I do try to maintain a friendly association with all our donors, because, of course, the more positive experience they have with us ensures that we can call on them again if need be. Besides, it's just good business. I don't really have to explain or justify that, do I?"

"Of course not," Ralph agrees. "But has your conduct with Mr. Lane deviated from your usual donor interaction?"

I take a measured breath. "While it's true that I've developed a close tie with Mr. Lane outside of our business relationship, it has no bearing whatsoever on the Foundation or on Parker's dream. Mr. Lane was extremely interested in participating from our first meeting, although I admit that initially he had to convince me that he could provide an appropriate interaction with Parker. He personally provided several ideas, and he finally assured me that he is more than able to provide not only Parker with a dream of a lifetime, but something that will benefit several other children directly and the Foundation in general." I can't help my pride in Kennedy from showing; he's truly jumped in with both feet, and his dedication is inspiring.

"And just how did he 'convince' you?" Nadia scoffs, earning her a glare from several Board members. "You were dead set against his involvement when we left our first meeting with him. But then you're suddenly meeting privately with him in New York and here in your office . . . and God knows where else. Why don't you just admit it, Abby? It was the other way around! *You* were the one who had to convince *him*. And it's fairly obvious how you did it."

"Oh, please!" April interjects hotly, her eyes snapping with uncharacteristic temper. "What a load of horse—"

"That's simply not true," I assert calmly, cutting her off with a gentle hand on her forearm. While I appreciate April's support, this is something I need to do myself. "It was pure coincidence that I ran into Mr. Lane in New York, but it gave him a chance to present some of his ideas for Parker for my consideration," I continue, looking at the faces around the table.

"But that's not all you've been discussing with *Mr. Lane*, is it?" Nadia sneers. "Looking for a more glamorous life, are we? You jet off to party with rock stars, leaving the rest of us to do your work for you. Nice. Did you think about how your staff was handling your work load while you were riding around in limousines?"

"I think what Ms. Baskov is trying to say," another Board member interjects while casting a warning glance at Nadia, "is that your recent vacation was very last minute. Did you receive any adverse feedback from the staff regarding the timing? Did anyone register any complaints?"

"Are you kidding? Most of us were in shock that she *finally* took some vacation time," April teases. "But of course, she couldn't completely unplug; she still fit in a few video conferences when the time zones cooperated. And the emails never stopped."

A few chuckles register around the room, but it's clear Nadia isn't giving up yet. She reaches forward and slides a stack of photos toward me that I reluctantly reach to pick up as she continues, "You're always harping about maintaining a 'proper public persona' because what we do reflects on the organization as a whole. Not exactly the best impression you're promoting there. I wonder what Parker and his family would think? What our *other donors* would think?"

My brow furrowed in confusion, I flip through the photos. There were a few fuzzy photos of Kennedy and I that I'd already seen, thanks to Maddie. Thank god the photographer who captured us on the terrace under the stars was too far away to get a detailed shot. Next were a few clear shots of Sean in all his drunken glory at some club.

I can't help my chuckle at the look on his face; he's everything Kennedy said and more. But then I gasp softly as I flip to the last two photos. The first is a clear shot of Kennedy and I standing outside the pub after our Abbey Road excursion. My arms are wrapped around his neck as he holds me close to him, and my heart leaps to see the tender expression on his face as he looks at me. It's breathtaking.

How could I help but fall in love with this beautiful, complex man?

Seeing the emotion on his face, I scold myself again for taking so long to admit how I felt about him. He had taken the risk, put himself out there from the beginning, and patiently waited for me to catch up. He truly is amazing. I'll never deny my heart—or his—again.

I turn to the second photo and freeze.

It's a shot of what happened next; when I took Kennedy's face between my hands and kissed the stuffing out of him. Holy crap, that's hot. I can feel my face heat as my blood races through my veins, my body clearly remembering the moment.

I clear my throat, conscious of the eyes on me. "Where did you get these?" I ask softly, a smile playing about my lips and my eyes still on the photo.

"They were uploaded to Twitter this morning by a random tourist," one of the other Board members offers.

"We're not sure if you've been identified yet, but it's only a matter of time. Ms. Baskov provided them as part of her, ah, information packet."

"I see. Well, thank you. I hadn't seen these yet. It was inevitable that there would be some clear photos, I suppose." At least my hair looked good that day. I set the photos back on the table and face the group with a serene smile on my face.

"I've already worked with my team in anticipation of when Abby would be identified, and we have a simple statement prepared," April chimes in. "Basically, it reads, 'her private life is private, but we'd love to give you some information about the Foundation and our upcoming events.' It won't be a problem."

There are murmurs of approval from around the table, but Nadia ignores them and glares at me. "That's it?" she demands. "That's all you have to say for yourself, Abby?"

"I don't see anything here that warrants further explanation," I retort, quirking an eyebrow at her. "I've already said that I have a close tie with Kennedy—Mr. Lane. It came about separately from his participation with us, and it will not affect Parker's dream or the Foundation in any way. If it becomes detrimental to the Foundation in the future, I would expect to address the situation with Mr. Shepherd and the rest of the Board at that time. But until then, I don't see a problem."

Nadia's eyes narrow and she opens her mouth to speak, but Ralph beats her to it. "So, you deny Ms. Baskov's charges of impropriety and stand by your account of the matter?"

I gaze back steadily into Ralph's wizened gray eyes. "I do."

He looks at me solemnly. "Abigail, I think you'd agree that if these allegations were true, it would be a very serious matter for the Board."

"Yes."

Ralph looks questioningly around the table at his fellow Board members, who give him slight nods. When he looks back at me, he looks resolved. "It would be a serious matter, indeed, if it were true . . ."

Nadia leans forward slightly in her seat, her eyes gleaming in anticipation as he continues, "But I don't believe it is."

Nadia gapes at him, her smugness evaporating. "*What?*"

"I'm pleased to say that this organization has never been in better shape," he affirms, smiling warmly at me. "As April says, your work ethic is legendary, as are your professional ethics. I speak for the Board as a whole when I say we see no need to discuss this further." I let out a breath and return his grin as the rest of the Board members regard us with no little amusement.

"Shall we take a brief break before beginning the main agenda?" April suggests smoothly, paying no attention to Nadia, whose face is turning redder by the second.

"I think that's a fine idea. Besides, didn't you tell me you had treats for the meeting, Abigail?" Ralph asks with a twinkle in his eye.

"Oh, yes, I do," I chirp and reach down for the small gift bag I'd brought in with me. I pull out an assortment of Hob Nobs, shortbread, some yummy little ginger cookies I found at a shop in Piccadilly, and a few other English treats I brought back with me. Then I pull out the last package and set it in front of Ralph with a flourish.

"You remembered!" He picked up the package of three small ceramic crocks bearing the distinctive Fortnum and Mason logo with obvious delight. "Thank you for picking it up for me—I just love this stuff."

The red in Nadia's face is slowly turning to white as the rest of the Board members busy themselves with getting coffee and chatting with the staff members who have now joined us. No one is paying her any mind as she sits there, seething. She slowly turns toward me, but before she can say anything, one of our other Board members, a fifty-something CEO of a California insurance company, steps over with an admiring smile.

"*Bravo*, Abigail," she comments good-naturedly. "That was a seriously hot kiss. You two look so happy together." Then she gives me an impish grin and whispers conspiratorially, loud enough for Nadia to hear,

"Now, do you think you could get me an introduction to his drummer?"

That seems to be the final straw for Nadia, who excuses

herself quietly and steps out.

AFTER THE SHOWDOWN THIS MORNING, everything pro-
ceeded as expected, although Nadia never returned. I heard at
lunch that she was sulking in her office.

The Board had been suitably impressed with the plans so far
for Parker's concert, as well as the things Kennedy had already
done for him and the other patients in his hospital wing. The rest
of the reports we presented were equally successful and some
good decisions had been made.

Ralph approaches me with a broad smile. "Well done," he
compliments, and I grin in acknowledgement. "Are you ready for
stage two?"

"Yes, but are you sure you want to do it this way?" I ask with
concern. "It could be much simpler, you know."

"I'm fully aware that you could handle it yourself and handle it well. But my way neutralizes her and leaves you and the
Foundation in the clear. Besides, I'll be getting something out of
it, too, you know, at least for a few months."

"Okay, okay." I hold up my hands. "Have it your way. I guess
I'd better head back to my office and put on my surprised face."
I pause and look at him sincerely. "Thanks for today, Ralph. I ap-
preciate it."

He chuckles and nudges my shoulder with his. "No
problem."

I smile fondly at his departing figure. He really is a dear
man. We are so lucky to have him on the Board. I gather my
materials and my thoughts and head back to my office. Tess is
on the phone when I get there, so I simply give her a little salute
and head inside. My desk phone rings before I can even sit down,
but when I answer, there is only silence for a few beats before the

caller hangs up.

"Oh, for the love of . . ." I bang the receiver gently against my forehead in frustration. Not here, too? "Tess," I call through the open door. "Please tell me you have a name for whoever that was."

She pops her head in. "I'm sorry, Abby, I didn't put that one through. Whoever it was must have your direct line."

Wearily, I wave to her in acknowledgement and frown at the phone as I set the receiver down. I've already canceled my home phone and blocked every crank call on my cell, but it would be a major pain to have to change my office number. There are several significant donors who have my number, not to mention all the board members. I wish whoever this was would fuck the hell off.

I don't have time now to worry about it, though, because Nadia is at the door. "A word, Abby?" she asks in a too-sweet voice, earning her a scowl from Tessa. "In private." I manage to stifle a sigh.

"All right. Leave the door open, please, Tess." I remain standing behind my desk, hands gripping the back of my chair, while Nadia sits casually on my sofa.

"You may have won the battle, but you shouldn't get too comfortable." She crosses her legs and tosses her fine blond hair over her shoulder.

"What you fail to realize is that there is no battle to be won." I shake my head in disappointment. "I don't understand why you've gone down this road. We've always worked so well together."

"That was before you started stepping on my turf," she snipes and my eyes widen.

"What on earth are you talking about?"

"You've been all over this project from the beginning."

Venom drips from her words. "You insisted on coming to the initial meeting with me, and it just snowballed from there. At least you could have the decency to admit it. You wanted Kennedy for yourself."

I stare at her, honestly mystified at the change in her. "Nadia, I assure you—"

"Oh, keep your 'assurances' to yourself." She waves one of her finely manicured hands at me. "I don't give a shit anymore. Whatever you think you have with him isn't going to last beyond the concert anyway. He must be living out some kind of librarian fantasy or something."

I can't help my snort. I don't know about a library, but there was a mention about laying me out on the boardroom table.

"Okay, let's finish this. What did you want to say?" I ask, finally out of patience. I'll go with Ralph's plan, but that doesn't mean I'm going to sit here and listen to whatever crap is going to spill out of her mouth while it plays out.

"Fine. I'm giving my two weeks' notice."

I cock an eyebrow at her smug smile. "I'd say I'm disappointed that it's come to this, but you wouldn't believe me."

"You'd be right." She sniffs disdainfully. "I got a better offer." I wait but she just sits there, like the cat that got the canary.

"And? Don't pretend you're not dying to tell me where you're going."

"I'll be leading the charitable giving department at Ralph's firm, actually." I raise my eyebrows, as if I'm impressed. "He needs someone to revamp their efforts, and I'm just the person to do it."

Sure you are. If only you knew. "I wish you luck," I say simply. There really isn't anything more to say.

"Thank you." She smirks and rises gracefully from the sofa. "Good luck with Parker's dream. Of course, my team has already worked out the rough bits, so it should be smooth sailing for you now."

I manage to refrain from making the snarky comment that's dying to come out as she turns and struts to the door. Just before she leaves, she tosses one last comment over her shoulder. "Tell Kennedy I'll give him a call in a few months. Now that he's willing to do charity work, I'm sure I can offer him something *much* more interesting."

I roll my eyes; nothing she says is worth the breath of a reply. Barely five seconds pass before April storms in. "Her team," she scoffs. "Right, like they've done *all* the work so far."

"Let it go," I advise with a shrug. "We both know the truth, as does the Board. My problem now is to decide on her replacement. Any suggestions?"

"Yes, but . . ." She eyes me carefully. "Okay, I know you've turned taking the high road into an art form, but why do you not look surprised by any of this?" I simply smirk at her, and then she laughs. "You knew, didn't you? Did you cook this up with Ralph?"

"No. It was his idea," I admit. "He suggested 'hiring her away from us' to save me from firing her, or having her quit outright. Who knows what havoc she'd wreck if she was running around loose? This way, she can't try to sue us or me for unlawful termination or gross moral turpitude, or anything else she'd try to pull out of her ass."

"None of that would stick, of course." She purses her lips, no doubt thinking about the headlines such a lawsuit would conjure. "It would have been a bitch to deal with when we had Parker's concert coming up."

"That was Ralph's thought as well," I confirm. "I'm not sure if she read her new employment agreement closely enough, or if she just doesn't think I know anything about it, but she's been banned from making any comments or sharing *any* information about me, Kennedy, or anything having to do with the Foundation without Ralph's permission."

"This was all settled before the meeting, wasn't it? Did all the other Board members know in advance about what she was trying to do this morning?"

"Yep. Ralph had briefed everyone prior to the meeting. He felt that if the Board made a show of listening to her concerns, then that was one less thing she could protest later. She complained, they listened, they didn't agree, story over. We all move on."

April chuckles. "She'd be so pissed if she knew he was playing her like that."

"Which is why it will stay between us and Ralph." I can't help my smirk, thinking of Nadia's haughty last words. She has no idea of the shit-storm Ralph will rain down on her if she steps over the line at his place. "Do you think you can oversee Giving until we replace her?"

"Sure, but I don't expect any problems. Despite Nadia's recent insanity, she ran a good department. Her people are solid."

We chat for a few minutes on a possible replacement for Nadia, then bid each other goodnight. After also sending Tess home, I quickly pull myself together and head outside to grab a cable car. I flip my trench coat collar up to ward off the chilly evening and check my cell phone. There's nothing from Kennedy since his earlier text saying he was boarding a plane and would be out of reach for a while. I text him anyway, telling him I love him and to let me know when he lands.

I let my thoughts drift during the ride home, and before I know it, I'm approaching my building. All I want to do now is curl up with a nice glass of wine and let Maddie and Dylan distract me over some Thai food.

Thinking back to the asinine things Nadia said during the meeting, I sigh as I make my way to my door and let myself inside. She was fixated solely on his looks and his fame and obviously assumed I was, too. Everything she said demonstrated how little she knows me—and she certainly doesn't know Kennedy.

Despite the lavish lifestyle his success has afforded him, it isn't really important to him. Admittedly, having security and a private jet is helpful, but all the rest? The endless parties and promotion, the grueling schedule, and the groupies trailing along like ducklings . . . It all seems more of a burden to him than a boon. He accepts it because it's what people expect from rock stars, but it's not who he is. People like Nadia are only interested in the cover—they don't care about the book.

There are plenty of celebrities who have worked with us simply for the good press. They don't really care about whatever cause they're championing. It's just part of a marketing plan that their agents approved. Some don't know *anything* about what they're doing—they just jump on the bandwagon because it's the hot cause on Twitter or Instagram.

Then, there are people like Kennedy. Yes, the concert will be huge and visible, and will take social media by storm. But it's the things he's done for Parker personally that no one will know about that makes it special. The video chats and new guitar so that they can play together. He wants to use his success to help others, and that's what sets him—and those like him—apart.

I shake my head as I change into jeans and one of Kennedy's old Redfall shirts, trying to halt my subconscious rambling. I'm too tired to make much sense right now. And I'm missing Kennedy fiercely. I've never felt anything like this; it's like I'm missing my other half.

chapter twenty

kennedy

"YOU WANT TO TALK ABOUT it?" Sean asks from across the aisle as we jet from France to Germany. "It's good to get your feelings out, so my shrink says." Sean's admission is greeted with silence as we all soak in his words, exchanging surprised glances.

"You're seeing a shrink?" Matt asks after a long beat, lifting a brow.

"I am indeed. She's hotter than hell, too. Got this put-together-hair-in-a-bun-reading-glasses-sexy-as-fuck thing going on." He waves his hands around in the air as if he could conjure her up right here. "Damn."

"Of course she does. Couldn't just pick some boring older guy with a sweater vest, could you?" Cam teases.

"Hey! I'll have you know I had no prior knowledge of her hotness."

"And if you had known?" I ask.

"I would have insisted it be her."

Once our laughter dies down, Matt clears his throat, starting in on the subject we've all been avoiding. "What's the latest on Brodie?"

Tucker shifts uncomfortably in his seat as all eyes turn to him. "He's in rehab in London."

"How's he doing?" I ask. After the incident with Abby, and then seeing him in the hospital, I had wanted nothing more than to wash my hands entirely of Brodie, but I know I can't. He's part of our past, part of the reason we are where we are, and despite everything that has happened, I don't want him to be another statistic. I know he's on a long road to recovery, but at least he's on the path, and that gives me some glimmer of hope that maybe he'll take it all the way to the end.

"It's hard to tell. I think he's got a ways to go." It's all we're going to get out of Tucker. I know he's deliberately being vague in an attempt to shield us all from the reality. If it were up to Tucker, Brodie would have been gone a long time ago. If I had listened to him, maybe—

"I need to tell you guys something," Cameron says, fidgeting with the hem of his jacket. "I saw Brodie in London after you told us what happened with Abby."

I feel my jaw set. "What?"

"Yeah. We hit it a little too hard. He was blowing off steam, and I guess I was, too."

"Sean thought you were dead at one point," Matt fires at him. "Would it have killed you to check in with us?"

"I was too out of it. We were doing a lot . . . smack, blow . . . you name it." He takes his time glancing at each one of us. "I fucked up. I don't know what else to say. I should have been with you guys, and I wasn't."

"So this was just an experiment? Thought you'd chase the dragon a bit in London, hmm?" Sean glares at him. "See what all the fuss was about?"

"Look who's talking," Cameron grinds out.

"Enough." Tucker's voice echoes through the cabin,

silencing us quickly. "You're done now, right? No more of that shit. And if you want, I've got a few names of places that can help."

"Sure, thanks, man." There's a tension in his words that I want to question, but really, I have no right to. All of us have been there in one way or another. Sometimes it's destructive and antagonistic, but there's been one truth to us that I don't think can be said for a lot of other bands out there. We battle through, and break free to the other side, a little battered, but a lot stronger than we were before.

There's a firm shove from Matt to Cam's shoulder, and then they settle into their seats, locking down in their own thoughts. An uneasy peace has been restored once more.

DEATH IS INEVITABLE. IT'S THE one thing we all know is going to happen. So why does it come as a shock?

We're sitting backstage, utterly stunned as twenty thousand people chant, scream, and beg for us. The Lanxess Arena in Cologne is alive and buzzing, pulsing with a heartbeat all its own even as another has been extinguished.

The letter we received from Brodie came an hour ago. It was short and to the point. Much like the person who wrote it.

Guys-

Light it up. I know you can, and you always will.

I can't do this anymore. It's all on me. You always wanted more, but I'm not cut out for this. I've only got one thing left—sorry.

—Brodie

We shouldn't be shocked, but we are. Despite the writing on the wall we all saw in bright, bold, flashing neon colors, utter shock is the state we're in.

A sharp knock breaks the tense silence in the room, and

I look up to see Tucker open the door a crack before letting Dawson in.

The roar of the crowd in the arena increases as the man, the legend fills the room with his presence. His battered leather jacket is back in place, his silver hair a little wilder than we've seen it, his expression the same as it always has been—stern, confident, never wavering.

"I know what this feels like," Dawson starts. "I've been there. More than once." He levels us each a knowing look. "But you've got a job to do, and from what I know of Brodie, he would have wanted you to do it. Hell, he would have kicked your ass if you didn't." His gaze lingers on me. "Be out there in ten."

No more words are needed as he brushes past Tucker and into the hallway, the door closing firmly behind him.

"Fuck." Cam rakes a shaky hand through his hair, and I push up from my slouched position on the chair. Even though I'm numb, I take my role once more. Make the hard decisions, rev them up when all they want to do is disappear.

"We're going to do this one for him." Matt shoots me a wary glance, but I don't back down. "Not because of who he was at the end, but because of who he was when we met him. Remember that? He thought we could do anything. He never doubted us once, and he never held back. So tonight, we won't either."

Sean slips his arm around my shoulder. "Fucking right. Let's do this!" Tucker opens the door and the three of them file out, quickly encased by the security team.

"You need another minute?" Tucker asks, waiting at the door.

I give him a nod, and he slips out, letting the door close quietly. Feeling the frenetic energy of the crowd riot through me, I try to calm the chaos currently rattling around in my head.

How did this fucking happen? I just walked away from

Brodie in France. Who did he have outside of us? Who was there to help him when he couldn't help himself? Why didn't he call? *You told him to stay away.*

I'm pacing a hole in the floor, my mouth dry as my gaze hits the drink table. There's a kaleidoscope of energy drinks as far as the eye can see. Not a drop of alcohol in sight as specifically instructed by me. How fucking ironic is that?

I fumble for my phone and dial Abby. She's the only thing I need. I need her voice and her strength. I need to hear her tell me it's going to be okay. That I can do this. *She's* the reason I can do this.

But when the call connects, her voice is off. My heart drops when I hear her voice crack, and I know immediately something's wrong.

♪ ♩ ♪ ♩

abigail

"READY?" I STOP IN FRONT of Tessa's desk; I've asked her to join me for a late lunch, wanting to discuss my hopes regarding Nadia's replacement.

She finishes typing something on her keyboard and gives me a smile as she reaches for her coat. "All set."

We make our way downstairs and outside, enjoying the clean air coming off the bay. Fall is right around the corner, and you can almost feel summer loosening its grip. We stride briskly to a small café on Geary and quickly find seats near the window. Once we've received our salads, Tess gives me a curious smile.

"You've seemed distracted this morning. Is there anything wrong?"

"Not wrong, just busy. Nadia's leaving left a big hole."

She scowls, her usual response to any mention of our former

co-worker. "I still can't believe she did that—said those things to you." She stabs a cherry tomato as if she wished it was Nadia. "What a bitch."

I stifle a laugh. One of the things I love about Tess is her sense of loyalty. "If she truly felt that way, then it's good she left. I look at it as an opportunity."

"How many candidates do you have lined up for her position? Are you going to poach someone from Make-A-Wish?"

"That's what I wanted to talk to you about." I lean forward and dump some sweetener in my iced tea. "How would you like to toss your hat in the ring?"

She freezes and stares at me, her fork suspended halfway to her mouth. "Seriously?" At my nod, she sets her fork down and sits up straighter. "I think I would love to. But, Abby, what about someone who's already on the Giving team?" She frowns. "Wouldn't that make more sense?"

I sip my tea, meeting her gaze over the rim of my glass. "We haven't announced it yet, but two of Nadia's senior people are following her to her new job. Those that remain aren't ready to take on the manager position."

"But you think I am?" A myriad of emotions flicker on her face; excitement, pride, worry, and a little bit of fear.

"I think you may be. I'd hate to lose you as an assistant, Tess, but I don't want to hold you back, either."

She tucks a strand of her dark hair behind her ear. "I don't have any management experience."

"Not formally, no. But think about everything you've done since you've been with us. Plus, all the charity work you were involved in at Stanford."

"But you'll look like you're playing favorites."

I hold up a hand. "I'm not the only one making the decision. Ralph, April, and Duane will weigh in, too. Just think about it,

Tess. I promise I won't think poorly of you if you decide you don't want to apply."

We let the conversation drift to some of the current dream projects. Tess is bubbling with ideas, which is the very reason I wanted to plant the seed. Capable doesn't begin to describe her. In addition to being the perfect assistant, she's always right there on the front lines, providing sage advice and insight to every dream fulfillment. She's so busy, I'm not sure she ever takes a step back to realize how integral she is to what we do.

Eventually, we need to head back to the office. Tess excuses herself to the restroom while I pay the check, and I tell her I'll meet her outside.

I gaze up at the cloudy sky for a moment and enjoy the fresh air. But my moment ends with the shrill ringing of my phone.

I root around in my purse for a moment and finally locate it. "Abigail Walker," I answer easily, but there's no reply. Damn it! Frowning, I'm about hang up when I hear it.

"Abby."

The hair on the back of my neck stands up. I know that voice. I still dream of it occasionally when I'm stressed or upset. Dreams of terror, violence, and blood. My mouth opens, but no sound comes out.

"You're looking good, babe." My eyes shoot open. I turn and my breath leaves me in a whoosh, my eyes disbelieving when I spy him standing a few feet away.

Lucas.

Although he's shorter than Kennedy by a couple inches, he makes up for it in musculature. He's obviously made good use of the prison weight room. Everything about him looks hard. His once shaggy dark brown locks are now buzzed close to his scalp. His face is leaner, his jaw sticking out pugnaciously. And his eyes . . . those soft hazel eyes I used to get lost in have turned to flint. There's no spark, no life in those eyes.

"How are you?" His deep voice has an edge that speaks of too many cigarettes. I keep staring, as my hand holding my phone falls limply down to my side.

"What . . ." I swallow thickly, my mouth suddenly parched. Then realization hits me hard. "It's been you—you're the one who's been calling and hanging up," I accuse, my eyes narrowing.

"Guilty." He gives me a half-smile that I used to find endearing, but now just pisses me off. "I've wanted to talk to you, but didn't know what to say."

"You've been hanging up on me for weeks! That's not being tongue-tied," I snap. "That's harassment."

"I'm sorry!" He holds his hands out and chuckles. "Yeah, I know. It's kind of a joke?" he offers, with a shrug. "I wasn't sure what you'd do when you saw me."

"A joke. Great." I cross my arms protectively. "What are you doing here, Lucas? Are you stalking me?" I take a step back, my flight mode definitely winning over fight at the moment.

"Not stalking," he replies with a scowl. "I've just been trying to figure out the best way to approach you. I've thought about this a long time, Abby, and I don't want to screw it up."

"Screw what up?" My brain is finally beginning to function again, but I can't think of a single thing that Lucas could screw up worse than he already did years ago. "What are you talking about?"

"I want to make amends," he says with an odd formality. The phrase rings a bell somewhere in my memory, and I gape at him.

"You're working a recovery program?" I'm astonished. It's never occurred to me that he'd join AA, or NA or whatever-A, and get help. He always used to scorn the idea.

"Yeah. I'm in NA. The list of people I've wronged is pretty

long, but besides my parents, you're at the top of it. You and Frank."

I suck in a harsh breath. "Stay away from my father. You're the reason he had to leave the force, the reason he has trouble reaching up with his left arm. You're the reason he was almost killed. Stay away from him!" I clench my fists, trying to get myself under control when I realize I'm almost yelling at him. We're drawing curious looks from a few passersby, and I feel myself automatically adopt the passive expression I reserve for unpleasant work discussions.

"Okay, okay!" he says quickly, taking a step toward me. I immediately back up a step to maintain distance between us, but find myself bumped up against a short wrought iron fence that borders a small planter full of colorful geraniums. Shooting a look at the café, I wonder what the hell is keeping Tess. How long does it take to pee, anyway?

"I'll leave Frank alone. But you're another matter. I had to see you." The hardness in his eyes lifts for a moment, replaced by a longing that I don't want to see.

"Why?" The word escapes before I can stop it; I'm afraid of the answer.

"I loved you, Abby. I still do, despite everything that's happened. I always have, ever since you first started tutoring me." He looks at me, his distress clear on his face, and I feel the bottom drop out of my stomach.

"No—no, Lucas. You can't. Not anymore," I whisper, shaken. "It's over. Long, long over."

"I know we can't be together anymore. I'm not stupid, our history aside," he says with a hollow chuckle. "Shit. You never even came to see me in jail, never even wrote me a letter, and I still love you. Why didn't you write to me? After everything we'd been through, I would have thought I at least rated a letter!"

"And say what?" I stare in exasperation, my gut roiling. "'Gee, you almost got me and my dad killed by a crazed drug dealer, but come see me when you get out of the slammer?' What the hell?" My chest heaves from the effort it takes to get the words out. "I only went to the apartment that day because you kept begging to see me, and I thought we could settle things between us once and for all. And look what happened!"

"I never meant for either of you to get hurt. It was an accident that you chose that moment finally to come over. If you'd seen me when I first asked you, it never would have happened!"

"Oh, so it's *my* fault?" I ask incredulously, holding my arms out in amazement. "You have to be kidding me!"

He pinches the bridge of his nose and grits his teeth. "No, of course not," he grates. He takes a deep breath, obviously trying to gain control of his emotions. "That's not what I meant. I just . . . Look, this isn't easy to say. Cut me some slack here. I'm trying to apologize."

I can't do this anymore. I have to get out of here. My skin is crawling, my heart is beating a mile a minute, and my stomach's doing somersaults. A small part of me wonders if I'm having a panic attack.

"Fine. I accept your apology. Now, I have to get to a meeting, so if you'll excuse me . . ." I want to leave, but I can't make my feet move. I'm trembling all over, and I hate that he can see it.

He looks me over slowly. "Oh, that's right. Working in a swanky office—executive director for some conglomerate, right? What's that dream company about, anyway? Do you schedule dream vacations for rich clients?"

"Of course not." I shake my head at the ridiculousness of his question. "It's a charity for terminally ill children."

He has the grace to look ashamed. "I should have figured you'd end up doing something like that. Well, you're obviously doing well," he snorts, his voice tinged with resentment. "All buttoned up and proper, wearing fancy clothes. Although, I miss the girl in jeans and one of my old Bears sweatshirts."

"I've grown up," I say coldly. "And I have my own Bears sweatshirts to wear. I don't need yours."

He kicks at a crumpled cup on the sidewalk. "Yeah, I can see that. You've definitely moved on."

"Yes, I have. You should, too." My tone is flat. "Now leave me alone. I have my own life, and you're not a part of it anymore."

"What if I want to be? Just as a friend?" He looks at me forlornly, but with an underlying frustration that frightens me.

"No, Lucas," I say, shaking my head sadly. "You've done what you came here to do. Can't you please leave it at that? What we had is long over. Just let it go. *Please.*"

"Abby . . ." He takes a quick step forward and grabs my arm, the anguish in his eyes ripping at my heart.

"What's going on?" I sigh in relief at Tessa's confused, but wary voice. Lucas releases my arm as if it burns him and backs away swiftly as Tess steps to my side. "Abby, are you all right?"

"I'm fine," I say automatically. "Lucas was . . . He's someone I used to know in college. He was just leaving." I can see the pain in his eyes at my words, and I'm sure it matches my own. It's like my heart is breaking for him all over again.

"Yeah. Nice seeing you again, Abby. Take care of yourself." He clenches his jaw, his eyes glistening, as he steps further away.

"Be happy, Lucas," I whisper, squeezing my phone so hard I'm surprised it hasn't cracked.

His lips curl in a tight smile, and with a sharp nod, he turns and strides off down the street and around the corner.

It's only after he's out of sight that my body gives up. My trembling becomes a violent shaking, and my hands release my purse, the contents skittering across the pavement. "Holy shit—Abby!" Tess shouts in alarm as I double over. I manage to turn to the poor geraniums next to me just in time for my lunch to evacuate.

Tess quickly gathers my things as I retch into the planter. Luckily, my hair is up, so at least I don't have to worry about it getting in the way. "Who was that guy? What did he do to you?" she begins, but I shake my head and wipe my mouth with a tissue from my pocket.

Poor Lucas. I had loved him, but my love wasn't what he'd needed. My vision blurs as I choke on old regrets.

My phone begins ringing, and I close my eyes. There's no way I can deal with anything else. But when I see that it's Kennedy calling, I can't answer fast enough. "Hello?" I have the wrought iron fence in a death grip, and I rest my forehead against the cold metal.

Kennedy's concerned voice vibrates down the line. "Abby? Baby, what's wrong? You don't sound yourself."

"I'm fine. I just felt a little sick after lunch." Now was not the time to get into everything that had happened with Lucas, especially with Tess watching me like a mother hen. I hold the phone away and turn to my friend.

"Would you mind seeing if they have any bottles of water for sale in there?" I whisper.

"Of course. I'll be right back," she promises and then reenters the café, giving me a moment of privacy.

"Abby?" I can hear a thrumming in the background, like he's in a tunnel or something; I glance at my watch, trying to work out the time change.

"Where are you? Aren't you supposed to be on stage right now?" I ignore the curious glances of people who are probably wondering what a woman in a business suit is doing perched precariously on a planter of flowers that don't smell that great now.

"We're in Cologne. I need to get out there, but I had to talk to you first." He sounds as wrung out as I feel, and I'm instantly alarmed, knowing he's delaying a show for an arena-full of people just to talk to me.

My voice softens, full of worry. "Kennedy, what's wrong? What's happened?"

"It's Brodie." His hollow voice fills me with dread. "He's dead. Killed himself. Said he couldn't do it anymore."

"Oh my God," I breathe, blinking in disbelief. "When? Where?"

"I'm not sure when, but he arranged for us to get the note before our show."

Anger surges through me. That asshole—did he intentionally time it to screw with their heads before a show? It wouldn't surprise me. I take a deep breath—this isn't what he needs now. I set my confrontation with Lucas and my anger toward Brodie aside and marshal my thoughts.

"What if there was something I could have done?" His voice heavy with regret. "I encouraged him to get help, but what if I hadn't fired him? Not that I'd ever have him around you anymore after what he did."

I close my eyes, trying to channel my strength over the nebulous cellular connection to the shaken man in Germany. "There's nothing more you could have done. Brodie made his own path. This was his decision, and it had nothing to do with you. You know this."

His defeated sigh makes my heart ache. "Yeah, I know," he whispers. "I just feel responsible, somehow."

"You listen to me," I start firmly. "You are in no way responsible for his decisions—or anyone else's decisions, you hear me? Brodie, Cam, Sean, whomever—they own whatever choices they make in this crazy life you all lead. You are only responsible for your own decisions, and you are a strong enough man to make the right ones."

A soft groan of longing echoes down the line, wrapping around me like a warm blanket. "Fuck, baby, I wish you were with me right now."

"Me, too," I whisper, melting a little at the neediness in his voice. "But it's going to be okay. I promise. You're going to get through the rest of this tour so you can come home to me."

"Can't happen soon enough, gorgeous." I can hear someone calling for him and his vague answer. And I know our time is up.

"I love you."

He laughs, but there's no humor in it. "I don't know why."

"Because under that bravado beats the heart of a truly not-so-bad-guy," I quip and am rewarded by a more genuine laugh this time.

"I don't deserve you—don't reply to that," he says quickly, his smile in his voice. "I don't think I can stand anymore honesty right now."

"Now, go out there and give the good people of Cologne the show they've been waiting for." I glance up to see that Tess has rejoined me. "I love you, Kennedy. And it's going to be okay."

"Thanks, baby. I love you, too. I'll call you after the show." The call disconnects, and I sigh as I take the water bottle from Tess.

"Everything okay?" she asks cautiously. I give her a wry smile.

"Yeah. He got some bad news today."

I sit on the edge of the planter for a few minutes as I sip my water. I'm exhausted. Heartsick and still shaken over Lucas, and full of empathy and yearning for Kennedy. "Tess, I'm sorry, but I'm going to call it a day." All I want to do right now is change into my sweats and the Redfall shirt I filched from Kennedy, and curl up on my couch.

"Okay, but we're getting you a cab." I don't argue with her. We step to the curb to flag a taxi. She tilts her head at me. "Did you tell Kennedy what happened with that guy? I've never seen you like this, Abby."

She gives me a knowing expression. "He'll want to know. He obviously loves you," she says softly.

Warmth blooms in my heart, quickly easing my lingering anxiety, and I smile. "He does."

chapter twenty-one

kennedy

"YOU SERIOUSLY GOT YOUR CAR repainted?" I ask Adam while I pace on the stage at the Mercedes-Benz arena in Berlin, waiting as an army of roadies work through another glitch in the sound system.

Time has slipped away from us again during rehearsal, and Dawson has his hands full keeping us on track. It's been this since we got the news about Brodie. There's an undercurrent of unease between the four of us as we each deal with what happened in our own ways. We seem to just pull it together for show time, and deliver what's expected of us. We're living the dream, the one Brodie always wanted for us.

That night in Cologne, we blew the roof off the stadium. Four encores and the frenzied crowd still wasn't satisfied. After it was all over, Cameron disappeared, resurfacing just in time for the flight out in the morning.

Somewhere in the middle of the night, Matt found the next love of his life, and Sean got fresh ink. Etched and flowing beside the series of skulls and music notes on his left arm, Brodie's words—*Light It Up*. That night, Tucker and I spent four hours in the gym. It's the first time he wanted to quit before I did.

And so it goes. Day by day.

Adam's laugh brings a welcome grin. My mood—all of our moods—have been decidedly dark. It's not a good place for any of us to dwell. The darkness is dangerous to all of us for different reasons. That's why I need Adam. I need him, Parker, and Abby. Anyone who can stop me from getting pulled under.

" 'Course I did. Told you I'd spread the word. What better way than on my car? *Rock the Dream*, loud and proud for all the NASCAR lovers to see."

I take a seat at the end of the stage, my legs dangling down into the empty VIP area that will be pulsing with energy in a few hours.

"You're going to get me backstage passes, right?" Adam asks seriously.

I tilt my head back with a laugh. It's good to feel something—anything than the constant state of numbness we've all been in. "I'm pretty sure I can make that happen."

"Had to ask. I don't know how this stuff works with it being a charity and everything," he mumbles.

"It's a concert put on by my band. You'll always have tickets and backstage passes. Don't ever doubt that. Plus, you're introducing some of the bands."

"I am? See? You do love me!" I hear Sean start up again on the drums. "Mom and Dad still coming?"

"As crazy as it sounds, they are." I've called them a couple of times since we've been in Germany.

Conversations with Dad are much easier than those with Mom. I've talked to her twice, and both times it was stilted and painful, but we're trying and that's got to count for something. The fact that they're coming to the concert is a bit of miracle in my opinion. I know it's mostly Dad's doing, but I'll take it.

"That's good. And am I finally going to meet the elusive Abby?" he adds excitedly. I smile at her name. How I got to be so lucky to have Abby in my life, I'll never know. The last couple of weeks away from her are worse than the first, and I know it's only going to get harder. Being an ocean away is killing me.

There's also been a growing sense of accountability since the realization of Brodie's death has started to sink in. Accountability to the band, to the promise I made to Parker, and to our fans, but most importantly, to her. How many times have I told her I don't want to be that person she met at the Fairmont? How many conversations have we had about what's important to us? It's in the forefront of my mind every single day, and it helps to keep the temptation at bay.

"You're definitely going to meet her." Dawson signals me from one of the massive amps, duty calls once more. "I've got to go. Sound checks are back on."

"Knock 'em dead. See you soon."

I pause to take a picture of the empty stadium, sending it off to Abby. Tonight, I'll send her one of it packed with a heartbeat all its own. Each picture, each text, each conversation we have means I'm one step closer to getting back to her where I belong. My home.

ON A HUMID, OVERCAST THURSDAY, the four of us pile out of the back of a rented SUV in Brodie's home town of Tulsa. The crowd is thinner than normal, but it's still there in all its inappropriate, screaming glory. Demands are shouted for autographs, for pictures, for a momentary brush with fame. The scene is familiar, but in front of a funeral home, it's wildly misplaced.

Tucker shields us from the worst of it, forming a human

barrier between us and the pulsing throng who doesn't give a shit about Brodie. The carved wooden doors close heavily behind us, as Sean adjusts his three-piece suit. It's not a normal sight, the four of us together dressed up like this. Sean's even dyed his hair brown for the somber occasion.

A portly fiftysomething man waddles over to us, pausing as he takes in Matt's neck tattoo. His eyes widen slightly as he stops beside us, but he snaps back into business mode quickly.

He extends a pudgy hand, and I take it, trying not to cringe at his sweaty palm. He repeats the process with the rest of the band and Tucker, introducing himself as Derrick Morris before ushering us forward.

"Can you point me in the direction of Brodie's family? I'd like to pass on my condolences," I say quietly, willing my racing heart to calm the fuck down.

"There's no one here. I'm sorry," Derrick answers, stopping us all in our tracks.

"No one?" Matt repeats, clearly in shock.

"What the fuck?" Cam's voice carries through to the hushed room as he cranes his head in. Tucker nudges him back, stepping into the room to give it a scan before he lets us through. There's less than twenty people all mingling together at the back, away from the simple silver urn that sits atop an ornate pedestal. Rows and rows of empty seats spread out in front of us, and my heart takes a dive.

Scanning the sparse crowd, I recognize a few faces as we draw attention. There's a couple of other managers I've seen and met over the years and one of the members of a short-lived hipster band Brodie managed in his early days. A few of them give us an obligatory head nod.

The funeral director gives us a grim smile. "If there's no one here, then who arranged all of this?" Sean asks.

"Mr. Dixon's cousin. Unfortunately, he couldn't make it. The family lives in New Hampshire," Derrick hastens to add. "They're asking for donations to be made to the Anxiety and Depression Association."

I lift a brow as Cameron glances over at me. The reality hits me that we never really knew Brodie at all. The overwhelming scent of flowers washes over me as we move down the aisle, stirring memories I've tried to drown out over the years with Brodie's help. No amount of alcohol is enough to erase the sound of Mom sobbing against Dad's shoulder. No drug can erase the uncharacteristic sight of Adam breaking down at Robin's funeral. I'll never be able to forget the hushed sympathetic murmurs of an overflowing room of well-wishers and friends who loved Robin because it was impossible not to.

The realization that Brodie has literally no family who would want to show up to pay their last respects hits me hard. Were we really the closest people to him? A pang of guilt slices through me.

My feet are like bricks as Tucker guides us toward the front of the room. He waits for us to file into the empty seats before sinking down to the one closest to the aisle. It's suddenly a million degrees in here. My throat constricts, and I curl my hands into fists, the blood pounding relentlessly in my ears.

From a concealed side door, a subdued man of the cloth shuffles to the front, and the hushed muttering dies down behind us. He's an older gentleman, probably pushing seventy if the thinning, gray hair and gnarled, shaking hands are any indication.

The pastor's words wash over me, and they're simultaneously poignant and meaningless. This man didn't know Brodie— he admitted as much. He never even laid eyes on him, yet his description of a determined, strong-willed man ring true. The whole thing barely lasts ten minutes, and that includes the heavy organ music played before he invited us all to bow our heads and remember him.

Looking out to a room of empty seats, he asks if anyone wants to share a few words. Silence greets him, and I feel my leg bounce with pent up energy. I start to rise, but I'm pushed back into my seat by Cameron. He's up and striding to the front of the room, his mind made up.

The pastor seems to cower away from Cam, fading into a seat while Cam adjusts the microphone at the podium to his height and clears his throat.

"For those of you who don't know me, my name is Cameron Chapman. I've known . . ." He pauses, taking a deep breath before continuing. "I *knew* Brodie for a long time. He managed our tours, which isn't an easy task. We're a train wreck a lot of the time." A few subdued laughs echo through the room before he continues.

"Getting four guys like us to show up on time for anything was the least of Brodie's challenges. But he never complained. He'd just barrel through whatever we threw at him with an attitude of his own. He never backed down. Lesser men might have been intimidated by us, but he wasn't. If anything, it just made him more determined." Cam pauses, glancing over at us.

"Beyond that though, I got to know Brodie a bit, as much as anyone could. He was a driven man who always had faith in us no matter what. He was there for some of our greatest achievements, and for some of our more epic nights of mayhem." A low hoot rings through from the back of the room. Cam shoves his hands into the front pockets of his suit jacket. "Truth is, I think all of us want to escape from life from time to time, and everyone tries to find different ways to do that." His gaze locks to mine before he continues.

"We're never going to know why Brodie wanted to end it

the way he did, but I can tell you that he went out the way he always lived his life; on his own terms, and maybe we can all learn something from that." Taking both hands out of his pockets, he grips either side of the podium. "It's easy to try to take some blame for this, or to try to blame each other, but he wouldn't have wanted that, and that isn't going to bring him back. Instead of dwelling on his death and how horrible it is, maybe we can see this as a new way of looking at life." I glance at Sean and he catches my gaze, giving me a half grin.

"Maybe we just need to let go of old habits and bad memories. The fact that we're still here after everything that's happened means something. And I think we need to try to remember that whatever struggle Brodie was going through, it's finally over, and the man can find some peace."

"I WISH YOU WOULD HAVE told me. I would have been there." Abby's voice is quiet as her fingers comb through the chaos of my hair. Outside her open window, life carries on. A car speeds by, and the distant sound of a dog barking complaints into the night echoes from a few streets over. Finally, after all the bullshit of the last few weeks, I'm right where I should be. Right where I need to be.

I tighten my grip on her waist, glancing up from my prime position against the soft swell of her breasts.

"I don't want you anywhere near that kind of shit, baby." She scoots up to sit back against the headboard, brushing a wayward strand of her hair from her face. Her cheeks are flushed, her breathing still elevated, and her skin reddened from the stubble on my jaw. She looks gloriously fucked.

"And I don't get a say?" she protests, crossing her arms over her tits, obscuring them from my view.

I scrub a hand down my face before moving to sit at the edge of the bed. "Did you forget what he did to you?"

"No, but that doesn't mean I wouldn't have wanted to be there for you. That's what people do who love each other."

I huff, hanging my head in my hands before turning to look at her once more. "Like I was here for you when Lucas came around, you mean?"

That earns me an uncharacteristic scowl. "Stop it. You were touring, and you couldn't have possibly known he'd show up. I'm still trying to wrap my head around it."

"Fuck." I rake my hand through my hair in frustration before closing the distance between us, cupping her face between my hands. "Let's just get out of here. Me and you." I trail my thumb over her cheek, and she leans into my touch. "Go somewhere away from all of this fucking bullshit. I can call for the jet. We can leave right now. Tonight."

Her eyes search mine, and I can see her consider it for a brief moment before she kills my master plan. "Running isn't going to change it," she says gently.

"No. But it would sure beat the hell out of dealing with it for a while. I'm fucking tired, you know? I just found you, and every time we turn around it's another fucking crisis."

"And we're dealing them," she says emphatically, her hands closing around my wrists. "We're stronger because we're getting through them together."

I rest my forehead against hers, breathing her in. "I know. You're right."

"Of course I am," she whispers. "Now, let me welcome you home again."

abigail

I PEEK OVER AT HIM and smile. He's slouched in the passenger seat, eyes closed and face tilted up, absorbing the morning sunlight. His long lashes brush his cheekbones softly, and he looks so beautiful, it's all I can do to keep from leaning over and . . . I tighten my hands on the steering wheel to anchor myself. Shifting in my seat to ease the slight ache he's left me with this morning, I smirk and hum softly to myself.

After thoroughly celebrating our reunion during the night, I'd woken feeling much more rested than I'd expected. As I quickly dressed while he was finishing up in the shower, I'd decided that maybe getting away for a quick overnight somewhere wouldn't be a bad idea after all. Just a short respite in a soothing environment to recharge before the controlled chaos of the concert. And I happened to know just where we could go.

"I haven't ridden in a convertible in forever," he muses, finally opening his eyes and smiling over at me.

"I love it; I don't even care if it's overcast. As long as it's not raining, the top's down—period. I don't think I could drive anything else." I smoothly change lanes, reveling in the engine's power.

"Well, there's not much call for convertibles in Minnesota, not with our winters," he jokes, before turning a bit wistful. "And since we hit it big, it's mostly been those SUVs Tucker keeps renting."

I look at him in surprise. "You don't have a car?" From what he's said, his home in Bodega Bay sounds pretty isolated. He wouldn't call a cab just to go to the grocery store, would he?

"Yeah, but not a convertible." He rakes a hand through his hair, but it does nothing to tame his longish locks as they blow around in the open air. "They just sit in the garage, mostly."

They—of course he has more than one. "What are they?" Visions of him behind the wheel of something sleek, fast, and foreign come to mind.

"A 1968 Mustang Fastback that Matty refurbished, and I just had a Tesla delivered about six months ago."

I laugh and glance over at him. "Matt knows about cars? And a Tesla?"

"Hey, they're sweet cars," he defends with a laugh. "Besides, they're better for the environment."

I frown, looking at my gas gauge, but then shrug. "When they come out with a hybrid convertible, I'll consider it."

"Um, actually, I think Tesla makes an electric one," he says, giving me a sly glance. "When's your birthday again?"

My jaw drops, and he laughs. "Not until October, hot shot, so calm down. You are not buying me a car."

"Abby," he whines, looking at me with exasperation.

"Mmm. Well, we're almost here, so we'll have to table this conversation for later."

My nerves make an appearance as I slow down to the speed limit as we enter town. I note that Kennedy pulls on his Ray Bans as he slouches down a little more in the seat, and I frown in concern, realizing that having the top down is a double-edged sword. He's exposed, and if someone recognizes him, this getaway will have been for nothing. For a second, I contemplate pulling over to raise the roof, but before I hit the turn signal he lays a gentle hand on my thigh. "Just drive, baby. I like having the top down, too. I'll be fine," he assures me with a smile.

I step up the pace a little as I navigate to the long driveway on the outskirts of town. Within a few minutes, I pull up in front of the farmhouse and turn nervously to Kennedy. "Well, this is it. What do you think?"

"It's amazing. It's the quintessential country B and B." He

grins, but when he pulls off his sunglasses I can see his own nerves showing. "Um, are you sure this is okay with them?"

"Of course. You just might want to guard your eardrums when you meet my mom." He lifts a brow. "Don't you want to do this? I mean, if not, let me know now."

"No! No, this is great. It's just . . ." He drags a hand through his hair and chuckles apprehensively. "I want them to like me, you know?"

I cup his cheek and lean closer. "They're going to love you. And not just because they're fans, but because you're you. How can they help but love you? Especially knowing that I do?" A shy smile curves his lips before he presses them against mine in a soft kiss. He reaches and cups the back of my head, his long fingers tangling in my windblown hair, and begins to deepen the kiss . . . until we startle apart at the sound of a screen door slamming.

"Oh, you're here! Frank! They're here!" I smile apologetically at Kennedy before opening my door and stepping out of my car, just as Mom makes it to the gravel driveway. I'm immediately enveloped in a hug, the scents of vanilla and cinnamon surrounding me. She's wearing a burgundy wrap top and crisp chinos, in the new consultant-approved colors of the establishment. She looks very California chic, but still my mom. She pulls away and takes me by the shoulders, a smile eclipsing her face, but her eyes are glued to the tall man behind me. I take a deep breath and step back to stand next to him.

"Um, Mom, let me introduce you. This is Kennedy Lane," I offer, trying not to sound anxious. "Kennedy, my mom, Terri."

My mother stares at him like she's just seen the sun, but Kennedy simply smiles politely. "Nice to meet you, Mrs. Walker. It's a beautiful place you have here."

Thankfully, she snaps out of her daze and takes his offered

hand. "Oh, please, call me Terri. Mrs. Walker makes me feel ancient," she gushes, and I hide my smirk as she struggles to maintain a calm façade. "It's so nice to finally meet you, Kennedy. When Abby first told me about this mystery donor, I knew there was something special going on with whoever it was. And now that I know the mystery donor is *you*. Well, I can see I was right. I mean, how could she help it? You're even better in person than on your album covers."

She winks—actually *winks* at him—and Kennedy chuckles as I feel my face flame. "Mom—"

"Holy fuck, she wasn't kidding." My father's shocked exclamation interrupts me and causes all three of us to look up at his stunned face as he stands at the edge of the porch. Dad gapes at us for a few seconds, before he barrels down the steps, walks straight up to Kennedy with uncharacteristic boldness, and starts pumping his hand. "Frank Walker. Damned nice to meet you, Mr. Lane. Your *Flaming Solstice* album was genius, sheer genius."

Kennedy bites back a laugh. "Uh, thank you, Frank. Call me Kennedy." He gently removes his hand from my father's enthusiastic grip as my mother simply rolls her eyes.

"I was worried about this," she mutters to me, and then says more normally, "Frank, honey, Kennedy has to play with that hand, you know."

"Oh, right. Um, sorry," Dad says, his cheeks pinking. Mom jumps into action.

"Abby, why don't you take Kennedy in the house? We'll meet you in the dining room. I need to have a few words with your father," she suggests sweetly, although her eyes are boring into my father's.

"No problem." I unconsciously take Kennedy's hand to lead him in the house, not realizing until too late that the simple action has probably made my mother's day; her eyes light up as if she's won the lottery, but I know she's only happy for me. She was distressed when she heard about Lucas's sudden appearance and is equally thrilled that I've taken this opportunity to bring Kennedy to meet them.

I lead him through the cozy sitting room and, past the stairs leading to the guest rooms, to door with a discreet "Staff Only" sign. Behind it lie Dad's study and my room. They have only one other couple staying with them right now, and Mom assured me on the phone this morning that they're newlyweds who have barely stepped out of their room for two days.

"Where's your parent's room?" Kennedy asks casually, stepping up to the broad windows that line the dining room and give a panoramic view of the surrounding vineyards.

"They're at the other end of the main floor, which is a good thing, believe me," I mention with a shudder. "You don't want to know what goes on in there."

He laughs and leers at me. "I don't think they'll want to know what will happen in your room tonight, either."

"What's happening tonight, dear?" Mom's voice floats to us as she and Dad join us.

"Oh, I was just mentioning to Abby that I'd heard the 'Niners game is on television tonight," Kennedy says smoothly. "I thought it'd be nice to relax and catch the game."

Dad lights up like a Christmas tree. "You like football, Kennedy? That would be great!"

"Football, ugh," Mom sighs dramatically, rolling her eyes. "I swear, I don't see what's so exciting about a bunch of grown men chasing a stupid ball that doesn't even roll properly."

"Um, Terri, Abby's been telling me that you've made a bunch of improvements to the place lately," Kennedy interjects smoothly. "Would you mind showing me around?"

"Oh!" Mom blinks at him, her impending rant neatly

derailed. "I'd love to show you. Raphael—he's our consultant—has been an absolute godsend!" She takes his arm to lead him through the house, and I catch his eye over the top of her head; he sends me a mischievous wink, to which I mouth, "Kiss ass." He swallows his laugh, and I trail along behind them as Mom chatters away.

AFTER MOM TALKS HIS EAR off, we are able to escape for a few hours for a lengthy hike around the property, even daring to venture into the farmer's market at the outskirts of town. Miraculously, no one recognizes Kennedy—that we know of at least. It's beyond relaxing to be able to behave like a normal couple, walking around and chatting about normal, everyday things. No crowds of groupies or hyper bandmates. Just us.

By the time we make it back to the inn, Kennedy almost looks like a new man. The tenseness around his eyes and the tightness in his shoulders has disappeared, and he playfully swings our joined hands back and forth as we head up the back kitchens steps. I can't help my giggle when we step into the kitchen with our wares; Dad has shed his regulation khakis and polo shirt for worn blue jeans and an ancient Redfall T-shirt, and he's shuffling awkwardly by the sink.

"Uh, it's almost game time, Kennedy; that is, if you're still interested," he mumbles, trying unsuccessfully to hide his excitement.

"Wouldn't miss it." He plucks a few bags of chips out of one of the grocery sacks and offers them to him with a winning smile. "I hope you don't mind, but I don't often have the chance to indulge these days—Tucker would have a cow if he knew I was eating this stuff."

Dad eyes the collection of Cheetos, fried pork rinds, and

kettle chips with surprise. "Man after my own heart," he mutters, a smile playing about his lips. "Abby? You joining us?"

"Ah, I'll be in for the second half, Dad," I promise, glancing at my mother. "I don't want to abandon Mom in the kitchen." I don't get to see my Mom that often, and I know she'd appreciate the help. And although it's just the four of us—the newlyweds finally left their room to seek dinner in town—it's not fair to make her cook for everyone.

On his way past me, Kennedy leans in close. "You sure?" he asks quietly, his eyes concerned. "Would you rather I stay and help?" Sweet man. I shake my head quickly and give him a quick kiss. "No, go bond with my Dad," I assure him. "I'll be in to get you shortly."

He gives me a cheeky grin and turns to where my dad is beckoning.

IT'S ALMOST HALFTIME WHEN DINNER is ready, so I head down to Dad's study to fetch the men. But their low, serious voices catch my ear.

"I almost jumped on a plane when she told me, to hell with the show in Berlin," Kennedy was saying. The frustration in his voice causes me to pause in the doorway, just out of sight. It sounds like Kennedy is on the sofa with his back to the door, while Dad is, no doubt, in his beloved Barcalounger.

My father grunts softly. "I can't believe he just showed up like that. I tell you, I almost died a thousand deaths when I saw that animal with his arm around her neck and a gun pointed at her head."

My stomach lurches and my hand flies to my throat; they're talking about Lucas. My brow furrows at Dad's obvious distress as he continues, "And that kid just stood there! He'd put my baby's life in danger, and then just stood there watching it happen like a-"

"Fuckwit," Kennedy grumbles, and I hear Dad snort.

"Exactly. When I saw the open door and heard the yelling, I knew it would be bad. But to walk in on *that*." He pauses, and I can only hear the play-by-play announcer on the television for a few minutes. The emotion in my father's voice when he resumes speaking brings tears to my eyes. "When I hit the floor, I didn't even feel the bullet in my shoulder. Afterward, I thought someone had ripped my arm off, it hurt so damn much. But at the time, the only thing in my brain was that I had to stay conscious as I took aim . . . That this was the most important shot of my life, and I'd better make it a good one or else my baby girl was going to . . ." He clears his throat roughly, and Kennedy takes a ragged breath.

"I thank God that your aim was true, Frank," Kennedy says hoarsely, and my heart leaps to my throat. To hear Dad recount the worst day in my life is heart wrenching, but to hear the pain in Kennedy's voice as well is almost too much.

I'm about to step into the room, when my father's firm voice stops me. "So, are you going to be good to my girl? Don't think that I'm so much of a fan that I wouldn't kick your ass if you do her wrong."

My eyes fly open in alarm. Wanting to spare Kennedy from any more fatherly "advice," I round the corner, only to stop in my tracks when I find Dad's eyes fixed on me over Kennedy's shoulder. He must have heard me at the door.

"You have nothing to fear," Kennedy says surely. Dad's eyes flicker back to Kennedy's, but I can't move. "I know my life is unpredictable to say the least, but I promise that I'll protect Abby from the craziness as best I can. She's . . . I can't even describe it." He chuckles wryly. "She's everything I ever wanted and more. I don't know what else to say without sounding like some sappy cliché. She's everything to me, Frank. I love her."

I let out a breath and glide to Kennedy's side automatically. He glances at me, his blue eyes shining and a soft smile curling his beautiful lips. I'm melting a little inside, until Dad's gruff snort breaks our moment.

"That's all I need to know," he mutters, his mustache quivering with his suppressed smile. "Let's go eat."

DINNER IS LIGHTHEARTED, WITH MORE of my mother's stories about Raphael the Consultant and some of the more eccentric guests they've hosted. "I finally had to tell her that, although I was more than willing to accommodate a vegan diet, I wouldn't do the same for her Pomeranians. The little shits chewed up one of my best comforters," Mom growls. "I wasn't going to feed them for the privilege."

Kennedy tries to stifle a yawn, but my mother catches him. "Oh, I didn't realize it was that late. You've missed the second half of your game."

"Eh, they lost anyway," Dad grumbles, not-so-secretly pocketing his smartphone as he rises from his seat. Mom shoots him a look.

"Well, I'm so glad you both could join us for the day. It's been wonderful to meet you Kennedy," she gushes. She refuses our offers to do anything more than help clear the table, saying she'll pop everything in the dishwasher in the morning, and Kennedy excuses himself to fetch our bags from the car. Once we're alone, she pulls me into a hug.

"I'm so happy for you, sweetie," she says in my ear. "He's marvelous, and he's absolutely smitten with you." She pulls back and smiles lovingly, smoothing my hair back from my forehead.

"You have an interesting time ahead of you, but you're more than up to the task. Just enjoy your time together, trust in yourselves, and everything will work out as it should."

I give her a grateful smile. "Thanks, Mom. And thanks for letting us invade for the day."

"Pssh, no thanks needed, sweetie. We're thrilled that you were both able to be here. So, I'll see you in the morning for breakfast before you leave, yes? Good—sleep well, you two." She gives me an innocent look that immediately makes me wonder what she's up to; but before I can question her, Kennedy returns with our bags and she wanders off to lock up for the night.

"Hmm." I look after Mom for a minute, before following Kennedy down the hall to our room. I see him step inside and stop abruptly.

"Hey, Abby?" Kennedy calls softly, his voice tinged with amusement. "Is this what I think it is?"

"What?" I hurry my pace and step into the room, expecting to see one of my mother's quirky towel animals that are her current obsession sitting on the bed. Instead, my mouth drops open in horror.

"Oh my God!" Sitting in the middle of the room, in all its glory, is my parent's tantra chair. "Oh my God, oh my God," I chant, my embarrassment growing when I see the small card bearing Mom's distinctive scrawl sitting atop it with the direction, "Use me."

I snatch up a sheet that is acting as a dust cover over a short stack of wine crates and swiftly cover the monstrosity, but Kennedy's bark of laughter draws my eyes back to the crates.

They aren't crates.

I'm staring at the broken pieces of *another* tantra chair, one that has obviously already succumbed to my parent's ardor. My mortification is complete. I squeeze my eyes shut, as if by doing so the mess will magically disappear, and feel Kennedy's strong arms slip around me.

"Hey, she even left us an instruction manual," he teases, his voice barely holding back his laughter.

"No, no, just hell no," I shoot back, my own laughter finally winning out over my embarrassment. I fix him with a saucy look over my shoulder. "I wouldn't mind trying one someday in the future, though."

His eyebrows shoot up at my declaration, and I giggle at his speechless state. He looks like an eager teenage boy who just saw porn for the first time. I take my overnight bag out of his slack hand and sashay into the ensuite washroom, leaving him standing there gaping at me.

SOMETIME DURING THE NIGHT, I find myself staring at the ceiling. I don't know if it's the quiet, or the fact that I'm overly warm, trapped as I am in Kennedy's scorching embrace. We didn't make love tonight, content simply to curl up in each other's arms. Okay, mostly it was because I couldn't quite bring myself to have sex in my parents' house after the encounter with the 'chair of love'. It was a little difficult for him to squeeze his long frame comfortably into the humble double bed my parents keep for me here, but he didn't complain.

I manage to extricate myself without waking him and gingerly get out of bed. Snatching his discarded shirt off the floor, I slip it on and pad soundlessly to the window to peak through the blinds. It's a beautiful, cloudless night.

"Abby?" I turn at his sleepy murmur. "You okay?"

"I'm fine," I assure him quietly, and then smile at his deliciously rumpled state. "How would you like to go for a walk? I want to show you something."

"Now?"

"It's the best time."

He blinks a few times, but nods, a slow smile curving his lips. He slides his legs over the edge of the bed, leans over to retrieve his jeans from the floor, and slips them on. Standing, he scratches his chest distractedly before pulling another shirt from his bag. I smile at his drowsy disorientation and take his hand. Grabbing an old, faded quilt off a stack near the bedroom door, I lead him carefully through the silent house and out the kitchen door. "Don't we need shoes?" he whispers, still not quite awake.

"Not unless you're squeamish about walking barefoot on grass," I tease, and he growls playfully, giving me a quick pinch on the ass. I squeak out a giggle and skip ahead a few steps, before taking his hand again and leading him silently away from the house. There's just enough light from the quarter moon to allow me to see where we're going. In a few minutes, we reach my little knoll; on the far side, I lay out the quilt with a practiced hand and sit. I smile up at him and pat the soft fabric beside me until he joins me.

He glances over his shoulder toward the house. "They can't see us here. This is my secret spot," I inform him with mock seriousness.

"Secret, eh?" he says with a smirk. I shrug.

"Well, not really. I used to sit here a lot when they first bought this place after Dad was shot, and I usually find my way here whenever I visit. It's a nice place to sit and think."

He reaches an arm around my shoulders and pulls me close to give me a gentle kiss against my temple. Warm air, full of the earthy, dry aroma of the surrounding vineyards, floats over us. With a soft sigh, I lean into his warmth, and we lay quietly while we gaze up at the sparkling sky. It's like all the stars in the heavens have come out to play just for us.

"It reminds me of the winters back home when I was a kid. Adam and I would trudge out to the backyard and lie on the snow watching the stars come out until Mom hollered for us to get our butts inside before we froze to death." He chuckles. "This is considerably warmer."

I smile. "That's a nice memory." Rolling onto my side, I prop my head up on one hand, while the other slides up under his T-shirt to caress his firm chest. "Want to make another nice memory?"

He sucks in a breath and a slow grin spreads across his face. "What about your nervousness about having sex in your parent's house?"

"We're not in my parent's house; we're in the backyard." He smirks and reaches to grab the back of my head, his fingers tangling in my hair.

"So we are," he whispers, before firmly pulling my lips down to his. My heart pounds in my chest as we tussle together on the old quilt, kissing and groping each other like a couple of teenagers. Kennedy's lips are a contradiction—soft and firm at the same time—and they leave a scorching trail across my throat. I gasp when I feel his hand squeeze my bare ass hard.

"Commando, Abigail?" he purrs. "What a naughty girl. One would think you were planning this."

"Maybe I was." I pull away just a bit so I can reach down and flick open the buttons on his fly. In seconds, I'm holding his heavy, warm flesh, and I tug gently. Letting out a deep groan of pleasure, he flips me on my back and climbs between my legs. In an instant, he pulls his jeans down to his knees, lines himself up, and plunges inside me, muffling my startled exclamation with his mouth. I wrap my legs around his waist and dig my heels into his ass, relishing the feel of his hard body and powerful thrusts that threaten to send me scooting off the aged quilt. "Fuck, you feel good. Jesus, Abby."

"Harder," I beg, clutching his shoulders. My shirt bunches up around my waist as we rock together almost violently. Every nerve ending is tingling, and I'd feel like I'm floating except for his relentless pounding that anchors me to the earth. My blood sings in my veins, and I can tell I won't be able to hang on much longer. Threading my fingers in his soft hair, I pull his face down to mine, and try to pour every ounce of love I have for him into my kiss. His deep growl is my reward, and I soon find myself at the edge. A whimper escapes me—I want to hold on—but his intense whisper is my undoing.

"Come on, gorgeous. Let me see you." I explode around him, thankfully retaining enough presence of mind to enjoy the sight of him quickly following. He collapses on top of me for a moment, covering me in his warmth, until rolling to the side, panting heavily.

The rustling of the vines in the light breeze lulls me. "Do you want to go back to bed?" I murmur, my eyelids drooping. Kennedy grabs the edges of the thick quilt, fashioning a cocoon of warmth around us.

He positions my head on his shoulder, and I can feel his lips against my forehead. "In a minute," he promises.

I WAKE WITH A START. It's much cooler now and my feet, which are sticking out the bottom of our quilted burrito, are chilled, but that's not what woke me. Kennedy is awake, and the muffled sound he makes has me raising my head in alarm.

He's staring at the enormous expanse of stars above us, anguish etched on his handsome face. When he realizes I'm awake, he wraps us up tighter in the quilt.

"Kennedy! What is it?"

"Nothing." He blinks and swallows thickly, roughly rubbing at his eyes with his free hand. "I'm fine."

"Clearly, you are not." I cup his cheek. "Did you have a dream?"

"No, I've just been thinking." He looks at me, clearly conflicted, but also troubled. "I was thinking about Brodie and the way he died. I was also thinking about my talk with your dad. The way he described the day he was shot, and how he felt when he opened that door and saw you." He clenches his jaw, trying to control his emotions. "He told me a lot more about that day before you walked in the room. And I was just thinking I could have lost you before I ever met you."

I blink at him, feeling helpless. "You can't lose what you haven't found yet. Regardless, you didn't lose me. I'm here now and we're together," I soothe him, but he suddenly clutches me tighter, burying his face in my hair.

"I know. But you're wrong. Even though we hadn't yet met, I think I would have known—somehow—that I'd always be missing something in my life, something important. My missing piece. Because you're fucking everything to me, Abby. And I can't bear the thought that I might do something someday that would put you in danger like that asshat, Lucas."

His voice is a tormented whisper against my neck. "I know I can't keep blaming myself for what happened to Robin. The fact is that she's gone, and we'll never get her back. Maybe our argument had something to do with her accident. Maybe I upset her so much that she took that curve too tightly, or maybe it would have happened anyway. I'll never know. I can only hope that if I did somehow influence it, that she's forgiven me."

"It was an accident. A terrible accident. I know she *has* forgiven you," I say softly, but with conviction. He looks at me suddenly, his brow furrowed with his grief.

"How do you know?"

"Because she loved you."

His eyes open wide for a moment, as if the thought is almost too much for him to accept, before he swallows and gives me a shaky nod. "I swear to you that I'm not going to make those mistakes again. I've got every reason to shape up—my parents, Adam, Tucker, the guys, and even Parker. But you . . . You're the best reason. Every fucking day, I'll keep fighting. I'll never be perfect, but I promise that I won't let you down."

My spirit soars at the love and determination in his voice, but I shake my head gently and give him a soft smile. "I'm honored that you include me in that list, but you're wrong. *You*, Kennedy; *you're* the best reason to keep fighting. You owe it to yourself, because you're worth it."

He pulls me to him fiercely, his face pressed against my neck, and I hold him securely, offering him my strength and acceptance. My heart aches with love for this incredible man, and I murmur soft assurances to him as we lay there under the broad blanket of night. When he finally raises his face, he presses his lips reverently to mine. There's not enough light to see his tears, but I can taste their saltiness on his oh-so-soft lips.

Our kiss intensifies, but instead of our earlier passionate fervor, this is about comfort and caring. Slowly, he pulls me on top of him and lowers me down with a tenderness that's breathtaking. The expression on his face as he watches me move above him is full of such adoration and intense desire that it almost stops my heart. With the quilt protecting us from the now-cool air, we're in our own little bubble under the pre-dawn sky, worshipping each other slowly with lips, hands, and hearts. Our movements are fluid and loving, but bring us to an even more poignant pinnacle.

When we're finally spent and lying once again in each

other's arms, I look up at him expectantly and nod toward the house. "Ready? We don't have much time before it starts getting light."

He gives me a peaceful smile that tells me so much more. "Ready."

chapter twenty-two

kennedy

I'VE ALWAYS SAID THERE ARE a few days in your life that define who you are. Sometimes, it's not easy to recognize them. They start simply, mundane even with breakfast and coffee, and the grind of all the things you do on a daily basis. Then, it hits you right in the gut when you least expect it, knocking you on your ass and changing your life.

This is one of those days.

"Are you ready?" Abby's hand slides down the back of my leather jacket as we stand outside the closed door in a wing of the hospital no one wants to see.

I've had a lot of Skype sessions with Parker over the last couple of weeks, but being behind the safety of a computer screen is one thing. Now, he's just beyond the light beige door, and he has no idea I'm here. His parents know, and the hospital staff; the thirty-minute briefing and subsequent sanitization of my hands took a layer of skin off, I'm sure. It's not a complaint—it can't be here, where children are fighting for their lives. I have zero to complain about. My life is a gift. What Cameron said at Brodie's funeral is right. The fact that I'm still here after all the fucked up shit I've been through means something. I just hope Parker isn't disappointed.

The meeting with his parents is still fresh and raw in my mind. I know what it's like to lose a family member. It's a haunting, agonizing loss you never get over. But dealing with the intensity of treating this fucking disease is also brutal, and it's obviously taken a huge toll on them.

David, Parker's dad, was less than enthusiastic at first when we met this morning, and I don't blame him. He's protective of his son, as he should be.

Parker's mom, Joyce, was the polar opposite. She took my hand, her eyes brimming with tears. "Thank you," she whispered in my ear, her arms a vise around my neck as she crushed herself against me.

I gave Abby a concerned glance, but quickly pulled her into a gentle hug. "Hey, no thanking me is needed. I'm glad I'm here."

"You got the media with you?" David had asked, clearly sizing me up. He's only forty, but looks much older. Parker's illness has had far-reaching effects. It looks like David hasn't slept in weeks.

"No. It's just Abby, Tucker, my security guard, and me."

David looked unconvinced, but shook my offered hand. "Thought you might use this meeting for a photo opp." His tone was clipped, tension rioting through him. I understood the skepticism. Abby and I had talked about this. Some celebrities use charity events as a PR stunt only. They don't really give a shit about what cause they're supporting, only that their name will be flashed for the masses to see. Any press is good press and all that.

"There will be enough press at the concert. I wanted to meet him without all the craziness, you know?"

David nodded, swallowing back some barely restrained emotion, his expression softening. "I'm sorry. That was out of line. You're a good man, Kennedy. This whole thing, it's been a blessing, really. Parker was . . ." His face paled, and Joyce took his hand and squeezed, providing him the strength he needed. "He wasn't doing very well. For a while there, we just didn't know. I mean it could still take a turn, you never know with this. But then, the foundation called, and we met with Abby, and now . . . Well, it means the world to him, and to us. I don't think you'll ever know what this done for us and for him. You've given us back our son."

My jaw set as I tried to hold back my own emotions. Abby attempted to prepare me for this, for meeting them. She said it would affect me, but I really hadn't believed or understood her until now. These people, the things they said . . . It was all too much. They were treating me like some kind of hero, when the real hero is Parker. He's the one who has survived; he's beating the odds in the face of a disease that no one should ever have to deal with.

"It means just as much to me. I just hope he has a good day. And that we're able to raise a shitload of money," I added, trying to lighten the mood.

That earned me a laugh at least.

"We're up over the three million mark now," Abby reported, steering the conversation away from the minefield we were in. "And that's before the concert is televised. I'd say you're well on your way."

Abby's hand squeezing mine brings me back to the present, and I meet her gaze.

"I'm ready as I'll ever be." The nurse that's been shepherding us around the hospital gives me a bright smile and pushes the door open, as my heart hammers inside my chest. A faint guitar strum drifts into the hallway and I smile at Abby, whispering,

"He's practicing."

"His mom says it's all he wants to do when he's not sleeping."

"You awake in here, Parker?" the nurse asks, stepping into the room.

"Yep. Just playing. Kennedy says it's important to practice." I recognize Parker's voice immediately, and I try to hold back a laugh, glancing at Tucker with a grin.

"Does he? Maybe he'd like to tell you that in person," the nurse teases.

"I can't believe I'm going to meet him next week."

"How about not waiting until then?" I push through into the room, stopping at the foot of his bed.

Parker's big blue eyes widen, his dry lips dropping open as he stares at me in disbelief. I've seen a lot of looks over the years from fans, but this? This does something to me, deep down and into my soul. "Holy sh—"

"Don't be picking up my bad habits now," I warn with a laugh.

"Is it really . . . Are you really here?" he stammers.

"Looks that way, bud." I shuffle forward, setting the guitar case on the floor and leaning it against the end of the bed.

"Am I allowed to hug you?"

The nurse smiles when I glance quickly at her. "Of course you are." His tiny, frail body scrambles across the bed, and he practically launches himself at me, his thin arms flying around my neck. As gently as I can, I wrap my arms around him, closing my eyes as he hugs me with every ounce of the limited strength he has. I can feel the distinct outline of his spine, the clear definition of his shoulder blade.

"It's good to finally meet you, Park," I manage, my voice soft and shaky as he pulls back from me.

"You're here!" he shouts, and I can see a spark in his eyes, like I've seen in our Skype sessions. It gives me hope. Despite the fact that the Redfall shirt he's wearing is hanging off him, and he's pale as a ghost, there's sheer energy vibrating through him. His mood is infectious, and I marvel at the strength this eleven-year-old has in the face of a daunting disease. He's stronger than most adults I know.

"I sure am. Had some time off, you know?"

"And you wanted to come here?" he asks, pulling a face.

"I can't think of another place I'd rather be."

"You'd be the only one," he mumbles, scooting back across the bed, but keeping hold of my hand. "Oh, this is my mom and dad."

We go through the mock introductions, pretending like we haven't already met as Parker looks on, beaming a smile.

"This is Tucker." Parker's eyes widen as he glances over to Tucker.

"Your security guy. Cool!" Parker looks just as excited to meet Tucker.

"Yeah, he's more like a brother, but he is kind of cool." Ignoring my comment, Tucker holds his hand out and Parker shakes it.

"Whoa. You're really strong," Parker comments in awe, his eyes widening as he takes in the sheer size of Tucker.

"You've got a good grip there, too, Parker. Have you been working out?" Tucker grins, sitting on the bed beside him.

"Just playing the guitar a lot. Maybe that's making me stronger?" he asks, looking hopefully between Tucker and me.

"I'm sure it is." The confirmation from Tucker seems to send his enthusiasm higher. He's practically bouncing on the bed. I try to remember what Abby said. To not focus on the equipment in the room, or his bald head effectively concealed by a *Rock the*

Dream bandanna, but I can't help it. At least he's not hooked up to any of the machines. I'm taking that as a good sign.

"Hey, Abby!" Parker's voice cracks a bit as he finally notices her. "Want to take a walk, Kennedy?" he asks, pushing up from the bed, looking ready to take on the world.

"Well . . ." I look to his parents and the nurse for guidance, but there's none to be found. They seem enthralled by him, as if they're seeing something they don't see very often. "Only if you're rested. Remember what I said, right? You can't put on a concert or practice if you're tired, and you don't want to disappoint people. That's one of the big rules."

"I've been in bed all day, just playing the guitar. And, Nurse Claire says I need to walk."

"Well, if Nurse Claire says it's okay, then lead the way."

"YOU KNOW HOW YOU'RE ALWAYS asking about what I would do if I wasn't following your sorry ass around?" Tucker's voice drifts to me as he spots me at the bench press in my gym at my house in Bodega Bay.

After spending most of the morning with Parker and the some of the kids at the hospital, we reluctantly dropped Abby off at her place. I fucking hate leaving when my time with her is so limited, but we made a compromise; something I haven't been very good at in the past.

It's given me time to go to another AA meeting while she spends a few hours getting caught up on foundation business. It isn't any easier than it was the first time, but I also know it's therapeutic. People gathering together because they want to, not because they've been ordered to seems to cut through the bullshit I experienced when I was in rehab. I know there's not a magic bullet for this. It took me years to get here, it's going to take a lifetime commitment outside of random meetings to remain sober.

"You getting bored of me finally?" He answers my smirk with one of his own, squirting the water from the bottle at my face as I push the bar up again.

"Every damn day, sunshine. Seriously, though, seeing Parker today, seeing all of them actually gave me an idea. There's not a lot of physical activity going on in there."

My muscles complain as I push the bar up, finishing the third rep of twelve as instructed by the drill sergeant himself. "A lot of them can't do much."

He nods, easily lifting the bar from me and setting it down as if it carries the weight of a feather. "Yeah, but when they can, what about a program? It could start with simple exercises in bed and progress as they get better. It can't hurt, right?" His voice is hopeful, excited. It's not something I hear a lot from Tucker. He's normally so stoic, so focused. It's refreshing to see a different side of him for a change.

I sit up on the bench, trying to control my breathing. He's added forty pounds today, claiming I can handle it. I'm not so sure about that. My muscles shake in agreement or protest; I'm not sure which. "I think that's a great idea."

"I wonder if the hospital has funding for that sort of thing?" He passes me a towel, and I wipe the sweat pouring down my face.

"I'm not sure, but even if they don't, you won't need funding. I'll help. We could put a whole proposal together. Some sort of musical/fitness treatment regime. The Lane-Pearson Program."

He laughs darkly, shaking his head and moving to the free weights. "You mean the Pearson-Lane Program."

"Silly me. What was I thinking?" Pushing up from the bench,

I join him at the weights.

"As usual, you weren't. When are you going to realize that you're just a pretty face, and I'm the brains behind this operation?"

"I DON'T THINK I'LL EVER get used to this view."

"Mmm. Me either." Abby's hair swirls in the wind picking up off the Pacific as she turns back to watch the surf kiss the shore. The light is fading, the sun slowly disappearing into the ocean, a vista of orange coating the sky.

After picking her up in the Fastback this afternoon, we enjoyed the ride back, taking in the coastline views. We stopped at one of the sleepy towns along the way, picking up fresh produce from one of the local stands, and indulging in the best fish and chips you'll find this side of London.

There was not a single adventurous thing about it. No paparazzi, no screaming fans, no drama, nothing to do but just be, and it was perfect.

Now, the familiar sounds of Queen's *Night at the Opera* album spill out the open patio doors, and I grin listening to Freddie croon about the love of his life. I recognize every groove on the record. They're deep and worn with countless turns on the table. Abby was beyond excited about the house, but my vinyl collection had her seeing stars.

"If I lived here, I'd never leave." She sounds wistful, her voice full of longing.

I drop my gaze over her delectable body, barely encased in a dark blue bikini that blows my mind. "You don't have to." She laughs and turns around to lean back against the rail. "Move in with me." Her eyes widen, her mouth dropping open. "Speechless again, Miss Walker? I like being able to do that."

Pushing off the lounger, I cross the deck to lean my bare torso against her, my hands braced on the railing on either side of her waist, and brush my nose over the curve of her neck. Her pulse flies under my touch, and fuck, she smells so good. Warm and inviting and like home.

I feel her shiver with excitement under my touch as I sing along with Freddie, begging the love of my life not to leave me.

She bites back a grin with a shake of her head. "That's unfair," she whispers, drawing her hand down my side. "You can't bribe me with that voice. You know what it does to me."

"Say yes. We can make love all day and fuck all night," I whisper under her ear, slowly reaching behind her neck to pull the tie from her bikini top, freeing her glorious tits.

"And I bet you're going to explain the difference between those two, right?" Her shaky breath fans my face, her palm making a circuit back around my shoulder.

"Are you asking me to?" Gliding both hands up her trim waist, I cup her breasts, holding her gaze as the calloused pads of my fingers tease her hardened nipples.

"I'm hoping you'll show me."

"I'm pretty sure I have several times already today." I press a kiss under her ear. "Yesterday." Slowly, I sweep my tongue along her lower lip. "Day before that." Her breathing hitches and I lower to pull a nipple into my mouth. "Etcetera."

She lets out a sexy little moan, and my voice mixes with Freddie's against her tempting skin. The sensual feel of her hand trailing down my back electrifies me, pure, raw energy buzzing between us. "I can always use a refresher."

"So greedy. Which would you like, then, hmm?" I mumble, pulling my thumb over her plump bottom lip, feeling the cool breeze from the ocean skim over us. She has no idea what she does to me, how much I need her.

"I think I'd like you to fuck me," she whispers, sounding slightly embarrassed as she buries her face against my shoulder.

I lean back, cupping her chin with my hand, and tilt her head back so her eyes meet mine. "Don't ever feel embarrassed about asking for what you want. Not with me, baby. You know I'd give you the world if I could."

Tightening my arms around her, I hold her against me, watching the tide roll in, wishing I could bottle this feeling to take with me when we're apart. Closing my eyes, I press a kiss to her temple, smiling as she practically melts against my chest.

Taking a firm squeeze of her ass, I start to work on the strings of her bikini, tugging them free as she grinds back against me.

"Kennedy? Son?" My eyes snap open as I hear the faint, but distinct voice of my father, followed quickly by another.

"Bro? You home?" Adam's booming voice echoes through the house, floating out to us, and Abby tenses in my arms.

"Fuck's sake. I forgot they were coming." I groan, dropping my forehead to her shoulder.

"Your parents are here?" she whispers, pushing me back and turning to face me. Her eyes are wild, panicked, her cheeks flushed, hair a mess from the wind and my hands.

"And my brother and his fiancée." I flash her a smile, and she hauls off and hits me in the chest.

"Oh my God, Kennedy! Look at me."

"Oh, I am." I rake my gaze over her, and she huffs in exasperation. "I'll stall them."

"I can't meet your family like this!" Her voice sounds frantic, and I can't hold back the laugh. I toss her my worn AC/DC T-shirt with a grin.

Glancing inside the house, I see Adam making his way into the living room, before heading down the hallway. Hovering in the kitchen, Sara sets down a large bag on the counter and I smile as I see Mom take a tentative look around, her eyes falling to the piano at the far end of the room. "You've probably got three minutes, four tops."

She glares at me, but I can see her holding back a grin. "You're so going to pay for this." Bristling with that feistiness I love, she ties the string on her bikini bottoms at her hip.

"Can't wait, baby."

I throw her a wink and step back into the house. "Dad? Adam? Did I hear you guys?"

♪ ♩ ♪ ♩

abigail

HOLY FUCKING SHIT.

Part of me is mortified and another part—a part that has lain dormant for years until the force of nature that is Kennedy Lane burst into my life—is smug as shit about being caught with my pants down. Literally.

Checking to make sure my bikini is secure, I pull Kennedy's shirt over my head. The damn thing hangs almost to my knees. I'm going to look like I'm naked underneath, but it covers me better than my bikini. Dragging my fingers through my hair, I try to calm myself as best I can. I look around frantically, as if a hair elastic is going to magically appear, to no avail. Oh well, no ponytail for me.

I hear voices coming closer as Kennedy greets his parents, and I know my time is up. There's no way I can sneak around to the master bedroom from here without them seeing me. Squaring my shoulders, I know there's only one thing to do—own it.

I step into the great room and brace myself, a winning smile on my lips. A thin woman with caramel-colored hair wrapped in a bun stares at me in shock. She retains the vestiges of what was once a great beauty, but I recognize how her grief has taken its toll on her. It's a sight I'm unfortunately very familiar with. I see it every time I meet another sick child's parent.

"Ah, there you are." Kennedy gives me an encouraging smile and steps closer, slipping a hand around my waist.

"Mom, this is Abigail Walker," he says, his voice ringing with a combination of pride and smugness as his eyes twinkle at my undressed state. "Abby, my mother, Helena."

She's dressed in linen slacks and a stylish scoop-necked shirt, looking neat as a pin despite having just stepped off a plane. Her eyes flicker down to my bare legs, and I try not to wince as her brow crinkles in a frown. Plastering a professional smile on my face, I extend my hand and step forward confidently. "It's lovely to meet you, Mrs. Lane," I say warmly, as if I'm wearing a business suit instead of standing here half-naked. "Please forgive my appearance—we were, um, swimming."

The dark-haired woman standing to one side raises a skeptical eyebrow, although she looks amused instead of censorious. "Swimming, huh?"

"Yes, swimming." I ignore Kennedy's smirk at my blatant lie and stick my chin out, as if daring anyone to contradict me. "Kennedy's been so busy lately; he must have forgotten to mention you were arriving today, otherwise we would have been more prepared." I shoot him a look before smiling again at his mother, who regards me with wonder before scowling at her son.

"Good Lord, Kennedy. Please tell me you didn't just spring your family on your girlfriend like a dirty bomb," she scolds, as his father coughs into his hand behind her. Kennedy's eyes widen in surprise.

"Hey, this is the first time you guys have been to visit," he says defensively. "It's not like—"

"All the more reason for you to have discussed this with her first." After leveling him with another look that would have made a lesser man quail, she smiles politely at me. "It's a pleasure, Abigail. And this is my husband, Graham, and our future daughter-in-law, Sara. I'm not sure where Adam has wandered off."

Graham is as handsome as his son, although the past few years have obviously taken their toll on him as well. But, his blue eyes are vibrant, and he smiles warmly as he takes my hand in his. "Nice to meet you, Abby. I'd like to say we've heard all about you, but . . ."

"But besides what Adam and the Internet has told us about you, we've heard very little," Helena finishes, casting a meaningful glance at her son.

"Hey!" he protests, and I giggle as Helena rolls her eyes at him. "I told you about her."

He's cut off by a booming voice coming from the hallway. "Oh, there you are!" A giant bear of a man, who can only be his brother, enters the living room and stares at me in confusion. "Aw, fuck, man," he mutters in disappointment. "You've got a groupie here? Don't tell me you're two-timing Abby?"

My smile becomes brittle as Kennedy takes two steps and smacks Adam on the shoulder. "This *is* Abby, fuckwit."

"Boys," his father admonishes, but his lips are quirking with restrained amusement.

"Nice to meet you," I say as graciously as I can, while Adam just gapes at me. I shift awkwardly on my feet, the state of my dampening bikini bottoms becoming uncomfortable. "If you all will please excuse me a moment, I'd like to, um, rinse off the sand and saltwater. Kennedy, why don't you get them settled in, and I'll join you in a few minutes?"

"Sure you don't need help?" he says teasingly, taking a step toward me, but stops in his tracks when I narrow my eyes at him. "Let me show you guys the guest rooms first," he continues gingerly, looking somewhat sheepish.

I smile at him sweetly and, with as much dignity as I can muster, glide off down the hall toward his bedroom. As soon as I'm out of view, I tear down the hall and just manage not to slam the door in my haste. Leaning back against it, I finally release the laughter that has been fighting its way out. That was . . . not as bad as it could have been. But I still plan on making Kennedy pay for it later.

I can't wait.

AFTER THE FASTEST SHOWER IN history, I rejoin them in the living room, dressed in more appropriate twill capris, flat sandals, and a sleeveless, pale blue button-down. I pause for a moment at the threshold of the living room when I see that Kennedy isn't there, but at the welcoming smile of his father, I proceed and take a seat in the lone remaining armchair. It feels a bit like I'm on trial.

Adam beams at me. "Now you look more like your pictures," he teases, casting a sly glance at Kennedy as he strides in barefoot, his hands full of water bottles. "All that bare skin confused me; I'd thought we'd walked in on some kind of orgy for a minute."

"Only in your dreams, Adam," Sara, retorts dryly. She nods at me in greeting, her eyes appraising. Her clothing is clearly designer, but casual, and I instantly like her no-nonsense persona. "So, Abby, are you from California originally, or are you a transplant like Kennedy?"

"Born and bred," I confirm. "I grew up in Half Moon Bay,

just a little south of where I live now in San Francisco." Kennedy hands water bottles to his father and Adam, and then walks over to give me a bottle, too, before sitting nonchalantly on the arm of my chair. I catch Helena watching with undisguised interest as he circles his arm around my shoulders. Thank God he found some jeans and a shirt to put on, so at least I won't be tempted by his abs in front of his mother.

We make the kind of small talk that people do when they're trying to get to know each other, and I willingly share stories of growing up on the California coast as the daughter of a policeman. Helena and Graham watch me like I'm some kind of rare bird, while Sara is reserved, but friendly. Adam is the most open and gregarious, however I have the feeling they are all evaluating me on one level or another. I'm the first woman Kennedy has introduced to his family since that idiot broke his heart years ago, which secretly thrills me. I can't blame them being cautious. He was hardly a saint before he met me, and the kind of girls he'd been with were as interested in his checkbook as they were in his cock.

But that was before.

They're chuckling at my description of my dad's touch of fanboy-mania when I took Kennedy to Napa. "Your parents sound awesome," Adam laughs. "Will we get to meet them at the concert?"

I hesitate, not sure if Kennedy had thought that far ahead, but he squeezes my shoulder supportively. "Absolutely. They'll both be there," he chimes in. "Frank's main sport is football, but he's a NASCAR nut, too. He was telling me that last win of yours was a thing a beauty."

Adam's eyes light up, while Sara gives a playful groan. "Thanks for that, Kennedy. Just what his ego needs."

"Can you tell us a little about your organization and this

concert, Abby?" Helena asks with a hesitant smile. "It's been so long since we've heard Kennedy play live, I'm not sure what to expect."

I can feel Kennedy tense beside me, so I casually rest a hand on his thigh and launch into a brief description of *What's Your Dream*. My enthusiasm is hard to temper when I begin describing the concert particulars, and Kennedy eagerly jumps in to add his own comments about some of the acts. Eventually, we begin talking over each other and laughing, not realizing how focused we are on each other until his father laughs at Sara's comment.

"*Rock the Dream* is plastered all over your brother's car now." Sara nudges Kennedy in the arm.

I nod and smile warmly at Adam. "And thank you for that. The extra attention that has garnered is making a difference." I look up at Kennedy, and my heart skips a beat to see his deep blue eyes gazing back at me. "This dream fulfillment has become the biggest thing we've ever done. Kennedy has been wonderful—his involvement has gotten us places in just a few weeks that would have taken months otherwise. The concert will end up helping hundreds of kids, not just Parker."

"It's a wonderful thing you're doing, son." Graham's deep voice resonates with a paternal pride. "We can't wait to see it."

Kennedy swallows nervously, shifting next to me. "Well, all those guys owe me favors . . . It's about time for them to repay," he jokes, but I can see in his eyes how much his father's praise means to him.

"It's not just the concert," I blurt, suddenly wanting them to know how much of himself he's poured into this. How it's not just a simple calling in of favors. "Kennedy's been working with Parker over Skype while he's been on the road."

His parents' eyes shoot open in surprise. "You have?" Helena asks him shakily, but Kennedy only swallows thickly, his hand clutching my shoulder like a lifeline. In turn, I squeeze his leg slightly, letting him know it's okay.

"He encourages Parker with his guitar lessons and generally gives him something to look forward to. The nurses say it's really made a difference in how well he takes his chemo. I think Parker's mother wants to nominate Kennedy for sainthood."

Kennedy barks out a harsh laugh. "And, I think we all know that would truly be a miracle," Kennedy says wryly, rubbing a hand on the back of his neck. "I'm the least saintly person I know." Looking back at his amazed family, he shrugs the praise off.

"It's the least I can do. I'm shuttled around in private jets, anything I want at my fingertips, while he's stuck in a shitty hospital bed with a life-threatening disease that's affected his whole family. If spending a few hours with him on Skype will make him feel even a little better, it's worth it."

His mother sniffs, her face blotchy, and Kennedy squirms with embarrassment. Even Graham looks teary for a moment and I'm suddenly struck with the fact that it must be years since they've seen Kennedy being so open and *involved*. I quickly think back to the first time I met him in the Fairmont; the man I know and love now is light-years from the train wreck he was then. If that's all they've seen for years, then it's no wonder they're looking at him like some kind of fog has lifted from them all.

Adam breaks the awkward silence by slapping his hands on his thighs and standing. "Hey, is it okay if we walk down to the water? I kind of want to check out the swimming area Abby was talking about earlier."

"Yeah, sure," Kennedy says. He stands and holds a hand out for me. "How about it, baby?"

"Actually, I think I'm going to go check out the kitchen and see what I can pull together for dinner." Since I didn't know about guests, I'm not sure what we have left in the way of food. Kennedy's kitchen was as barren as the desert when we arrived a few days ago, and we only picked up enough for the two of us.

"Hey, don't sweat it. If we don't have enough, I'll have something brought in. Or we can go out." He lowers his voice to a murmur. "I don't expect you to cook for my family. I'm sorry I forgot to tell you they were coming."

"It's okay." I smile softly. "I'll check it out, and if we're out of luck, we'll let your Mom decide. Okay?"

He turns to face his family, my hand still in his. "Mom? Dad? How about a little sea air?"

"Oh, I'll help Abby," Helena says quickly, rising to her feet. "But I'm sure your father wants to join you, don't you dear?" A look passes between them, and Graham immediately stands. "Yes, definitely," he agrees with enthusiasm.

Adam leads them out onto the deck, exclaiming at the view, and I turn to head into the spacious kitchen. I busy myself surveying the contents of the refrigerator, wondering what I can pull together at such short notice, when I hear a noise behind me. "These might help," Helena says softly, holding out the bag I saw earlier. "We brought a few groceries with us. Graham has a sensitive stomach these days, so I thought it wise to bring what he needed. I hope that was all right."

"Of course," I say in surprise. "Kennedy wants you to be comfortable here. I'm sure he'd want you to bring whatever you need." We share a smile and she unloads the bag. "Hmm, how about a nice pasta alfredo?" I suggest as I eye the contents. "My mother has a great recipe that's creamy yummy, but not too rich, so it doesn't sit in your belly like a bomb all night."

She laughs, and it's a much brighter sound than I'd heard earlier. "Sounds perfect."

We sort out ingredients for the pasta, a salad, and bread,

each busy in our own tasks. Her shoulders look so thin beneath her blouse, and I wonder if she's well.

"You're very comfortable in his kitchen," she observes. I glance over to see her eyeing me speculatively.

"I enjoy cooking," I offer, and then laugh lightly. "This kitchen is much larger than mine; it's been great to work in."

"I can't believe how different he is, how much better he looks," she says softly, glancing over at me. "The look on his face when you two were talking about the event . . . He's smiling like he did when he was a little boy."

I find a grater and begin preparing the Parmesan. "I wasn't exaggerating earlier; he's truly been amazing. He cares so much about making this event perfect. He's put his heart into it."

"He's done all this for you?"

I look at her sharply. "No, he's done it for Parker, and the other kids." She cocks an eyebrow at me, and I sigh in acknowledgement. "Perhaps I'm part of it, too," I concede. "But it's mostly about Parker. And you."

"Me?" she blurts, shocked.

"Yes, you, his father, Adam . . . and Robin," I say, ignoring her sharp intake of breath. "He's doing it for all of you, as well as himself. I think it's struck at something deep inside of him, and it's helping him find strength he didn't know he has."

She slices vegetables for the salad quietly, frowning as she considers my words. "Robin was such a beautiful girl. She was pretty, yes, but it was her spirit that shone so brightly," she says, her voice strained. "Everyone loved her. All three of them were close, but there was something special between her and Kennedy. She was always his biggest supporter, but she also held him accountable. When his music took off and he began to reap the benefits of his success, she always encouraged him to do more."

Setting her knife down, she turns to me. "She wanted him

to start a charity that could benefit people who weren't as lucky. But she also wanted him to do it so that he wouldn't lose himself as the voices clamoring for his attention grew louder. She knew, better than I did, how easily Kennedy could get swallowed up." She looks down and grips the kitchen counter, her anguish written on her face.

"He's a grown man, and he's responsible for his choices," I say gently, wanting to ease her pain. "You can't blame yourself for his poor decisions."

"I blamed him for Robin," she whispers, hanging her head. "I thought that if he hadn't argued with her, if he had done what she asked that night, she would never have been in that car." She takes a deep breath, and my heart aches for the pain that has held this whole family in thrall.

"Blame is a tricky thing." Resting my hands on the countertop, I avert my eyes from where she stands rigidly, grappling with the past. "It's one thing to acknowledge facts," I murmur, thinking of Lucas's overdue debt to his dealer that ended up putting Dad and I in harm's way. "But to blame someone. . . . Once it starts, it can grow and fester, and never let you move beyond it. It's easy to be caught in a vicious cycle you can't break out of, to the detriment of all."

"Yes," she agrees softly and looks at me directly, her eyes glistening. "Robin always wanted more for Kennedy. I'm happier than I can say that it looks like he may finally be getting it."

I give her a watery smile, and she takes a step, reaching out to embrace me, but freezes when we hear notes drifting in from the piano. A flicker of recognition lights her face, and she turns abruptly to walk out of the kitchen, leaving me to trail behind. Kennedy sits at the piano, playing something I've never heard before. It's lyrical and haunting, and one of the most beautiful pieces I've ever heard.

Hovering at the kitchen door, I watch as Helena slowly glides across the room to stand slightly behind him and rests a hand on his shoulder. When he comes to the end of the piece, he reaches up for her hand; I can hear her faint, wistful sob as he pulls her down next to him, wrapping his arms around her. I clap my hand over my mouth, afraid that I might make a noise to spoil the moment, when his eyes meet mine across the room, hope and relief written on his face. I give him an encouraging smile, and then retreat to the kitchen to give them their privacy.

Leaning against the doorframe, my heart swells with the love I saw between mother and son. Hopefully, this time together for the concert would do the same for Kennedy's family as I wished it would bring a measure of for Parker's family, and all of the other kids and families involved.

Healing.

chapter twenty-three

kennedy

"ARE WE ALL FINALLY IN agreement with the order?" Nicole's exasperated voice carries through the boardroom of Abby's office. "Speak now or forever hold your peace."

"Fuck no," Matt complains, stalking to the whiteboard. Reaching for a red marker, he draws a series of angry lines under a few of the names. "In what alternate universe do The Vandels go before Lennon Acer?"

"The one in which the demographic of eighteen to twenty-four year olds watches the most television." I can hear the patience in Tess's voice fading. We've been at it for the entire afternoon, hashing out the order of performances for the concert over a table laden with Chinese takeout.

It's a small army in here; Abby and her team, Nicole, Tucker, and the band, minus one very absent Cameron. Dawson was even here for a few minutes, along with the television producer. You'd think this would be an easy task to coordinate, but no. I don't know how Nic does shit like this on a daily basis. She's got the patience of a saint.

We've got to juggle competing schedules of more than twenty different high maintenance performers and satellite feeds from locations around the globe. There are interviews and planned backstage peeks, comedy skits, and obscene demands by A-list actors who are only appearing to say, "And now, welcome so and so." It's fucking beyond ridiculous. Who the hell needs their own room with designer water, a catered, vegan-friendly meal from Spago, and a crystal bowl filled with roasted almonds for fifteen seconds of air time? Some of these celebrities are insane.

"We've been over this. The Vandels are the hottest band in that demographic right now. We're putting them on when we get the most viewers, which means more donations," Tess challenges, not backing down one bit.

Matt barely contains a growl of frustration as he takes a step toward her. "Are you implying we appeal to a more geriatric crowd?"

I lean back in my chair, amused at the show these two have been putting on over the last few hours. It's rare that a woman stands up to Matt and speaks her mind. It's refreshing to see. Somehow, in the space of the afternoon, Tess has gotten under his skin.

"Why can't you just listen for once?" Tess protests, her hands defiantly balled into fists at her hips.

"Remind me again. You're just an assistant, right?" Matt provokes her once more.

Tess narrows her eyes, closing the distance between them, and poking her finger against his chest. "And you're just the bass player, right?"

"Grasshopper, relax and listen to the lovely Tess," Sean chimes in, doing nothing to defuse the situation. "Do we really give a rat's ass at this point? We'll be on stage all night regardless of the order, mate."

"A-fucking-men. Words of wisdom from the Brit finally," I mutter, opening up another fortune cookie from the box. Abby catches my gaze across the table and grins.

"Landon will be gloating that he's going first. Plus he's doing the song at the end with you," Matt fires back, turning to glance in my direction, hoping I'll throw him a bone.

"Don't care." I read the fortune, tossing the tiny slip of paper across the table to Abby.

"It's all about the big finish anyway, Matty. The grand finale. You want to end with a bang, yeah? You know how that goes . . . or maybe you don't? Do you have trouble finishing? Hmm?" Sean pokes the bear that is Matt once more, unable to contain his smirk.

Nic throws her hands up in frustration as the rest of us crack up, Tess included. "We're going with this order." She motions to the whiteboard, her hands flailing wildly. "So suck it up. All of you."

Sean pushes his chair back, standing up to give her a salute. "Ma'am, yes ma'am!"

Tess narrows her eyes at Matt and he responds in kind, sticking his tongue out at her like some twelve-year-old. There's no mistaking the audible gasp from her as her eyes widen at his tongue piercing, and he plunks down into his chair. I think it's safe to say he's won this round. I wonder how long it will be before they hook up.

"Let's talk about the missing link," Nic starts, clearing her throat.

The mood in the rooms takes a noticeable dive, and Sean is the first to speak. "When's the last time any of us spoke to Cam?"

"At the funeral." Sean holds my gaze across the table, nodding.

"Me, too," Matt adds.

"He's going to be there. Cam wouldn't let us down." I try to muster up a convincing tone, but I'd be lying if I said I wasn't worried.

Cameron has fallen off the face of the earth again. He's been unresponsive to any of our calls and texts. Rumors are flying that he's off on a binge somewhere. It's publicity we don't need right now with the concert less than forty-eight hours away.

"He's in rehab." Tucker's deep voice slices through the room. Relief washes through me and Abby meets my gaze across the table, offering me a small smile of encouragement. Thank fuck, she's here to help calm the chaos. "That piece of information doesn't leave this room," Tucker adds, glancing at Abby's team.

"Of course not," April confirms for the group. I smile at the determination in her voice. Abby has a great group of people working for her. This kind of loyalty is hard to find. "What goes on in here stays in here." Tucker nods, relaxing slightly from his post beside the door.

"And you were going to tell us this when?" Sean asks after a long beat, narrowing his eyes.

"I'm telling you now. It's . . . intensive, this one. Not supposed to be any contact for the first little while. He's being put through the paces."

"You should have told us," Matt complains, straightening in his chair.

"You should have asked," Tucker counters.

"You're right," Sean interrupts Matt before he can start another rant.

"I'd like that on a flashing neon sign please." Tucker grins before taking a long sip from his green energy drink.

Holding Nicole's gaze, I give her the answer they all need to hear. "He'll be there."

Satisfied for the moment, she scrolls through her tablet.

"Okay. Then let's switch to security. Tucker, how much over budget are we?"

"THIS IS YOUR HOUSE?" PARKER'S voice seems to have climbed about three octaves as he roams to the bank of windows that face the ocean.

"Yep. It is."

After the limo ride to my place, we were greeted by Mom and Dad, and Adam and Sara, with the band's video and photography crew already setting up shop inside.

Parker seems as taken with Adam as he is with the whole day so far. I think it may have been Adam's promise to take him for a ride in his car one day that vaulted him into hero territory.

"I haven't been home in so long," Parker comments wistfully, stopping at the piano, and staring out to the ocean.

At his words, I see Parker's dad, David, almost lose it for the first time today, and I move quickly across the room to join Parker at the piano. "Do you want to see the ocean, Park?"

"Can I?" He starts to turn back to seek permission, but I steer him away from what I know is an impending breakdown about to happen with his parents. I'm not sure how any of us are going to make it through the rest of the day, but I know we need to find a way.

"You sure can."

I guide him outside and down the stairs, aware of the camera crew following us. Parker laughs when his shoes hit the sand, and he looks up at me tentatively. "Can I take off my shoes?"

"I think you have to at the beach, right? It's like a rule or something." I toe off my boots, and sit on the bottom step to roll my jeans up, pulling off my socks in the process.

Parker plunks himself down in the sand, tugging off his

Converse sneakers and socks, and rolling his jeans up as far as he can.

Standing, he shyly reaches his hand out to me, and I take it without hesitating, moving along the sand towards the roar of the surf. The sand is warm and inviting under our feet, but his laugh as we make our way to the shore warms my heart more.

For a few minutes, we're quiet, both of us gazing out to the ocean, and I feel his hand tighten around mine. "Thanks for today, Kennedy," he starts, his eyes fixed on the surf. "I'm not sure if I said it yet."

My heart tightens at his words. "You don't have to thank me, Park. I should be thanking you."

"Hey, can we lie down?" he asks, switching gears completely.

"Are you tired?" I glance down at him in concern, and he shakes his head.

"I mean in the sand."

With a laugh, I catch sight of the camera crew, filming just off to the side. "We can do whatever you want."

Without missing a beat, he's down on his back, the waves lapping over his feet and shins. "Come on!"

I glance up to the house, and smile at the audience we've drawn. The band—Cam included now—Tucker, Parker's parents, and my parents, are all on the deck, watching us intently. I offer them a shrug before lowering down beside him, stretching my legs out.

The first few waves are cold, as evidenced by the squeal from Parker each time another rolls over our legs. I feel his hand reach for mine, slowly closing with a firm squeeze.

"Coolest thing ever," he says quietly.

MOVING ALONG THE EXTENSIVE HALLWAY on the second

floor, I have to give my head a shake at the ridiculous size of my house. One person doesn't need nine bedrooms and over seventeen-thousand square feet, but right now, I'm glad for it. Parker and his family can get some well-deserved rest for a few hours and not hear anything that goes on in the rest of the house.

I smile at the sound of his excited voice, stopping to listen outside of the door to the bedroom we've set him up in. He's chattering away, sounding like he's on hyper-drive, and both of his parents indulge him. "Listen!" he shouts, and the room falls silent. "You can hear the ocean."

"You can see it too, bud. This view is something else." His dad's voice trails, and I lean into the room.

"Everybody comfortable in here?"

Parker looks so tiny and frail in the monster of a bed that dominates the room. I watch as Nurse Claire gingerly unwraps a blood-pressure cuff from his thin arm, giving me a warm smile.

"We're doing great." Her words ease my worry slightly, but I also know that today has already been over the top for Parker with the press conference this morning at the hospital, and the drive in the limo here. The last thing I want is for him to get run down because we've overdone it.

"Did you get enough to eat?" I make my way over to the bed and take a seat on the edge, glancing at the spread laid out on the large coffee table set by the windows. Under Parker's doctor's advice we stuck with what he's used to. It would be tempting to give him a Michelin star five-course meal, but his tender stomach would never be able to handle it.

Parker lifts the empty smoothie glass with a smile before setting it on the nightstand. "This is way better than that pink junk at the hospital. Is this what you have before a concert?"

Joyce smiles, climbing into the bed beside her son. "It's exactly what I have. It's full of protein and energy. Just what you need before a big night." I can see him fighting exhaustion. Joyce gently removes the bandana from his head, setting it to the side. He looks so vulnerable like this, and I fight to rein in the emotions threatening to overwhelm me. "You know what else you need?"

He lets out a sigh, settling back against the plush pillows on the bed. "You're going to tell me I need rest, right?"

"You do, bud. I mean, what kind of a rock star packs it in at nine thirty because he's too tired to stay up?"

His eyes widen. "That's an hour past my normal bedtime!"

"You rebel."

Leaving Parker and his parents to rest, I lead Claire back downstairs. She sets her bag on the edge of the kitchen island before moving back beside me. "You're a good man, Kennedy." Without another word, she turns away, heading out to the patio.

"Don't let that go to your head, mate." Sean's voice rings from across the room, and I turn to find my three bandmates lingering outside the staircase that leads to the studio. We all know what we need to do. It's as simple as taking a breath. This is how we deal with the curveballs life seems intent on throwing at us; it's how we fight temptation that taunts us at every turn. We need to play.

"We doing this or what?" Cam asks with a smirk. I can tell the past few weeks haven't been easy for him. If this rehab facility is as intense as Tucker alluded to, I can understand why. It's what I don't see that gives me hope. The lifeless, red-rimmed eyes are gone, the greyish tinge to his skin replaced with a bit of color.

I know there's no magical solution when you're trying to kick a habit. Mine was found with Abby, with Parker, and with finally starting to forgive myself for what happened with Robin. Cam needs to find his own reasons, and I can only hope that he's starting to do just that.

"Well, you showed up so we better. Never know when we might see you again." Matt's only half teasing.

Cam nudges me in the shoulder as I move to punch in the code to open the studio doors. "You look better," I offer.

"I'm getting there." It's a muttered admission, but I'll take it.

"I think we all are."

"Yeah, yeah. Everyone is forgiven, and we all love each other again, yada, yada, yada. Can we play some fucking rock-and-roll now?" Sean asks, smacking Cam on the shoulder. Sean's dyed his hair bright blue today, and Cam can't seem to resist poking at it with an amused grin.

Sean shrugs him off, descending into the studio. Matt and Cameron follow quickly behind him, but Nic's voice stops me.

"I need five minutes before you disappear into your rock-and-roll man cave."

I laugh, turning back to see Nic and Abby approaching. "What's up?" I can feel the adrenaline spike as Cam strums a few chords, my heart pounding harder at the sight of Abby.

I also can't resist taking her hand and pulling her in for a lingering kiss. "Missed you," I mumble, pressing her against my side.

"Just no," Nic complains, and I feel Abby smile against my lips before she pulls back.

"We've been talking to Landon" Abby begins, and I lift a brow.

"On a first name basis are you now?"

"Oh, yes," Nic starts with a smirk. "Mr. Ravine has been very sweet and accommodating." Nicole knows exactly what she's doing, trying to get a reaction out of me, and she flashes me a grin.

"I just bet he has," I mutter, glancing down at Abby.

Abby doesn't miss a beat, continuing on, "You two will be performing toward the end of the concert, and I thought maybe we could run a video. We have a lot of great shots from today we could add. And then your mom said we should put some pictures of yours in there, too." I can hear the excitement in Abby's voice, and I love that she's come up with this idea.

I scan the room, looking for Mom, but come up empty. "Mom's got old pictures of me with her?" I ask, slightly horrified. Abby doesn't need to see any of those, particularly the ones of me naked running around with a cowboy hat on in the yard when I was three. The guys would never let me live it down.

"She said she has a bunch up on Dropbox and to not look so surprised when I told you that."

"I can pull some from the other guys, and Tucker, too," Nic adds. "I think we should try to get you all in there if we can."

"On one condition," I start. Nicole adjusts her glasses, glancing at me over her ever-present tablet. "Pictures of both of you get in there too."

Abby starts to protest, but I place my fingers over her perfect lips. "Non-negotiable. None of this would be happening without the two of you."

Abby nods, pressing a gentle kiss to my fingers. "I'll see what I can do."

"That's my girl."

"Now go," Abby urges, pushing me in the direction of the studio. "Make music."

♪ ♩ ♪ ♩

abigail

"I GUESS WE HAVE OUR marching orders."

My smirk mirrors Nicole's. "Apparently so," I agree. "But, luckily, we get to choose which of our own photos get included. And only one of each of us."

"Damn straight." She taps a few keys on her tablet. "We'll put them in because he insisted, but we're not the show, they are. Right?"

"Right." I knew she and I would be on the same page. "But we need to get hopping if we want it ready for tonight."

"On it," she says tersely and looks up from her tablet to give me a cheeky grin. "And you need to call your buddy Landon, back."

"Yeah, yeah." I roll my eyes. "I'll meet you in Kennedy's office in ten." I give her a friendly push in the direction of the office, and shake my head as her laughter floats back to me. Okay, so I was a little excited to be talking to Landon, but that doesn't mean she needs to wind Kennedy up about it.

I want to do that.

Wandering down to the kitchen, I pull a couple bottles of iced tea out of the fridge for us and then head out to the deck for a breath of fresh air before I join Nicole. Bracing one hand on the railing, I savor the sea breeze on my face and feel my shoulders relax a little.

Graham is sitting on the beach reading and looking far more relaxed than when I first met him. It seems the beach has been a healing balm for everyone today at some point. I watch the waves below and feel my heart expand as I remember watching Kennedy and Parker laughing as the water washed over their toes.

Parker was virtually incandescent with joy. He's beginning to look up to Kennedy like a favorite uncle or something; I wonder if my rock god realizes that. He's been amazing all day, but when they were standing in the surf, hand-in-hand . . . I quickly swipe away some dampness in my eyes. Kennedy is going to make a wonderful father someday.

♪ ♩ ♪ ♩

A SIGH OF RELIEF ESCAPES me. I'm so, so glad that Cameron made it in time. I'm not sure what the future holds for the guys after they finish this tour, but they work too well together, know each other too well, for them to break up contrary to the tabloid rumors.

Turning, I make my way with my bottles back inside and to the office. On my way, I pass Helena and Sara sitting on the sofa in the living room, their heads together over a laptop as they search for photos of Kennedy for the montage. Although she's still tentative toward Kennedy, I can see the heartache and grief she's been clinging to the last few years thawing and falling away as the days go by. The spark in her eyes when she offered the photos of a young Kennedy warmed my heart, and Nicole and I both eagerly accepted. This concert has become a labor of love in more ways than one.

"Oh, I buzzed April and Tess in through the gate a few minutes ago," Nic mentions as I walk in the office, which has turned into whirlwind of controlled chaos. She accepts the bottle of iced tea with a grateful smile. "I have to say, it's been a godsend to work with your staff on this. They're awesome."

I chuckle. "The feeling is mutual, believe me. I think April wants to adopt you."

She smirks and gestures to the room and the many framed concert posters and photos of the band—both promotional and in action during shows—that cover the walls. "And leave all this? I think Kennedy would have a nervous breakdown."

"Don't tell me that's the latest rumor?" April says drily, as she and Tess arrive, their arms full.

"No one's breaking down anywhere," I assure her, and take the bag full of shirts bearing the *'Rock the Dream'* slogan out of

Tess's hand. We're selling them at the show, but these are for us to wear tonight. Pulling one out, I inspect it to ensure the Foundation's logo isn't screwed up.

"Don't worry—it looks good," she confirms, and then adds oh-so-casually, "So, um, where's the fearsome foursome? Have they headed over to the stadium already?"

Nicole snorts in amusement, her eyes glued to her laptop, and I cock an eyebrow at my assistant. "You're not fooling anyone, you know."

"What do you mean?" Tess asks, her voice suddenly an octave higher.

"We mean that you're really only interested in *one* member of the 'fearsome foursome'," April answers for me, a smile quirking her lips. "That was quite a display you two put on back at the office. We're thinking of starting a pool about which one of you caves first."

Tess's face reddens and she's about to protest, but Nicole cuts her off before she can get started. "But not until after the show, okay? We've got too much to do before tonight. Could you please give the caterer a call and double check that they received the supply of bandanas for the green room?" She taps furiously on her tablet. "Oh and make sure they got that last minute beverage request from Kate Mara straightened out."

Tess tilts her chin up, marches from the room with dignity, ignoring our quiet giggles. April winks at me. "Twenty bucks says they don't last the week," she whispers under her breath.

I laugh. "No bet. I'll be surprised if they make it forty-eight hours."

AFTER ANOTHER CONVERSATION WITH THE flirtatious Landon and a few hours perfecting the photo montage, my phone chimes, alerting me to the latest arrivals to the house. I can't help the nerves fluttering in my stomach. This event has become so big on so many levels. It's a bit unnerving to have so much of my private and professional lives colliding. I pull down my concert T-shirt and check the mirror. I'm too nervous for tonight to deal with my hair, so I've tied it back into a loose braid. Between that, my jeans and my favorite New York stiletto boots, Ralph may not recognize me tonight.

I hear Adam's voice in the foyer, and I know I'd better get out there. I scurry out of Kennedy's bedroom and down the hall where the voices are getting louder. Turning a corner, a smile breaks out on my face when I see my parents. Mom has traded in her floaty skirts for a pair of jeans and a black tank top under a sheer blouse, while Dad is once again sporting his old Redfall shirt.

"Abby!" Mom throws her arms around me and hugs me tightly, oblivious to the Lanes standing off to the side. "You look wonderful, sweetie."

"I was beginning to wonder if you guys were going to make it in time to go with us," I say with relief. I'd been working on a separate transportation plan in my head if they hadn't arrived in time.

"Oh, well," she starts with a dismissive wave of her hand. "You know that GPS thingy isn't always reliable."

"It *would be* reliable if you entered the right address the *first* time," Dad grumbles, shooting her a look that she blithely ignores.

"This house is incredible! It's nicer than anything I've seen on HGTV," she gushes before surrendering me to Dad's gruff embrace.

"Yeah, trust Kennedy to have the nicest digs on the beach," Adam jokes, but cuts off when Helena gives him a look.

"It's a fine investment, Adam," she informs him crisply. "Far better than your dozen fancy cars that depreciate by half the minute you drive them off the lot. You'd think you'd get enough of cars just doing your job."

"Never! And, it's only a half-dozen," he retorts with a grin, undeterred. "Besides, I bought them for Sara."

"Even the Lamborghini?" Sara asks dubiously, stepping up beside him. "And the Maserati?"

He gives her a sly grin and wraps his arms around her. "Well, maybe not *those* two."

"Uh, Mom, Dad? Let me introduce Kennedy's family. This is Graham, Helena, Sara, and Mr. Hot Car Guy is Adam," I say with a sweep of my hand. "And, these are my parents, Frank and Terri." Hands are shaken all around, until my mother surprises Helena by drawing her into a hug.

"I'm so happy to meet you all! You must be so proud of Kennedy," she exclaims. "He was a delight when he came to visit us last week. He left me the loveliest note to thank me for the offer of our—"

"Mom!" I blurt, suddenly afraid of what she was going to say, but she merely laughs at me.

"Equipment, dear," she says with a wink. "I was going to say equipment. Not that they used it, but it's the thought that counts." She turns back to a confused Helena. "Anyway, when I read that sweet note, I knew that boy had been brought up right."

Graham chuckles. "We tried." He steps closer to his wife and slips an arm around her waist.

"And as for your question, we're proud of both our boys," Helena says, her eyes flicker over my shoulder. I glance around to see Nicole and Kennedy join us. "I haven't shown it enough the last few years," she continues, looking at Kennedy as her voice gains strength. "But I'm incredibly proud of them, and never more than now."

Kennedy clears his throat, a shy smile playing around his lips as he loops an arm around my shoulders. "Frank, Terri, I'm glad you could make it," he says, reaching out with his free hand to shake Dad's.

"I'm sorry we were a little late. We wouldn't miss it for the world!" My mother beams at us; she's practically vibrating with excitement

"I'm sorry, Mom. I'd show you around, but we don't have a lot of time now. We all need to get over to the stadium," I say apologetically. "Let me show you to your room." I gesture to their bags beside Dad, but Helena stops me.

"Oh, let me," she offers graciously, smiling with a little more energy than she's shown before. "Your room is near ours." She leads my mom down the other hall, Dad and Graham dutifully following with the bags. Adam mutters something into Sara's ear that makes her smile, and they slip off into the kitchen, leaving us with Nicole.

"Are you guys ready?" I look up into Kennedy's sparkling blue eyes, and I can see that his session in the "rock-and-roll man cave" must have been fruitful. He has that calm look that only comes after he's figured out a tune that's been trying to work its way out of him.

He nods and pulls me into a hug. "Of course. I love it when we all come together like that. It's an incredible feeling."

"I can tell." Then my smile becomes impish. "The only other time you look so satisfied is after sex, and unless there's something between you and Sean I don't know about..."

Nicole snorts beside us, but a loud laugh interrupts us. "He wishes he could get a piece of me," Sean declares loudly, leading the remaining group in. "He got close a few years ago in Budapest."

"Nah, that was Cam," Kennedy retorts, and dodges a swing from the guitarist. He pulls me in front of him like a human shield, ignoring my laughter at their ridiculousness. Cam gives him a stink-eye and leans up against the wall. He looks relaxed and very pleased with himself. They all do, actually. It must have been a really good session.

"So, are we doing this thing, or what?" Cameron asks, but startles into silence when Matt grabs his arm, his eyes wide.

"What the fuck is that?" Matt demands, looking in horror at something behind me. I turn to see April and Tess have joined us. Tess is tapping something on her tablet, seemingly oblivious, and rocking a flaming pink Vandels tank top. She glances up at me, as if suddenly aware of our gaze, and only the barest hint of a smile tells me that she knows exactly what she's doing.

"What?" she asks innocently, while Matt practically growls on my other side.

"That." He points at her chest. "What the fuck is that?"

She gives him a devilish smirk. "Well, if I have to explain what they are, you must not be the Casanova they say you are," she hums. He glares at her.

"I'd be more than happy to tear that fucking thing off you and give you a demonstra—hey!" He winces from Cam's slap on the back of his head.

"Watch your language, asshole," he hisses, tossing his head toward where Parker and his parents are now standing with Nurse Claire. Kennedy groans.

"*Both* of you watch it," he warns, but all three stop what they're doing at my laugh.

Joyce giggles. "See what I have to live with?" Nicole laments, and then waves her arms toward the door. "Okay, let's get moving! Parker, you and your parents and Nurse Claire get to ride with the band, all right?"

"Cool!" Parker grins and eagerly pulls his father's hand toward the door. His nap has obviously recharged his batteries. Kennedy and I follow them and the band outside, where Tucker and two stretch limos await. Kennedy didn't spare any expense.

"Wow! Do we get to ride in the limo again?" Parker asks, a hopeful smile stretching across his face. Kennedy squats down next to him.

"This night is just getting started, Park. We need to arrive in proper rock-star style, don't you think?"

He pumps his little fist, and lets Cam and Sean usher him and David toward the first limo. We watch as Tucker gets them settled for a second, and then Kennedy pulls me into another hug. "See you in a little while," he hums against my lips. He gives me a soft kiss that sets my head spinning. "Are you going to be okay with all of them?"

The plan is for me to follow with the families and Nic in the second limo, and for April and Tess to drive separately. Maddie and Dylan are meeting us there. "Of course. As long as my mother doesn't start talking about anybody's sex life," I add wryly. He chuckles and gives me another kiss, his hands sliding down . . .

"Hey, sunshine!" Tucker calls from the limo. "Let's get this show on the road. You've only got a few thousand people waiting on you."

Smiling up into his beautiful eyes, I give him a light push against his chest. "Get going, you. I'll see you soon."

"Can't wait," he whispers. He trails a finger down my cheek in farewell, and then turns and sprints over to the limo, arms held out wide, to the delight of the little boy waiting inside.

chapter twenty-four

kennedy

"CAN YOU BELIEVE SHE WAS fucking wearing a Vandels T-shirt?" Matt's annoyed voice bellows through the back of the stretch limo as we wind our way to the stadium. His leg bounces off nervous energy as he shakes his head. It's actually quite amusing to see him like this.

"Matty, watch your mouth. There are virgin ears present." Sean smirks at him before turning to Parker's parents. "I apologize for the Neanderthal. You really can't take him anywhere."

David gives a short laugh, but doesn't look bothered. "Don't apologize. Everyone is always so careful with Parker all the time; they're almost afraid to say anything. It's nice to see normal for a change."

Sean barks out a laugh. "Mate, if you wanted normal, you're in the wrong car."

Joyce smiles from her spot across from us. She's obviously exhausted from the day, from the months and years of living under the cloud they all have been under for so long, but she also looks genuinely happy.

Parker's laugh drifts down to us from the sunroof. He's been perched up there with Cam for the better part of the drive. I'm looking forward to hearing his reaction when the police escort that will lead us the final miles to the stadium comes into view.

"Joyce, darling," Sean starts, bringing me out of my thoughts. "I want you and David to spend a weekend at my place in Malibu."

Joyce's eyes widen, and she immediately shakes her head. "That's very sweet, but we really couldn't."

"Sean's a lot of things, but sweet isn't one of them." Sean flips me the finger at my comment, and receives a swift smack on the back of the head from Tucker.

"Hey! What was that for?"

"We're trying to be civilized remember, genius?" Tucker taunts him.

Sean scowls, but turns back to Joyce and David quickly. "When's the last time you two went away together? Had a meal outside of the hospital?" His voice lowers and he leans forward, obviously not wanting Parker to hear this particular conversation.

David glances down at his wife with a look of longing. "I can't remember. Months . . . probably longer."

"I can't leave him there alone," Joyce replies softly, her eyes glossing over.

"Ah, but there's the beauty of it. He wouldn't be alone. We'd be there, yeah?" Sean turns back to Matt and me.

"Absolutely." It's a firm confirmation from Matt.

Joyce looks between the three of us in disbelief. "Come on. It would be fun. Like a big old sleepover with Uncle Sean and his less awesome friends. What could possibly go wrong? Oh! I'll get a tent and everything." Sean rubs his hands together in excitement.

"I don't know . . ." Joyce hedges, and I see David squeeze her hand.

"It's right on the beach," Sean encourages. "Quiet, secluded, all the rooms you could ever want to do whatever you want in." Another stealthy punch from Tucker lands on Sean's shoulder, and he brushes it off.

"Thank you, but—"

Joyce's protest is silenced as David interrupts, "We'd love to."

"Brilliant! Where do you think the best place is to buy a tent, then?" Sean reaches into the inner pocket of his leather jacket for his cell phone, quickly getting immersed in his latest mission.

"I mean, where's the loyalty?" Matt mumbles after a few minutes of silence, glancing out the window.

"Are you still on about the lovely Tess, grasshopper?" Sean asks, clearly amused. "There'll be thousands of people wearing different shirts. Why is hers all of a sudden so important to you?"

"It's not; it's just she should be wearing one of ours, you know?"

"Women rarely do what they should," Sean comments, scrolling through his phone.

"Really? I've never found that to be case," Matt fires back at him.

Sean snorts, glancing up from his phone. "Right, because most of them just fall all over you? Cater to your every whim?"

"Guys, not here," Tucker warns.

"Mom!" Parker's excited voice is heard above us, and Joyce looks up to the sunroof.

"You okay, honey?"

"Come here!" Joyce flashes me a look of concern as Cam moves down from the sunroof, sinking back into his seat.

"You'll both probably want to see this," Cameron suggests, offering her his hand as she stands to join her son for a view from the sunroof.

David turns to peer out the tinted window. "Holy shit," he mumbles before joining Joyce and Parker at the sunroof.

Tucker smiles at me as the crowds that have lined the streets for hours in preparation of our arrival come into view. It's a sight we've all gotten used to and take for granted. Seeing it from Parker's perspective is beyond humbling. The cheers and screams rise in a crescendo as the motorcade approaches the stadium. The police sirens squeal a few times in succession as if the throng needed another indication that we're making our way closer.

A sea of brightly colored signs that would typically feature Redfall's name have Parker's name and the *Rock the Dream* hashtag emblazoned on them instead. Sean hits me in the leg, pointing to a massive bright yellow homemade sign, held up high by six little kids, the words *Fuck Cancer* loud and proud in big black letters.

Sean lets out one of his trademark howls and hangs out the window. Tucker lets out a sigh, leaning across Nurse Claire's lap to grab hold of his jacket. "Every damn time," he mutters before raising his voice so Sean can hear, "Don't make me buckle you in!"

abigail

"I THINK SOMEONE'S SMITTEN."

I roll my eyes at Tess's teasing observation as we make our way backstage before the beginning of the concert. "Don't be ridiculous. He's merely being polite."

"Right," she says with a smirk. "Polite. All the 'accidental' arm brushes were him just being polite. He was practically jumping around you like an eager puppy!"

"Whatever." I shake my head at her. Okay, so maybe Landon

did seem a bit *enthusiastic* when we were going over the redone video for the finale, but it's not like anything will come of it. "I'm not going to make a big deal of it. He's doing us a huge favor by letting us mess with his video."

"You may not want to make a big deal of it, but Kennedy may break a guitar over his head if he doesn't tone it down."

Rolling my eyes again, I hear April's voice in my ear. "Can you please swing by the press room again? *Rolling Stone* finally deigned to grace us with its presence."

I bite back a laugh. April has had a serious thing against *Rolling Stone* since they killed an article they were going to do for a dream we did last year due to some infighting between editors. She'll never let *them* know that—she's too much of a profession-al—but that doesn't stop her sarcasm from showing with me.

"Sure. I'll be there in ten," I promise, talking into my new, high-tech headset. We're all wired for this event. Normally, we'd have clunkier headsets, but after Kennedy complained at the "ar-chaic pieces of shit" our tech guy was loading up at the office, some sleek, feather-light European earpieces magically appeared when we arrived tonight.

Some women get diamonds, some get enough AV gear to cause even the most fervent techno-nerd to dance with joy.

I TAKE OFF TOWARD THE pressroom we have set up back-stage, via the phone room. I spy my mother sitting close to Hel-ena as they man a couple of phones taking donation calls. At the moment, though, they're giggling wickedly until they see me across the room. They give me a couple of finger waves, their faces pictures of innocence. I return the wave, shaking my head in amusement as I continue to the pressroom. Considering my mother's unpredictable filter, putting those two together may have been a colossal mistake.

"Do you think they've been drinking?" I mutter, and Tess laughs, glancing back at them over her shoulder.

"Of course not," she says, nudging my shoulder. "I think it's more likely that there's more to Kennedy's mom than meets the eye."

I laugh. "True. He must have inherited his moves from somewhere." I expect her to make some kind of smartass comment, but instead, she purses her lips in thought.

"There's only one person's moves I'm wondering about right now," she mumbles, her cheeks pinking.

"Let me guess, a certain bassist with a tongue piercing?" I tease lightly, and her blush becomes deeper. I smile smugly, but let it go, not wanting to embarrass her further. Besides, I've got *Rolling Stone* to deal with now.

WE APPROACH THE PRESSROOM AND find a dozen or so reporters milling about, typing furiously on laptops, or interviewing some of the celebrity presenters or performers. I know there are probably a dozen more sitting out in the press section in the crowd. April waves me over to where she stands with a tall, lithe man with grey eyes and dark hair drawn into a man bun.

April makes the introductions and the reporter flicks on his digital recorder.

"Thanks for sparing a few minutes. I know you're busy tonight," he begins politely. "April has already briefed me on the particulars for tonight, but I wanted to ask you a few specifics, if I could." I nod and he continues. "Whose idea was it for the Jensen boy to join Redfall on stage tonight?"

"It was Kennedy's suggestion, actually," I answer with a smile. "The entire band was onboard with it, but Kennedy was the initiator. He's been working with Parker for weeks on the song they'll play."

He cocks an eyebrow at me. "And what piece is that?"

"You'll have to stick around to find out. It's a surprise." I grin at him, thinking of how excited Parker is about playing with Kennedy. "But it's important to remember that it's all up to Parker. If he wants to play with Kennedy, he'll have that opportunity."

"Who wouldn't want to play with Kennedy?" he asks, his voice disbelieving, and then he purses his lips. "Do you mean he may not have the energy for it? Everything that's been happening today must be very taxing on such a sick kid."

"Parker has had medical supervision the entire time, as well as the constant support of his parents," I answer smoothly. "This has been a dream of his for years, and we're more than happy to do anything we can to fulfill it. But it ultimately comes down to what he wants. If he feels uncomfortable with standing on stage in front of that crowd for an instant, we can make other arrangements for him. It's all about him, and everyone involved understands that."

"And all of this was his dream?" He gestures to the vast room around us. "This is quite a dream for one little boy."

"Parker wanted to spend the day with Kennedy, and he has," I explain calmly, knowing exactly what he's suggesting. However, this isn't my first rodeo. "Kennedy wanted to make it something that could help kids beyond Parker as well. His original idea was for a small concert, but once some of his friends in the business heard about it, it started growing like wildfire. They all understand what's at stake for Parker and children with similar ailments, and were more than willing to give their time and talent."

"I'm sure you've heard the rumors that Redfall's participation—beyond Kennedy, that is—might not actually happen.

What with Cam's sudden disappearance and all."

"I'm sorry; I didn't hear a question there," I reply mildly before April can interject. She glares at the reporter, but he simply smirks at me and clears his throat.

"Where's he been?"

I smile benignly. "You'll have to ask Nicole Hays; she handles Redfall's information. However, I can tell you that every member of Redfall has been looking forward to tonight's show. They're very committed."

"Would their commitment have anything to do with the fact you're dating Kennedy Lane?"

My heart skips a beat as it always does when I think of Kennedy and me together, but I keep my cool. "My private life is just that—private. It has no bearing on today's event, or Parker's dream fulfillment. As to the commitment of the band, why wouldn't they want to participate?" My smile becomes more confident as I point to the phone room next door. "It's a tremendous cause. All these people, as well as the ones on stage and in the audience, and those calling and donating, understand what we're trying to do here. The energy is incredible. Who wouldn't want to be a part of trying to help these kids, vulnerable kids whose childhoods are being stolen.

"The money we're raising tonight will go toward fulfilling a hundred other children's dreams, but also to several associations that are working to find cures. April has a full list of the recipients. With this single benefit concert, hundreds of children will find relief from their illnesses, even if only for one day. We are incredibly grateful for everyone who has had a hand in making tonight possible. It's turned out to be the biggest dream fulfillment we've ever been a part of, both in terms of scale and complexity of the event and the number of children it will help. If you've seen the smiles on the faces of the kids in the audience from Parker's unit, you'll know we've been successful. And as I asked earlier, who wouldn't want to be a part of that?"

He scratches his cheek, his hard edges softening a bit. Then he gives me a knowing smile and tries one more time. "So, no confirmation of you and Kennedy?"

"My personal life isn't news. But all of this is," I repeat patiently with a sweeping gesture around the room.

He chuckles and gives me a more sincere smile. "Okay, I think that will do for now. Thanks for your time, Abigail."

"You're welcome." I nod and leave him in April's capable hands. It's not until I'm around the corner and out of sight that I take a breath and let it out in a whoosh.

"Good job," Tess says admiringly.

"Thanks. It's getting harder to pass on the Kennedy questions, though," I admit. "Sometimes it's difficult to keep myself from just blurting it out."

"I can imagine. If it's any consolation, I think it's just as hard for him. He was watching you from the green room when you were talking to that guy from Vibe earlier." She laughs. "I think he was about to gnaw his knuckles off."

I can't help my smile; it's nice to know that he's as affected by me as I am by him. There have been times today when I've barely been able to restrain myself from dragging him off to a secluded room so I can have my way with him. He's just so . . . *commanding* when he's doing an interview or is on stage, striding around like he owns the place. He oozes confidence, authority, and so much friggin' *sexual energy* that I can barely stand it.

And he wants me to move in with him! I was afraid to believe he was serious when he first asked me; it would be a dream come true to wake up every morning to the glorious sights of Kennedy and the Pacific Ocean. But, I love my job. It's my calling, just as making music is Kennedy's.

♪ ♩ ♪ ♩

"BEAUTIFUL ABIGAIL!" SEAN GREETS ME from where he's stretched out on one of the sofas that are scattered around their green room. He has a pair of drumsticks in his hands and is beating out some incredibly complicated rhythm on his knee. Cam is draped across a recliner not far away and he gives me a little salute, while Matt is too busy glaring at my companion to notice me. Tess pretends to ignore him, but I hear her breath catch when she sees him. I can't wait to see what the future holds for these two.

"Hi, guys. Where's Kennedy?" I ask, looking around. Cameron points at the ceiling, where the stage looms over our heads. "He's going over some things with Nicole for the finale," he drawls and returns to scribbling in something, a journal perhaps?

"Oh, good. The video is ready—your parents really came through for us."

Sean sits bolt upright as if he touched a live current. "Our parents?"

"Yes. Didn't Kennedy explain what we were doing?" At their blank looks, I smirk at them. "We interspersed photos of Parker, Kennedy, and all of you as you were growing up. It was quite enlightening."

"You've talked to my mum?" Sean whispers, his face panicked. I nod, a grin spreading across my face.

"And she was most accommodating." I love the photo she sent of little Sean sitting on the kitchen floor and banging on the pots arranged like a drum kit around him. "You were obviously destined for this life. I was surprised about the red hair, though. Your parents let you dye it that young?" His mouth drops open in horror, and I congratulate myself for catching him speechless for the first time. Cam snickers at his expression, so I turn toward him.

"I also love the photo of you, Cam, with the long bleached-blond bangs in your prep school uniform," I inform him, which cuts him off cold. "You were the epitome of middle-school cool."

Sean barks out a laugh, but Cam merely flips him off. "What about Matt and Kennedy?" he demands. "You wouldn't have let them off the hook."

"They are both amply represented, we promise. It was actually Kennedy's mom's idea to use your photos as well as Kennedy's," Tess pipes up with a mischievous grin.

"What did Tom send?" Matt's worried grumble reaches us, but only I turn toward him, since Tess is studiously tapping at her tablet.

"A sweet picture of you hugging a giant white Newfoundland, for one." His eyes widen, and I hold my hands up defensively. "Guys, trust me. I'd never do anything to embarrass you. Well, maybe Sean, but not the rest of you."

Sean seems to have recovered from his shock enough to grin slyly at me, rubbing his hands together. "What about HRH's photos? Oh, please tell me you have something especially precious of him."

"You'll have to wait and see." I glance at my watch, as Sean throws his head back.

"Aw, come *on*, MP. You're no fun at all—"

"Okay, out with it," I suddenly demand, my hands on my hips. "What the hell does MP stand for? Come on—dazzle me with your brilliance."

Matt chuckles softly behind me as Sean stares with a mixture of adolescent delight and shock. He opens his mouth, but is cut off when Cam barks out a laugh. "Kennedy's been so whipped since he met you, we figured you must have a Magical Pussy to keep him in line," he drawls, slouching back in his seat and propping an ankle on the opposite knee.

All eyes are on me, and I'm proud that—for once in my life—my blush isn't giving me away. Instead, I nod thoughtfully. "Well, if the shoe fits," I murmur, giving a knowing shrug.

Sean hoots with laughter and points at me. "Okay, you can stay. I approve."

"Like you have any say in the matter, you idiot," Matt scoffs, just as one of the assistants sticks his head in the door.

"Redfall!" he barks. "You're on in ten."

A COUPLE HOURS LATER, I'M almost dead on my feet. My face feels permanently stretched by the smile I've worn all evening.

"Abby! It's time." April beckons me, and I hurry to join her as we trot up the stairs. She pushes open a door and we emerge on the stadium floor to the left of the stage. "Are you sure you want to watch from out here? We can watch from the wings with Parker's parents."

"I know, but I want to see this from the audience. This is what it's all about." I've been looking forward to this moment all night. It wouldn't be the same without the energy of the crowd surrounding me.

Waving to a few staffers as we walk, I find myself pulled into a quick hug by Ralph when we reach one of the VIP sections. "Abigail, you've outdone yourself," he gushes. His *Rock the Dream* shirt is wildly out of character for him, but I love his dedication. "Everything has gone like clockwork."

I laugh. "I'm glad it looks like it from this side. It's not just me, though; the whole team has really gone above and beyond. They're the ones who deserve your praise, along with

Kennedy's assistant, Nicole." There are always a few glitches at an event like this, especially with all the personalities involved, but we've worked them out. We'll go over them during the event post-mortem.

"Speaking of Kennedy," he says sheepishly. "Do you think he'd sign an autograph for my granddaughter? It's killing her that she couldn't be here—she came down with chicken pox—so I thought that might ease the sting a bit."

"I'm sure he'd be happy to." I look up at the stage, where a small army of roadies bustles around. "Although it might take a couple of days for him to regain his energy after tonight." He's truly been amazing; he wasn't kidding when he said he'd be playing for four hours. He's been onstage more than he's been off it, either playing with one of the legends who volunteered their time, backing up others. He's been like a kid in a candy store. Considering some of the names who have played tonight, maybe that's exactly how he's felt.

Scanning the section, I feel a tremendous sense of satisfaction wash over me. Everyone we love is here. Dad and Graham, looking as excited as the kids and holding up their cell phones instead of the traditional lighters. Mom and Helena with their heads together and laughing. Helena looks ten years younger than she did when she first arrived at Kennedy's home, with a sparkle in her eyes that I sense has been missing for some time.

Sara is snuggled into Adam's side, his arm protectively slung around her shoulders. Dylan smiles indulgently at Maddie as she bounces excitedly next to him in anticipation of the next act.

I strain to try to see Kennedy on the darkened stage. I know he's probably preparing for the last number in the wings somewhere, but I can't help it. I *need* to see him.

My emotions are all over the place. I've never felt so proud, so humbled, so overwhelmed by one of our projects, and I need the focus that only Kennedy can give me right now.

Then the stage clears and an excited whoop rises from the audience in anticipation. I'm practically vibrating with expectation, my heart pounding, and when I see Kennedy and Parker rise from the center of the stage under the spotlight, everything else falls away. My attention zeroes in on their two forms, one standing tall and strong, the other small and frail, and both with hearts as big as the sea.

chapter twenty-five

kennedy

THE SWEAT SOAKS THROUGH ANOTHER shirt, and I pull it over my head, dropping it to the growing pile while we wait backstage. We've only got a few minutes until the live feed from the Foo Fighters is over, and the grand finale begins.

I see Nicole carefully leading Parker over to join us as I tug on a new shirt. "What do you think so far? I saw you rocking out there in the front row." Tucker passes me an energy drink, and I take a long sip.

Parker beams at me, his parents watching from the wings. "It's so great!" he gushes, practically vibrating with excitement.

"I'm glad you're having fun. You ready for our turn now?"

He glances down at his Converse. "I'm kind of nervous," he says quietly, and I crouch down beside him.

"Hey. I still get nervous every single time, bud. Being scared is part of what makes this so great. But you know what?"

"What?" he asks, looking at me cautiously.

"I'm never out there by myself. I have three guys backing me up." Parker glances at my band, standing behind me. "We're always there for each other, and when we make mistakes, we're there to support each other. And the really great thing is, you don't just have three guys. You've got an entire stadium backing you up."

He tentatively takes hold of his guitar. "What if I mess up?"

"I'll be there to help you. We all will. We've got your back, okay?" Slowly, he lifts the strap of the guitar over his shoulder, glancing at his parents.

"Okay."

Dawson appears at the stairs with Tucker. "Knock 'em dead, kid."

"I'll try," Parker replies, letting out a laugh when Sean picks him up and carries him to the lift under the stage that we'll both rise up from.

"We're live in thirty, Kennedy," the disembodied voice of the producer drifts through my earpiece, and I join Parker on the platform.

"Remember, it's just like we practiced, okay? It will be dark when we rise up, and then the spotlight will come on. I'll count you in." I adjust the cord from his guitar that leads to an amp, and he gives me a quick nod.

"Hey, Park?" I give his hand a squeeze, hearing the crowd roar to life as the Foo Fighters' satellite feed comes to an end.

"Yeah?"

"Remember to breathe and enjoy it. You got this."

He grins over at me as the producer counts back from five, the crowd chanting his name over and over. Slowly the platform rises, and he looks up at me in anticipation before focusing his gaze on his fingers.

"Three, two, one, hit it."

The familiar intro riff of "Sweet Home Alabama" that I could play in my sleep echoes through the stadium, and it's all

Parker, playing like a pro as a hush falls over the crowd. The spotlights illuminate his tiny figure, clad in a *Rock the Dream* shirt, a Redfall bandana secured on his head, and I feel a rush of pride.

I anticipate where he's going to miss a few chords and join him, the rest of the band kicking in as Matt's voice fills the stadium. Parker's smile when he glances up at me after the intro is all I need to see. It's everything—every hope, every dream, every wish that I could have had for him answered with that smile.

And then, he does something I never would have predicted. As the band and I take over, he unplugs from the amp, sliding the guitar behind his back, and he prowls the length the stage as if he's done it a thousand times before, urging the crowd to sing along with us.

Matt and Cam move up to play on either side of him, following his lead as he takes control of the stadium and every single person in it. He urges one side to sing to the chorus, and then races to the other side of the stage to get them to try to sing it louder.

Glancing to the side of the stage, I see his parents waving their arms in the air, cheering him on, singing along with the crowd. On and on it goes, the crowd indulging him, feeding off his boundless energy, captivated by this little boy who somehow has beat the odds and inspired us all.

Sean brings us to a marathon conclusion before joining us at the end of the stage. He passes Parker his drumsticks, and he wastes no time, sending them sailing through the air. Taking his hand, I throw Parker's arm up high as we all bow, the frantic demands of an encore already starting before we've even made it off the stage.

Parker is literally bouncing as he races off to the open arms of Joyce, crushing himself against her. "Did you see? Did you, Mom?"

"You were amazing," she manages, taking a stealthy wipe of tears as they stream down her cheeks.

I catch sight of Dawson leading Landon up to join us in the darkness of the stage. Good thing he's donating fifty grand, or I'd be tempted to pound the shit out of him. Even in the mayhem of the night, the extra time he's spent with Abby hasn't escaped me. Fucker better watch himself.

"You were brilliant," Landon says enthusiastically, holding his hand up for a high five. Parker reaches up to slap it, beaming back at his parents and Claire.

"I messed up a bit, but—" Parker starts.

"I didn't hear a thing wrong with that," Landon corrects him.

"You were awesome, Park. You owned that stage," David assures him.

Parker laughs, keeping a tight hold of his dad's hand. "I did, didn't I?"

"Damn right, you did!" Sean's voice booms as the roadies arrange the baby grand piano in the center of the stage under the cover of darkness. Landon and I have only had a few brief conversations about our performance, but if there's anything I know about him, it's that he's always a professional about his work.

"All ready then?" Landon asks adjusting his guitar, the chants growing louder from the impatient crowd. "I saw the video Abigail and her team did. It's really quite something."

"You're ahead of me, then. I haven't seen it yet."

"Well, you'll like it . . ." He pauses, issuing me a slight smirk. "Maybe not the part where you're running under the sprinkler naked, but otherwise, you'll like it."

He strides to the darkened stage, taking his place beside the piano, leaving me scowling after him.

"You're the Steel Revenger!" Parker's voice practically

squeals, and I turn back to see him staring at Trey Ransom, the actor who plays the comic-book hero.

"I should have brought the suit, right?" Ransom shakes his head. "I knew I was forgetting something." Without missing a beat, he turns and holds his hand out to me. "Big fan," he says, shaking my hand before adjusting the vintage black Redfall concert-tee he's wearing. "Saw you back in 2010. It was . . ." He holds his fists up to his temples and opens them up. "Mind blowing."

"Glad you liked it."

Nicole appears from the hallway, looking beyond exasperated. "You need to get out there, now. Introduction time." She pushes Ransom to the stairs, and he glances back over his shoulder at me.

"She always like this?"

"No. Sometimes she's worse."

The raw, electric energy fuels my adrenaline as I follow him out to the stage and sit at the piano, bathed in the darkness of the stage. The frenzied crowd senses we are reaching the end of the night. Tonight has been everything I hoped for, particularly for Parker, but also for my family.

I never would have imagined that the simple act of meeting Abby and Parker would change everything. Parker will never really know what he's done, how he's given us all hope.

Landon and I start in on the first few notes of his song, and the stadium erupts once more, as the giant screens flash with the video that Abby and the team spent the better part of the morning on. I'm blind to it all, the details a blur. I'm lost again in the place that has never failed me, leaving it all on the stage, to give the crowd what they came here to experience.

The first round of fireworks burst in the darkened sky overhead as we end the song, and Landon waves a reluctant good-bye to the crowd, making his way off the stage. While the throng focuses on the spectacular light show above, the black curtain draws across the stage, and I collect my guitar from a waiting roadie.

"I was just telling Parker here that he must be up past his bedtime," Cameron teases, earning him a mega-watt grin from Parker. "See? You're a rock star already."

"We'll be done soon, bud," I offer, when he holds up his palm for a high-five. "Just one more song, and then we'll bring you out for a final bow, okay?"

His big blue eyes seem to light up. "Cool! And these fireworks are awesome," he adds, turning his face up to watch the display.

Bathed in the blue haze of the spotlight that practically blinds me, the sky bursts with a final epic display of red and gold. It only takes a few seconds for the crowd to acknowledge me as I move back to the front of the stage.

"You didn't think we were done, did you?" More ear-shattering chants answer me, and I can't help but laugh as I adjust the mic stand.

"If you've ever been to a Redfall concert, you know we never really say good-bye, just that we'll be seeing you again real soon." Slowly, I start strumming what to most would sound like random notes, but is actually a stripped back version of "Born to Run".

"I wanted to take just a minute to thank all the volunteers behind scenes, who have worked for weeks to put this together. Dawson and Nicole, our roadies and crew, Tucker and his burly band of security." That earns me a wave of laughter, and a few catcalls. "Yeah, yeah. I know you all think they're hot." More shrieks from the crying gaggle of girls up front. "A big thank you to the team at the *What's Your Dream* foundation for giving us all the opportunity to meet Parker and his family." I let my gaze wander to section I know Abby is in.

"To the nurses, the doctors, and the hospital staff who work every single day, dedicating their lives to these kids, a thank-you will never be enough. To the fine women and men of the San Francisco police and fire departments who have allowed us to break noise bylaws, thanks for putting up with us . . .

"For the artists who took the time to be with us tonight and for Parker, the kids here tonight and the ones who can't be here, and for everyone watching and supporting us tonight, keep on rocking . . . This is "Born to Run"."

Wasting no time, I start in on the acoustic first verse of the song I learned to play in my parent's living room. For the next few glorious moments, I'm hit with memories. I can see Robin sitting with her legs tucked underneath her on the shag carpet, telling me to play it again. Adam and his gang of skinny teenaged friends crowded in the garage in the middle of an icy Minnesota winter, hearing me play for the first time. All the years and miles logged with the band, playing in dingy bars, the hours of practice, of blood, sweat and tears flash by, and I hear the raw emotion break in my voice.

I play for Parker, all the kids like him, and the ones who will never experience a night like this. I play for Robin, and somewhere I hope she's looking down, and that she's proud of me. And, I play for Abby who's the reason I'm even still standing here, and the reason I know that I will be for a very long time to come.

I pause to the ear-piercing screams before the curtain pulls away and the crowd ignites, Sean exploding at the drums to take the band through the rest of the classic song, giving it our own fuel-injected twist. We play like it's the last time we'll ever get the chance to, and we do exactly what Brodie always told us to, we light it up.

♪ ♩ ♪ ♩

"YOU SURE YOU WON'T TAKE me up on my offer? I can get you guys a suite at a hotel," I try to persuade once more as Claire quietly shuts Parker's hospital room door, leaving Abby and me alone with his parents.

The hospital is in stark contrast to the events of the day; eerily quiet and empty when we finally arrived back shortly after midnight. The after party was a bit of a whirlwind, but still scaled back compared to what we're used to. It gave me time to talk to Ralph while Abby saw to making sure Parker met everyone he wanted to. A few signed autographs and photos for Ralph's granddaughter and I had what I needed from him as well—some well-deserved time off for Abby. I try to stifle a grin at my last minute getaway plan. I hope to hell that she'll like this surprise.

"I want to wake up with him tomorrow," Joyce answers with a tired smile before she engulfs me in a tight hug. "Thank you so much . . . I don't know what else to say." Her voice is muffled against my shirt, and I give her a gentle squeeze.

"Hey, no crying, and you don't have to thank me or say anything." She pulls back, wiping the tears from her face. "Promise me you'll call if you need anything. Day or night. I don't care when it is, or what you need. Just call, okay?"

She nods quickly before pulling Abby against her. "I'll call him in the morning and see how he's doing." My voice is quiet in the muted light of the room, catching a glimpse of David. I can see the telltale signs of a chin quiver I've grown accustomed to seeing over the past few hours.

David claps my shoulder with a firm squeeze. "Thank you, Kennedy. He'll never forget today, and neither will we."

Fighting to hold in my own rioting emotions, I take a final glance at Parker, his tiny body safely tucked under the crisp white hospital sheet, peacefully sleeping away. His Redfall bandana is strategically placed on the table beside his bed, along with one of the many pictures our own team of photographers took today. This one, of Parker and me playing Sweet Home Alabama side by side with the crowd going wild at the edge of the stage.

"I won't forget either."

"YOU WERE AMAZING TODAY," ABBY whispers as she tucks in beside me on the leather seat in the back of the limo. I press a kiss to the top of her head, breathing her in. We're finally alone, having sent Tucker off to track down the rest of the band and whatever random entourage they've picked up along the way.

"Right back at you, baby." She answers with a giggle, glancing up at me from her prime location on my chest. "You know, I can be even more amazing."

"Is that right?" Her palm slides up my thigh, tightening in all the right places. "Whatever do you mean?"

"Little tease. Let me show you." I slide both of my hands to her hips, lifting her up to straddle my lap, my palms sliding to squeeze her perfect ass.

"Here?" Her eyes widen as she glances back at the privacy screen, quickly turning back to me. "Now?"

"Mhmm. Two of my favorite words. Here . . ." My lips trail a circuit along the column of her neck, my tongue teasing at her warm skin. "Now."

Her fingers sink into my hair, tugging like she can't get enough. She's taking what she wants, and I love every single delicious second of it. Deliberately, she grinds against my lap, right where I need her most, and I struggle to release the button on her jeans.

"Think you can be quiet?" There's a roughness to my voice

brought on by four solid hours of singing, and the sheer desire that burns hot through my veins.

She takes a sharp breath, leaning back with a quick nod before launching her lips back to mine. It's a pure, raw craving between us that shows no signs of letting up. She meets every stroke of my tongue, every desperate touch, fumbling with the metal buckle on my belt as I lift my hips so she can finally tug my jeans down.

"So good," she mumbles, her hand closing around my hardened length, my head dropping back to the seat with a needy groan. Outside the tinted windows, the lights of the city blur past as we wind our way through the streets, and she sets a firm and equally agonizing pace.

It's always intense, but tonight, the addicting energy that sparks between us seems more powerful. My hands are everywhere, stroking her thighs, tugging at the end of her sexy braid before she drops to the carpeted floor between my legs, closing her perfect mouth around the head of my throbbing cock.

"Jesus fuck." I gently brush the pads of my fingers along her jaw before palming the back of her neck, urging her forward. Judging from the moan that vibrates around my length, she doesn't seem to mind. Lifting her big, hazel eyes to mine causes another wave of desire to roll through me.

"I need to be inside you." Dragging her tongue up the underside of my length just about sends me over the edge, but then she makes a show of sitting back on the adjacent seat. Slowly, painfully slowly just to drive me out my damn mind, she lowers the zipper on one boot, tugging it off, her heated gaze never leaving mine.

"One day, I'll fuck you in just those boots."

"You keep saying that," she teases as the other boot joins its mate on the floor. Thank fuck for the size of this limo as I'm treated to the insanely erotic sight of Abby tugging her jeans down. While my hand passes over my cock in long, slow strokes, she glides her fingers over her bare and exposed pussy.

"Were you like this the whole time?" Sliding to the edge of the seat, I cover her hand with my own, coaxing both of our fingers over her clit. "Bare and wet and ready for me?" Teasing our fingers inside her, her ragged breathing hitches to the sensation as she rolls her hips, her tongue darting out to wet her lips.

Unable to resist, I lean forward and grip her hips, my fingers digging roughly against her smooth skin as I pull her onto my lap and down over my aching cock. The hedonistic need to claim her overwhelms me when she clenches around my throbbing length, meeting every forceful punch of my hips; so warm and tight, and so fucking perfect.

She claws at my shoulders before gripping the plush leather on the seat behind me, her head thrown back, mouth dropped open as our desperate rhythm builds. I slide my palms to take hold of her sweet ass, squeezing and urging her faster as I pound into her.

There will be time . . . lots of time for warm, gentle and tender, but now, we're both too far gone for that. I can feel it building, that rush of white heat, my muscles tensing as each kiss grows wilder, each press of my palm over her hip and against her thigh more frantic.

Her taste explodes in my mouth, her tongue brushing urgently with my own. She's the air I breathe, and I claim her mouth, her pussy, every single inch of her delectable skin in the only way I can.

"Kennedy . . ." It's a mumbled plea against my lips as she stretches one arm up, her palm pressing to the ceiling of the limo, arching her back away from me in a stuttered cry. I wish to fuck we had at least gotten around to losing her shirt for this so I could bury my face in her tits. But, maybe it says more about us that we couldn't wait.

"What you do to me, baby," I mutter as I feel that delicious tremble around my aching length when she finally lets go. She tries to stifle her scream against my neck. I plant my feet on the floor of the limo, my hips bucking forward with my own release as I bury myself inside her over and over.

We're a tangle of needy hands and joined groans, trying to get impossibly closer. Her arms wrap around my neck, and she practically melts into me, resting her forehead to mine. Leaning back, I grip her chin, my own breathing labored as I take her in; cheeks flushed in that glorious just fucked way.

"We're going to do that again . . . real soon," I mumble through a shaky breath.

"Promise?" It's a whispered word against my lips.

"Promise."

LOSING TRACK OF TIME IS easy when I'm in the solitude of my recording studio. With Abby back at the office and the band dispersed until the Australian leg of the tour, I'm alone. Even Mom and Dad have taken off to Abby's parents' place to spend a few days before heading home. Things are getting better with them. We're not perfect, but we're making progress.

Our families spent a couple of days together at my place, and we settled into a rhythm of sorts. Meals were made together, evenings typically were around the piano where I'd catch Mom's eye and a silent moment would pass between us. There were common, everyday conversations that end up tying people together in ways you can't expect.

But through all of this, there's a nagging guilt gnawing away at me. Do I really deserve to be this happy? The scars all of us

have are wounds that will never really, truly heal. While I'm trying to stop blaming myself for Robin's accident, I'll never get
over losing her. A part of me, a part of all of us died with her,
and the best that we can do now is try to make whatever time we
have mean something. That's what I'm committing myself to do.

I've always said I wanted more. I've learned now that can't
be found in a hangover or with some strung out junkie in a shady
bar. It can't be found at the bottom of a bottle. That demon
of temptation will try to trick you, tempt you, make you think
you're invincible. And it's so easy to forget—forget about the
people you're hurting, and the lost patches of time you'll never
get back.

Then one day, you wake up and you don't recognize the
stranger staring back at you in the mirror. You forget about
promises you made to the people you love. Temptation is a vis-
cous cycle, and it's always going to be there. For Cam, Matt,
Sean, and for me. We've each battled and lost, and battled again.
And we're still here, scarred and bruised, but each of us finding
our own reasons to fight for another day.

For me, it's Parker. It's rebuilding with my family, my band,
and Tucker. It's finding my heart and soul. Ours has been a whirlwind, a test, a scorching, intense desire. I've gone from never
wanting to leave the numbness I was wandering in to craving
every single emotion Abby brings out in me. It's a love that is
all-consuming, a place outside of the stage where I'm lost and
found at the same time, where I can breathe again because of
her.

Adjusting the headphones, I switch the recording light on
and get lost once more. I play about all the mistakes and the
miracles, and all of that wide-open glorious future that stretches
out in front of us. I play about the darkness, the temptation that
will always be with me, but mostly, I play about the only woman

who's ever really seen me, knows my fears and doubts and darkest side . . . the one who saved me from myself.

♪ ♩ ♪ ♩

abigail

"WHAT'S UP NEXT?" I LOOK over at Tessa, who's chewing on a pencil pensively as she looks out the window, instead of at her clipboard. "Hello? Earth to Tessa?"

She startles and abruptly turns away from the window, her eyes immediately roving over her notes. I look at her with concern. She's been unusually distracted since the concert. "Tess, are you all right?"

"Of course," she says quickly, looking at me with wide-eyed innocence. Flashing me a too-bright smile, she sits across from me at my desk and flips a page. "Shall we go through the details so far for the Browne dream?"

I let her take me through the schedule, involving a deal with the New York City Ballet to allow a young lymphoma patient to perform a brief cameo during a performance of the Nutcracker. Her scarf shifts, and I stifle a gasp when my eyes spy the faint love bites that trail down her neck toward her chest. Now I understand why she's been wearing turtlenecks for the last three days.

Her voice trails off when she notices where my gaze rests. "What?" She nervously pulls her scarf back up to cover the marks and I smirk.

"Anything you want to tell me, hmm?" I tease, cocking an eyebrow at her as her blush deepens. "Or about *anyone*?" She's usually dying to tell me about her latest conquest; I'm surprised I haven't heard about this one. From the looks of those marks, it must have been a wild night.

"Oh, you know, just some guy I met the other night," she says dismissively, and before I can quiz her further, there's a tap at the door just before it opens and April sticks her head inside.

"Can you come down and talk to the guys from ESPN for a minute? They're here for the Joey Anderson dream."

"Right." I rise to my feet, tossing a teasing glance at Tess. "We'll finish this later, okay? I want to hear every juicy detail."

"Um, sure." She gives me a wry smile. "I'll be going with you to the airport, so you can grill me then."

"Perfect." I give her a wink, and then follow April down the hall toward her office. It's only a few days after the concert, but we can't stop to rest; there are dozens of other children's dreams in line to fulfill. Although it will certainly be easier now, thanks to the concert and the generosity of Kennedy and those who donated in Parker's name. My heart skips a beat, and I pull out my phone to fire off a quick text to my rocker, just to let him know I'm thinking about him . . . As if that's a surprise.

I'm always thinking of him.

"OH ABBY, WE'RE HAVING SO much fun!" my mother gushes over the phone. "That Graham is a live wire after a few bottles of wine."

I grimace. God only knows what's been going on in Napa. I love that Kennedy's and my parents are getting along so well, but if mom has been offering that damn sex chair to them, I don't want to know about it. "Erm, that's great, Mom. When are they leaving?"

"Tomorrow, unfortunately. But they've invited us to fly out to visit them in Redwood Falls." I hear something rattle in the background, and my father grumbling. "So, what's up with you? Has Kennedy recovered after the concert yet? That poor man's voice was almost nonexistent at the end of the night."

"He's fine. Tucker has this mystery concoction of tea, honey, and some spicy herbal mixture that snaps him back in shape pretty quickly." I can't help my smile; even though I probably shouldn't because it means he's overused it, a part of me secretly loves Kennedy's deep, raspy voice and the way it sounds murmuring dirty things in my ear. Shaking my head, I pull my thoughts back. "I was just calling to let you know I'll be out of town of a couple days. April and I are flying down to San Diego to meet with some people for another dream."

I can hear her smile in her voice. "Thanks for letting us know, sweetie. I like knowing where you are, just in case." I do know that; Mom doesn't worry about much, but she does get a little anxious when I travel, especially to different time zones. "Abby, that was an incredible thing you all did," my mother says in all seriousness. "Seeing Kennedy with that little boy . . ." I can hear her soft sigh. "He was wonderful with him. You've given them something they'll remember for their entire lives. I know I don't say it often enough, but I'm proud of you, sweetie. You've turned into an amazing woman, and I—your father and I—couldn't be prouder of you."

My throat closes with emotion from her unexpected praise, and I swallow thickly. "Thanks, Mom. I love you."

"Oh, I love you, too, Abby," she replies. "Never forget that." She clears her throat, and then asks more casually, "What's Kennedy going to do while you're gone?"

"Well, I don't know," I say, confused. "He can do whatever he wants, I suppose. I think he mentioned helping Tucker with something, but I don't know the particulars." Considering how pouty he was when I went back to the office, I was a little disappointed with his calm reaction to my news about my trip. I expected him to cajole me into staying, especially since I had to cancel dinner with him. I hated to do it, considering he'd be leaving again soon—too soon, actually—but April needs me on this one. If she hadn't practically pleaded with me, I wouldn't be going. I want to spend every moment I can with him before he leaves. But given his almost perfunctory acceptance of my trip . . .

It's not all about you, Abby, I silently chastise myself. The man has given me his undivided attention for days—he's probably looking forward to a little alone time.

"Oh, that's nice. Well, tell him that I took care of that thing for him," she says cryptically, immediately raising my suspicions. My mother doesn't do cryptic well.

"What do you mean?" I ask, but she just laughs. "Just something he wanted me to take care of for his parents, sweetie," she says hurriedly, which tells me there's more to it than that. Good Lord, what is she up to now? "I'll talk to you when you get back. Have a nice trip!"

She hangs up, leaving me staring at the phone. I love my mom, but I swear, sometimes I think she'll give me more grey hairs than any kids I may have someday.

SITTING ACROSS FROM ME IN the Town car, Tessa rattles off the particulars for our meeting tomorrow in San Diego. She's a little nervous, but April and I ignore it and listen dutifully. Now that things are calming down after the concert, April and I agreed that it was time to step things up for Tess and offer her the opportunity of taking over Nadia's position as Giving Director. Normally, we'd do a search for someone with more Foundation experience, but Tessa knows the position almost better than we do. The way she stepped up during the prep for the show demonstrated that she's more than ready for more responsibility.

Although I'll miss her as my assistant, it would be unfair of me not to consider her if she was willing. And, after she got over her shock, she eagerly assured me she was when I suggested it to her this afternoon. I can't wait to see her in action.

I chuckle to myself as I picture the look on Matt's face when she stood up to him in the boardroom. That was something to see. Even Kennedy was impressed. The other members of Redfall scattered to the winds following the big event, as they typically do, he says. Although I've managed to build an easy rapport with them, I still don't know much about their private lives. Each one is so different, but when they come together . . . Kennedy has tried to describe the feeling he gets when he's onstage with them, when everything's clicking between them and they don't even have to think. They're like some kind of freaky hive brain or something. It doesn't matter how it happens. All I know is that when they play together, it's a wonder to behold.

Tess falls silent, leaving us to our own devices for a few minutes before we get to the airport. As the San Francisco scenery flashes by, my mind wanders. I can't believe the turn my life has taken. A few months ago, all I looked forward to were Wine Wednesdays with Maddie and my work. Now, although I still love my work, it's taken a backseat to something—*someone*—I've never imagined in my wildest dreams. Kennedy . . . with his strength and courage to fight his demons, his passionate intensity, and his loving adoration has turned my life upside down. He barged into my regimented existence and made me see that there's more to life than what I'd been allowing myself. Despite our shaky start, I wouldn't trade our journey for anything.

He's talked about taking a few months off after Redfall finishes its world tour, and has made it abundantly clear that he expects me to be a part of that. And he wasn't kidding about my moving in with him. He's even said that he'd buy a condo in the city so we can stay here during the week while I'm working, and then head out to Bodega Bay on weekends. I haven't agreed yet; I don't know why I'm dragging my feet. I suppose that I should be resistant to giving up my apartment and the independence it symbolizes. And some would say we're moving too fast. But, honestly? None of that really matters. I'm thrilled by the thought of waking up every morning with him and beginning our next stage, wherever that might lead us. A part of me will miss seeing Maddie so often, but she's moving on, too. She and Dylan are madly in love, and she's over at his place more often than not. I know they'll make it permanent one day soon.

So what am I waiting for? If I think about it too much, it scares me how much Kennedy has come to mean to me so quickly. I need him like I need air to breathe. I crave the closeness we've developed; it's something I never knew I was missing.

By the time the airport signs come into view, my mood has plummeted. Jeez, I haven't even set foot on the plane yet and I'm already missing Kennedy like crazy. Why did I agree to this trip again? Oh yeah, because I'm a responsible adult, that's why.

Humph. Sometimes, being responsible sucks.

I'm surprised though when, instead of pulling up to the terminal like normal, we take a side road into a tunnel. "Where are we going?" I ask the driver, slightly panicked. My panic turns to confusion when we emerge on the tarmac, heading toward a row of what look like private planes.

I look over at April in consternation, but she merely gives me a calm smile. "A certain someone thought you'd be more comfortable in a private jet," she explains, and I laugh. It doesn't take a genius to figure out who that certain someone could be. I shake my head at Kennedy's largesse. That man has more money than sense sometimes, but I love him anyway.

The car smoothly pulls up next to a black SUV sitting near

the foot of one of those stairways that leads up to the open doorway of a small jet. The three of us get out and retrieve our overnight bags from the driver. But, when I turn, I stare in shock when I see Kennedy emerge from the plane and jauntily walk down the stairs towards us. He's dressed all in black again, from his tight shirt to his kick-ass boots, looking like sex incarnate.

"What the hell?" I whisper, my feet rooted to the spot. I can't move, not even when he walks right up to me, cups my face in his large hands, and gives me a kiss that would make me blush to my roots if I weren't so surprised.

"There's been a slight change in plans," he says, looking beyond pleased with himself. I just shake my head, smiling in confusion.

"Are you coming with us?" I ask, my confusion morphing into suspicion when a smug-looking Maddie climbs out of the SUV with Tucker, who looks more resigned than pleased. "What's going on?"

He deftly takes my carry-on from me. "I'm not going with you; you're coming with me." My gaze snaps back to his, his blue eyes sparkling with mischief.

"What?" I exclaim. "Where? I can't go with you! Our plane leaves in an hour." I spin to look at a grinning April and Tess who are still standing next to the car.

"No, *our* plane leaves in an hour," my former assistant corrects me, exchanging a smirk with April. "We're going to San Diego, and you're going to wherever it is Kennedy is taking you."

I look incredulously at all of them. "Are you serious?" My stammering is cut off when Kennedy slips an arm around my waist, propelling me toward the stairs. Maddie and April quickly step up on either side of us.

"Kennedy cleared it with Ralph; you're good to go," April informs me as Kennedy marches us forward. "And I packed for you," Maddie chimes in. "Your mom called me. Everything is already loaded on the plane. With that, plus what you have in your carry-on, you should be ready for anything."

"Which is perfect, because anything is what could happen," Kennedy finishes, giving me a wink. "Ladies, my heartfelt thanks. Come on, baby—your coach awaits." My heart hammers in my chest at the suddenness of it all. I barely have time to thank them all before we're climbing, with Kennedy helping me negotiate the metal steps in my high heels. Just before I let him pull me inside, I turn and wave back to my girls who are standing on the tarmac, grinning up at us and waving.

"Clock's ticking." Kennedy pulls me inside and my eyes widen again to see the luxurious interior. It's all sleek design, high-tech gadgets, and pale wood. As many times as I've flown in first class, this is something else. He indicates a seat next to the window and, after I've sunk into the soft leather, quickly sits next to me and turns to take my hands in his. The intensity in his gaze is mesmerizing; I have to remind myself to breathe.

"Where are we going?" I ask breathlessly.

A slow smile spreads across his face. "It's a surprise. And don't worry," he says quickly. "I gave Maddie some parameters, so whatever you have in your suitcase will work."

"Work for what?" His enthusiasm and excitement is infectious, and now that I'm finally coming to terms with being "kidnapped," my smile matches his.

"Somewhere tropical. Where we can be naked for days, if we want." At my intake of breath, he chuckles. "Abby, you deserve a break. *We* deserve a break. A chance to get away from it all . . . no phones, no interviews, no board meetings. No responsibilities. It's just us. It's only for a few days, but I didn't want to wait until we were done with the tour." He looks at me tentatively. "I hope you're okay with that."

"Now you ask me?" I gesture to our plush surroundings with a laugh, and then smile reassuringly. "I'm more than okay, Kennedy. And I love that you wanted to do this. It's amazing. Thank you."

He smiles in relief and drags a hand through his hair. "Thank fuck. I hadn't really thought about what I'd do if you were pissed about it."

We laugh just as the flight attendant steps toward us to ensure that we're buckled in for takeoff. After he wanders back toward the cockpit to take his own seat, I squeeze Kennedy's hand, drawing his attention. "By the way, I want to move in with you," I say matter-of-factly. His answering smile is like the sun coming up. He pulls our joined hands to his mouth and kisses my knuckles.

I'm vaguely aware of the pilot saying something over the intercom, but my attention is solely on the handsome face leaning in for another kiss.

"Ready, gorgeous?"

After all these years, now I know how it feels when someone helps your dreams come true. I take a deep breath and smile, my heart bursting. "Yes. Let's go."

The Redfall adventures continue. A sneak peek at "Dare to Dream," book two of *The Dream Series,* coming soon. *Content subject to change.*

chapter one

matt

A DULL JACKHAMMER BEATS RELENTLESSLY in my head as I slowly become aware of frenzied movement beside the bed. I can't even imagine trying to open my eyes. Just the thought is painful. Why did I let the Brit talk me into tequila? You would think I'd have learned by now.

You're a stupid fuck . . . Too dumb to remember to come home on time.

I squeeze my eyes tighter, trying to drown out the memory of my poor excuse for a mother's shrill voice. No amount of time seems to let me forget my childhood. That doesn't mean I won't stop trying.

"Shit . . ." It's a whispered, under-the-breath curse from a panicked female voice, bringing me back to the torture of the morning. I turn my head slowly in the direction of the sound with a groan. A headache the likes of which I haven't had in a while has taken up residence with no plans to vacate any time soon.

Greeted by an eerie silence broken only by the sound of the

AC in the hotel room switching on, I struggle to put together the sketchy puzzle that is the night before.

The day with my band, Redfall and the classic concert we held in support of the *What's Your Dream* foundation is something that will be etched in my memory forever. Parker Jensen, an eleven-year-old kid fighting leukemia, had his rock-and-roll dream fulfilled by spending a day with his idol, legendary rocker and our frontman, Kennedy Lane.

We came close to losing Kennedy to the demons he's battled since an accident took his sister's life a few years ago. But being involved in something like this changes you, makes you look at life in a different way. I don't think Parker will ever know that he's the one who did the saving.

So, the day and the concert, I'll always remember. The rest of the night, though? A bit of a hazy mystery. I remember Sean Murphy, our borderline insane drummer, dragging a group of us out to celebrate. It started in the limo with a few members of the charity foundation's team, including the delectable, but equally infuriating Tess Baker. Long, black hair, curves that drive me insane, sarcastic mouth on her I'd like to put to better use. There's no denying we get under each other's skin. A more frustrating woman I have yet to meet. She seems to know every single button to push to get a reaction out of me.

The limo cruised the steep streets of San Fran as we indulged in expensive champagne before Sean demanded that we stop outside a gentleman's club. Cue the ensuing battle of wills with Tess where she accused us of setting the woman's movement back a few decades.

Snippets of the alcohol-induced rant flash back to me.

"We love women, all of them, don't we, grasshopper?" Sean is always so helpful.

"Come in and see it for yourself before you pass your high

and mighty judgment." And Tess did. Marched her sweet ass right up to the doors and demanded entry from the linebacker-sized bouncers. I wonder if there's anything she'll back down from.

Being famous comes with a few perks that I'll never complain about, and one of them is getting in anywhere, anytime, no questions asked. So our little entourage, already half shit-faced, spilled into the high-end club so that Tess could she for herself that the women weren't being forced to do anything they didn't want to.

This particular club is one Sean and I have been to a few times. They cater to the elite, to the rich, to the ones who need and demand confidentiality. It's five-star meals and the most expensive liquor money can buy. It's top industry DJs, a high quality burlesque show, and uber-exclusive lounge areas.

I think Tess was expecting sticky floors and drunken frat boys catcalling women who were chained up. What she did see rendered her speechless, and what a fucking sight that was. It may be the one and only time in the couple of days I've known her to be at a loss for words.

Safely tucked into one of the white leather VIP booths is about the time we broke into the Tres Quatro Cinco. Sean opened up a tab to pay for a few bottles of the expensive tequila and rounds of whatever poison anyone wanted. Everything after that point is a blur; a nasty, pinpricking, and painful blur.

Bits and pieces are here and there; hushed, wicked words whispered close to Tess's ear, the touch of her hand against my thigh, her twirling beneath a lamppost under a cable car sign. But the blanks between are greater than the rest of the foggy picture.

I have no idea how we made it back to the Fairmont. I run a shaky hand over my face, hearing more rustling from beside the bed.

"Where is it?" Her husky voice, filled with urgency, teases my consciousness.

My mouth is dry, feeling like it's full of cotton, and preventing me from actually attempting to speak. Something definitely happened last night. There are flashes of her practically pouncing on me in the elevator, drunken, uncoordinated limbs grabbing at my shirt, the pair of us stumbling into the hotel room.

I can smell her on my fingers, still taste her on my tongue, and feel her hand clumsily reaching into my jeans.

"So stupid . . ." It's the last thing I hear.

acknowledgements

TO MANDY—THE WHOLE REASON WE started this was for you. You continue to inspire us, to support us, and to be just as *passionate* as we are. You are an amazing friend, and we couldn't imagine doing this without you.

Much love to the Facebook Dream Team. A daily source of visual inspiration that never fails to rock our world.

To Jada, thank you for your gift of bringing our rocker to life! You're incredible, and we love seeing each and every beautiful work you create.

To Lauren, thank you for your patience and your guidance. We'd like to promise not to be wordy in the future, but we all know that would be a lie.

To Christine, thank you for making this beautiful.

To our pre-readers—Mandy, Lynsey, Patty, Corinne, and Tami. Thank you for taking the time to read and re-read. Your enthusiasm and support keeps us going!

Many thanks to the wonderful authors who gave us support in the early days of the writing and publishing process. We'd be lost without S.L. Scott, Melanie Moreland, and Harper Bentley. Ladies, we love and support you.

A world of thanks to the fandom—the bloggers, Twitterloves, Facebook friends, and review sites that found this story back in the early days. You are an amazing group that has inspired countless stories including this one. Thanks for sticking with us, and we hope you enjoy this journey as much as we did.

To our families, thank you doesn't seem enough. Your love and support while we tackled this adventure is quite simply legendary.

Lastly, to you, the reader. Thank you for being curious, thank you for reading, and rock on, friends. Rock on.

about the authors

ABOUT SIX YEARS AGO, A Canadian vegetarian and an American carnivore bonded over a shared love of shoes, wine, and good storytelling.

Leslie Carson lives in Ottawa, with her busy family and seems to spend more time at the hockey rink than outside of it.

From her home near Portland, B.B. Miller spends her days with family and friends in search of the perfect pear martini.

Together, they enjoy visiting random vineyards and writing about the romantic adventures of good and bad boys.

They would love to hear from you.

www.ingramcontent.com/pod-product-compliance
Lightning Source LLC
Chambersburg PA
CBHW070614260626

47161CB00007B/2429

9780999824620 8